"BewAre tHe nInTh of AV"

The terrorist's message said nothing more—but it left a great deal to be feared. For the Ninth of Av was the blackest day in Jewish history . . . the day when disaster after disaster had stricken the Jewish people—including the destruction of the Holy Temple.

It was the ultimate threat of destruction, aimed straight at the heart of a nation and a people. This, Dr. Paul Richardson soon learned as his visit to Jerusalem turned into a frantic effort to stop the icily cryptic warning from becoming a reality. And in a desperate search for the man or woman, Jew or Arab, who had marked this unholy day in blood, Richardson's enemies were everywhere. . . .

The Jerusalem Code

The Jerusalem Code

HAROLD L. KLAWANS

A SIGNET BOOK

NEW AMERICAN LIBRARY

PUBLISHER'S NOTE

This book is a work of fiction. Names, characters, places, and incidents either are the product of the author's imagination or are used fictitiously, and any resemblance to actual persons, living or dead, events, or locales is entirely coincidental.

Copyright © 1988 by Harold L. Klawans, M.D.

SIGNET TRADEMARK REG. U.S. PAT. OFF. AND FOREIGN
COUNTRIES
REGISTERED TRADEMARK—MARCA REGISTRADA
HECHO EN CHICAGO, U.S.A.

SIGNET, SIGNET CLASSIC, MENTOR, ONYX, PLUME,
MERIDIAN and NAL BOOKS are published by NAL
PENGUIN INC., 1633 Broadway, New York, New York 10019

First Printing, October, 1988

1 2 3 4 5 6 7 8 9

PRINTED IN THE UNITED STATES OF AMERICA

1

"How the hell can you go to Israel at a time like this?"

In a way, Paul Richardson was relieved that the question had finally been asked. He knew that everyone wanted to ask it: the residents, the medical students, the secretaries, even more than a few of his patients. Why Israel of all places? And why now? He was chairman of the Department of Neurology at Austin Flint Medical School. He belonged here in Chicago, not Jerusalem. It was Arnold Chiari, using the prerogative he had acquired during his long tenure as Paul's student, resident, associate, and friend, who walked into Paul's office on the day Paul was to depart and voiced their collective concern and bewilderment. But expecting the question did not make it any easier to answer.

The older neurologist made no response, but instead continued to gaze out his window at the skyline of downtown Chicago, which was just beginning to emerge from the early-morning haze. Usually Bud Chiari understood such a failure to reply as a clear signal to change the subject and did so, but not this time. "Paul," he insisted, "How can you go now?"

Paul knew he had to answer. He could no longer avoid the subject. "Bud," he began, "why should I change our plans and not go?"

"For God's sake, Paul, there's a war going on. Half of the entire Israeli army must be in Lebanon, and don't tell me it's just an incursion. It's not and you know it. It's a real shooting war."

"I know that. Better than you do. But the war is in Lebanon. We'll be in Jerusalem. There won't be any problems there."

"Are you sure of that? How far is it from Lebanon to Jerusalem?"

"Yes, I'm sure." Paul nodded, ignoring the second question. Was he also ignoring reality? When he had planned this trip, Israel had been at peace, or as much at peace as could be expected for Israel. That had all changed abruptly in the last two days. First a group of PLO terrorists had machine-gunned Shlomo Argov, Israel's ambassador to Great Britain, as he stepped out of a fashionable London hotel. Another act of terrorism, no worse than many others. But this one somehow seemed to be too much; the straw that broke the camel's back. The Israeli camel. And most unexpectedly. Israel invaded Lebanon. In two days the Israeli army had stormed its way deep inside Lebanon, striking at the PLO camps which had shelled settlements in Israel.

"Will you and your kids be safe?" Chiari reiterated. "Absolutely?"

Paul continued to gaze out the window. The bright June sun was beginning to burn off the summer haze. There would be no such fogs in Jerusalem. Nor in Beirut. How far was it from Jerusalem to Beirut? Paul wondered. As far as it was from Chicago to Milwaukee? No, a bit further than that. Green Bay? No, not quite that far.

Bud did not let up. Paul's going to Israel now made no sense at all to him. Paul could delay his sabbatical or he could go somewhere else. All he was going to do was begin work on a textbook. He could do that anywhere. He didn't have to walk into the middle of a war. "What if Syria enters the war and attacks Israel? How many minutes does it take a MIG to fly from Damascus to Jerusalem?"

"Syria won't attack Israel," Paul said quietly but firmly.

"How can you be so damn certain of that?"

Paul went back to his desk. He no longer peered out the window. He did not look at Chiari. Bud had been his favorite student and resident and was now his closest friend at the medical center. They thought about so many things in the same way. Not just neurology, which, after all, Paul had taught the younger physician, but most other aspects of their lives. But this Bud did not understand. How could he be expected to? He had not gone through what Paul had. And he was not Jewish.

Paul shuffled through his desk, found a cigar, and lit

it. As he took the first few puffs, he looked at the pictures hanging on the walls of his office. Each of them had been carefully chosen and represented a part of his life. He would miss them more than he would miss the skyline.

He fixed his gaze on a small ceramic tile he and Bobbie had bought on their first trip to Jerusalem, in 1971, at a small shop on the Via Dolorosa, the Way of the Cross, the pathway Jesus had taken to reach his crucifixion. That street and the shop were both in the Arab quarter of the city, a quarter filled with Muslims. Its owner was an Armenian Christian. The shop was no more than a stone's throw away from the Church of the Holy Sepulcher, where Jesus had been buried. And this Armenian shop on a Christian street in a Muslim neighborhood, like the rest of the Old City, was now governed by the Israelis, by Jews.

The tile was a reproduction of the oldest existing map of Jerusalem, a mosaic on the floor of a Byzantine church somewhere deep in Jordan. Paul had never seen the church nor its floor, and probably never would. The tile was cracked. He should replace it, but he knew he wouldn't. Bobbie had loved the tile. She had bought it for him.

"Paul, if it were just you, I suppose I could understand your going. But you are not going by yourself. You're taking your two kids."

"They are two of the reasons I have to go."

"Paul, they're still kids," Bud complained.

"They're old enough," Paul replied.

"How old is old enough, Paul?"

"Carolyn's sixteen already and Joshua's thirteen."

Bud knew their ages. He had merely asked that question to remind Paul that his kids were just that, kids, not adults. Paul did not need reminding.

Paul did not wait for another question. "We have to go. We have to get away as a family. The three of us. We have to leave that house. We have to leave Highland Park. We have to get away from all of those memories and be together."

"I can understand that." Bud paused. "Bobbie's been . . . dead for only four months. The three of you need more time together. But why Israel?"

"That is where we all want to go. Carolyn is going to

go to camp there. This way she can be with me and Joshua for a few weeks, and then be with her friends and still come back to us for weekends.''

Bud did not seem very impressed by this.

''And besides, I have work to do there.''

''You could do your work anywhere.''

Paul wished that Bud were right. But he wasn't. Paul could not work anywhere. He could not do any work at all here. He hadn't done anything worthwhile since Bobbie died. He knew that. Bud knew that. Hell, Bud had been covering for him for four months. That couldn't go on. Paul had to be able to do his own work, to do those things that made his life worthwhile. He had to be able to pick up the pieces.

''You could work in London,'' Bud suggested.

''No.''

''In Paris.''

''No.''

''Why not in Amsterdam?''

''No.''

''Why not?''

''No. It has to be Israel.''

''Why?''

''My sister, Pat, is there. Her husband, Jonathan, was my college roommate, my closest friend. They moved to Israel in 1972. I need to be with them. We all do.''

Arnold Chiari knew the discussion was over and that he had lost.

''Do me one favor, Paul.''

''What's that?''

''Don't get involved in any murders or terrorist plots.''

''Me?'' Paul said in mock innocence.

''Paul, aside from teaching neurology, there is nothing you enjoy more than playing detective.''

Bud was right about that. Paul had played amateur sleuth before, and loved every minute of it. And he'd done it very well. But that had been in Chicago. ''Don't worry. I'll keep my nose out of such things. After all, I'll be in Israel, not Chicago. I'll be an outsider.'' Paul was no longer looking at Bud, thus did not see that there was no need to say any more. ''I need to be there. I have work to do there. I have to be there this summer. Now.

If there is anything I can do to help out . . .'' Paul stopped. He knew he had said more than he had to say.

Neither doctor spoke for several moments and then Arnold Chiari ended the farewell, ''Take care of yourself!''

''I will. And you can take care of my beloved White Sox.''

''I won't do that. I may share your love for neurology, but I detest baseball. I'll run your department for you, but I won't watch a single inning.''

''No one's perfect.'' Paul smiled. ''Stop worrying, Bud. I'll come back in one piece. Now, get out of here and let me finish my work so that I can go home and pick up the kids and get to O'Hare on time.''

It took Paul over two hours to finish all the work that had piled up on his desk. When he was done, his desk was clearer than it had been in years. He had dictated over a dozen letters, five memos, and one brief research report. He had proofread one abstract to be submitted to an international meeting to be held next February in Puerto Rico. He then returned several phone calls from patients, looked at all the pictures one last time, and left his office.

In his reception room he ran into an old patient.

''Mr. Greenberg, I wasn't expecting to see you today. I didn't think I had any appointments, but I have time.''

''I have no appointment, Dr. Richardson.''

''No?''

''No. I came here to give you an errand to do.''

''An errand?''

''Yes. There is an old tradition dating back at least a thousand years, that anyone who makes a journey, and on that journey carries out an act of tzedaka, charity, for another Jew, will travel safely. So I am here to give you eighteen dollars for the rebuilding of synagogues in the old Jewish quarter.''

''Thank you,'' Paul replied. He recognized the significance of both the mission and the amount of money. The number eighteen mystically represented two Hebrew letters which spelled out the word *''chai,''* meaning ''life.'' Hence ''eighteen'' also meant ''life.''

''It is I who should thank you for helping me carry out this act of charity.''

Paul took the eighteen dollar bills, put a paper clip on them, and put them in his wallet. It was time to go.

Jonathan and Pat met them at Ben Gurion Airport. It was an emotional scene, mixing both joy and tears. The two families had not seen each other in three years. And when this scene had been planned, Bobbie had still been alive. No one mentioned her at the airport. Everyone thought about her.

They loaded the luggage onto the van and all climbed in.

"Where to?" Jonathan asked.

"Let me off at the Central Bus Station," Paul replied. "I . . ." he began. He couldn't say any more. The Weisses would let him off and then take Carolyn and Joshua to their home at Neve Ilan.

As soon as he saw the wall of the Old City, Paul knew he had made the right decision. He had had to come to Israel, without Bobbie. It was one more act of grieving he had to work his way through.

Jerusalem.

The soul of Judaism for three thousand years. The World's Holiest City.

Jerusalem.

Paul and Bobbie had often talked of moving to Israel, of becoming citizens of the Jewish state. Bobbie had been sure that was what she had wanted to do with her life. Paul had been much less sure, more ambivalent, and now that Bobbie had been killed in that auto accident, and he was alone with their children, the question remained unresolved. This lingering doubt was one reason why he had had to come to Israel. He hadn't mentioned that reason to Bud. There had been no need to. But it was there nonetheless, and it was time to resolve it.

He entered the Old City through the Jaffa Gate, past the walls built by the Ottoman ruler Suleyman the Second, in the sixteenth century, on the foundations of earlier Roman and Crusader walls. Paul knew the history of each building, of each remnant. As he paused, it was as if he could hear the voices of each era competing to be heard, demanding to be felt.

The modern Jaffa Gate, a breach in the ancient walls created so that the Kaiser could enter the city triumphantly in 1890, led him into Citadel Square. To his right was the Citadel itself, a Mameluke structure erected upon a Crusade fortress and buttressed by foundations built by Herod himself. Without looking, Paul knew that the road to the right went to the Armenian quarter, while to the left was the Imperial Hotel, where the Kaiser had stayed during his visit. Unfortunately, not much remodeling had been done since the Kaiser had signed out. Up a small alleyway he could see a marble column carved by the Tenth Roman Legion, which had been stationed here after Jerusalem had been destroyed on the orders of Hadrian. He remembered taking a picture of Joshua there when he had been only three or four years old and trying to teach him exactly who the Romans had been. So many voices clamored to be heard, so many spirits. But those voices would be for other times. And there would be time, but now there was only one voice which counted. He plunged straight ahead, down a narrow street of Arab-owned shops, past the Crusader Hall, now used as a vegetable market, up a narrow street to the left, past the rubble of the rebuilding of the Jewish quarter, and there it was, in front of him.

The Western Wall.

The Wailing Wall.

For Jews this was the heart of Jerusalem, the most important spot in God's city.

The Wall is the only remnant of the Temple. It was never actually part of the Temple itself, which had been built on the top of Mount Moriah. This wall was only part of a retaining wall completed by Herod in order to enlarge the Temple Mount. When Titus had destroyed the Temple and pushed its ruins off the mount, all that was left was the retaining wall. Ever since, Jews had come here to a small remnant of that wall to pray, to lament, to dream of someday having Jerusalem back. That dream had finally come true. But Paul Richardson came here not in triumph but to pray and lament for all those Jews past and present who had been unable to pray at the Temple, and especially for one in particular.

Paul stood at the Wall and thought about the Wall, and about Bobbie, and about the history of the Temples. Each

Jew knew of two Temples from childhood, but there had also been a Third Temple, shrouded in mystery. Paul knew he had to investigate that mystery. No harm in that. Delving into this ancient issue would not violate his promise to Bud Chiari.

While Paul stood in front of Herod's massive wall, the body of Nahum Eckstein lay on a metal table in the pathology laboratory of Maimonides Hospital. Overhead hung a bright fluorescent light, a microphone, and a scale.

Rabbi Nahum Eckstein had had a peculiar relationship to the object of Paul's pilgrimage. He had been the leader of the Guardians of the City. The Guardians could trace their history all the way back to the time of the Crusades. Over the centuries, they had made it their business to preserve a Jewish presence within the Holy City. Century after century, fighting one hostile force and then another, the Guardians did whatever had to be done to assure that Jews could live in Jerusalem.

That mission had changed in 1967. All of Jerusalem was once again under Jewish control. For the first time since the destruction of the Holy Temple by the Romans in the year 70, Jews were both welcome and safe in Jerusalem. Under such circumstances, the Guardians seemed to most Jews to have become superfluous. The Israel Defense Force was more than merely adequate to protect Jerusalem. But the Guardians did not disappear. Instead, they expanded their horizon. The presence that they now felt needed to be safeguarded was no longer restricted to Jerusalem. After all, God, blessed be His Name, had given Moses and the descendants of Israel the entire Promised Land, not just the Holy City. This small group of underground fighters now became a highly visible faction of religious-political fanatics agitating for Jewish control of all the lands once possessed by the Twelve Tribes of Israel.

Seven people were now gathered around the body of the former leader of the Guardians. Despite the relatively large number of observers, there was no conversation, no gallows humor. The doors to the room were locked. The six men and one woman all knew Eckstein's political history. They also knew his medical history.

Three weeks after suffering through a mild upper-respiratory-tract infection, Nahum Eckstein had noticed a numbness and then a weakness of his feet. In a few days his legs became weak, and then he could no longer walk or even get out of a chair. His friends physically carried him to Maimonides Hospital. By the time he arrived at the hospital, he had difficulty using his arms. The next morning, he could not lift his head off the bed; his arms and legs were completely paralyzed; his speech was slurred. He could only move his diaphragm and chest wall a short distance, not enough to move in and out of his lungs the air he needed to survive.

Once he had been admitted to the Neurology Department of Maimonides Hospital, a diagnosis of Guillain-Barré syndrome had been made. They all knew that Guillain-Barré, or G.B., as it is called by those who prefer acronyms to eponyms, was caused by inflammation of the nerves, which results in progressive weakness and paralysis. This weakness most often begins in the legs and then works its way up the body to involve the arms, the face, and, at times, the muscles that control breathing, so that the patient can no longer breathe.

That is what had happened to Nahum Eckstein. Not too many years before, he would have died. Respirators which can completely take over respiration are not as old as the State of Israel. But they are common enough now, and one had been used to keep the rabbi alive. Then on June 8, 1982, at six-forty-five A.M., as the Israeli army stormed northward into Lebanon, Nahum Eckstein had been found dead. The respirator which had been preserving his life somehow was no longer plugged in to the electrical outlet of the intensive-care unit.

Three men stood out from the others; two were the pathologists in their surgical greens and plastic butcher aprons, and one was a man in a black suit wearing a round black hat. The senior pathologist, Yitzak Cohen, was about fifty-five, with short gray hair, thick glasses with wire rims which emphasized his steely gray eyes, and a face marked by scars of old acne. He spoke in short curt sentences, and with a tone that carried authority. The other pathologist was much younger, in his late twenties, with long black hair and a smooth face. He spoke only rarely, and when he did, his voice was soft and his sentences often incomplete.

The others all wore the long white coats of physicians. Finally one looked at his watch. This was Avram Schiff, chairman of the Department of Neurology at Maimonides Hospital. The rabbi had been his patient and the same responsibility that had been his during the rabbi's life continued after the rabbi's death. Avram Schiff had never been one to shrink away from responsibility, and he didn't now. "It's time to start," he announced.

With unexpected suddenness, Yitzak Cohen made three quick incisions, three long cuts, forming a deep Y. From the right shoulder to the sternum. From the left shoulder to the sternum. Down the middle of the sternum. Deep, rapid cuts down to the bone. The physicians gathered closer to the table. The man without a white coat had already stepped back so that he was no longer truly a part of the group. The young pathologist picked up the three-inch circular electric saw and began to divide the sternum. Above the high-pitched whir, Yitzak Cohen began to dictate his report into the microphone that dangled down from the ceiling.

"Autopsy number : 5742–87.

"Nahum Eckstein.

"Age sixty-two.

"Time of death: six-forty-five A.M., 17 Sivan 5742.

"Time of autopsy: four-forty-five P.M., 17 Sivan 5742.

"The body is that of a sixty-two-year-old male who appears to be his stated age."

From where he stood, the man in black could hear only the whir.

The entire autopsy took a little over two hours. Each time another cut was made in the body, the man in black seemed to cringe. Each time an organ was removed, he scowled. Within those two hours, all of the organs were removed, weighed, examined, sampled, and then put back into the various cavities of the body.

One of the physicians was a heart specialist. Chaim Abramowitz was chairman of Cardiology at Maimonides and he spent over an hour performing a detailed study of the heart that the pathologists had removed. Once he was done, he returned the heart to the pathologists, who then replaced it in the body. A number of small liquid-filled bottles stood in a row on a long counter in front of Yitzak Cohen. Each of the bottles had a fragment of tissue floating in a bath of clear fluid. Each also had a tag attached to it:

"5742–87 Heart."

"5742–87 Kidney."

"5742–87 Liver."

There was another set of similar bottles on a similar counter across the room. The red-haired woman, Rivkah Geller, chairman of Pharmacology and Toxicology, was carefully labeling this set of containers. While the bottles themselves were no different from the ones in front of Yitzak Cohen, the contents were quite different. These held no fragments of tissue, just different-colored fluids:

"5742–87 Blood, taken from the right atrium of the heart."

"5742–87 Urine."

"5742–87 Bile."

"5742–87 Gastric contents."

Having finished with these, she turned to another set of bottles with clear fluid and small bits of tissue and began the same process:

"5742–87 Liver."

"5742–87 Kidney."

Finally only one task remained, the removal of the brain and the spinal cord.

Once again Dr. Cohen picked up the scalpel. He made a deep incision around the back of the skull from just in front and just above the right ear to just in front and just above the left ear. One deft cut. Just as quickly, he peeled the scalp off the bone of the skull so that it hung down in front of the wooden block supporting the head of the lifeless form.

The whir was much louder this time, and higher-pitched. More penetrating. Even the two pathologists felt uneasy. It lasted only a few minutes and then the younger pathologist removed the top of the skull, exposing the coverings of the brain. Yitzak Cohen took a small scalpel with a new, sharp blade and started to cut through the outer lining of the brain.

"Do you have to remove the brain?" It was the first thing the man in black had said.

"Yes, Rabbi," Dr. Cohen answered.

The rabbi was not a physician. He did not understand what made the brain and the spinal cord different from all the other organs. He did not know that the brain had the consistency of melting Jell-O and that any attempt to cut it and study it before it had been properly fixed would merely destroy it without giving any useful information. He did not understand that each area of the nervous system had its own function. The brain is not like the liver, where each area is like every other area. Examining one section is as good as examining them all. The brain is not like that. To study the brain, the entire organ is needed.

The very concept of removing the entire brain and not putting it back was repulsive to the rabbi. Removing a piece of tissue was in itself a sacrilege. This was too much. He left.

Later that evening in a small dark room in an old building somewhere in Jerusalem, a thin intense man quietly cut up newspaper headlines, one letter at a time.

A B.
An e.
A w.
An A.
An r.
An e.
A t.
An H.
An e.
An n.
An I.
Another n.
A T.
An h.
An o.
An f.
An A.
A V.

Then he pasted the letters on a piece of writing paper: "BewAre tHe nInTh of AV."

Twice more he repeated the same procedure, cutting and pasting the same letters. Carefully he addressed three envelopes in childlike block Hebrew, then sealed them.

By now his cloth gloves were dark with newsprint. He turned off the one small lamp and went out to deliver the letters.

It was just after six when Paul got back to the Central Bus Station and into the line for the 85 bus to Pat and Jonathan's home in Neve Ilan. Other passengers collected rapidly. Many were listening to small transistor radios. Everyone was talking about the war. From the snatches he heard and understood, most Israelis supported the government. Some vigorously, others reluctantly. They had put up with more than enough for too many years. How long could the world expect them to allow the PLO to sit safely in Lebanon and send its Russian-made rockets crashing into Israel whenever and as often as it wished? How many could Cuba launch before America reacted? The war itself was going as well as could be expected. The major enemy was clearly Syria. Syria controlled most of Lebanon and much of the PLO. Twenty more Syrian MIGs had been shot down in the skies of Lebanon. The ancient town of Sidon was under siege. It was a historic moment which Paul fully appreciated. For the first time in almost three thousand years, Jews were besieging a Philistine stronghold. The road from Beirut to Damascus was all but under Israeli control. But aside from these gratifying reports, there was another issue to face. How many Israelis were dead? How many were wounded? All wars cost, but Israel was so small that lives lost were never merely statistical body counts. They were real people. The announcer's voice did not vary, but the list of the dead came out as a dirge. Most of those killed had been junior officers leading their troops. The list of dead was read out. Name, Rank, Age, Home. No need to give religion. So many. So young. Sixteen in all. Would it be worth the cost?

Once the news was over, the crowd relaxed. Perhaps there would be a cease-fire soon. They seemed to be more relaxed than people in a train station in Chicago with its threats of pick-pockets and muggers. Yet they all knew that the dangers were more significant. The Central Bus Station was an easy site for a terrorist bomb. The milling crowds could never be searched. The relaxed atmosphere was misleading. the slouching soldiers with

automatic weapons over their shoulders were not all just
killing time. As he waited in line, one of the soldiers
asked Paul if the shopping bag resting against the bench
in front of him was his. It wasn't. Quickly the others in
the disorganized queue were asked the same question and
all gave the same response. Suddenly dozens of alert efficient soldiers appeared from out of the crowd and the
station was cleared. In less than a minute the bomb squad
appeared. As the asbestos suited experts approached the
lonely paper bag someone broke out of the crowd. A
seventy year old, short, bustling woman clamoring for
attention. It was her bag. She had to go to the bathroom
and it was too heavy to carry with her. The bomb squad
departed, the soldiers disappeared into the once again
noisy crowd and the queue reformed with Paul Richardson somehow further from the front than he had been
before. Nothing more than a story to tell when he got
home.

The 85 bus drove into its stall at the bus station and
everyone quickly boarded. The hoarse vendors made their
last pitches for Popsicles, "arctic, arctic, lemon arctic,"
rolls, "bagela, bagela, bagela," and newspapers, "yediyot, yediyot." Paul Richardson passed up the first two
but bought a newspaper as the bus pulled out.

The death of Nahum Eckstein was buried on the fourth
page. Paul did not get to it until he finished reading the
war news. The story began with a long description of
Eckstein's checkered career as he moved from hero of
the underground working against the British to reactionary outcast whose name was respected only in certain
zealot circles. It was the last paragraph that attracted
Paul's attention and puzzled him. The article quoted
Avram Schiff, the head of Neurology at Maimonides
Hospital. According to Dr. Schiff, Nahum Eckstein had
died of Guillain-Barré syndrome. But very few patients
died of Guillain-Barré these days. Not with modern respiratory care. In fact, virtually no one died of Guillain-
Barré anymore. It was still possible to die from the
complications, certainly. A patient weakened by G.B.
might die of pulmonary embolism or perhaps of pneumonia, but not of Guillain-Barré itself. Maybe Avram
Schiff had neglected to mention the pneumonia or perhaps the reporter hadn't understood the significance of

the complication, or the role it must have played in the actual terminal event. As well as he could remember, Paul had never seen anyone actually die from Guillain-Barré syndrome. He was so caught up in his own thoughts that he almost missed the last line of the story: "An autopsy will be performed." Once he read this simple sentence, he found it to be even stranger than attributing the death to G.B.

The background hum of conversations came to a complete and sudden halt. Fragments of Hebrew, Arabic, Yiddish, and some languages Paul could not easily place no longer filled the air. The bus had just left the friendly Arab village of Abu Gosh and was turning slowly on the narrow, winding road through the Judean Hills. It was at this exact spot just one year earlier that some not-so-friendly Arabs had machine-gunned another 85 bus, killing and maiming several passengers, including a pregnant woman and her never-to-be-born child. Like Nahum Eckstein, they too had died in Maimonides Hospital. There was no marker on the road. But the collective memories of the passengers pinpointed the spot.

The hiatus was brief. As soon as the bus had negotiated the turn and regained its usual speed, the conversations began again. In less than two minutes Paul got off at Neve Ilan.

2

It was now after nine. Dinner was over. Carolyn and Joshua were ready for bed, but the mixture of exhaustion and excitement did not permit them to go to sleep. Instead, they sat and talked, half-dazed in the warmth of what was to everyone else a cool evening.

Pat had changed in the last three years. She was still warm and giving, and it was her warmth that was reflected in Carolyn's half-closed eyes. But Pat now had a greater sense of strength and determination than Paul remembered. She had not been his kid sister in years, but he had never felt her inner strength this clearly until he watched her with his two children. She did not skirt the issue that still troubled them. She was their aunt, not a substitute mother. But if they ever needed to talk, to cry, to be hugged, to be loved, an aunt might be just what they needed.

It was.

Paul saw the tears in Carolyn's eyes. She had cried only once that he could remember, at the funeral. She had told him she didn't want to cry in front of Joshua. Tonight that didn't seem to matter.

Pat smiled at her brother and nodded. It was time for him to leave. The kids needed to be alone with Pat. For the first time Paul understood why his niece and nephew had not been home to welcome them. He grabbed one more of Pat's cookies, took one last sip of coffee, kissed everyone good night, and went out to talk with Jonathan.

He walked down the solitary roadway of Neve Ilan until he reached the guard post. The gate had been lowered across the narrow blacktop road entering the settlement. The black-and-white barrier reminded Paul of the crossing gate he had gotten for his Lionel train set when he was nine years old. But this was no mere game being played here. A clear, cool evening had descended on the Judean Hills. Clear, cool, and quiet. There would be no more buses stopping at Neve Ilan until six-fifty-five in the morning. A few people would be coming back from Jerusalem later, but their bus would let them off on the highway three-quarters of a mile down the hill. One of the two guards would drive down to meet them. It wasn't that the walk up the gentle slope was particularly arduous, but it was safer that way. Here on what had been the border between Israel and Jordan until 1967, one could take very little for granted.

Neve Ilan was a moshav, the first cousin to a kibbutz. Like a kibbutz a moshav is an economic cooperative in which everyone works in industries owned by the cooperative. But each of the families has its own small town house and each family remains as a traditional family unit. To an outsider a moshav looks much like any other small village of some several hundred people perched on a small rock-strewn hilltop.

Each night two settlers from Neve Ilan shared guard duty. Such was the way of life in settlements, even those in the heart of Israel, just ten miles from Jerusalem. It had been that way before 1948, when the British protected only themselves, and the Arabs needed no protection, and it remained a necessary part of everyday life. And now, with a war going on, who knew what might occur?

Jonathan was at the gate. The two men greeted each other and leaned on the gate, staring down the road into the star-filled sky. The contrast between the two old friends was as strong as the bond between them. Both had changed over the years. Richardson was an inch under six feet tall, and though he had not put on any weight over the years, even he recognized how his sedentary life as a professor in a medical school had contributed to a significant shift in the distribution of his body weight, so that he looked heavier and shorter than ever. His face remained smooth and rounded. His hair had receded several inches. Jonathan Weiss, on the other hand, now seemed taller than his six feet, five inches, and thinner. Yet Paul was sure his old college roommate had not lost any weight.

The Mediterranean sun had already descended below

the horizon and it was now completely dark. Neither man seemed to be in a hurry to talk. Paul loved watching the stars over Jerusalem. There seemed to be so many more than there were in the sky above Highland Park.

"How many times have you been here to Neve Ilan?"

"Three."

"Three." Jonathan shook his head. "I thought it was more."

"No, only three. Nineteen-seventy-four, 'seventy-six, and 'seventy-nine. The first two times, we only came out for a few days. In 'seventy-nine we stayed for three weeks."

"You've watched us grow."

They both listened to some dogs barking down the hill, in the direction of the Finnish kibbutz. In the distance they could hear a truck lumbering up the highway. It was Paul who interrupted the silence. "It's strange how we ended up."

"Strange?"

"Yes, strange. Here you are with your Ph.D. in theoretical mathematics, raising turkeys, and me, the premedical student who wanted to be a neighborhood physician, what do I do? I teach and do research in a medical school."

"That's not what's strange."

"No?"

"What's strange is why you aren't here, especially now."

"I am here."

"You know what I mean. We both know that survival of Israel is one of the few things that really matters in this crazy world. So why aren't you a part of it?"

"If I knew that, I wouldn't be here now." In the darkness Paul couldn't see the puzzled look on Jonathan's face. He could only make out his profile. If he added a white beard, he would look like one of the patriarchs. "It's just that if I knew for sure, I'd either go somewhere else whenever I have time off, or I'd already be living here like you, raising turkeys—"

"We do a hell of a lot more than raise turkeys," Jonathan interrupted with more than a trace of anger in his voice.

"I know that. Raising turkeys is just symbolic of the

differences in our lives. You do what you do because your country needs that specific job to be done by you. I do what I do because it's what I like to do.''

"Is it?''

"You know darn—'' Without any warning Jonathan interrupted Paul by holding up his hand.

"What's the—?'' Paul began again.

"Shush.''

Jonathan heard a noise. Exactly what, he wasn't sure.

Paul saw the tension mount in his friend's body. He too tried to listen as hard as he could. He heard something now; they both did.

Footsteps.

Coming up the road toward them was the sound of half-muffled boots.

"Shalom,'' Paul called out.

"Shalom, Jonathan,'' a voice called back to them.

Jonathan's entire body relaxed and a smile crossed his lips. It was the other guard. All three men spoke quietly for a few moments. Then Jonathan and Paul walked off together, Jonathan with his Uzi submachine gun over his shoulder, Paul an unarmed visitor.

Even more stars were visible in the sky, and it was becoming chilly, as it did even in summer in the Judean Hills. They turned uphill and walked to the western edge of the summit. In the distance were the lights of Tel Aviv, and beyond them, the blackness of the Mediterranean.

"Tell me about it.''

"What's to tell? She was killed in an accident by a drunken driver. She was dead before they got her to a hospital. We never got to see her before . . .'' He paused, swallowed, and went on. "The kids wanted to be here this summer with Pat and you.'' He hesitated again. "So did I. So we came.''

"Dammit, Paul! There is more to it than that. Those are a mere set of facts. She was not one of your patients who just happened to die.''

Jonathan had done it. He always did. Paul couldn't fool him. He'd never been able to. Thank God.

His armor had been pierced, his bravado shattered. He began to cry. He, too, had not cried since the funeral. It took almost an hour, but Paul spilled out his grief, his insecurities, his doubts that he could be enough of a family for Carolyn and Joshua, his worries about their ability to come to terms with what had happened. Jonathan listened. He said very little. An occasional word of encouragement, a rare question.

Paul's voice became hoarse.

And then there was nothing more to say.

"You should have come sooner."

"The kids had to finish school."

"Perhaps," Jonathan conceded. "We've all learned to deal with death here. It's never easy. And it's never the same. But we are here."

Paul nodded. Thank God.

Jonathan understood that it was time to change the subject. "What will you do all summer?" he asked.

"I'm not sure. I brought some research data with me, which I want to write up, and I may do a little work on an outline for a textbook."

"That official work should take you, all told, about a week and a half. You must have been planning to do something else."

"I'm going to read everything I can about the Third Temple."

"The Third Temple? What Third Temple?"

"Our Third Temple. Right there on Temple Mount," Paul explained.

"Paul, there have only been two Temples."

"Only two Temples were ever completed, but a third was started.

"When was that?"

"In 363."

"In Roman Jerusalem? Jews weren't even allowed into Jerusalem then."

"Except on the ninth day of Av to mourn the destroyed Temples."

"So how could we rebuild the Temple?" Jonathan asked.

"We didn't."

"Then who did?"

"Julian, the Apostate," Paul replied.

"Why would any Roman emperor, even if he was an apostate, want to build the Jews a temple?"

"Julian was a pagan. He believed in the old gods, not in any one god, and certainly not in the god of the Christians. Even though he had been raised as a Christian, Julian didn't accept Christianity. He wanted to suppress Christianity and bring back paganism.''

"Paganism!''

"That's right. Paganism. Although Julian would never have used that term. He called himself a Hellene, not a pagan—a believer in the old gods, in that old-time religion, in the gods who had made Rome great. The new god had never done anything for Rome. In fact, Julian knew that the Romans had crucified Jesus and was convinced that Rome was very unlikely to derive much benefit from him.''

"Why would a pagan want to rebuild the Temple to the God of the Jews? We rejected all their idols and all their gods.''

"Because he hated Christianity.''

"I'm not sure I'm following this.''

"Look, Julian fervently believed in the old religion, but how could he reestablish it? First he had to discredit Jesus and the Christian church. How could he do that?''

"A rhetorical question, I presume.''

"Correct. He could discredit Jesus and the church by making liars out of them. Julian was a bright guy. Pagan writers call him Julian the Philosopher. He knew church history. He knew that Jesus had taught that the Second Temple would be destroyed and that not one stone would be left standing upon another and that the church was teaching that the Jews were scattered across the face of the earth because they had rejected Jesus. They weren't teaching that we had killed Jesus yet, since they were operating in the Roman world where everyone knew that crucifixion was solely a Roman form of capital punishment. Jews stoned people for their capital sins against God. What would be an easier way to show up Jesus and the church than to rebuild the Temple? If the Temple were there, then the prophecy of Jesus was wrong, or at least only applied for three hundred years, and if the Jews came back to their Temple and their land, the bishops were liars. So he started to rebuild the Temple.''

"What happened?''

"That's what I want to find out. Apparently things didn't go well. Soon after construction began, it stopped. According to Christian authorities, the bowels of the earth opened up and great balls of fire erupted, destroyed the building site, and formed a great cross in the sky.''

"A true miracle." Jonathan chuckled.

"For true believers, yes."

"You don't—"

"Of course not. But something happened, something important. I'm pretty sure of that. Even some of the pagan writers agree on that, and I'm going to spend some time here reading about it in various old sources."

"Why?"

"Why?"

"Yes, why do you care so much about an obscure Roman emperor and an unimportant page in history?"

Again a question only Jonathan would have known existed and that had to be answered.

"Because I don't know what happened. Because no one knows what really happened. Because it happened sixteen hundred years ago and no one else cares and I can get lost in it and not think about . . . anything else."

"Paul, that's the wrong thing to do."

"Is it?"

"Yes. You should be binding yourself to life, to *this* Israel, not burying yourself in the past. Look at what we have done here."

"It's what I can do now. Later, who knows? I certainly don't." Paul hesitated. "It might feel good to be involved."

"It does. Believe me, it does."

Paul believed him.

They walked back around the southern border of the settlement and got back to the gate in time for the other guard to drive down to the bus stop. It was ten o'clock and time for the news. Jonathan fished a small radio out of his knapsack and flicked it on. The two old friends listened carefully. There was nothing new being reported from Lebanon. The army was close to carrying out its primary mission of cleaning out southern Lebanon and freeing northern Israel of the persistent threat of sudden death from PLO rockets, shells, and infiltrators. The Russian-made surface-to-surface missiles had a range of forty kilometers. Israel had now taken complete control of forty kilometers of land north of what had been the old border. Israel's northern settlements were now safe for the first time in decades. Some Israelis believed that this was enough. Others, the majority, wanted to move on and destroy the PLO once and for all; as if Israel's Arab enemies and non-Arab friends would allow that to happen. They only half-listened to the rest of the broadcast: threats of retribution by terrorists and radical Arab states, the usual denunciation of Israel by Russia, the expected condemnations by supposed friends, support by Washington, the continued inflation and new taxes to help pay for the campaign into Lebanon. Funeral arrangements had been made for Rabbi Nahum Eckstein.

"How would Eckstein have felt about your Third Temple?" Jonathan asked.

"I don't know. I don't think there were any Guardians of the city then. Jews weren't officially allowed to live in the city, so there was no one to guard."

"I think that Rabbi Eckstein would have liked it," Jonathan replied.

"Why?"

"He was a strange man. Spoke only Yiddish except when studying the Bible, since he believed that Hebrew was a holy language. But he believed in Israel and fought for it despite his differences with the state. He wasn't one of those reactionaries who believed that only the Messiah can bring about a Jewish state in Israel. His two sons both died in the Yom Kippur War in 'seventy-three. His only daughter lives on the border, just this side of Lebanon.

"I'm not sure there were any Jews like that then."

The vehicle was returning and it was time for Paul to turn in. The two men looked at each other and for the first time hugged one another. As Paul turned and walked up the hill, Jonathan said softly, "I'm glad you're here. Two months is better than a few days or weeks. Perhaps you will be able to work something out."

Paul Richardson was up long before the early sunrise. His biological clock had not yet adjusted to his new environment.

The children were both asleep. He did not know when his sister had put them to bed. They were already fast asleep when he had left Jonathan and come home. The small attached cottage they had rented was identical to every other house on the hilltop. Downstairs there were a narrow kitchen with a two-burner gas stove and a small refrigerator and a large all-purpose living area. Upstairs were a bathroom and three modest bedrooms, one for each of them. The furnishings varied from frugal to Spartan, their style from Israeli pseudo-Scandinavian to early hand-me-down. It was a far cry from Highland Park.

Paul put on the teakettle, boiled some water, and made instant coffee for himself. It was not long before Carolyn and Joshua were up. He made breakfast for the three of them and they listened to the morning news. More air battles had taken place over Lebanon. Twenty-two more Russian-built MIGs had been shot down. Syria was losing them faster than Russia could supply them.

As soon as the news ended, Jonathan came in through the open patio door. The children hugged their uncle warmly.

"What are you two going to do all summer?"

Carolyn answered first. She was going on a six-week seminar with other Americans, friends of hers who had all gone to the same Jewish camp together in Wisconsin. It wouldn't start for almost two weeks.

"Until then?" Jonathan inquired.

"Nothing special."

"How would you like to work around here until then?" Jonathan asked.

"I'd like to," Carolyn answered.

"We need you. Eighteen of our men have been called up."

"I'll do whatever I can to help," Carolyn said. It was the most enthusiasm she had shown in months. Was it that she felt more needed here? Or was it that she had been able to share her feelings with her aunt?

"Are they being sent into Lebanon?" Paul asked.

"Some," Jonathan answered. "Some are on the Golan Heights or the West Bank. With them gone, we're short on manpower."

"Can I help too?" Joshua asked. "I'll be here all summer."

"Sure."

"What will we do?" Carolyn asked.

"I'm not sure. I'll ask the woman in charge of the

work schedule and we'll set something up. Work for teenagers, sixteen and thirteen years old.''

"By the way, I'm here too," Paul said.

"I actually came by to see you."

"I would never have guessed it."

"I made a phone call just now to a friend of mine, Eleazar Danin. His family has lived here for seven or eight generations, or maybe more. He grew up in the Old City, before 'forty-eight, and has lots of friends from that time: Jews, Christians, Arabs. Friends who have spent their lives in love with Jerusalem. Like Danin himself. Together they must know more about Jerusalem than any library. I told him about your project and about you and he said he'd like to meet you. He said if you were going to be in Jerusalem today, you could come by his office at three."

"Do you really think I should bother him? I don't even know him."

"Yes. He wants to meet you and see if he can help you."

"Thanks, Jonathan. Maybe he can show me where to go for the right sources."

The letter with its childish scrawl arrived on the desk of Eleazar Danin at nine-thirty that morning. It had no stamp on it and had apparently been put into the mailbox sometime after he had gone home the day before. Most likely an ad or an announcement of some sort, Eleazar thought as he carelessly opened the letter.

BewAre tHe nInTh of AV

He grabbed his phone, hoping that the letter was not an announcement.

At exactly the same time, Paul Richardson walked down to the central building of the moshav to use the pay phone. First he bought the necessary tokens and then he got in line to use the phone to call Avram Schiff, the head of Neurology at Maimonides Hospital. He had set aside two hours for this task. It would not have taken any more time to drive there and back or take a cab, but hazardous as the Israeli roadways were, the phones represented even more of a challenge. Paul loved that chal-

lenge. He could not just reach into his pocket and put a
coin in the phone. He had to use a token, which, of
course, he had to buy at the post office, when it was
open. According to Jonathan, there was one advantage to
the tokens: inflation went up eight percent each month
and the tokens ten percent. That made them a great in-
vestment. Only in Israel.

He could not just dial 0 and reach a friendly operator.
No 411 would be followed by courteous information. And
the phone books were useless. When brand new they were
inadequate, and no one had a new phone book.

As soon as you apply for a phone, you are given a
phone number, which is then listed in the phone book.
The phone itself you do not get for three, maybe four
years, just the number. Somehow, somewhere, it rings,
but you can't answer it since you don't have a phone.
Since you don't answer it, you must be out, so people
don't even stop by to say hello. Some system.

Paul was fourth in line. Everyone else made a number
of calls, to friends, to relatives, never any business calls.
The purpose of all the calls was the same. News. Not
war news. Health news. Was Ari safe? Had they heard
from Shlomo? Yes. Thank God. Jack was safe. The same
prayerful litany over and over.

It was Paul's turn.

On the third try he got through to an office in Maimonides Hospital. Not the Neurology office, but someone who actually knew Neurology's number, had dialed
it recently, and gotten an answer. They gave him the
number. It took him only two more tries and he got Neurology. Professor Schiff was there. They exchanged the
appropriate polite greetings and then Avram Schiff asked,
"How soon can you start working?"

"Start working? I wasn't planning to . . ."

"True, you weren't. But I want you to do some teaching for us, since we are short on staff. Two or three times
a week."

"If you need me, I'll help any way I can."

"Good. You can start tomorrow. Are the afternoons
good for you?"

"Sure."

"Say, one to three or three-thirty."

"Fine."

"Get here about twelve-thirty so we can talk a bit."
Dr. Schiff paused and his voice got softer and colder.
"Ahm . . . there's one other thing."

"Yes?"

"The dean wants to meet with you at four o'clock."

"Okay. I'd like to say hello to him. He's an old friend
of one of our rheumatologists."

"This is not just to say hello."

"No?"

"No. You know about Rabbi Nahum Eckstein's
death?"

"Of course. It's been on the news and in the papers."

"Then you understand?"

"No."

"The dean has appointed a select committee to go over
the details of his death and review the autopsy findings,
and he'd like you as an outsider with an international
reputation—"

"Of sorts."

Avram Schiff ignored the interruption. "He'd like you
to serve on the committee."

"Sure."

"Don't answer so quickly. It might take some time."

"I'll do it, Avram, but there is one thing I don't understand."

"What's that?"

"Nahum Eckstein was Orthodox, wasn't he?"

"Of course."

"Then how did you get to do an autopsy? Orthodox
Jews usually don't permit such things."

"The law demanded it."

"Demanded it?"

"Yes. See you tomorrow."

Demanded it. What a strange choice of words. Yet
Avram, like many educated people who learned English
in college or later, was always precise in his choice of
words.

Demanded it. Paul repeated the phrase to himself. Why
would the law demand it?

Before he left for Jerusalem, he stopped by to see Pat
and Jonathan again. Their house was identical to the one
Paul had rented, but it was furnished as a real home so

that it was hard to recognize that beneath the surface it was twin to the Richardsons'.

Jonathan was up, having slept a few hours, and was starting to shave. As he lathered his face, Paul asked him, "What's the government's stand on autopsies here?"

"Pretty traditional." Jonathan began shaving.

"Meaning . . ."

"An autopsy is viewed as a desecration of the dead and is only permitted to save the life of another patient."

"That's it?"

"Yes. That's it."

"What about medical schools? Students have to learn anatomy, don't they?" Paul asked.

"Not from the bodies of Orthodox Jews."

"True."

"To the Orthodox, no one is permitted to derive benefit from the deceased."

"Then how come they did an autopsy of Nahum Eckstein?"

"They did?"

"Yes. Avram Schiff told me. It was even in the paper."

"Are you sure?" Jonathan asked.

"Yes. Avram said the law demanded it."

"You must have misunderstood. The law only demands an autopsy in cases of murder or suspected murder."

Paul did not think he had misunderstood. But if the rabbi had been murdered, why was there a select committee? Perhaps he had misunderstood. Or perhaps Jonathan didn't know the law that well. Jonathan was not a physician. There might be some other reason. "Perhaps," Paul said.

But if the rabbi hadn't been murdered, why had there been an autopsy? What other reason was there?

More questions that could only be answered later.

Paul left his teenagers with their aunt and took the bus into Jerusalem. He found the building he was looking for without any difficulty.

The office was on the second floor of an old building just off Jaffa Road, far enough off to be away from the constant bustle of shoppers and traffic. The plain thick wooden door had only two lines of lettering:

ELEAZAR DANIN
CONSULTANT

Paul knocked on the door, and when he heard a buzzer releasing the lock, he opened it.

There were two women behind old wooden desks in the office, and another solid wooden door. Metal file cabinets lined the wall on either side of the door. A man in khaki pants, army boots, and an open sport shirt leaned on a chair against one wall, covered with maps of Jerusalem. A carbine was cradled in his lap. The windows opposite were open, and Paul could see the thick metal bars outside.

One of the secretaries smiled at him, so he told her his name.

"Mr. Danin is expecting you. Go right in."

Another buzz with a different tone, and as Richardson opened the door, the two secretaries began to type again.

"Shalom. Welcome to Jerusalem, Dr. Richardson."

"Shalom and thank you," Paul responded.

Eleazar Danin's office was small. So was Danin himself. He was no more than five-foot-seven, with a slight build. Paul guessed that he was in his early fifties, with a full head of gray hair and in excellent physical condition, not more than a few pounds overweight. All four walls of the office were covered with maps, often several thick.

"Our mutual friend has told me a great deal about you." Danin began.

"You have an advantage, then, because he told me very little about you."

"An advantage which makes you uncomfortable?"

"A little."

"Let me even things up, then. Would you like some tea perhaps?"

"Yes."

Danin pushed a button and spoke briefly on the intercom. He turned back to Paul. "I, like you, am a consultant, but our fields are a bit different. You are an expert on the topography of the brain. I on the topography of Jerusalem. You give consultations on the brain. I give consultations on Jerusalem for architects, city planners, and"—he paused briefly—"internal security."

"That explains the armed guard." Paul hesitated, then decided to be blunt. "May I assume that city planning and architecture are only a sideline?"

"Yes and no. They take up most of my time. They pay the rent. But you are correct. They are not what I do."

"May I ask another question?"

"Yes."

"The training of a neurologist is well-defined. What we have to learn is rather clear-cut. But in your field, I assume, there are no residency programs."

"No. No," Eleazar said laughingly.

"How, then, does one become a consultant in your field?"

"A good question. I was born and raised in the Old City. I lived there until I was twenty-one. I knew every nook and cranny of it. After the War of Independence I studied archaeology and cartography, and here I am. Your training was more traditional."

"I'm afraid so."

"But the results were far from traditional."

"How so?"

"Very few neurologists have solved major murders."

"How do you know about that?"

"First of all, it's my business to know. But to answer your question, two ways. From Jonathan Weiss. And . . ." He paused as if unsure he should go on. "And I called a friend of mine who is a detective in Chicago. We worked together on a rather sensitive matter once."

The soft voice, which had been pleasant, now lost all of its conversational qualities. The words became harsher, harder. "Tell me, Professor Richardson, what happened on Tisha B'Av?"

This Paul could not answer without hesitating. "Tisha B'Av" was Hebrew for the ninth day of the month of Av. One of the most awesome of all days in the Jewish calendar. He knew the traditional teachings.

"According to the Mishna, five things. The decree that the generation that Moses led out of Egypt would not enter the Promised Land but would wander in the desert for forty years. The destruction of both the First and the Second Temple. The fall of Betar, the last stronghold of the second revolt against the Romans. And finally, the plowing under of Jerusalem by Hadrian."

"Very good." Danin sounded almost like a pleased teacher.

"That's not all."

"No?"

"No. In 1492, we were expelled from Spain on Tisha B'Av."

Danin nodded his agreement.

"Let me ask you a question," Paul went on without waiting for a reply. "What famous event did not happen on Tisha B'Av?"

"I'm not sure I know what you mean."

"Something scheduled to happen on that day was put off for no known reason."

"I don't know."

"Christopher Columbus was scheduled to sail out of Barcelona on the morning of Tisha B'Av in 1492," Richardson explained. "The *Niña,* the *Pinta,* and the *Santa Maria* were all loaded, the crews were aboard, the weather was clear, the winds were favorable. Without any explanation, Columbus put off the departure until the next day."

"Are you certain?"

"Yes. I don't think this means that Columbus was really a Jew, and like all Jews, unwilling to begin anything new on a day of recurring tragedies. But he was probably from a family of converted Jews who, for half-forgotten reasons, maintained some Jewish fears, traditions, and rituals. Like the first Spanish governor of San Antonio, who had a special bowl for ritually cleansing his hands before dinner each Friday night. A Jewish ritual without any Spanish or Catholic counterpart. He just did it because he had been taught to by his parents. He didn't know why. Neither did Columbus."

"You ask better questions than I do, Professor Richardson."

"No, not better. Different. You basically are a policeman, of sorts."

"Of sorts."

"As a policeman you ask questions to increase your knowledge. Your goal is to find out what people have seen or done or heard, to get at facts or versions of the truth that will in some way help you.

"I, on the other hand, am a teacher. I ask questions to

find out what people don't know, to define the limits of their knowledge and understanding. Only if I know that can I teach them something new.''

"Paul. I can call you Paul, can't I?''

"Certainly, Eleazar.''

Danin's tone was lighter now. "I'm sure we can help each other. Jonathan told me about your project, the Third Temple. It might be difficult to find everything you need to learn, but I do know many people, Jews, Christians, Arabs, who know a great deal about Jerusalem and its many almost hidden libraries. I'm sure some of them will help you.''

"That's very kind of you.''

"I'm not kind. I expect something in return.''

"What's that?''

"I want you to apply your brain, your approach, to a little problem with which I am faced. Normally I would not bother you, but these are not normal times. We are short on manpower. More important, we are short on brains. I think you might be able to help us.'' With that, he reached into the top drawer of his desk and pulled out a folded piece of cheap white writing paper, opened it up, and handed it to Richardson.

It contained three words. Each letter individually cut from a newspaper: "BewAre tHe nInTh of AV.''

"What do you make of it?''

"A warning.''

"Why a warning?''

"If it were just a reminder, it would be 'Remember,' not 'Beware.' ''

"That's what we thought. What else other than the obvious use of newsprint?''

Paul had nothing more to add, so instead he asked a question. "Does the author have to be Jewish?''

"No. He merely has to know about Tisha B'Av. This is not the U.S. Any educated person living in Israel would know about Tisha B'Av.''

"Why did he send it to you, Eleazar?''

"I wasn't the only one to get one.''

"Who else got one?''

"The mayor and the publisher of the Jerusalem *Post.*''

"That might explain why he chose English and not Hebrew.''

"Possibly. He might have used English in the hope of getting English-language news coverage, which of course he would never get for a single crank letter."

"But why you?"

"I'm not sure. I'm involved in security planning whenever we have a major event or whenever there's an important visitor here or anywhere within twenty or thirty miles."

"Does everyone know that?"

"Everyone that we wish didn't."

"Do you take the threat seriously?"

"We take every threat seriously. Very seriously. We have no other choice. Especially not now."

3

"Dad, how far have we walked?"

"About two and a half miles."

"That's about four kilometers, isn't it?"

"Right."

"That's not bad for an hour and a quarter," Joshua said, looking at his watch.

"No, it isn't, considering all these hills. Come on, Josh. Finish your drink and we'll get where we're heading for and then we'll walk back home."

Neither Paul nor Joshua said much the next twenty minutes. The sun was beginning to get hot as it rose above the crest of the surrounding hills, but they continued their trek until they reached the top of the hill and stood facing a pair of buildings.

"We have arrived." With that Paul stopped, removed his White Sox cap, mopped his brow, and then gazed at the modern church in front of him.

Joshua followed suit, but his gaze was one of disbelief. "Where are we, Dad?"

"It's a place called Day Hatzar."

"And we walked all the way up here to look at that concrete statue of Mary?" Joshua asked as he pointed to the tower which jutted out of the hill in front of them.

"That and the building."

"Dad, you've got to be kidding. There are older and more interesting-looking churches in Highland Park."

Paul was kidding. He hoped that his voice didn't betray him. "Older, yeah. But more interesting? Don't forget, we are in the Land of Israel."

When Joshua said nothing, his father continued, "This building, by the way, is not a church; it's a convent."

"There's a convent in Highland Park too."

"True, but this convent, although not even sixty years

old, is built upon the ruins of a fifth-century Byzantine church, and many of the original mosaics are still there, so we will take a look at them.''

"Dad, I'm not big on mosaic floors.''

"One other thing, Joshua. Before there was an ugly statue of Mary here sticking out like a sore thumb and before there was a convent here, back before they built a church here, this place had another name: Kiryat Yearim.''

"Kiryat Yearim.'' Joshua's excited voice echoed his father's words.

"Yes.''

"Are you sure?''

"Of course.''

"You mean we are standing on the place where King David danced before the Ark?''

"Yes.''

"The real Ark.''

Paul smiled. This was the only reason they had come here.

"The Ark,'' Joshua repeated.

Before his father could say any more, the thirteen-year-old began to pace back and forth across the open ground, looking not at the building, but at the ground.

"He didn't leave any souvenirs behind.''

"What's that?''

"I said you won't find any souvenirs.''

"I know that, it's just that this is one of the few places the Ark ever rested, Dad, and this is where David danced.''

Paul smiled and said no more. It took more than ten minutes before Joshua had finally stopped his pacing, which was almost a dance itself.

"Josh, do you know how the Ark got here?''

"The Philistines gave it back.''

"That's right, but why?''

"To get rid of a plague or something.''

"You're amazing. I never knew such things at your age.'' Paul shook his head and the two of them sat down together on a broken section of an ancient marble column.

"Joshua, your namesake, had set the Ark up at Shilah, and it remained there until it was captured by the Philistines. But wherever they took it, they were beset by misfortune. Ashdod. Gath. Ekron. Each place the same story. They were attacked by some sort of plague. Finally, in total desperation, the Philistines' own priests told them that they had to return the Ark in order to end the plague. So they returned it. First it rested at Beth Shem, then here, and here David danced before it as he rejoiced at its having been returned to the Children of Israel.''

"Dad, what happened to the Ark?"

"No one really knows. Tradition tells us two different stories. The second book of the Maccabees says that God warned the Prophet Jeremiah that the Babylonians would destroy the Temple. So Jeremiah took the Ark, the original Ark, made according to the instructions given by God to Moses, and the Altar of Incense from the Holy of Holies and buried them in a cave on Mount Sinai.''

"But . . ."

"Why do you look so distressed?"

"If they're at Mount Sinai, it means we just gave the Ark back to the Egyptians."

"Yes, but don't worry. They don't know it's there. It is hidden in a cave. And they didn't disturb it before we took the Sinai in 1967 and won't now."

Joshua was only partially relieved by this reassurance. "What's the other story?"

"The other story involves King Josiah. Josiah was King of Judah at the time of Jeremiah and had been greatly influenced by Jeremiah. He led a great religious renaissance. He repaired the Temple. But he, too, was worried about the fate of Jerusalem and the Ark. The Babylonians were threatening to invade. He supposedly took all of the major contents of the Holy of Holies—everything: the Ark, complete with the tablets of the Ten Commandments and several other things, the breastplate of the high priest, a pot of manna, and I forget what else, and hid them all in a subterranean passage under the Temple."

"Which one do you believe, Dad?"

"Mount Sinai."

"Why?"

"I just think it's more appropriate that the Ark and the Ten Commandments were returned to Mount Sinai to wait for God's next move."

"Not me."

"No?"

"No. I like the other version better."

"You may be right. There is an old story that when they were building the Second Temple, a priest noted a pile of elevated stones in an underground room full of stored wood. He immediately knew what he had found and raced to tell others, but was struck dead."

"Wow."

"That's what he said."

Joshua did not laugh at his father's joke, but thought for a moment before he spoke. "That's not why I believe it's inside the Temple Mount."

"Okay, what's your reason?"

"I think the Ark should be on Temple Mount. That's where it belongs."

"You may be right. In any case, the Ark was not left inside the Temple. Twenty-two years after Josiah died, when the Babylonians captured the Temple, the Ark was not there."

Paul put his arm around his son's shoulder and they began walking down the hillside. They had never seen the mosaics, but that wasn't why he had brought Joshua there. Paul, like his son, had no particular interest in Byzantine mosaics. It was the Ark that he cared about.

On another, more famous hill some twelve miles to the east of Neve Ilan, just on the other side of Jerusalem, just below the Intercontinental Hotel, three workmen, each wearing a skullcap, quickly dug a grave while one man clothed all in black and wearing a round black hat watched. Had anyone who had watched the autopsy been there, he would have immediately recognized him. From that spot on the southern slope of the Mount of Olives they could not see Temple Mount with its two Muslim crowns—the golden Dome of the Rock and the silver cupola of the El Aksa Mosque. All they could see was the edge of the wilderness of the Judean desert stretching south and east toward the Dead Sea and Ammon.

Once again the man dressed all in black who had been at the autopsy was standing off to the side, a few yards away from the action. This time, however, his face showed no disapproval. About a dozen khaki-clad armed men lounged around the area. Near the crest of the hill above them, their officer stood conferring with a man whose gray hair flowed in the wind.

The gravediggers, oblivious of the onlookers, finished their work and departed. The man in black inspected the grave site, looked up at the two men on the hillside above him, and left.

It was the young officer who broke the silence. "God, I hope there's no trouble."

"I don't think there will be. No Arabs will try anything in the open, and overnight we searched every inch for bombs."

"The crowd—"

"There will be no crowd."

"But—"

"Believe me. No crowd. His family, a few close friends and associates, a few long-standing enemies." Eleazar Danin looked down the Mount of Olives, gazed at the Temple Mount ever so briefly, and then focused on the groups of soldiers scattered on the hillside even as far as the turreted tomb of Absalom, the son of David, in the valley far below. "Your men will outnumber the mourners by at least three to one. And some of the mourners will even be under your orders." Eleazar Danin was confident there would be no problem. He had done his best to make certain of it. And now he had just stopped by to be doubly certain. Everything seemed to be under control. But in Jerusalem it was often difficult to be absolutely certain.

The young officer did not have to wait very long to see if the predictions of peace and quiet would prove to be valid. It was possible that the increased mobilization of the Israel Defense Force would keep the PLO in hiding. But the army never took anything for granted. After all, the village of Silwan, less than five hundred meters down the road from Absalom's pillar, was a PLO stronghold. Or had been before the advance into Lebanon. He wished he were up there, really doing something for his country, instead of guarding a fanatic's funeral.

Less than an hour later, a small procession walked slowly down the hill to the newly opened grave site. Six bearded men entirely clad in black, with broad-rimmed black hats and long flowing black coats, carried the simple casket of unfinished wood. The lieutenant counted carefully. In all, there were twenty-seven mourners.

When the short procession reached the grave, a few words were said and the casket was lowered into the earth.

Each mourner took a handful of dirt, threw it into the grave on top of the casket, and walked back up the hillside. Eleazar Danin had been right. There had been no trouble. It had been quiet on the Mount of Olives.

It had not been so peaceful in Gaza that morning. As Arab workmen got on their buses to go to work in Israel, a PLO hand grenade went off in the square. A wordless warning. Inarticulate perhaps, but nonetheless effective. No Arabs from Gaza went to work that day. Construction in much of Jerusalem came to a standstill. It was an effective protest organized with an efficiency even the Mafia would have admired. The PLO had learned much from their Russian teachers.

In some ways it was like being back home in Chicago. Paul had a long white coat on and was seated at one end of a narrow conference room. Three more white-coated figures were scatterd on chairs around the room. Two wore the long white coats of residents, the other the shorter white coat of a medical student.

Just like home, the professor waiting for the last student to show up so he could get started. Thank God they all knew enough English that he didn't have to try to teach in Hebrew. Now, if he could only remember who was who . . .

A second student, short, muscular, and with a crew cut, burst into the room. He appeared to Paul to be about twenty-eight or twenty-nine. "I'm sorry I'm late, but I just brought some spinal fluid over to Bacteriology. We are so shorthanded and—" He stopped his explanation short when Paul smiled and motioned him to sit down.

"Sit down. Catch your breath. I'm Paul Richardson and you are . . ."

"Yuri Aharoni."

"Okay, Yuri, let me tell you all a little about my style of teaching and what we're going to be doing together for the next month or so. According to your chief, Professor Schiff, an old friend of mine, the present situation would leave you with no one to run your teaching rounds for a while, so I'm going to pinch-hit, ah . . . substitute and make rounds with you two or three times a week. You can pick any case or even two cases you want to present, and I'll lead a discussion. I won't lecture you. No spoon feeding.'' Paul stopped again, unsure that everyone understood his last idiom. He hesitated and then explained again just a bit more carefully—he was not in Chicago. ''I will not teach you word for word, step by step. Instead, I'll ask questions to find out what you know and don't know, especially what you don't know, and then I'll try to help you learn something new. Please don't be embarrassed when I ask you a question you can't answer. That's what I'm supposed to do. If I can't find out what you don't know, I can't teach you, and that's what I get paid to do—except I'm not getting paid. One more thing. I'm terrible with names, so when we get started, begin by reminding me of who you are each time I ask you a question. Let's get started; I'm supposed to have a meeting with the dean this afternoon as soon as we're done.''

Everyone turned and looked toward the other end of the small room as one of the Israelis finally said something. ''Professor Richardson?''

''Dr. Richardson is okay.''

''Professor Richardson, I'm Dr. Rashem and I'm the chief resident on Neurology. Before we start, can I ask you a few things?''

Paul looked at the senior resident as he spoke. Dr. Rashem was darker than anyone else in the room and was at least six feet tall, with a short black mustache. Paul tried to remember the Hebrew word for ''mustache,'' but could not. He didn't like such formality, but if that was what they were used to . . . ''Certainly, Dr. Rashem. Ask whatever you want.''

''Would you like the students or the residents to present the cases?''

''The students, if possible.''

Dr. Rashem nodded and asked another question. ''Do you also want to see the patients yourself?''

''Of course.''

"Well, I guess Yuri will present the first patient. Yuri is our paratrooper from the Galilee."

That was a word that said so much: a paratrooper. Israel had universal military training. Everyone went into the army, but no one was drafted into the paratroops. That was strictly volunteer. More training. More years of active duty. More hazardous missions.

Yuri was a paratrooper.

He was also from the Galilee. The north of Israel, where PLO rocket attacks had long been a way of life.

A paratrooper from the Galilee. That one matter-of-fact statement had told Paul all he needed to know about Yuri's background. Paul settled back in his chair to listen to the presentation. The patient was a thirty-four-year-old woman with weakness of her right arm and a swollen, somewhat painful right shoulder. She had been in good health all her life. She was right-handed. According to the history she had given Yuri, she was not entirely sure when her problem started, but her right hand had slowly become weaker over the past four years, and over the last year or two her right shoulder had become swollen and had begun to ache. Yuri's examination of Mrs. Sassoon had confirmed the weakness of her right arm, especially of the muscles around her shoulder.

Paul interrupted the student. "Was there any sensory loss?"

"Yes, but I couldn't make much sense out of it."

Paul turned to the chief resident. "Did one of the residents examine Mrs. Sassoon?"

"Yes. I did, Professor."

The utter formality of the chief resident was too much for Paul. "What's your first name?" he asked.

"Hassan," the resident answered.

Hassan! A Muslim name. Paul had not expected to be working with any Muslims. Not here, not now. He knew that there were Muslim students and residents and physicians in Israel, but he had never thought that he would be teaching them.

Paul inadvertently stared back at the swarthy young man. He couldn't stop himself. Hassan appeared to be younger than the other resident, as young as the medical students—mid-twenties at the most. The dark, piercing eyes of the resident stared back.

"Yes, my name is Hassan. Hassan Rashem. I am from Abu Gosh. My family has lived there for so many generations even the village leaders lost count. I am an Arab, like John here." With that, he nodded toward the other male student seated next to Yuri. "But not a Christian one, a more traditional believer."

It couldn't be easy being "a more traditional believer" in Israel during a war. Perhaps the strain was getting to Hassan. This was not exactly what Paul wanted to discuss. At least not now and not in this setting.

"What were your sensory findings?"

"The only loss I could find was in pain sensation over both shoulders and down the right arm," Dr. Rashem responded.

"That was all?"

"Yes."

"No position-sense loss?"

"No."

"Or touch?"

"No."

"Or vibration?"

"No."

"How about temperature?"

Hassan shook his head. "I did not test that."

"Very interesting," Paul commented out loud. "Tell me about the shoulder, Yuri."

"The joint is about twice normal size," the student answered.

"Tender?"

"Yes."

"As tender as it should be, considering its size?"

"I'm not sure."

"Let's go see Mrs. Sassoon."

In the room, Dr. Richardson went over Rachel Sassoon's history with her and then examined her. She was thin, anxious, and smoked incessantly, holding her cigarette in her left hand.

What he found on his direct examination was no different from what Yuri and Hassan had reported to him. Weakness of the right arm, loss of pinprick sensation over both shoulders and down the right arm. He carefully examined her right shoulder. The joint was at least twice the normal size. He could move it easily, and the movement caused only slight twinges of pain.

Once they were back in the conference room, Paul wasted no time getting the discussion started. He turned first to a medical student, the short, thin one who wore a cross that Paul could just make out above his open collar and whose name was . . . Paul looked directly at him and the student supplied the answer. "I'm John Haddad. I'm from Jerusalem. My family has been here since the Crusades . . ."

John felt Hassan Rashem's stare and stopped. Paul directed the discussion toward medicine.

"John, what do you call that kind of joint? Do you know?"

John just shook his head. Paul looked at Yuri, but he didn't know the answer either.

"Hassan, do you know?"

"No."

He turned to the other resident, a dark young woman who sat back quietly, almost as if she were a spectator at a chess match, but she just shook her head without even introducing herself. It was almost as if she were concerned that the noise of her voice would somehow be a distraction.

"Well, I think she has a Charcot joint," Paul told them.

"Dr. Richardson," Hassan spoke up. "She has pain I thought a Charcot joint had to be painless, that the patient would have no pain."

"Most such joints are painless. They are caused by a loss or marked decrease in pain sensation, but sometimes the patient still has pain in the shoulder, like Mrs. Sassoon. The key to a Charcot joint is that the patient has much less pain than one would expect. This is certainly true of our patient. That shoulder is enormous and the pain is minimal." Paul paused. Time to change gears. He led them through a discussion of the diseases that could produce a Charcot joint. In ten minutes, they came up with four possible causes. Paul wrote them out on the blackboard:

1. Syphilis.
2. Tumor of the spinal cord.

3. Cyst of the spinal cord.
4. Injury of the nerves to the arm.

Then they discussed the evaluation which should be carried out. They would start with X rays of the neck to see if there was any evidence of a tumor. Such X rays were unlikely to show anything, but they were safe and easy and it was possible they would give an answer. If the X rays were negative, they would do electrical studies on the nerves going to the arm, and if these were also negative, they would have to do a myelogram to see the spinal cord itself.

Paul sat back down. The case was over.

"Dr. Richardson."

"Yes, Hassan."

"You did not test her ability to sense temperature."

"I didn't have to."

"Why not?"

"I knew it was decreased. I should have drawn your attention to it at the bedside. Thank you for reminding me. What was she doing when we walked in?"

It was the resident whose name he did not know who answered, "Smoking."

"Yes, smoking, and in which hand did she have her cigarette?"

Once again the dark young woman began to answer, but Paul stopped her. "I missed your name before."

"Dalia, Dalia Avni."

"Well, Dalia, let's see if one of the students was as acute an observer as you were." With that, he looked at the first student.

"Her left hand . . . I guess," Yuri responded.

"A good guess, Yuri, but one should not guess about observations. Now, why was she holding her cigarette in her left hand?"

"Because her right hand is too weak."

"Another guess. Not as good. You examined her. Is she too weak to hold a cigarette?"

"No."

"Then why?"

This time, Paul answered his own question. "On her right hand she has scars, burns she got from holding cigarettes too long because she couldn't feel their heat, because she had lost her ability to sense heat. There is no other explanation for such burns.''

He was done. He had made his point. Observation. Deduction. Understanding. He too understood one more fact. It was not strange that Hassan looked younger than the other residents. He was a citizen of Israel and therefore eligible to be educated by the state, even go to medical school, but unlike the others, he hadn't spent several years in the army first. Only Jewish Israelis had to do that. Not Arab Israelis.

It was Dalia who presented the second patient, Mrs. Fahoum, a thirty-six-year-old Lebanese woman who had been in good health until some three weeks earlier. (Did she say Lebanese? How had a Lebanese patient gotten here? Now?) He listened closely to get the exact details. The major problem had been a rather abrupt and marked change in her personality. Her family became frightened by her increasingly strange behavior. She became paranoid. Then she had a seizure and she became less and less responsive. This all took less than a week. That was two weeks ago, before Israel's invasion of Lebanon. A peaceful time, punctuated only by intermittent PLO shelling of the northern settlements. Mrs. Fahoum had been brought to Israel by her family.

"Across the border?" Richardson wondered out loud.

"Sure," Dalia explained. "We used to call it 'The Good Fence.' It's been going on for years. Any Lebanese Muslim or Christian who was sick and couldn't get help in Lebanon could come across the border and get medical care here."

"Most of the patients get taken care of up north right near the border, or in Haifa," Dr. Rashem added, "but we get six or eight patients a year in Neurology."

Paul nodded. There was so much the world didn't know! Muslim Lebanese coming to Israel for medical care and getting that care. They didn't get such treatment from the Syrians.

The service had evaluated the patient well. She had a form of inflammation of the brain, an encephalitis caused by a common virus, herpes simplex, the same virus that causes canker sores. In occasional patients, the herpes virus did much more than cause a small painful blister on the inside of the mouth. In those unfortunate few, it managed to enter the brain, and once there, it caused much more harm that it did in the mouth. Encephalitis resulted in personality changes, seizures, and frequently death. They had made the correct diagnosis and already started her on the best treatment, a drug called Arabinoside-A. The discussion was brief. There was little Paul could add to what they already knew and were doing correctly.

While Paul was enjoying himself, Eleazar Danin was not. The voice on the other end of the line spoke in a clipped, harsh tone. They had checked the other two copies as thoroughly as they had his. No, more thoroughly, if that was conceivable. There were no fingerprints on any of them. The paper was of the cheapest, commonest sort, sold thoughout the entire country in tablets and used by students everywhere. It was absolutely untraceable. The glue? Again, inexpensive, common. No, ubiquitous and untraceable. The lettering? From last Sunday's Jerusalem *Post*—the largest-selling newspaper in the country.

All of Eleazar Danin's worst apprehensions had been borne out. Nothing could be traced, nothing at all. This was not the work of some crackpot. "What about the handwriting?" he asked.

"If you could call that handwriting." Eleazar made no reply and the other speaker continued, "We're not sure whether it was done by a naturally left-handed person writing with his right hand or by a clever right-hander mimicking the style of a seven-year-old—a seven-year-old with significant hand-eye-coordination problems, at that."

The phone call was over. Eleazar leaned back on his chair, folded his hands behind his head, and gazed at the maps on his wall. Altogether it did not surprise him. His letter had been dropped into his mailbox while something had been held in front of the video camera that monitored it. That had been no accident.

He had never seriously believed that it was a prank or merely the effort of some harmless lunatic. This was well-planned, well-thought-out, and so far, well-executed. He only hoped that the rest of the plan, whatever it was, would not be as well-planned or as well-thought-out or as well-executed. It was his job to prevent that last step. If he could.

One of the walls of the dean's conference room was lined with portraits of the prime ministers of Israel. Dean Yehuda Ben Zvi sat near the end of the conference room under Begin. Avram Schiff, to his left, was under Rabin, while Paul Richardson sat in the chair next to Golda Meir. On a second wall there were other formal portraits, Herzl of course, and Chaim Weitzman and David Ben-Gurion, and some Paul Richardson did not recognize. It was Yehuda Ben Zvi who spoke first. "I'm not sure how much Avram has told you about this matter, Professor Richardson."

"Not much."

"Then it is best if I start at the beginning. As you know, a rather well-known patient died here this week—Rabbi Nahum Eckstein. Since the circumstances of his death were somewhat, shall I say, unusual, we decided to have an inquiry into all of the circumstances. He had a very serious neurological problem, and we would like you, as an internationally known neurologist, to sit on the committee."

"I'm not sure I understand. I'm not especially trained in neuropathology. Perhaps I have studied pathology a bit more than most neurologists, but I'm not a neuropathologist. If you're trying to make an exact diagnosis as to what kind of neurologic disease killed him, you already have an excellent neuropathologist here—Yitzak Cohen. He's a heck of a lot better than I am."

"He is on the committee, but the question is not just one of pathology."

"Was there some question of a poison or toxin of some sort?"

"We don't think so."

"Then I'm still confused."

"I'm just a poor general surgeon. Neurology has always been somewhat beyond me. Perhaps Avram can explain it better."

Paul turned to look at his old friend.

"Nahum Eckstein was sixty-two years old, and aside from some history of mildly elevated blood pressure, he had been in excellent health," the chairman of Neurology began. "Then he developed ascending weakness and paralysis, which spread rapidly for a few days—feet, legs, arm, neck, face . . ."

"Sounds pretty much like Guillain-Barré syndrome."

"That's what we thought when we admitted him to Neurology. And then he died."

"People do die of respiratory failure from G.B. You have to watch their respiration very carefully. Hell, you know that. At any sign of respiratory failure you put them on a respirator."

"Rabbi Eckstein was on a respirator," Avram responded.

"Did he develop pneumonia?"

"No."

"Then why did he—?"

It was the dean who broke in at this point. "He was found with his respirator unplugged."

"You're kidding."

"I wish we were," the dean answered.

It was Avram Schiff who went on. "He was in the intensive-care unit. He was stable. There was no sign of pneumonia." Avram took a deep breath. "It was one of those hectic days. The staff was working on two cardiac arrests at once, and when they got back to their other patients, he was dead."

"I'm not sure what there is here for a neurologist to investigate. This sounds to me like a police matter, not a medical problem."

"Yes and no," Avram Schiff continued softly. "Certainly someone pulled out his plug and we found him dead. Things were very confused. Someone may have found him dead and pulled the plug intentionally, but without a doctor's order, and now is afraid to admit it." Professor Schiff paused and then went on more slowly, less certainly. "It is quite possible his disease killed him."

Paul began to say something, but stopped as his friend continued.

"We thought he had G.B., but we weren't sure. I've seen a lot of cases of G.B., as I'm sure you have."

Paul nodded and Avram continued. "I've never seen a patient who was totally unable to trigger a respirator at all. Have you?"

Paul shook his head slowly.

"Neither has anyone here. So perhaps he didn't have G.B. but some sort of rare ascending inflammation that directly involved his brain stem and paralyzed his respiratory centers. I had just checked him over. He was getting worse. He had no movements at all. Not even eye movements. His blood pressure and pulse were getting erratic. The vital centers of his brain stem most likely were gone, and he may have been essentially dead."

"And whoever pulled the plug was merely terminating unnecessary life-support systems?" The sarcasm in Paul's voice was obvious to both of his listeners.

It was the dean's turn to respond. "That is not so far-fetched. Religious extremists are not rare here. Some zealots believe that removing life supports from someone who cannot recover is a commandment from God and that continuing such supports is a desecration."

"A mercy killing."

"No, not a killing at all. Not an act of mercy, but a necessary act to preserve the sanctity of the human body."

"Like not doing an autopsy?" Paul wondered aloud. The dean nodded.

"Can I ask a few more questions?" Paul inquired.

"Of course." It was the dean who responded.

"Let me be sure if I understand this. The committee is to make a full inquiry into all aspects of his death, and as far as you see it, there were three possibilities. One: murder. Two: sudden death and then the respirator was unplugged, inadvertently or not, and whoever unplugged it may be afraid he or she made a mistake in the midst of all the confusion of the ICU and isn't saying anything. Three: he was not retrievable and the unplugging, intentional or not, did not influence the final outcome."

Both Professor Schiff and Dean Ben Zvi nodded this time.

"An interesting problem! Will the committee be free to come to its conclusion without outside pressure?"

Paul looked at the dean as he asked this question.

"Yes."

"Will we be completely autonomous?"

"Yes."

"No interference?"

"None. You will even have whatever budget you need."

"And you want me because of my name?"

"Yes and no. There is no question that we want your name, the name of someone of stature on the final report, someone who is not involved in the internal affairs of Israel. But also we respect your opinion and experience. You are not here to put a rubber stamp on a whitewash."

"What if I have a different opinion from the others? Can I write a minority report?"

"Anyone can. We hope to have one single report, but there can also be one or more minority reports."

The intensity of Paul's rapid-fire questions disappeared as he went on. "Who else is on the committee?"

"Some of them you already know. Avram, our chairman of Neurosurgery, Romain Bernhard, and Yitzak Cohen, our neuropathologist. These men you know."

"Yes."

"The others are Chaim Abramowitz from Cardiology, Rivkah Geller from Pharmacology, and Rabbi Aaron Levi. He was an old friend of Nahum Eckstein's. They grew up together in the Old City, went to the same yeshiva, fought together, mourned together, but after 'fortyeight they split politically. They remained friends by never talking politics. He spoke at the funeral of one of Nahum's sons. I have rarely been so moved."

For a few moments no one spoke.

"Is that the entire committee?"

"Yes."

"Who is the chairman?"

It was Avram who spoke up. "I've polled the others; we were hoping you would be."

"I haven't even accepted membership yet, much less the chairmanship."

"But you will." The dean's remark was halfway between a statement and a question.

They were right. He would accept. But he didn't understand why Rabbi Levi was on the committee.

"It is not so difficult to understand. Such committees must have at least one lay person."

Paul nodded. "So do some of our committees. And it's usually either a lawyer or a clergyman."

"In Israel, we use a rabbi. They fill both roles," the dean explained. "They are experts on Jewish law."

That much Paul knew.

"One last question."

"Yes, Paul."

"Did it have to be a Jew?"

"No," the dean answered. "We have Arabs here in all capacities—from physicians on down the line. Both Muslims and Christians. They are all citizens of Israel and work here. But most of us here are Jews."

Paul left his meeting with the dean just in time to catch a bus to the Central Bus Station. Once there, he picked up a copy of the Jerusalem *Post* and found a seat on the five-thirty bus. He scanned the headlines. A cease-fire had been declared. Paul hoped it would last, but doubted it. In this part of the world cease-fires came and went at an alarming rate. The Arabs had not honored them in the past. Why should this time be any different? Perhaps they could set a new record for most consecutive days of cease-fires voted by the UN. What was the old record? Twelve? No, that was consecutive hits. Pinky Higgins. Later tied by Walt Dropo. He quickly read the war news, then riffled through the pages unsuccessfully looking for some news of his White Sox. There were no baseball scores at all in the paper. An English-language newspaper without baseball scores. Maybe that's why the politics in this country got so heated: no pennant races, no New York Yankees to hate, just real enemies.

He put the paper down just as the bus pulled out. He would be home with Carolyn and Joshua in just twenty-five minutes. How had he gotten involved in all these things? Teaching two or three times a week was one thing, but that plus the select committee was too much. He was here to spend time with his kids, not to be chairman of a select committee. Even the name smacked of controversy. He wasn't even sure he cared who had killed Nahum Eckstein, or more correctly, if anyone really had killed him at all. He wanted to spend time with Carolyn and Joshua and find out about Julian and the Third Temple for Bobbie. Bobbie. He had been so busy he had not thought about Bobbie all day. That must have been the first day when he hadn't. She would have remembered the Hebrew word for "mustache." He had too many other problems to worry about. Beware the ninth of Av. He had not thought about that warning at all. Like all Jews, he would be wary that day. When the bus stopped at Abu Gosh, an old Arab, bent by the years and weathered by time and the sun, got off the bus. Paul remembered the word himself. *"Safom,"* the Hebrew word for "mustache."

It could have been an Arab who killed Nahum Eckstein, a member of the PLO, an underground terrorist. After all, the PLO had just machine-gunned the Israeli ambassador to Great Britain.

With that, the bus arrived at Neve Ilan. Carolyn and Joshua were waiting at the bus stop. Carolyn had made dinner for the three of them.

Long after dinner, while the kids were getting ready for bed, Paul sat down at the old typewriter he had borrowed from Jonathan for the summer and typed a letter to Arnold Chiari asking him to have the library at Austin Flint send him copies of all the recent articles on Guillain-Barré syndrome. He also told Bud what he was up to. Suddenly Paul was dubious that he would ever get any work done on the proposed textbook. That could wait until next year.

Next year in Chicago.

4

As soon as he woke up on Friday morning, Paul knew that it was not a day to be spent worrying about Nahum Eckstein, or Guillain-Barré syndrome, or Tisha B'Av, or the patients he had seen on teaching rounds. Or Julian, for that matter. Those were all subjects that he could get around to later in the summer. By the time he finished his second cup of coffee, the sun was high overhead. According to the news, the cease-fire with the Syrians was more or less holding. By now it was apparent that the real enemy was not the PLO but Syria, and Syria seemed more interested in gobbling up Lebanon and fighting Israel than in supporting the Palestinians. Within Israel, dissenters who opposed the invasion were becoming increasingly vocal. They called themselves the Peace Now movement. This sort of criticism from inside during a war was something new. At least it showed that democracy worked in Israel. Paul wondered if the dissenters might not be leftover American radicals from the sixties who had moved here and found a new cause, or if they were home-grown. They were a small but vocal minority. A painful thorn. He would spend his day with Carolyn and Joshua. He would worry about Israel's internal political problems on another day.

The day went by very quickly. In the morning he and Joshua played catch and then the three of them played cards, cleaned up the house, and had lunch. After lunch they went next door to help Pat prepare for the Sabbath, their first Sabbath together in Israel. For them it would be a traditional religious Sabbath, a true Jewish Shabbat. A day of rest and religion.

Their first Shabbat in Israel began at sundown, with services followed by an almost traditional Friday-night dinner. The one break with tradition was the substitution of turkey for chicken. After all, Neve Ilan did not raise chickens.

After dinner, they said the usual prayer and sang a few songs and the younger set went out. They had other people to see and more important things to do.

"Carolyn seems happier," Paul observed.

"She is. She doesn't have to worry about you and Joshua so much here. She doesn't have to try to be the woman of the family," Pat informed him.

"She told you all that?"

Pat nodded. "And Joshua can just be thirteen without worrying about letting you down."

"But I never—"

"Of course not. He assumed a new role. Just as Carolyn did."

"As we all did. I hope they go back to something closer to what they were before Bobbie died." He had said that without hesitating. It was a step in the right direction.

The three adults sat outside and watched the stars and talked of the moshav and the war in Lebanon and finally everything that Paul was doing.

"What about your textbook?" Jonathan asked.

"I can do that in Chicago."

"That was true before you left."

"Not really. Before I left I was so muddled in trying to figure out my role that I couldn't get anything done. I was immobilized by my grief. Now I have a sense of work I have to do. I think that will stay with me."

The next morning the moshav awakened slowly and softly. There were no buses driving in and out. Little if any traffic could be heard on the highway. No trucks. No buses. An occasional private car. By nine-thirty the soft chanting of the morning service could be heard rising up from the community center.

In the afternoon, while Joshua and Carolyn went on a hike with the other teenagers from the moshav, Paul sat down with the packet of documents that Dean Ben Zvi had given him just two days earlier. It was addressed to him as Chairman of the Select Committee of Inquiry.

That SOB, he knew that Paul was going to accept the job and had already had the memo typed up.

The memo contained a full list of the membership of the committee.

Paul Richardson, M.D., Chairman
Visiting Professor, Department of Neurology

Yitzak Cohen, M.D.
Chairman, Department of Pathology

Romain Bernhard, M.D.
Chairman, Department of Neurosurgery

Avram Schiff, M.D.
Chairman, Department of Neurology

Chaim Abramowitz, M.D.
Chairman, Department of Cardiology

Rivkah Geller, M.D., Ph.D.
Chairman, Department of Pharmacology and Toxicology.

Rabbi Aaron Levi

Their first meeting would be June 13 in the dean's conference room. And the final report was due on the first day of August, one day after Tisha B'Av.

Paul had not realized that he had agreed to that deadline.

There was also a thick file of papers meant just for the chairman. These were the curricula vitae of the members of the committee.

Paul quickly shuffled through the sheaf of papers. Although there were six other members on the committee, there were only five C.V.'s. Dean Ben Zvi, it seemed, did not have a curriculum vitae for Rabbi Levi. Paul paid particular attention to two of the biographies: Rivkah Geller and Romain Bernhard. Both were names he had run across before.

Rivkah Geller was a widely acknowledged authority on a number of poisons. He had read several of her publications. The fact that he would be learning about the life of an author he had both studied and quoted in his own papers increased his interest.

She was a native Israeli, a sabra, born in Haifa in 1934, which made her just forty-eight. Her parents had come from Hungary to Israel in 1933. A good time to have left Hungary, Paul thought. A good decision for all the Gellers, past, present, and future. She had two brothers and two sisters and was herself unmarried. She had an M.D. and a Ph.D., both from Hebrew University. She also had an impressive list of publications, most of which concerned the effects of toxic substances on the brain, and had been chairman of the Department of Pharmacology and Toxicology since 1968. Chairman at age thirty-four. A major accomplishment for anyone, in any country. Here, where she must have spent at least two years in the army, it was even more impressive. No wonder she had no time to get married. In his mind, he created his own image of her. Forty-eight years old. A true sabra, tough on the outside, like the fruit of the desert cactus from which the name was derived. Strong, appearing older than her stated age, and dedicated to her work, totally dedicated. Not dividing her attentions between family and husband and work. Just work and Israel. That was more than enough for anyone.

Paul turned to the next C.V. It belonged to Romain Bernhard. He had been in charge of Neurosurgery at Maimonides for decades. Paul knew him by reputation, not because of any publications he had read.

Born Paris, 1916.

M.D. Paris, 1939.

War experience: Free French Army 1940–1945, Israel Defense Force 1948, 1951–. That meant that Bernhard was still in the active reserves.

Again the facts left out as much as they told. He had finished medical school just in time to enter the army and had spent the war in the Free French Army as a physician. He himself had personally missed the Holocaust. Only his family, his relatives, his friends, anyone who stayed in France had undoubtedly been directly involved. His brief bibliography included a tribute to Clovis Vincent. Vincent had been Bernhard's teacher for a couple of years after the war. Vincent was a name Paul recognized. He had been the founder of Israeli neurosurgery. Vincent had been a student of Babinski, one of the greatest figures in the history of neurology, discoverer of the most important of all neurologic signs, the Babinski sign. Babinski had always maintained that his most important contribution had not been the twenty-eight-line article describing the sign but his role in making Vincent into a neurosurgeon. An unbroken line. Babinski to Vincent to Bernhard. Training with him would be like studying piano with a direct musical descendant of Beethoven or Liszt.

Paul now had only three more C.V.'s to digest. They belonged to Chaim Abramowitz, Yitzak Cohen, and Avram Schiff. He didn't feel like reading through all three of them. He skimmed Avram's. The others he would read some other time. He had first met Avram at a neurochemistry meeting in Milan in 1969. Other than meeting some people, it hadn't been much of a meeting.

He and Paul had become friends. Not so much because their personalities blended, because they did not. Avram tended to be aloof, stiff, standoffish. A man for proper ritual and distance. Paul was as open as he could be with other professionals.

Nor did their research interests coincide. But one interest did. Israel and especially Israeli neurology. Paul wanted to do whatever he could to help both. So did Avram. When Paul had been editing his first book, Avram had suggested two Israelis who could write excellent chapters. That had been only the start. And in the next decade such interactions had developed into a mutual respect that was almost a friendship, but not quite. They spent hours together at meetings discussing projects, but had no dinners together. Paul had never been to Schiff's home. They had become close colleagues who maintained their distance because they both seemed to be most comfortable that way.

Paul had never learned the details of Avram's life. He knew that Avram was a survivor of the Holocaust, but Avram had never volunteered the precise facts and Paul had not asked. He felt strange reading the bare outline, as if he were invading Avram's privacy. True, it was a public document he was reading, but somehow it was not exactly kosher. Some things should not be shared in this way. He hardly read it. The contrast between Romain and Avram struck him. Two survivors, but with such different

histories. One in the Free French Army, one in Tre-
blinka, the model concentration camp.

The last paper in the packet was a copy of a brief memo
to the other six members of the committee which had
been sent to them along with a copy of Paul's C.V. It
was the one Paul had sent to Avram so that Avram could
make the various arrangements for his sabbatical. They
would all start out even except Rabbi Levi whose life
remained his own. Paul Richardson knew more about the
lives of the members of his committee than he did about
the life of Nahum Eckstein. Oh, well, they were supposed to be studying his death, not his life. Still, he'd
like to know more about Nahum Eckstein and about the
Guardians of the City. Perhaps Eleazar Danin could give
him some help.

It was time for the afternoon news. He flicked on the
radio. The Sabbath had been quiet in the north. No serious exchanges. A few rifle shots. No deaths.

After the news was over, his kids came home from
their hike, noisy and happy. It was not quiet again until
sundown, when Paul stood with Joshua and Carolyn and
watched the sun pass quickly below the horizon. It was
a Mediterranean sun, which disappeared rapidly but left
layers of color in shades of orange and purple in the haze
over Tel Aviv and the sea.

When the third star was visible, the Sabbath was officially over and the next week began. The teenagers of
Neve Ilan went off for a night in Jerusalem, where the
bustle of a free Saturday night replaced the quiet of the
Sabbath before the glow of the setting sun had disappeared. They would see a movie or visit an ice-cream
shop or buy a piece of Richie's kosher New York-style
pizza.

Not all of the houses of Jerusalem greeted the end
of the Sabbath with the same abandon. The home of
Rabbi Nahum Eckstein, in the rebuilt Jewish quarter of
the Old City, was once again open to friends and fellow
mourners.

Each visitor who came to pay his or her respects to the
family of Nahum Eckstein, to his widow, to his daughter,
repeated the same traditional words of comfort. ''May

you be comforted among the other mourners of Zion and Jerusalem.''

There was also activity going on in another house in Jerusalem that would have interested Paul Richardson, a solitary activity involving newspapers, scissors, and paste.

Slowly the scissors cut letters out of an old Jerusalem *Post:*

J
e
r
I
c
h
O

Three times the scissors cut out the same set of letters. Each set was then pasted onto an ordinary sheet of plain white paper. The letters were identical each time. The seemingly idiosyncratic use of the upper case was exactly the same in all three copies. These would soon concern many people, including Paul Richardson.

Each piece of paper was then carefully folded and put into a plain envelope. This time a stamp was put on each envelope.

Both of the residents and both of the students were waiting in the conference room when Paul arrived. He apologized for being five minutes late. He did not offer any excuses. He knew that he should have gotten up earlier. The problem was that eighteen men from the moshav, almost one-third of all of the adult males, were still on active duty in the army. There was work that had to be done, especially the planting of the seedlings in the hothouses. Carolyn and Joshua both volunteered to do whatever they could to help. It would be hard work, but they wanted to pitch in. Leaving their beds unmade and their rooms in a mess, they left the house at the crack of dawn. Paul did his part for the war effort by straightening up after them before he grabbed the bus for Jerusalem.

The group brought him up-to-date on the two patients

he had seen before: Mrs. Fahoum, the Lebanese woman with encephalitis, was no better. The neck X rays on Mrs. Sassoon were normal, but that was as they had expected.

John Haddad, his crucifix again showing above his open collar, told the story of the first patient, an eleven-year-old Arab girl who had a three-week history of not feeling right, of doing poorly in school, and of jerky movements of her arms and legs. Before he could detail the results of his examination, Paul suggested that they all go into the patient's room to observe the movements.

As soon as he entered the room, the abnormal movements were obvious to Paul. First he saw her right arm jerk, then her left wrist, the right shoulder, the right wrist, the right hip, the right side of her face, the right shoulder again, the right wrist, but not the same movement as before, the left side of her face, her neck, her left shoulder, her right shoulder. All that could be seen in less than four minutes. The movements formed no specific pattern, but they never stopped as they skipped from one site to another.

As soon as they returned to the conference room, Paul made each of the students describe what he had seen. Observation was the first step. Then, with the two residents, Hassan Rashem and Dalia Avni, he worked on the second step, diagnosis based upon observation. They both agreed that the girl probably had Sydenham's chorea, a mild, self-limited sort of inflammation of the brain causing abnormal involuntary movements. So far, so good. Next they discussed her treatment. Case one was completed.

It was Dalia Avni who then told him the brief but nonetheless unhappy tale of Zalman Cohen. As Paul watched her and listened, he realized just how pretty she was. She was slight, but in no way boyish or preadolescent. She had a full head of dark, curly hair and a small, sharply chiseled nose. How old had she said the patient was? He had better pay more attention. By the time she finished, Paul understood the entire case. So did everyone else. A man who was not very old had had a stroke and was now unable to speak. Paul taught them a little about the history of the neurological understanding of such problems and about the development of the term, aphasia, now used to describe a loss of speech. When he finished, Dalia asked him who had written the first description of aphasia. He replied that, as far as he knew, it was not a physician, but the great German author Goethe.

Paul took a bus back to the center of town and then walked over to Eleazar Danin's office.

Once he sat down in the office, Paul knew he was no longer the professor.

The role reversal was not as difficult this time. Danin asked the questions and Paul answered them. Danin started with direct questions seemingly designed to elicit only short declarative sentences. Not Paul's style at all. His style owed little to Ernest Hemingway. Perhaps it was not really Eleazar Danin's style either. Slowly but surely the questions became less abrupt, the answers more expansive, more philosophical, more meandering. Through it all, Paul tried to explain why he believed there had to be more than just one version of what had transpired in 363. The great city that had been Jerusalem had been transformed into a Roman garrison town. It even had a new name. Aelia Capitolina. It was just another backwater of the empire, not even the provincial capital. A city of a defeated God which was not yet dedicated to the new God. A city populated by Christians and pagans. That meant that there had been many pagan witnesses around when Julian ordered the Temple to be rebuilt, and they were still there when the rebuilding stopped. Or had they experienced something else? There were pagan historians in the fourth and fifth centuries, and Arab historians who relied on pagan sources. Somewhere there might be some information, some hints, some implications. Eleazer was no longer asking questions. Paul was talking on and on without any prompting.

As far as Paul could tell, Jerusalem, or Aelia Capitolina, differed in one important aspect from the other cities and villages in Judea. It had no Jewish population. Hadrian, after crushing the second revolt, had forbidden Jews to live within the city. They could not even appear within the city limits on fear of death, except one day each year—the eve of Tisha B'Av—to lament their fate. But there were many Jews in the area. In fact, there were more Jews than Christians. Perhaps there were even more Jews than there were pagans. They, too, must have left some record, some evidence. Certainly most Jewish sources that mentioned Julian spoke of him favorably. Somewhere, there must be some trace of this story. After all, Paul reasoned, the Third Temple certainly involved them.

Danin waited to absorb the entire narrative before he allowed himself to make any comments. "Three versions of the same truth. That's a luxury I cannot afford in my business."

"Nor in mine," Paul responded.

"Can you in the case of Nahum Eckstein?"

"You know about—" Paul started, but then stopped himself. Why shouldn't the range of Eleazar's knowledge, expertise, and consultative services extend as far as Maimonides Hospital?

After a brief pause it was Danin who went on. "Yes, I know about Nahum's untimely death. You see, my knowledge of old Jerusalem involves not only the streets and byways but also the peoples. Jews and non-Jews. Nahum and I both grew up in the Old City. He was a few years older than I. We were never great friends. Even if we had been the same age, we would never have been great friends. He was, I am told, in many ways a difficult man to have as a friend, a rigid idealist and stern moralist. But those things wouldn't have affected us as kids. We both grew up just a stone's throw from the great doomed synagogue. You never saw that synagogue, did you?"

"No," Paul answered as he shook his head.

"Of course not. You were too young then. How old were you in 1948? Eight? Nine?"

"Ten."

"An innocent age. In an innocent land. Things were not so innocent here."

Paul did not feel like sitting through a lecture, but he did not interrupt. Instead he listened politely. After all, Danin had listened to his stories. What were friends for, if not to listen to boring stories they already knew? It took about ten minutes. Eleazar paused and sighed. "That wonderful dome did not last very long after Jerusalem fell in 'forty-eight. Many a Sabbath I went there as a young boy and a young man. Then, after the war, the Arabs tore it down, brick by brick, for no good reason other than their own need to destroy it."

Eleazar paused once more. It was almost as if he were trying to conjure up the physical presence of the building, not just recall it. Paul could sense that the history lesson was not yet over.

"And not one voice complained in the UN. Did the Security Council ever debate what they had done? Of course not. Can you imagine that body considering the fate of some synagogue or another? No. But let one crazy Jew acting on his own fire a few shots in the Dome of the Rock. It's a crazy world, isn't it?" Without waiting for a reply, Eleazar went back to his own story.

"Our families and lives were separated even then. We . . . how should I say it? . . . went to different yeshivas together. We would be at morning services together at the synagogue, walk with our own small groups of fellow students down the narrow winding streets to the same old stone building, where we would enter separate doors into different worlds. His school was a classic yeshiva involved only in teaching Torah, mine a school which included Torah as part of its curriculum. He became a rabbi, I a . . ."

Paul filled in the word. "Consultant."

"Yes, a consultant." Eleazar's tone was once more of wondering than of nostalgia. "Each day our schools let out at the same time and we would walk back toward the synagogue together. There was very little mingling between the two groups, each sure that it was better, smarter than the other—they confident that they were learning what God wanted them to learn, we that we were learning what men needed to know." Danin paused before going on. "They are rebuilding that building to house schools again. I helped them locate the foundations of the old school. The Jordanians, the Palestinians, together after 'forty-eight, systematically went through the old Jewish quarter and destroyed each and every building. Hadrian, when he sowed the city over, could not have been more thorough. Even the Crusaders did less damage."

Paul suddenly thought of Mr. Greenberg and his eighteen dollars. *Chai*. Life. Eighteen dollars to help rebuild one of the old synagogues of the old Jewish quarter.

Eleazar Danin started again with less anger and more nostalgia this time. "Even among my liberated school-mates I was somewhat of a rebel. Several of my best friends were not Jewish. I met them at my father's store. My father, may he rest in peace, was not a rabbi. He had a dry-goods store in the Old City. His clientele included Jews, Muslims, and Christians of various sects. My clos-est friend was Vartan Boyajian." Danin paused for a mo-ment. "For centuries the Armenians have dominated the gold trade in this part of the world. Here longer than anyone really knows. That may go back as far as the Crusades. Vartan's father claims that he can trace the family back even further than that." Then he added, "His father's name is Sarkis, Sarkis Boyajian. You should meet him. He is the most respected jeweler in all of Jerusa-lem."

"I should meet a jeweler?"

"Calling him just a jeweler is like calling Einstein a petty customs official. If I am a policeman who, as you said, works to learn what is already known, and you are a teacher and scientist who works to find out what is not known, he could be called perhaps an accountant. No, an economist. He works to find out if things add up, if they are possible. He is somewhere between a theologian and an accountant. Sarkis knows more about the history of this city and its people than a whole generation of Ph.D.'s. He has spent his lifetime studying this city and its people where no professors have ever been. Using sources no professional would use. Family Bibles. The oral traditions of his neighbors."

"But I thought you said he was a jeweler."

"He is. He is said to have the best eye in the business. He still looks at jewels for his sons and grandsons. But mostly he reads, talks, and meditates. I'm not sure he will help you, however."

"Why not?"

"He has his own rules. For him to devote his time to anything, both the project and the purpose must fit within those rules. And he has not been well. Nothing that se-rious, I am told, but he is no longer a young man."

Suddenly the tone of Eleazar's voice changed. It became less friendly, more official. "My friend, you keep kosher?"

"Yes."

"Why?"

"Why?"

"Yes, why? Why do you keep kosher?"

"Because God instructed the Jewish people to keep kosher."

"That's the only reason?"

"Of course."

"Not because it's healthier?"

"No. There's no evidence that it's healthier, and even if there were, that would be irrelevant."

"Why did God give the Jewish people such rules?"

"To set us apart from others. It's a measure of our commitment, consciously repeated each and every day. Three times a day."

"Perhaps he will see you."

"Because I keep kosher?"

"No, that is irrelevant to him. He's not concerned about such issues. We are still friends, he still talks to me about things of common interest, and I no longer keep kosher."

"Why not?"

"I can no longer see any reason, any need for a set of rules to keep us separate and apart from other people. History . . . history and the other peoples have done that. Perhaps better than God. But that's not important. It's not because you keep kosher that he may spend some of his time with you, but because of the reason. I will see."

"Thank you."

Eleazar's nod waved off the thanks as unnecessary. "Tell me, Dr. Richardson"—the policeman was back to a tone that made Paul uncomfortable—"can a man die of more than one cause?"

"Theoretically or practically?"

"Practically."

"No."

"So you will find a single cause?"

"Yes."

"And you will all agree?"

"I hope so," Paul answered.

"I too hope for that. It will make my job easier."

Paul turned to Danin. "I'm not sure I'm concerned with making your job, whatever it is, any easier. I am only concerned with finding out the real sequence of events and the true cause of death."

"I'm sorry if I said—"

"Look, if it will make your job easier, I'll get you a copy of my C.V. so you will know my background better."

"That is not necessary. I already have a copy." As soon as he said it, Danin knew he had made a tactical error. His already having acquired Paul's C.V. had put Paul on the defensive. It had made Paul feel more than slightly paranoid, at a time when too many people were all too paranoid.

"Paul, I'm sorry. I wasn't spying on you. I genuinely wanted to help you and . . . have you help me. In my business I always have to run a few checks first just to be sure."

Paul grunted. He understood. He even knew it had been the right thing to do. It was just that it was not part of his usual life. But this was not Chicago, and extreme stresses and pressures did require greater caution.

"Paul, we have to be careful."

Paul nodded.

"And so should you."

"Me? Why? I'm just a tourist."

"Who is on a very sensitive committee."

"Yes."

"And who is working with me."

"In a way."

"And comes in and out of this office and can be seen doing that by our enemies."

That was true.

"And our friends."

"Am I really in danger?"

"Probably not, but if you notice anything peculiar or anyone acting strangely, be very careful."

"Whom should I worry about? Our friends or our enemies?"

"Both," Eleazar told him, and smiled.

The smile did not make Paul feel any better.

It was time for him to leave. Eleazar had work he had to do and Paul had a bus he had to catch. If he missed the five-thirty bus, he would have to wait until eight-thirty for the next one to Neve Ilan, or take one that would let him off on the highway one kilometer downhill. He didn't want to miss the five-thirty bus.

It was strange how easily he became adapted to the realities of Israel. He bought a newspaper in the bus station and studied the war news. There was more fighting in the north. More Israelis dead. The army was moving further into Lebanon, further from the border, closer to the Syrians, closer to Beirut. Israeli Prime Minister Begin was off to the U.S. to try to get Reagan's support. PLO Chairman Arafat was somewhere in Lebanon trying to rally his forces and hold his coalition together. He was both calling for revenge and proclaiming a Pyrrhic victory. Once again Paul looked in vain. There were no baseball scores, just the results of the World Cup soccer series. It was as if no one in all of Israel was concerned with what was happening to his White Sox. Didn't the editor know he was living in Jerusalem and buying a paper each and every day?

As he got on the bus, Paul realized that he recognized some of the faces. He had seen them before on the same bus. Fellow commuters. Israelis from Neve Ilan and neighboring communities. Arabs from Abu Gosh.

Friends.

And friends who might not be friends.

As he watched them he wondered if they might not be watching him.

As friends.

Or as enemies.

He was letting himself get carried away. No one was watching him. No one had any reason to. If only that were really true.

A little after six A.M., the medication nurse got to the bed of Zalman Cohen. Since he could neither speak nor understand, she said nothing to him. She merely checked her sheets of paper, drew up the fifteen milligrams of morphine, a healthy dose, she thought to herself, for such an old man. To her, anyone over fifty was old, and Mr. Cohen seemed over sixty and short of breath. That was only to be expected if you smoked all your life. She looked at the stains from cigarettes on his fingers and shook her head in disgust.

Fifteen milligrams, the doctor had ordered, and fifteen milligrams the patient would get.

Twenty minutes later, as the morphine was just beginning to reach its peak blood level, Mr. Cohen was sleeping and breathing slowly and shallowly. His breath became slower and more shallow and then stopped altogether.

No one realized he was dead until Yuri Aharoni came by to see him on morning rounds an hour later. An old man with a stroke who had died in his sleep. He must have had a heart attack in his sleep. It was probably better that way; he had had such a severe stroke, his speech might never have come back.

It wasn't until several hours later, when he was reviewing Mr. Cohen's records to dictate the final summary, that Dr. Hassan Rashem noted the order for morphine.

There had been no reason to give him any morphine at all.

Fifteen milligrams was too much for him.

He had been a heavy smoker for years.

He had severe emphysema.

Fifteen milligrams of morphine would suppress his breathing.

It could kill him.

It *had* killed him.

Rashem reached for the phone and called Professor Schiff.

5

It was a few minutes past four. Everyone was assembled in the conference room adjacent to the dean's office. They were seated at the conference table. Paul sat at the head of the table, carefully considering the exact words he should use in his opening remarks. As he hesitated, someone else preempted his prerogative.

"I think, Professor Richardson, that you and the other physicians here are all wasting your time as well as mine."

"Why is that, Rabbi Levi?" Paul asked in as friendly a tone as he could muster. He understood the need to have a nonphysician on the committee. If he himself were required to confirm some degree of credibility, so was the rabbi. After all, no one could accuse an Orthodox rabbi of plotting with physicians to gloss over the errors of other physicians. And this rabbi was an expert on Jewish law. What could be better? Paul would have preferred an expert on Israeli law. The two systems of law were not the same; they were at odds at times, and at those points of contention, the arguments were endless. This was one of those flashpoints: the desecration of the dead.

"Do you think it was a clear-cut murder and that we are merely gathered here to count the number of angels that can dance on the head of a pin?" Paul knew he had used a singularly ill-chosen metaphor but he continued despite his faux pas. "If that is what you are wondering, I am sure Avram can explain the medical issues to you better than I can."

The six physicians, all of whom were seated near the head of the table, looked to the other end of the table where the rabbi sat alone, separated by more than just the black suit and a half-dozen unoccupied chairs.

"It is not that, Professor," the rabbi began, "it's not

that at all.'' He then looked at each of the doctors as if he were a lawyer summing up a case to a set of jurors, a set of jurors with limited knowledge, at best.

''I do believe, as our esteemed chairman so eloquently phrased it, that we are merely counting the number of angels that can dance on the head of a pin—a diversion which Jewish scholars never felt was worthwhile, by the way.'' Paul winced, as did Avram. The others just continued to stare at the bearded, bright-eyed man as if awaiting an attack. ''But none of you, not a single one of you, really understands the issue. It is I who must explain it to you. Not just our American friend here, but I'm afraid all of you do not possess the knowledge that, as Jews, you should.''

Paul was certain that the shuffling of his feet was too loud for anyone to miss, but the rabbi paid no attention to it. ''You see, gentlemen, by law Rabbi Eckstein, may he rest in peace, was already dead whether or not his breathing machine, whatever you call it—''

''A respirator,'' Professor Bernhard informed the rabbi.

''Whatever. Such names mean nothing to me,'' the rabbi replied. He had not asked a question that required an answer.

''Whether or not that . . . respirator, as you call it, was working, whether it stopped working because of an accident or because someone intentionally removed the socket from the electrical outlet, or whether that was done by the Holy One, Blessed Be His Name, is not of any importance, for Rabbi Nahum Eckstein, may he be of sainted memory, was already dead according to the law. As a consequence, I feel that this should be our only meeting and that we should conclude that he already died and that the other act, be it savage, wanton, careless, or merciful, merely allowed his body and soul to go to their rest, which they have done despite the unforgivable sin of the desecration of his body.''

Paul wasn't sure where to start his response. It was Avram Schiff, who was seated on his right, who replied first.

''Rabbi, you are, I think, a bit confused. The medical definitions of death, while they differ somewhat from physician to physician, from country to country, have a certain core of components which are generally accepted. Most of these have to do with a complete absence of neurologic function and then evidence that the brain can never recover that function. If, for instance, the loss of brain function is due to some drug or toxin which can be cleared from the body, then the patient, despite having no brain function, is not dead, or better, cannot be pronounced dead, since he may perhaps recover.''

Rivkah Geller was visibly nodding her agreement.

The rabbi was not. ''Don't bother me with such notions. As I understand the facts here, Nahum Eckstein, may he rest in continuous peace and arise only for the coming of the Messiah, could not breathe. Am I right?''

''You are right,'' Avram responded.

''So he was dead. That is how our law defines death. Not the law of this government but *the law.*''

The physicians all began to speak at once, but the rabbi's voice became louder and silenced them. ''It has all been clearly explained by Rashi.

''You all must know who Rashi was. He was the greatest of all Biblical and Talmudic commentators, and he agreed. So did the greatest of all physicians, Moses ben Maimmon, after whom, I need not remind you, this hospital is named.''

For several moments no one said anything. It was left to the chairman to come up with a reply. ''Rabbi, you need not teach us who Rashi was, nor Maimonides. We may not be as familiar as you with the Mishnah or the Talmud, but we are not totally ignorant. I too have read Maimonides and I know that he believed that if there was no sign of breathing which could be detected at the nose, then the patient was dead. But that was over eight hundred years ago.''

''The law does not change that quickly.''

''But medicine does.'' Paul did not want to do anything to prolong this confrontation, but what other choice did he have?

''If what you say were true, then all of Professor Bernhard's patients would be dead during surgery, for under anesthesia they cannot breathe for themselves.'' The neurosurgeon's one nod signified his agreement.

As the rabbi began to answer this, he was attacked on

all fronts by Cardiology, Pathology, Neurology, and Pharmacology.

"Gentlemen, please!" Paul began to assert his authority. Confrontation was not the answer. "The rabbi has raised what he believes to be a major issue. I understand what he is saying, but unfortunately for you, Rabbi, it is, to use your term, not of any importance. I am sure you have less understanding of respirators than I do of Maimonides."

"I would not disagree," the rabbi readily admitted.

"Then let me explain respirators to you. They can work in one of two ways. One is called assist, meaning just that, the patient's own breathing starts the cycle and the machine merely assists the patient. The other is called automatic. In that mode the patient doesn't do anything. The machine does all the breathing. As I understand it, Rabbi Eckstein's respirator was on assist. Am I not right?"

It was Romain Bernhard who answered first. "You are correct."

Avram nodded and said, "That is true. When we found the respirator it was on assist."

"Rabbi, I and the others of us here appreciate what you are saying. But Rabbi Eckstein was capable of some respiration, as I understand it. So he was not dead. Can we now begin?"

As Paul looked at each of the other members of the panel, they nodded their agreement. When he looked at Rabbi Levi, the rabbi said softly, "May his family continue to be comforted among the mourners of Zion and Jerusalem and may the Holy One, Blessed Be His Name, forgive us our transgressions and presumptions."

It was an unorthodox benediction, but at least it was a benediction of sorts.

There were three items on the agenda that Dean Yehuda Ben Zvi had prepared and that Paul Richardson now passed out: the medical history of Nahum Eckstein, the results of the autopsy, and the schedule for future meetings. Paul called on Avram, on whose service Nahum Eckstein had died, to tell them the patient's history. Avram, in turn, passed a set of papers, each containing nineteen pages, to every member of the panel. "I have just given each of you a complete summary of the medical facts in this case. I will now spend the next twenty minutes or so briefly outlining the main clinical features, if I may."

"Go ahead, Avram," Paul agreed.

"Nahum Eckstein was a sixty-two-year-old . . ." The same formula, Paul thought to himself. "He first entered Maimonides Hospital on . . ."

Paul tried to listen closely even though he already knew most of the significant details. Avram Schiff omitted nothing. While he listened, Paul studied the faces of the other members of the committee. His committee, he reminded himself. He would have to get to know them better before they would seem like members of his committee.

As Avram got closer to the end of his recitation, Paul paid more attention. "At six-forty-five A.M. on June 8, while in the ICU, Nahum Eckstein was found dead. His respirator, which, when we looked at it, was, as Dr. Richardson pointed out, turned to assist, had somehow become unplugged. The neurological examination at that time revealed absolutely no evidence at all of any brain function. The details of that examination are listed in their entirety on page eighteen."

"It looks very complete to me," Paul said. "Do you agree, Professor Bernhard?"

"Yes," the senior neurosurgeon responded. "Most thorough indeed."

"That's what we thought," Avram went on. "He was neurologically dead, so any effort at resuscitation was out of the question."

For the first time, Chaim Abramowitz spoke up. "Dr. Richardson? Avram? I'm not sure I understand the issue. If he had G.B. syndrome, then he should have had a damn good chance of survival."

"That's right, Chaim," Avram answered.

"Then why are we here?"

"Let me answer that," Paul interceded. "Avram here and the other neurologist were not one hundred percent sure of their diagnosis. We often aren't . . . that's why we do autopsies." Faux pas number two. "There were some features here that were atypical and raised the possibility that there was permanent damage to the respiratory centers which may have been still progressing. If that were true, then the other vital centers which control blood pressure and heart rate are right there and would have been the next to give out, and he would have had no chance of survival.''

"In which case," Chaim responded, "pulling the plug may not have been an act of murder, I suppose."

"Correct, Chaim," Paul said. "Someone may have wanted to murder him or—"

"Stop the desecration of his body," the rabbi proposed.

"I guess so, Rabbi, but I would not have thought of it in those terms."

"I know that, Professor Richardson."

"—or," Paul continued, "it may have been an accident, or—"

This time it was Rivkah Geller who interrupted him. "I am not a clinician. It has been years since I took care of any patients. Perhaps it is my ignorance, for I never even took an internship, but how can an accident like that happen?"

"I guess I should answer," Chaim said. "After all, I see more people in the ICU than anyone else and actually was there that morning when it all happened. It was one of those ghastly days—or hours, to be more exact. We had two cardiac arrests at the same time and a patient in hemorrhagic shock. Everyone was running around like crazy. When it quieted down, one of the nurses went over to check on Rabbi Eckstein."

"Don't those respirators have an alarm or something?" Dr. Geller asked.

"Of course."

"Well, why didn't it go off?"

"The alarm only works when the machine is plugged in," Chaim explained.

Paul looked at his watch and took his prerogative as chairman: "I think it's time we began the second item. Yitzak . . ."

The pathologist, following Avram Schiff's example, handed out a set of papers entitled "Results of Gross Autopsy, Autopsy Number 5742–87." It was only six pages long.

"The body was that of a sixty-two-year-old male who appeared to be his stated age . . ."

Again the same formula.

"Gross inspection of the skin revealed no surgical scars, a small . . ."

As chairman, Paul tried to pay attention to each detail of the postmortem examination. It was not easy.

"The liver weighed twenty-one hundred grams. The edges were smooth . . ."

Yitzak worked his way through each organ of the body. It did not take as long as Paul had feared it might.

During the description of the kidney, Paul looked around the table and focused on Rivkah Geller. She was a tall woman, as he had imagined her. Perhaps just an inch or two shorter than he was. But other than that, his preconceived picture was all wrong. She looked younger than forty-eight. It was probably her red hair and her fair, smooth complexion that accounted for that. And she certainly was not heavy and did not look tough. More warm and concerned than tough. If anything, she was on the thin side, but with firm, high breasts. She concentrated on each of the pathologist's sentences, tapping a pencil against her lower lip and teeth. Paul began to wonder what it might be like to . . . God, he had not wondered about any woman, even as a mere academic question, since Bobbie had died. Why now? Was it just that he was no longer in Highland Park? Or was it time to start to think about his future? About women? No, not yet. The report was over.

"In essence, then, you found nothing," Paul said.

"In essence, some high blood pressure with mild changes in the heart, in both kidneys, and in the blood vessels. But, of course, these are only the gross findings," the pathologist responded.

"When will you have all of the microscopic findings?"

"About two weeks. It takes that long to do all the special stains. The slides may not be as good as I would like. The autopsy was delayed by . . . some differences in opinion."

It was getting late. They had to decide how often to meet. Weekly. When? That was a problem. They all had busy schedules. Paul didn't. He could meet whenever it was convenient for the others. It was decided that Avram would schedule the meetings as best he could and notify the others.

"In a week or so, we ought to be able to do the gross sections of the brain. Is that okay, Yitzak?"

"Yes. The brain and the spinal cord will be fixed by then."

"Good. After that, we will go over the results of the microscopic sections of the general autopsy. Then we can go over the slides of the brain and spinal cord. Our final meeting will be Sunday, August 1, at nine A.M. Let me see. Yes, that's the day after Tisha B'Av." Richardson paused for a moment to make sure no one had a problem with that date. The individual doctors were putting notes in their personal datebooks. No one said anything. "There are two other things I would like to do. I would like to meet with each of you individually so that I will know you better and will be better able to use your expertise, and you will get to know me better. And there is one last question I would like to ask you all. Who would have wanted to kill Rabbi Eckstein?"

"That's not the purpose of this committee."

"I know, Avram, but I am an outsider who is curious. Humor me."

It was the rabbi who spoke next. "If that is what you are going to discuss now, and your other business is done . . ."

"It is."

"Then I will leave."

After the rabbi had left, Chaim Abramowitz began, "It might be easier to ask who might have not wanted to kill him."

"Why?"

"Look, the Arabs hated him, and not just the PLO or other fanatics, like the ones who shot Argov, but most Arabs—even Israeli Arabs. They all considered him and his group to be a threat to them."

"A threat?" Paul asked.

"Very much so."

"How? In what way?"

"Those nuts believe that all the land, all the Biblical lands, belong to us. They were the ones who tried to prevent our giving Yamit back to Egypt." Seeing the puzzled look on Paul's face, Chaim went on to give a fuller explanation. It was not just the American English which made Paul feel a bond with Chaim as he listened, it was his relaxed American style. "Yamit was a settlement built in the Sinai after the 'sixty-seven war when the Sinai was ours. After Camp David, we gave the Sinai back to Egypt. We gave them Yamit. There were protesters who wouldn't leave. They had to be dragged out by the army."

"That's easy to understand," Paul said. "They had lived there for over a decade. They hated leaving their homes."

"But they were not the settlers. They were outsiders organized by groups like the Guardians," Chaim corrected him. He then detailed the story of how the Israel Defense Force had had to go from house to house pulling the Jews from Yamit. A peculiar prelude to house-to-house fighting in Sidon or maybe even Beirut. While Chaim Abramowitz talked, Paul wrote on a sheet of paper in front of him:

1. PLO
2. Moderate Arabs

Chaim went from one story to another. It seemed that even among his own followers, the Guardians of the City, Rabbi Eckstein had a number of bitter enemies who felt that he had gone too far. He had deserted their real goal, the preservation of Jewish Jerusalem. Worse, he had alienated them from so many other Israelis. They had always been the most Zionistic of the Zionists, loved and admired for what they did and believed. Now they were considered fanatics. Not zealots, but a lunatic fringe. To their credit, many of the same men who had been dragged kicking and biting out of Yamit were now fighting in Lebanon.

3. Guardians of the City

"And, or course," Chaim added, "there are Jewish radicals who are even more fanatic in their beliefs than Nahum Eckstein was in his. Whether these left-wing groups would kill another Jew, I don't know, but it's possible."

4. Jewish radicals

"Then, let me see. There are also some Christian groups who have felt very threatened by him and the State of Israel."

"Christians." Paul seemed surprised.

"Sure. After all, the Greek Orthodox bishop was thrown out of Israel a few years ago for smuggling arms for the PLO."

"You're exaggerating."

"No. As you well know, over the last thousand years we've had one hell of a lot more trouble from Christians than from Muslims."

"I guess—"

"Guess! The Crusades. The Inquisition. Hitler was a Christian . . ."

"Okay."

5. Christian fanatics

"I guess that's all," Chaim said after thinking for a moment.

"Except the most common motive of all." It was Professor Bernhard who interrupted their dialogue. "Most murders do not involve politics, even here in Israel. This is not Ireland."

"True," Richardson agreed.

"In fact, most are crimes of the heart, personal matters, not political events."

Richardson smiled. "Leave it to a Frenchman to remind us."

6. Personal—crime of the heart

As the doctors left, Romain Bernhard stayed behind.

"We have a patient in common."

"Yes."

"Mrs. Sassoon."

"Yes."

"She does not have a Charcot's joint." It was a statement of fact, of dogma.

"She doesn't? How can you be so sure?"

"Charcot trained Babinski. Babinski trained Vincent, and Vincent trained me."

Paul's expression showed that he had not been overly

impressed. The older physician continued, "Need I remind you that in his original paper on the subject, Charcot emphasized the total absence of pain?"

There was nothing for him to say. Medicine had changed so much in the hundred years that separated them from Charcot. What had been true for Charcot need not have been true for Babinski. Or Vincent, or Bernhard. And certainly not for Mrs. Sassoon. She had never read Charcot's paper. How did she know whether or not her arm was supposed to hurt? Hell, Paul had read that paper, but he had also seen patients with Charcot joints who had pain. More than just one such patient. Paul said no more.

The neurosurgeon left. He had issued his dictum. Paul studied his brief list as if it were a set of diagnoses.

1. PLO
2. Moderate Arabs
3. Guardians of the City
4. Jewish radicals
5. Christian fanatics
6. Personal—crime of the heart

A set of possible diagnoses.

But was diagnosis his job at this time? Maybe the dean and Avram were right. Perhaps it was none of his business. This was not his turf. He could not set the rules. Solving this one was not his problem. Without getting more facts, he couldn't hope to solve it, and fact-finding was off-limits to him. But at least he now knew the scope of the problem. All he had to do was decide whether or not there had been a murder.

He looked at his list again and then added another diagnostic possibility:

7. Accident

And then one more:

8. Intentional withdrawl of life-support systems for religious reasons

He crossed the last one off the list and picked up all his papers and turned off the light and closed the door.

Were these the same people who might be after him? No,
he doubted it. That list was short. It included only the
first five:

1. PLO
2. Moderate Arabs
3. Guardians of the City
4. Jewish radicals
5. Christian fanatics

No crimes of the heart. Unfortunately. Perhaps he
should include one more: accidents. In Israel, no one
is ever safe from accidents. Israelis all drive like mad-
men.

While the committee had held its first meeting, Eleazar
Danin was sipping tea and going through his mail. This
time, he did not rip the letter open. Instead, he carefully
examined it. He was sure that the childlike lettering was
identical. The letter had been mailed in Jerusalem. It was
postmarked by the Central Post Office. That would be no
help. He held the letter by its edges. He knew there was
no chance of there being any fingerprints on the letter,
any clue at all. Nevertheless, he held it by the edges and
took a knife out of his desk drawer and carefully opened
the envelope. Inside was the same cheap sheet of folded white paper with some letters glued to it. As he unfolded the paper he more than half-expected to see the
same message. But this one was much shorter. It contained only one word: "JerIchO."

One word. The name of the oldest city in Israel, perhaps in the world. Jericho with a capital I in the middle
and a capital O at the end.

Only one word. The newsprint looked the same to him.
He wasn't an expert, but it looked the same.

He reached into his top desk drawer again and pulled
out the other folded sheet, unfolded it, and put the two
sheets next to each other on his desk.

JerIchO
BewAre tHe nInTh of AV

Identical. Nothing had ever happened to Jericho on
Tisha B'Av. In the Sinai desert. In Jerusalem. In Spain,

the expulsion of the Jews is said to have occurred on Tisha B'Av. In Germany. In France. So many recorded disasters. But not in Jericho. Not yet. . . .

The bus from Maimonides Hospital left Paul Richardson off at the Jaffa Gate. The shop was on Muristani Road. Paul had no trouble finding it. It turned out to be a small jewelry shop on a quiet street leading off the Arab market toward the Church of the Holy Sepulcher.

The window of the shop was almost empty; a marked contrast to the crowded displays of those shops that catered solely to tourists. There were no signs offering to immortalize your name in Hebrew or English or Arabic in fourteen-karat gold for twenty dollars or in silver for six dollars. Here there were a few trays of gold bangles, thick ones, a few rings, a few pendants, and a great deal of dust.

It was difficult for Paul to estimate Sarkis Boyajian's age. The two men sat together in a small library on the second floor, above the jewelry shop. The room had only one tiny window which allowed very little light into the room. Other than the one window and of course the doorway itself, the room was lined almost entirely by bookshelves crowded with books and papers. The lettering of the various books gave witness to the breadth of the old Armenian's knowledge of languages. He not only read in many languages, but even in many alphabets. There were squared Armenian letters as well as Hebrew, Cyrillic, Roman, Arabic, and one or two that Paul did not recognize.

In contrast to the cluttered shelves, the one desk was almost barren. One open book, a small balance, a simple desk lamp, and three jeweler's eyepieces were all that were on it.

The man behind the desk sat quietly while Paul completed his survey of the room and its owner.

Mr. Boyajian was nearly bald and had a long, mostly gray beard, but his face was smooth, almost without wrinkles. His blue eyes quickly followed each move of Paul's eyes and his thin fingers moved almost constantly. Altogether he gave the appearance of an octogenarian of great youth.

The older man seemed to sense that his visitor had waited too long and did not know how to get started.

"Dr. Richardson, I am pleased to meet with you, as I am always pleased to meet anyone who has written something that I have found to be of value."

"You've read something of mine?" Paul was more surprised by this than by Boyajian's rather clipped British accent.

"Why do you look so surprised? After all, we do have libraries here in Jerusalem."

"But why would you read my papers? I write about parkinsonism and myoclonus and other, more obscure topics of no interest to nonphysicians."

"I have not read any of your medical papers, but a historical essay on the effect of some peculiar disease on the Roman Emperor Maximinus."

"Acromegaly." Paul smiled.

"Yes, acromegaly. It was most interesting."

"I'm glad you liked it. Did you accept my thesis?"

"If you want to know whether I believe that the deterioration and downfall of Maximinus was due to a tumor at the base of his brain as you suggested, or merely to his own degraded personality as Gibbon and also the ancient sources such as Herodian or Scriptores Historiae Augustae proposed, then I am afraid I must disappoint you." Mr. Boyajian's voice was almost sad.

"So you didn't find much merit in my arguments."

"On the contrary, I found them brilliant."

"But you do not accept my thesis as the true explanation of what happened to Maximinus."

"Of course not."

"But I don't understand."

"You do. I am sure. You are here in Jerusalem, the holiest city in the entire world, a city which has been the birthplace of so many truths. The streets of this city, including the one which leads to this shop, have been nurtured by the blood of martyrs who have died for different truths. There is no one truth. Especially not here."

"But you said you found my paper to be of value," Paul wondered aloud.

"Yes. Not because it told me the absolute truth about a man's life, but because it pointed out a possible truth, a new version that could well prove to be worth believing."

There were three sharp knocks on the door.

"That is my son. He has come to make me feel useful."

The older man said something in a language Paul didn't recognize but was certain was Armenian, and the man he had seen downstairs entered the room, walked over to the desk, and handed an envelope to his father. The older man opened the envelope and emptied a bright stone into his hand. He picked up one of the eyepieces, put it straight in his right eye, flicked on the desk lamp, studied the stone for a few seconds, turned off the light, put the eyepiece back on the table, put the stone into the envelope, wrote some numbers on the envelope, and handed it back to his son. The younger Boyajian left without reading what his father had written.

Once the door was closed, Mr. Boyajian gazed intently at his guest.

"You came to me with two recommendations."

"Two?"

"Your article and Eleazar Danin. Eleazar and my son grew up not far from each other in the Old City during the British Mandate. Some might say they were united by their dislike for our Arab neighbors and our distrust of the British whose love for the Arabs was as obvious as it was inexplicable. It was more than just that which brought the two sons and the two families together. It was something much deeper. Our people suffered a Holocaust of our own at the hands of the Turks."

"I know. The genocide against your people took place around World War One."

The older man went on as if he had not been interrupted. "Then, in 1942, the Grand Mufti of Jerusalem, may his soul forever burn in hell, in an act of wanton hatred, tried to organize army units to fight for the Nazis in Europe and assist in your people's Holocaust. . . . I am not a man of hatred, so let us say that we were brought together first by disgust."

Paul could think of no response that was not inadequate.

"How can I help you?" Mr. Boyajian did not wait for an answer. "Perhaps in two ways? First I not only have my own limited library but I probably have access to more private libraries than you do and I will help you there whenever I can."

"I'm very grateful. I'm sure that will be a great help to me."

"The second is quite different. I have lived here all my life. I have studied this city and its peoples and their histories and religions all of my adult life. I do not know what the truth is but I know whether or not something is worth believing. I cannot tell you what you should believe, but I can tell you whether something has a ring of truth in it."

Mr. Boyajian sensed that Paul was not sure he understood.

"As a Jew you must know very well the cost of truly believing in something."

"Yes, I think I do."

"Then you know that something must be truly worth believing if you are going to believe it." Again Sarkis Boyajian did not wait for a reply. "Now, Paul, tell me about your project. Eleazar told me it had something to do with Julian the Philosopher."

Yitzak Cohen took the covered pale gray crock off the shelf, removed the cover, and reached inside. He pulled out the cardboard identification tag and carefully read it: 5742–87.

He took the crock over to the sink, carefully lifted the brain and spinal cord out of it, and placed them on the cork-covered surface. He poured the cloudy formaldehyde out of the crock, refilled it with fresh formaldehyde, and lifted the brain and spinal cord back into the crock. After replacing the crock on the shelf, he took out his pocket datebook and wrote:

First formaldehyde fixation completed June 12.
Second formaldehyde fixation to be completed June 15.
Third formaldehyde fixation to be completed June 18.

The neuropathologist then sat at his desk and started sorting through a tray of small, irregularly shaped cubes of paraffin. Each wax shape was gray on the outside and contained a central core of whitish or reddish material. He carefully divided the pieces of paraffin into sets of two. He then divided the pairs of blocks. One he placed back into the original tray. The others he placed into a small box.

He wrote out a brief note to Dr. William MacNeal at the Armed Forces Institute of Pathology in Bethesda, Maryland. He had already called MacNeal and discussed the problem with him. MacNeal was an international expert on G.B. He would look at the material and send back a report. Yitzak then sealed and wrapped the box himself and took it to the post office.

As he took the bus back to Neve Ilan that evening, Paul tried to put together the events of his day. The more he thought about it, the more he liked what Romain Bernhard had said. After all, Israel was not Northern Ireland. Murder here didn't have to be a political event. Perhaps murder could even be nonpolitical in Ulster. That would make a good plot for a whodunit. A personally motivated murder masquerading as a terrorist killing in Belfast. If he ever got around to writing a novel, he might use that as an idea.

Unfortunately, what he found in his Jerusalem *Post* brought him back to reality. The reality of Israel. The Israel of Abraham's Tomb in Arab Hebron, of Rachel's Tomb, of the Little Town of Bethlehem. Three short paragraphs:

> The explosion-torn body of a Hebron man, Hamse al-Natche, was found yesterday in a flat in Abu Dis, in the Jerusalem area. Security forces found a gas canister and explosives near the body. They suspect Natche was killed while assembling a bomb, which exploded prematurely.
>
> In Sa'ir village north of Hebron, a soldier was slightly wounded yesterday when a hand grenade was thrown at an IDF patrol. A curfew was placed on the village following the attack, and a number of suspects were arrested.
>
> A Molotov cocktail was thrown yesterday at a bus transporting Israeli soldiers on the Bethlehem road near Rachel's Tomb. No one was hurt and no injuries were reported. Security forces arrested a woman from Hebron.

Paul might not be safe after all. Not because someone might be stalking him but because there were forces at work which seemed to have an irresistible momentum of their own. A momentum that threatened them all.

Romain Bernhard was wrong. Crimes of the heart were not the worry. Bernhard might be able to trace his descent to Charcot, but what had Charcot known of the Middle East?

Another morning. Another set of rounds.

There was only one new patient to be seen, and John Haddad presented the history. The patient was Amoz Tabezi, a fifty-two-year-old Libyan Jew who had come to Israel in 1949 at the age of nineteen. He had been in good health until the spring of this year, when his family noted that he was becoming very forgetful. Over the last two months his forgetfulness had progressed at an alarming rate. The neurologic exam revealed obvious and severe loss of intellectual function and occasional jerks of his arms and legs. It was the jerks of the arms that interested Paul. In his business the jerks were called myoclonus and the combination of dementia and myoclonus spelled one thing, Jakob-Creutzfeldt disease, a rare condition caused by a peculiar form of a virus. It could occasionally be spread from person to person by corneal transplants, but usually the means of transmission was unknown. It just seemed to occur.

The little girl, Avi Mashir, still had her abnormal movements. It was time to start her on some Haldol to suppress the movements.

He next asked about Zalman Cohen, the man with aphasia, but Dalia Avni was not there. He had not noticed her absence. He must be getting older than he realized. It was the chief resident who excused the others and stayed behind to answer his questions.

"What happened to Mr. Cohen?"

"He died."

"When?"

"The night before last."

"How?"

"He was given morphine."

"Yes?"

"And he had emphysema."

"So he stopped breathing," Paul completed the statement.

"Yes," Dr. Rashem said rather too coldly.

"But why was he given it?"

"We aren't sure."

"You're not sure?"

"No. We have been unable to reach Dr. Avni. She was the resident who took care of him. She apparently gave the order. But she is not here."

"When did she leave?"

"The night before last."

"When will she be back?"

"Who knows?"

What kind of a hospital was this, Paul wondered, where residents just disappeared? "Where the hell is she?"

"In Lebanon. She was called up."

At dinner that night the only topic was politics. Not Israeli politics but American politics. Even Pat, who rarely worried about political issues, was distraught.

Alexander Haig had resigned as Secretary of State.

Haig had been Israel's strongest supporter in the cabinet. Sometimes Israel's only supporter. It did not look good for Israel. Israel needed America's support financially, militarily, and as a friend. Israel had so very few of those, losing one never helped. That Paul understood all too clearly.

Both extremist factions were activated by Haig's resignation. The Peace Now group claimed that it proved that Israel was isolating itself and had to pull back. The right-wing elements knew that it confirmed how little Israel could rely on anyone else. They had to be in a position to determine their own future. The U.S. might not be there to help in a crisis.

Most Israelis heard the news and the debate and felt more and more unsure. Did this mean that Israel had lost its only friend in Reagan's administration?

Would Reagan's policy change?

Who would replace Haig?

What would happen?

Paul knew no more of the answers than they did. He hadn't even voted for Reagan. He had voted against Carter.

He was no less anxious than any of them. And no less worried.

6

Paul kept watching the addresses as he walked along Jaffa Road. He had the vague feeling that someone was following him, but that was preposterous. The national feeling of paranoia had become contagious. He stopped suddenly and turned around. In so doing he nearly collided with a teenage girl who had been hurrying along behind him.

"Sleekah," she said, excusing herself.

"Sleekah," Paul replied. He stood there and looked around. No one else had stopped. No one looked familiar. Or threatening. He turned around again and started reading the addresses: 33, 29, 27. That was the right address. It was a short, dark passageway decked out with garrish bilingual signs that led into a dark, secluded courtyard. There on the right side he located the restaurant. Taj. No customers were at any of its tables yet. It was early. Only six-thirty. He asked for a table for two and was seated in the back, under a formal picture of the former shah. That portrait served as a reminder of the happier times for Iran's Jews, who were once again suffering repression under Muslim fundamentalists.

Paul ordered a full bottle of Carmel Grenache Rosé. Chilled. Would '81 do? Yes. Then he sat back and waited. He tried to reconstruct the conversation that had resulted in his being where he was. He had called Dr. Geller to schedule a meeting for the two of them. He had done the same with Chaim Abramowitz and Yitzak Cohen. That was all well and good. On the phone she was most obliging, and somehow the result was a plan for them to meet tonight for dinner. He didn't think that he had been the one to suggest dinner. He knew he had not chosen the restaurant.

He did not know how long Dr. Geller had been standing across the table from him before he saw her. He was not sure how long he could have missed her. Her hair looked redder than before. Her long black Middle Eastern dress highlighted her fair skin.

"I'm sorry, Dr. Geller, I was just . . . reminiscing."

"That's okay, Paul. I was not standing here long. It is all right that I call you Paul?"

"Of course."

"And you can call me Rivkah."

"Please sit down." With that, he poured her a glass of wine and refilled his own.

"It is quite good," he added. "An 'eighty-one."

"Ah, yes. It was a good month."

Paul looked puzzled.

"It is a local joke about the quality of our vintage wines. Not a very good joke, I'm afraid."

The waiter came by and offered menus and told them about the day's special. Small chickens fixed on a skewer with Persian rice. They both ordered it.

It was not until the meal was over that they got down to business. While they ate they spoke of the heat, the new movies, the concert season, the things both friends and strangers can safely discuss. She asked Paul how his children were doing. She knew that he had two. How? It was on his C.V. And what were they doing this summer? Were they enjoying Israel? How were they adjusting to their loss? How did she . . . ? That, too, he guessed, must have been on his C.V.

Over coffee, it was Rivkah Geller who changed the subject.

"Paul, I wanted very much to talk to you about the diagnosis on Nahum Eckstein."

"Yes?"

"I am concerned about it."

"So are we all," Paul agreed.

"I think that I may be more concerned than any of the others with the exact diagnosis."

"Why?"

"As I said at the meeting, I'm not enough of a clinician to challenge Avram's neurologic diagnosis, nor yours. I'm so far away from my training in pathology that all I will be able to do is listen to Yitzak and agree. But I am a trained toxicologist, not just a pharmacologist."

"I know, I read your C.V. Your background and experience are impressive."

"Impressive?"

"Yes. To have become chairman of the department at age thirty-four, and your work on tetrodotoxin is classic, to say nothing of your study on—"

"Please, Paul."

"Okay, I'll stop. We didn't come here to discuss your C.V." He looked at the gray-green eyes that were staring straight at him. A few age lines were just discernible around the eyes. She wore almost no makeup. Her thin neck did show a few wrinkles. Altogether, he thought, she looks about ten years younger than her stated age. Still a very desirable woman.

"No," she agreed. "What really matters about a person is rarely on a C.V."

Paul was not sure he fully understood what she was getting at.

"Paul, I called several people last night about you."

"About me?"

"Yes, to see if I had the right . . . no, the clearance, to tell you this story."

"You mean whether I had the right to hear it," Paul interjected. "Clearance" was probably a more accurate term, but he intentionally did not use it.

"That is more correct."

"And do I?"

"Don't be offended. The story is some twenty years old and still classified as top-secret. It was back in the early sixties. It was called 'The Pickwick Project.' "

"Pickwick as in Dickens' Pickwick?"

"Identical. You must recall the fat boy in the book who would suddenly and inexplicably fall asleep during the day."

Paul did. After all, neurologists used the name of the book to describe such patients—the Pickwick syndrome. Dickens had been an outstanding observer. One hundred years later we were just beginning to understand why fat people like Joe slept all day long. It was not because they were fat. Lots of fat people stayed awake all day long. But certain fat people had severe difficulty sleeping at night—episodes of difficulty in breathing which woke them up time after time and resulted in excessive daytime sleeping. It was no longer called the Pickwick syndrome. It had a new name—sleep apnea. Sudden episodes of inability to breathe during sleep resulted in sudden movements which awakened the patients and finally led to daytime sleepiness because of the lack of continuous sleep at night. Sleep apnea.

"Sudden deep sleep. That was what we were looking for. It was so long ago. Several major wars ago. Some things have not changed since that time. Then, like today, we were surrounded by enemies who would not even recognize our right to exist. We were a small fledgling nation. We had defeated our neighbors in the War of Independence by the skin of our teeth and won the right to try to survive in this hostile world, but were we strong enough to survive? Could our army defend us? Today we know the answer to that question. But then we didn't, so we were desperate. We had great scientists here, great chemists. We became interested in chemical weapons—"

"Chemical warfare."

"But only on our own terms. We are very different from our neighbors. Two days ago our army stopped outside Sidon and Tyre to let civilians out, as we are now halted outside of Beirut." She hesitated. Paul did not have to be convinced. He understood and she recognized his understanding. "We would not use a true poison. What we wanted was more like a sedative. Something that would suddenly and effectively put people to sleep. A deep, sudden sleep. Hence, we chose the name 'Pickwick.' We tried to find a gas which would rapidly and safely cause deep sleep for several hours."

"A great way to win a war."

"Yes, in places like this where we and our enemy live next door, it would have been perfect. I worked on that project for several years, but we never solved one problem. The series of chemicals we worked on did cause sleep, but also caused a progressive paralysis and death. No matter how much we modified the chemicals, they still caused some degree of paralysis days or weeks later."

"So, what happened?"

"Then our army was victorious in the Six-Day War. We had other technologic advantages which seemed more worthwhile. Chemical weapons seemed less important and the project slowly ground to a halt. I think the last work was done in 'sixty-nine or 'seventy.''

"That's over twelve years ago," Paul thought out loud. If no one had worked on this in that long, he wondered what it could have to do with Nahum Eckstein.

Rivkah Geller anticipated his question and answered it before he asked. "The chemicals we developed still exist. They have a very long shelf life. They are almost indestructible if kept away from bright light, and they are still potent. The army was moving some three years ago and there was a spill. Two soldiers and a number of sheep died.''

"But how could Rabbi Eckstein have gotten this stuff?''

"You may not remember, but last fall there was a series of explosions at an arms depot north of Haifa.''

"I remember that. It even made the news in the U.S. It was supposed to have been an accident, an incendiary grenade went off by mistake.''

"That's what was officially said.''

"But?''

"There were many rumors.''

"The PLO?''

"That was one, of course. They might have wanted to destroy our supplies or perhaps to steal some for themselves. Although, at the rate the Russians and Syrians were giving them arms, they didn't have to steal them.''

"I know. According to the papers, the army has already captured over four thousand tons of PLO ammunition,'' Paul said.

"That is more than we have used in this entire campaign. So it's obvious that they did not need the few arms that were kept at that depot. And besides, it was not done in PLO style.''

"How is that?''

"No claims. No publicity, and no Israelis were even injured. It was done so that no one's life was endangered.''

"Then who?''

"The Guardians of the City.''

"Why the Guardians?''

"They of course did not need sophisticated arms even for their most harebrained schemes. But they knew the chemicals were stored there. No one knows exactly how much they knew about the chemicals themselves. After the explosions were over, two small containers of chemicals could not be found. If you have a gas that puts people to sleep and you want to throw all the Arabs out of some small village in an hour or two, it might come in very handy.''

"And you think the Guardians might have this stuff?''

"It's more than just possible.''

"Then how did Rabbi Eckstein get poisoned? Accidentally?''

The pharmacologist said nothing.

"Intentionally?''

Again she made no reply.

"By whom?''

She worded her reply very carefully. "Not all of them are as crazy as Nahum Eckstein was.''

"Some were even crazier, from what I've been told.''

Rivkah said nothing, but Paul knew she agreed.

"Tell me, can you measure this stuff?'' he asked.

"I think I can,'' she answered. "The missing ones were P971 and P972. We may be able to measure the levels in body tissues by very careful chemical techniques, including both thin-layer gas chromatography and mass spectroscopy. I am working on the methods and I'm hopeful that I will be able to measure them.''

"And tell if Rabbi Eckstein was poisoned before somebody pulled out the plug.''

"Yes.''

The cool air of the Jerusalem evening was reaching into the restaurant. Paul felt it and looked at his watch. He had to go.

Rivkah offered to drive him to the bus stop to meet his daughter and niece, who had also been in Jerusalem for the evening.

By eight-twenty, Paul and Rivkah were standing together at the bus stop. There was no sign of Carolyn and Adena.

At eight-twenty-five there was still no sign.

At eight-twenty-seven Paul recognized Carolyn's high-pitched laughter ringing from the entrance of the station. He had not heard that laughter in months. It sounded wonderful. It made him want to laugh or at least smile. It also brought some tears to his eyes.

"She is beautiful," Rivkah said.

Rivkah was right. Carolyn was beautiful. With a gorgeous smile. So much like her mother's had been. If only she could never stop smiling.

"Very beautiful," Rivkah continued.

Paul suddenly wondered how Rivkah knew which of the teenager girls was his daughter.

"You are fortunate. She looks like your wife."

Again, he wondered.

"You should follow her example and let yourself go. It would be nice to hear you laugh."

"Yes, it would. I'm going to try. If only to keep her smiling."

"No. You must laugh for yourself."

"Perhaps we will laugh together."

"Perhaps so," she said.

During the bus ride back to Neve Ilan, Paul tried to interest himself in the sport section of the *Herald Tribune* he had picked up specifically for that purpose. It was no use. The thirty-six-hour-old baseball scores did not exert the same fascination here in the middle of the Judean Hills that they did on the South Side of Chicago, especially since the White Sox had lost once again and Kansas City was in first place.

The change in the decor was obvious to Paul; the maps and plans of Jerusalem were now covered by maps of Jericho of every type—aerial maps, topographic maps, mineral maps, water maps, types of maps which Paul couldn't even recognize. There were maps of modern Jericho showing each individual building, maps of the Tel of Herodian Jericho, maps of ancient Jericho, maps of the ruins of Khirbat Mafjar, the Omayyad pleasure palace built at Jericho in the seventh century.

"I wanted to thank you for introducing me to Mr. Boyajian," Paul began.

Eleazar waved off Paul's thanks. "My pleasure, Paul."

"How," Paul asked, "did this Armenian jeweler from Jerusalem get his Oxford accent?"

"At Cambridge."

"Cambridge?"

"Yes. In the early twenties his family sent him to Europe to learn about gems. He was to study in Antwerp, Amsterdam, Brussels, London, all the great centers of the gem industry. Somehow he managed to spend most of those years at Cambridge learning ancient Semitic languages, early Bible study."

Paul looked at the maps and asked, "Are you now becoming a consultant on Jericho?"

"Unfortunately. Look at this." With that Eleazar Danin handed Paul the second letter.

JerIchO

Paul studied the one word. "I'm no expert, but it looks like the same type."

"It is. Same type. Same paper. Same glue, same childlike printing."

"Same person."

"Or persons."

"Well, at least you know when and where."

"I wish I was sure I knew. Do they mean the small Arab village which is today called Jericho, or the Jericho of Joshua's days, or the Jericho of the Omayyads. Which one?"

"And why Jericho?" Paul asked.

"I'm not sure I can afford to worry about why, Paul. Where, when, and who are sufficient problems for a poor policeman."

Paul looked at the word again:

JerIchO

Eleazar handed him the other note.

BewAre tHe nInTh of AV

"Were there three notes again?"

"Yes."

"Were all the notes identical?"

"Yes."

"All had the same capitals?"

"Yes. We thought of that." Eleazar looked at the notepad on his desk. "The capital letters are: B, A, H, I, T,

A, V, J, I, and O, while the lower-case letters are: e, w, r, e, t, e, n, n, h, o, f, e, r, c, and h. I've been playing with those two lists for hours and they make no sense to me at all.''

Paul wrote the letters on a piece of paper:

B A H I T A V J I O
e w r e t e n n h o f e r c h

He studied the letters for a few moments and then asked again, "Why Jericho? Nothing ever happened there on Tisha B'Av."

"Not yet."

Paul asked one last question as he got to the door.

"Another patient at Maimonides Hospital, on the Neurology service, died under strange circumstances."

"I know. Zalman Cohen."

"His death is not connected to Rabbi Eckstein's, is it?" Paul asked.

"I'm not certain."

"You mean it could be related?"

"Yes. It could."

"Why?"

"He was the last protester removed from Yamit."

In less than a week, Paul's freedom had disappeared. His life developed a routine, almost a regular schedule. Each morning he would take the first bus from Neve Ilan to Jerusalem, to the Central Bus Station; then he would wait for a different bus, to Maimonides Hospital, to Hebrew University, or to the Old City. Any real plans that he had for starting work on the outline for his textbook had now been shelved indefinitely.

Joshua and Carolyn divided their days between playing with their cousins and working on the moshav. The need for them to work was now less acute. Five men had returned from the army.

There was now time for Paul to begin reading about Julian the Philosopher. He started with the eloquent anti-Julian invectives of two early fathers of the Church, Gregory of Nazianus, himself a contemporary of Julian, and John Chrysostom, of the next generation. He delved into somewhat later historians, such as Sozomen and Rufinus. Slowly but surely he got the feel for the subject.

It was the last two years of Julian's reign when he was sole emperor that interested Paul. Julian left Constantinople in May 362 and set up temporary headquarters in Antioch, Syria. It was from here that he would set out for his ill-fated war against the Persians. It was here that he met with a group of leaders of the Jewish community. According to Rufinus, who apparently had access to the official records, the emperor had called the Jews to his court.

Julian asked the Jews, "Why do you not sacrifice to God, as required by the law of Moses?" The leaders of the Jewish delegation replied, "We are not allowed by our law to sacrifice animals outside the holy city of Jerusalem. Restore to us the city, rebuild the Temple and the Altar, and we shall offer sacrifices as in the days of old." Julian then responded, "I shall endeavor with utmost zeal to set up the Temple of the Most High God."

So the building of the Third Temple began.

All this not to support the Jews but to attack the Christians.

Mrs. Sassoon's clinical condition was unchanged. Following Paul's suggestion that she probably had a Charcot joint, they had started to evaluate her for the common causes of a Charcot joint.

"I thought Professor Bernhard said that she didn't have a Charcot joint and his authority for this was apparently Charcot himself," Paul said.

"We know," Hassan explained, "but we went over X rays of her shoulder with Radiology and they felt that a Charcot joint was a definite possibility and Professor Schiff . . ."

"Yes?" Paul looked up.

"He's pretty sure it's a Charcot joint. He thought it was a Charcot joint when he saw her as an outpatient and decided she should be admitted."

Avi Mashir was on Haldol and the movements were much reduced. She might go home soon.

Mrs. Fahoum, the Lebanese woman with encephalitis, was definitely better. At least they were able to treat one viral disease. She had been on Ara-A for almost a week and was improving at last.

No one mentioned Zalman Cohen, who had died. Nor Dalia Avni, who was still somewhere in Lebanon.

John began the presentation of one new patient. Mrs. Yousuf was a thirty-six-year-old Lebanese woman who was admitted because of progressive weakness of both sides of her face for two days. Now both sides were completely paralyzed. She had no known underlying diseases. In fact, until now she had been in excellent health. Other than the facial weakness, her general physical and detailed neurological exam were entirely normal. She had been examined by Dr. Avni just outside of Tyre and sent to Maimonides.

Slowly but surely Paul led them through the differential diagnosis and ways to evaluate a patient with bilateral facial weakness. There were a number of other diseases to consider and a number of tests to do, but the most likely diagnosis was G.B.

"Guillain-Barré syndrome," Paul started, "just like Rabbi Eckstein had." No one picked up his cue, so he continued. "He was just on the service here ten days ago . . ." Paul stopped. The rapport, the free give-and-take, the camaraderie, were gone. Was it fear? Hatred? Distrust? Guile? Perhaps they were merely ill-at-ease. It didn't matter, he was there to teach them, not analyze them. So he did just that.

On his way out of the hospital, he stopped by Avram Schiff's office, ostensibly to discuss Mrs. Sassoon and her Charcot joint and Romain Bernhard. But Paul really wanted to learn more about Zalman Cohen and Dalia Avni. So he began by asking about Dalia.

Had she really ordered morphine for Zalman Cohen? If she had, she had screwed up and killed a patient. If she hadn't, that was a different matter. Paul had worked in a hospital when a number of patients had been murdered suddenly, like this, one right after another. That had been the first murder case he'd helped the police solve. He told Avram that he had seen problems like this before.

"Like this!" Avram challenged him.

"Yes."

"What do you mean?"

"First Nahum Eckstein, then Zalman Cohen."

"Paul!"

"Yes."

"This is not America. Israelis don't go around murdering each other. We don't even know if anyone was murdered."

"No, we don't," Paul admitted. "But at least call in the police and get some cops here to supply some security until we are sure."

"We do not need to do that."

"Why not?"

"As I said, this is not America."

Paul understood. It was not America. In two ways. There were fewer murders and more security people. Eleazar Danin already knew about Zalman Cohen. It was not Chicago. The authorities here would not station uniformed cops in the hospital. Here they would use undercover agents of one sort or another. The uniformed policemen at Austin Flint hadn't done any good. Hopefully the Israelis would be more successful.

The cutting of newspapers had begun again.

An a.

A p.

An l.

Another a.

A G.

A U.

An e.

An o.

An N.

A B.

An o.

A T.

An h.

A y.

Another o.

A u.

An R.

An h.

A capital O.

A second lower-case u.

An s.
An e.
A capital S.
Slowly but steadily the letters were pasted into place
one at a time on a blank sheet of cheap white paper.

a plaGUe oN BoTh youR hOuseS

Two more times the process was repeated, and the three
sheets of paper were carefully folded and placed in envelopes which were then stamped, addressed, and taken
out to be mailed.

Events in the world were moving quickly. Alexander
Haig had been replaced as U.S. Secretary of State by
George Shultz, a longtime friend of the Arabs with ex-
tensive Arab business connections. His C.V. did not
seem to bode well for Israel. Israelis of all political per-
suasions were worried, even the half-dozen Communists
who feared that strengthening of U.S.-Arab ties might be
bad for the international Communist movement. The UN
plan to have Israel pull out of Lebanon entirely and leave
the PLO and Syrians in place had been vetoed by the
U.S. Perhaps, Paul hoped, George Shultz's Arab connections would not hurt Israel too much.

The cease-fire was being broken virtually hourly. The
advance into Lebanon had now become the longest war
in the history of Israel. The PLO had retreated into the
major cities, to seek refuge among civilians and behind
Syrians. Very few Syrians were going to expend themselves for their fellow Arabs. Even fewer Lebanese, if
they had any choice in the matter.

Most Israelis also hoped that it would not be necessary
to enter Beirut itself. That would involve house-to-house
combat, and that type of fighting would be all too costly.

Overall though, the fighting had become less intense,
and Israeli troops were being rotated home. Dr. Dalia
Avni was one of them.

7

It was the Sabbath again. Another week had passed. Paul got up quite early, made himself a cup of coffee, walked out onto the patio, and began to drink it as he watched the sun rise. He had not learned very much about the Third Temple yet. The warmth of the early-morning sun felt good. It was, he knew, the same sun that had risen over Jerusalem in the year 363 and even earlier. Over the first two Temples. And over Nineveh, whose forces had unsuccessfully besieged Jerusalem. And Babylon, whose armies had conquered Jerusalem and destroyed the Temple. Who still prayed at Nineveh? Who at Babylon? They had come here to conquer and destroy. Yet, Paul thought, we still pray here and they are all gone. Everyone still prays here. Each on his own Sabbath. On Friday or Saturday or Sunday. Pay your money and take your choice.

Had Rabbi Eckstein gone to the Wall on Sabbath to pray? Eckstein had been a leader of the Guardians of the City. To them, the right to pray at that ancient wall was a right that had to be preserved no matter what the costs might be. It had been such a pitiful right, in a way. A right to visit the retaining wall of a landfill project and to lament. No, not just to lament. For nineteen hundred years now Jews have come to pray here, Jews who spoke so many different tongues, but prayed in only one.

How would the Guardians of the City have known about the Pickwick Project—known enough about it to have stolen and been able to use one of its toxins?

Could Eckstein actually have been poisoned? It was possible. There were some toxins that could injure the nerves and cause a disease that resembled G.B. very closely. If Eckstein had been poisoned, was the plug pulled by the same people in order to finish off the job? Or by somebody else? Trying to discover who might have killed Eckstein was not Paul's job, nor why they did it. Just if. If and how. Somehow that seemed either backward or incomplete, or both.

"Dad, did you know that Hitler and Satan are equivalent?" Joshua had joined his father on the patio.

"Of course I know history," Paul replied, making a hasty recovery.

"Not history, Dad," Joshua explained. "Gematria. Aryeh taught me all about it after dinner last night."

"Gematria?"

Paul listened carefully while his thirteen-year-old enthusiastically explained Gematria to him. It was not that Joshua was really teaching him anything new. It was because of Gematria that he was still carrying eighteen dollar bills held together by a paper clip in his wallet. The *chai* with a value of eighteen that meant life. Paul listened as if it were all new to him. Joshua was so excited when he could tell his father about something strange that he had just discovered, and Paul was like any other father and loved his son's excitement and even more he loved seeing something anew through his son's mind.

It was, Joshua explained, a medieval Jewish mystical exercise in which each letter was given a numerical value. *Aleph* was one. *Bet* was two, and so forth. As a result, each word obtained a mystical numerical value and an even more mystical equivalence with other words of the same value. Hitler and Satan became one because they had the same value.

When he had finished, Paul wrote out a copy of the lists of letters from the warnings and gave it to Joshua to work on.

"Play with these letters."

"First I'll have to convert them to Hebrew."

"Go ahead." Joshua sat down on the patio and went to work and Paul went back to his own thoughts about Nahum Eckstein and the select committee, a subject equally mysterious but less mystical. Avram knew neurology and Yitzak was an excellent neuropathologist. They'd be able to do what they had to do. Would he be able to do what he wanted to do? Would he have the time? Perhaps with Sarkis Boyajian's help.

After lunch Paul walked through the neighboring hillsides to be by himself for a few minutes, but decided quickly that he'd rather read than be alone with his thoughts. As he approached his house, Paul could see Joshua playing catch with someone, but it was not someone he recognized. Was it a boy or a girl? A girl, he decided. Her back was to Paul. He didn't recognize the figure. It was much too thin to be Pat's. He got closer. It was Dalia.

"Dr. Avni."

"Shabbot shalom, Dr. Richardson."

"Dad, we've got three gloves. Can we all play for a while? In ten minutes I have to go with Aryeh and his class to the Roman fort, but we could play until then."

Paul looked at the young doctor. "If it is all right with Dr. Avni." She nodded, and for the next ten minutes they played three-cornered catch, quitting only when Joshua ran off for his walk through the hills. It had to be less depressing than Paul's had been.

"Dr. Avni, how did you learn to use a baseball glove, and play so well?"

"From some cousins, when I spent a summer in America."

"How was it up north?"

"Terrible. The day I got there, sixteen boys got killed. Three of them died in our aid station. They were all so young. They had so much to live for. One died while I was trying to stop his bleeding. He had been shot in the neck and the blood was spurting from his carotid . . . I'll never forget it. I . . . Will the world let this be our last war? Or will they side with the Arabs and their oil and try to destroy us again in some way?"

"I don't know."

His answer obviously did not satisfy her. This girl who sat back so quietly in his teaching conferences was alive with feeling, with a passion that bordered on fanaticism.

"Will your President Reagan support us at all now that Haig is gone? Will he make the Syrians leave Lebanon when we do? And the terrorists?"

Paul felt helpless to answer her questions and angry that he was helpless. "I don't know those answers, Dalia. I just don't know."

She heard his nonanswer and became equally frustrated. There was no reason to ask him any more questions.

"You had to attack the terrorists. They were too great a threat." He had not really said very much.

"Some of our own people are even worse than the terrorists. Those damn extremists. They're pulling us apart."

"Like Rabbi Eckstein?"

"Yes, like him."

"How?" he asked, not because he didn't know the answer but because he had changed roles. It wasn't the factual answer that he needed to hear; it was the depth of her feeling.

"He and his kind will destroy us, and for what? Some two-thousand-year-old dream."

"That dream is Zionism."

"Not the same Zionism I believe in."

"You don't have to worry about him anymore."

"There are others. Some of them are even worse."

"Such as?"

"Those idiots who occupied Yamit."

"Like Zalman Cohen?" he suggested. It was a leading question.

"What?"

"He was at Yamit?"

"I . . . I . . ." she stuttered.

"Didn't you know?"

"No."

He wanted very much to believe her, although he wasn't entirely certain why. He had probed enough to find out that her hatred ran deep. Deep enough to kill? He hoped it wasn't that deep.

"You did not come here to discuss politics with me," he said.

"No, I didn't. They said at the hospital that you wanted to see me about Mr. Cohen."

Paul nodded.

"I didn't write any order to give him morphine. I would never have done that. I may not be as good a physician as you are, and I probably never will be, but I'm not that stupid."

"I never said that you were."

"And I didn't know he was at Yamit," she repeated. "And I didn't pull Eckstein's plug either. I wasn't even in the hospital when it happened."

There was nothing more for either of them to say. After a few awkward moments Paul collected the gloves and took them into the house and Dalia walked down the hillside toward the highway to Jerusalem. He had witnessed both her hatred and her denial. The former had felt more real. The question was whether the latter was any less true.

He took out the list he had scribbled down at the committee meeting.

The differential diagnosis.

Accidental death was too much to be hoped for, as was a crime of the heart. That left five.

1. PLO
2. Moderate Arabs
3. Guardians of the City
4. Jewish radicals
5. Christian fanatics

The differential was not complete. He added one more.

6. Main-line middle-of-the-road Israelis.

That didn't add much. So far, his list included everyone but himself and his two kids.

Yitzak Cohen usually came into the hospital on the Sabbath. Not to see patients. As a pathologist he never saw patients except for their autopsies. He came in each week to finish up his work, to go over the microscopic slides of each postmortem, without being disturbed.

He finished up case 5742–86 and went into the preparation room to look for the next batch of slides: 5742–87.

The tissue blocks were not in the tray where he had left them. There was no one else there to help find them.

He called the senior lab technician at home. Yes, she had started work on them. Yes, in the usual way. Yes, she knew where she had left the tissue blocks. In the usual place. Just where he had looked.

So he looked again.

And again.

The blocks were gone.
His next call was to Yehuda Ben Zvi.

Eleazar Danin always stopped by his office at least once
on the Sabbath to make sure there were no urgent messages.

Today there were none, so his Sabbath could be a day
of rest.

Paul met with Sarkis that afternoon and told him what
he had learned about the meeting of Julian with the Jewish leaders in Antioch. Julian had announced his decision
to help the Jews rebuild their Temple and to return the
scattered Jews to Jerusalem. The plan had progressed and
a Roman overseer had been named, materials had been
collected, and work had been started.

"All you need now is a few details about the miracle."

"Yes, about the miracle." Paul's tone did not hide his
sarcasm.

"Do you know where to find such details?" Sarkis
asked.

"Not for sure."

"The St. Thoros library. Not only have we Armenians
been here longer than any other Christians, we also built
the first library. I will give you a letter of introduction to
Archbishop Boggharian. He will help you find the books
you need."

Yitzak Cohen called William MacNeal in Bethesda and
told him what had happened and requested his help.
MacNeal was most understanding. He had also been involved in cases with political ramifications and security
problems.

Once the blocks of tissue arrived, William MacNeal
would call the Israeli embassy. He would then take
enough of each block to do his own studies and the embassy would pick up the rest, about two-thirds of each
block, and bring them back by diplomatic pouch. Yitzak
was glad he had mailed them out personally.

"Is your computer programmed to do Gematria?"

"Of course not."

"That may be a mistake."

"Why?"

"My thirteen-year-old son has solved the mystery of the message by using Gematria."

"So?"

"B A H I T A V J I O transmuted became Menachem Begin."

"Begin!"

"Yes, Begin. So now you may know who the target is."

"You don't really believe in Gematria," Eleazar Danin declared in disbelief.

"No, it's a fun game for adolescents. Give a word a numerical value and it becomes the same as hundreds of other words. It's foolish. There are thousands of words and only a few numbers. You can then choose whichever one of the equivalent words meets your fancy. My son chose Begin."

"What were his other choices?"

"Well, I told him it had to be someone both famous and alive. So he came up with Mick Jagger, Begin, Chet Lemon—"

"Who?"

"A center-fielder we traded to Detroit—" the explanation seemed to shed little if any light—"and Isaac Singer."

"Singer."

"Yes, but he won't be in Israel on Tisha B'Av. Nor will Chet Lemon, nor Mick Jagger. Jagger was his initial choice. But we settled on Begin."

"That can't be right."

"Probably not, but who knows? But if it is Gematria, then whoever is sending them must be a Jew."

"If whoever did it believed in Gematria, why weren't the messages in Hebrew to start with?" Eleazar asked.

"Don't ask me."

"Is that all you came to tell me?" the consultant in security inquired.

"No. That wasn't all. Another idea occurred to me." Eleazar Danin stopped doodling and put down his pen.

"It's just possible that Jericho doesn't stand for the place, not Jericho the city, but that it represents a means or a method."

"How did you reach that conclusion?"

"It's not a conclusion; it's just an idea."

"So how did you get that idea?" Eleazar persisted.

Paul did his best to explain his logic. It was based on the Biblical history of Jericho. Jericho had been destroyed by Joshua and then cursed. It was not resettled until four or five hundred years later, and then only after the Prophet Elisha had cleansed the well.

"So?"

"The well had probably been infected or poisoned."

"Poisoned!"

"Yes, poisoned."

"No one would want to poison Jericho's water supply."

"What about Jerusalem's?"

"I hope not." Eleazar was becoming less comfortable.

"That's what the Yippies were planning to do in Chicago in 'sixty-eight. They threatened to put LSD into Lake Michigan. It could be done."

"Perhaps," the consultant conceded.

Danin was not as impressed as Paul thought he should have been.

"I also wanted to discuss another matter. I talked to Dr. Avni."

"Yes."

"She denies ever writing an order for morphine."

"So?"

"That may mean that Zalman Cohen was murdered and there is some conspiracy going on here."

"No, I doubt that," Danin replied, shaking his head ever so wisely.

"Why?"

"I have information that you do not have. It is very sensitive. I cannot let you see it. But I can tell you some of it. The part that may mean something to you. The terrorists who shot Ambassador Shlomo Argov in London had a prepared list of targets, and Nahum Eckstein was on that list."

Paul began to understand.

"But Zalman Cohen was not."

Paul understood. They already knew who had killed Nahum Eckstein, if he had really been killed. Not the exact person, maybe, but the group who had done it. They knew the motive. That was why finding the supposed murderer wasn't his problem. And that was also why Zalman Cohen had not been killed. Arab terrorists would not have had any reason to kill Zalman Cohen. They didn't even know that he existed, Danin concluded.

That was all wrong. They had the process all backward. You didn't pick the killers first and then see if the victims fit. You started the other way around, moving from victim to suspects. Suspects with opportunity and motive.

"Dr. Avni had a motive to kill Zalman Cohen," Paul said challengingly.

"Dalia?"

How did Danin know her first name? What more did he know about her? Paul told Danin what she had said about the right-wing extremists.

"Did she know that he was at Yamit?" Danin asked.

"She denied it," Paul replied automatically.

"Did you believe her?"

"I don't know."

"Why not, Paul?"

"She hates the right-wing extremists. She thinks they will destroy her country."

"She's not alone in that fear."

"No, I guess she isn't," Paul admitted.

"Even I feel much the same way. But, my friend, it's a long step from fear and dislike to murder."

"Perhaps."

"And she wasn't there when the—"

"Plug was pulled," Paul said, completing the phrase. "How did you know that?"

"It's part of my job."

"Oh."

"I trust her. She's no murderer."

"Oh," he repeated. What else did Eleazar know that Paul didn't? How well did he know Dalia? Eleazar didn't use first names for the others whom he only knew peripherally.

Dalia.

As Paul left the office, Danin wrote a brief note on a pad of white paper: "Begin—where on Tisha B'Av?"

The meeting began on time.

The brain was placed in the middle of a hard cork cutting board. The tips of the frontal lobe were facing Yitzak Cohen, who stood at the front of the table dressed in a surgical scrub suit and a plastic apron. On his hands he wore surgical gloves. A large butcher knife, a surgical scalpel, a probe, and a ruler were to the right of the brain. The other five doctors in their white coats were gathered around the front of the table. The man in black was not there. Instead he waited silently outside the room. There were some desecrations he would not condone by any hint of participation.

Yitzak Cohen picked up the brain, turned it over, and began to study the undersurface. A faint smell of formalin began to pervade the room.

Avram Schiff, Romain Bernhard, and Paul Richardson each looked carefully at the base of the brain. It seemed normal to each of them. Normal for a healthy sixty-two-year-old. A little hardening of the arteries, but nothing remarkable.

Yitzak Cohen cut off the brain stem with the scalpel, put it to the side, arranged the brain on the cutting board, took the butcher knife, and cut across the brain once, twice, three times, producing slices that were about one centimeter thick. The third slice cut across the cavities of the brain, and formalin gushed out of them, bringing tears to the eyes of the nonpathologists. He kept on cutting.

Within a few minutes he had sectioned both hemispheres. The slices of brain were carefully arranged on the table. Yitzak was now making cuts through the brain stem, that part of the brain that had controlled Nahum Eckstein's respiration for all but the last few days of his life. Despite the heavy odor of formalin, Avram and Paul inched even closer to the table. The stench irritated their noses as they studied each section.

Nahum Eckstein's brain was normal. Next, Yitzak took the spinal cord. He cut through its lining, and then, using the scalpel, made cuts across it at one-centimeter intervals. It also appeared to be entirely normal. The slides would be ready for presentation in two or three weeks.

Once the tissue had been put away, the smell of formalin began to recede and Rabbi Levi rejoined the committee. So did Dean Ben Zvi. He told them of the theft of the tissue blocks and of the second set which would soon be on the way back to Israel. He warned them to guard all materials very closely. All samples and tissues were now under continuous surveillance.

"Perhaps," Rabbi Levi said, interrupting him, "this theft of yours is not a theft as such, not an illegal act aimed at thwarting this committee."

"What else could it be?"

"An act of piety. An attempt to replace the missing elements of Rabbi Eckstein's body. May he rest in peace."

"I doubt that. They seem to have been stolen on the Sabbath."

"An act of such piety might take precedence."

"Like saving a life?" Paul asked.

"Is setting a soul at rest any less important?"

No one had a direct answer to this question, but the dean went on.

"All other materials are now under guard and will not be subject to such mysterious disappearances. You should all keep your papers, your notes, and what-have-you under lock and key." With that the meeting was over and everyone left the conference room but Paul Richardson and Rivkah Geller. Paul patiently waited for her to say whatever it was she had to say.

"I think that one of the Pickwick poisons caused Eckstein's disease."

"Have you found it in the tissue samples?"

"No."

"Then how can you be certain? There could still be evidence of inflammation in the slides."

Rivkah was not convinced. That was obvious to Paul, as were her anguish and her distress. He tried once again to reassure her. But his reassurances didn't help. Paul didn't want to add to her discomfort in any way, but there was one question he had to ask. "How could Eckstein, or any of the Guardians for that matter, have known about the Pickwick poisons?"

"From me," she blurted out with a combination of guilt and relief.

The tale was straightforward enough. When she was a student and then a resident, she had chosen not to get married, not to let anything stand in the way of her professional career. Paul was gratified that at least one guess of his had been right. But then, when she became a professor, in the late 'sixties, she had met a man. They had lived together for a number of years. Why hadn't they married? So many reasons. He was older. A survivor. Uninterested in marriage. She didn't care. She didn't want to raise a family. It lasted for eight years and then it was over. Somehow, this once gentle man found a home in the Guardians. That was one of the things that finally had driven them apart.

"And . . ."

"And he knew everything I had worked on. He knew everything about the Pickwick Project and was smart enough to know what it meant."

"And . . ."

"Fanatic enough to tell the others. Thank God he died. He had become so embittered."

"Are you sure he told others?"

"Yes."

"Why?"

"He told me he had. On his deathbed. As a farewell blessing."

Once again, Paul just barely missed the action. It took place at the Hilton Hotel, just beyond the Convention Center, two blocks from the central bus stop where he changed buses to go home.

"Three copies of the *International Herald Tribune,* please."

"That will be seventy-five shekels."

For all intents and purposes it had been just another tourist. One who needed three copies of the same paper. People from tour groups often bought more than one. The purchase was forgotten in less time than it took to ring it up on the cash register.

After dinner the three of them played cards. Just the three of them. The family, by themselves.

They played hearts.

And they talked. Mostly about the war. Joshua knew all of the technical details. He had been thrilled by the total failure of the Russian surface-to-air missiles. Israel had somehow managed to destroy all of the SAMs without the loss of a single plane. That was bad news for the Kremlin. They probably held a party in the Pentagon to celebrate. Both Joshua and the U.S. Joint Chiefs were also cheered by the superiority of the F-15 and F-16 fighters. They had never really been tested in combat before. They passed their test with flying colors. Joshua could not get over how the new Israeli tanks had outmaneuvered the supposedly invincible Russian T-72's. None of this fascinated Carolyn. But when Paul asked them if they would be willing to go into the Israel Defense Force and fight if they moved to Israel, it was Carolyn who answered first.

A simple yes, said quietly and sincerely. It was clearly something she had already considered.

Paul hardly heard Joshua's echoed and enthusiastic yes. It was his daughter's answer that made him realize that not all the decisions were his to make.

When they were eighteen they could come here on their own.

When she came to kiss him good night he asked her if she had ever thought of coming here on her own. Carolyn said she had. She didn't think she would. Not until Joshua was in college at least. Until then, they should all stay together.

Very little new had been learned about the patients.

Mrs. Sassoon's myelogram was scheduled to be done the next day.

Most of the results were back on Mrs. Yousuf. It looked very much like she had Guillain-Barré syndrome.

There were two other new patients to be discussed. One was a twenty-three-year-old woman who had delivered a normal healthy baby boy five days earlier and had run a low-grade fever for the next three days and complained of pain and tenderness. Yesterday the fever had suddenly reached 102 degrees, she was septic, and then she had a seizure. The patient had another seizure, then a third. She was treated vigorously with anticonvulsants but then had another seizure. This one involved her left side only, and now her left arm and leg were paralyzed.

They all knew the diagnosis.

Puerperal fever—a pelvic infection with thrombosis of pelvic veins followed by secondary spread of that thrombosis to the brain, resulting in seizures and now paralysis.

Could they have done anything more for Mrs. Leah Gandel?

No.

Was there anything else they could do now?

No, nothing more than they were already doing.

The reality of their helplessness was weighing heavily on all of them.

They were dealing with a young woman their own age, who was half-paralyzed. She had gone to high school with Dalia's younger sister. And there was nothing they could do.

The frustration was thick enough to cut. It was one thing to have events in the world that you could not control. Events that killed your friends. But that plus this— this personal failure to be able to save a life—was almost too much for them to tolerate.

They needed to be able to do something. Yuri and Dalia and even John Haddad.

But what?

And to whom?

Had Dalia already done something?

No. Paul didn't want to believe that. Through it all, Hassan Rashem sat almost passively, almost uninvolved.

As soon as rounds were over, Paul went next door to see if Avram Schiff was free. He was. He offered Paul coffee, and once they were served, the two neurologists sat back comfortably.

"The brain was normal, Avram."

"I know."

"The respiratory centers were entirely clean," Paul continued. "I doubt that the slides will show very much. They might, but I doubt it. He probably had severe G.B. Your clinical impression was correct."

"I don't know. I'm not as sure as you are. In most cases of G.B., the nerve roots are swollen. I looked very closely while Yitzak was cutting the spinal cords, and the roots looked normal to me."

"We'll have to see the slides," Paul said. "By the way," he went on, "I'm sure your lady has a syrinx causing her Charcot joint."

"So am I."

"Your neurosurgeon isn't."

"Bernhard?"

"Yes, Bernhard."

"Paul, don't jump to any conclusion about Romain. Just when you are sure he is nothing more than a pompous old man, he will surprise you."

"I hope so. I have a meeting with him in ten minutes. By the way, I was glad to hear that Dalia Avni didn't write an order for morphine. It must be a relief for you too, even though it means that someone intentionally gave him morphine and—"

"But you're wrong, Paul."

"Wrong?"

"The order was initialed by Dr. Avni. I have a Xerox copy of it right here if you'd like to see it."

"That's not necessary. What are you going to do?"

"We will have an official mortality review and then we will see."

"But she . . ."

"What?"

"Nothing." He didn't have to start any rumors. Her life was here. He was an outsider. He could always go home. Maybe she didn't really hate that much. At least he hoped she didn't. Besides, it wasn't his problem.

It was time to meet with Professor Bernhard. He shouldn't have been in such a hurry. The meeting resulted in none of the pleasant surprises Avram had promised him.

Romain was pleasant enough. His politeness bordered on solicitude.

He asked the right questions.

Did Paul enjoy teaching here?

Were the residents challenging?

The students?

The patients?

How did he find the hospital facilities?

The library?

The laboratories?

Did Romain hear the answers? Did he care? It was time for Paul to take charge. There were answers he needed to hear. This meeting was for his benefit, not the neurosurgeon's. "Professor Bernhard."

"Yes."

"Tell me, had you been consulted on Rabbi Eckstein?"

"No . . . not officially. Avram had mentioned his problem to me. That morning, in fact, just before he died, just outside the ICU. The question of a myelogram was discussed. We both thought that one would not be useful."

He, too, had been there. It must have been rather crowded in that ICU.

Suddenly Paul lost control of the conversation. Bernhard began asking the questions. Did he think Reagan would support Israel now that Haig was gone?

Would it not be best just to wipe out the entire PLO?

What would the effect of the new Secretary of State be? What was his name? Shultz. That sounded too Germanic for him.

Once and for all: "Professor Bernhard."

"Yes."

"About our committee."

"Oh, yes, the committee. I will speak to you frankly. I, for one, Professor Richardson, do not see much purpose in this entire procedure."

"Why?"

"Yitzak is an excellent neuropathologist. He will tell us if he died of a neurologic disease. And if he did, fine. If he didn't, that's fine too. It makes no difference to me. He is dead and we are all better off without him.

"Don't get me wrong. I will pursue the truth here. But don't expect me to be influenced personally by that truth."

"But someone may have killed him."

"I've seen men killed in worse ways, many of them, and no one did anything about it and the world didn't stop on its axis."

Paul hadn't learned anything that would help him in the deliberations of the committee. The other problem seemed more pressing. Romain could best be handled by ignoring him. But Dalia Avni. That was not so easy to disregard.

Why had Dalia lied to him? She might not have written the order, but she had countersigned it. Without her signature the nurses wouldn't have given the morphine. It was her responsibility. She had lied to him.

She had signed the order.

The order that had killed Zalman Cohen.

Had she also pulled the plug on Nahum Eckstein?

No. Eleazar had cleared her of that.

What did that mean?

Did it mean that she was innocent of that killing? If it was a killing.

But why had she lied?

To protect someone else? To protect herself? The terrorists who killed Eckstein would not have killed Zalman Cohen. If Eckstein was killed by terrorists. Maybe he was murdered by someone else? If he was murdered? Dammit. He was murdered. Paul had become convinced of that. But had Zalman Cohen been killed too? Could Dalia have signed that order intentionally? Knowing that it would kill him?

Paul wanted very much to be somewhere else, away from the plots and intrigues, away from the hatred. They should be saving lives or at least trying to.

He looked at his watch. It was time to go. He took a taxi across the city into East Jerusalem and across the crest of ridges overlooking the Temple Mount, to the top of the Mount of Olives to the Intercontinental Hotel. Joshua and Carolyn were waiting in the restaurant to have lunch with him while looking down upon the Temple Mount with its golden Dome of the Rock and the silver Dome of the El Aksa Mosque. It would be their last family excursion before Carolyn left to join her group for the summer. They had already been here two weeks. It had gone by so quickly.

"It was here," Paul told them, "that the Crusaders spent their first Sunday in Jerusalem. Right here on the top of the Mount of Olives.

"Here these great nobles from France, England, Italy, and Germany found a Christian hermit, an old man, who lived in a cave on the Mount of Olives undisturbed by the Muslims below. This old man blessed them and prophesied that if they would attack Jerusalem right then from right there, the attack would succeed. It would be God's will. The knights mounted their horses, charged down into Kidron Valley, and then attacked the eastern wall of Jerusalem."

"What happened, Dad?" Joshua asked.

"Guess."

"The Crusaders won."

"No. They got creamed. A prophetic blessing is no substitute for an adequate battle plan."

After lunch, they wandered down the Mount of Olives and Paul showed them the various shrines. It was hot, but the kids enjoyed it. As they walked, Paul tried to figure out which was worse, having a resident who negligently killed someone, or having patients being murdered. Probably the former. The latter would eventually run its course, the murderer would be uncovered, but a doctor who killed by mistake, by negligence, could keep on knocking patients off for a lifetime.

That was Avram's problem.

No, it was his problem too.

Getting rid of dangerous doctors was every physician's problem.

That was more his responsibility than worrying about who killed Nahum Eckstein.

He would have to talk with Dalia Avni again. He'd rather talk to Rivkah Geller. Perhaps they would have dinner again.

The afternoon mail had come. Eleazar Danin was almost relieved that another letter had come. He half-expected it to be hand-delivered on Sabbath, but instead it had been mailed.

a plaGUe oN BoTh youR hOuseS

Same scribble.
Same envelope.
Same paper.
Same glue, he was sure.
Same stamp.
Same postmark.
Now there were three:

BEWARE THE NINTH OF AV.
BewAre tHe nInTh of AV.
JERICHO.
JerIchO.

A PLAGUE ON BOTH YOUR HOUSES.
a plaGUe oN BoTh youR hOuseS.

Shakespeare. Even he knew the exact source of this quote. *Romeo and Juliet*. At least it was not from *The Merchant of Venice*.

Paul Richardson could be right. Jericho might not represent a place, but a means. Poisoning of a well with a plague. Not LSD, but some sort of bacterial contamination.

But what kind of plague?

Eleazar continued to study the third note. It had to be more than just letters to feed into the computer. More combinations. More Gematria. Both? Two. Two targets? Maybe it meant Begin and someone else. Two targets. Two people who would have to be given extra security on Tisha B'Av. But who? Which two? Begin and Jagger?

8

As soon as Paul sat down, Eleazar handed him the third warning. Paul did not just read it. He studied it.

a plaGUe oN BoTh youR hOuseS

"What do you make of our third message?"

"Obviously it's from Shakespeare. A direct quote, in fact. Even though he's the most quoted author in the English language, this choice to quote him must not be a coincidence." By now Paul was beginning to think aloud, to let his mind associate while he talked. This was what he always did at home in his lab meetings when he was trying out new solutions to some research problem. "Perhaps the first—'Beware the ninth of Av'—was a paraphrase from *Julius Caesar*. A variation on 'Beware the ides of March.' This one's from *Romeo and Juliet*. In *Caesar* the chief of state is assassinated. It's not the only death in the play, but it's the most important one. And the only one that takes place on the ides of March. In *Romeo* the final tragedy revolves around a fake poisoning followed by two suicides. One by poison and two by knives. Caesar was killed by knives."

"You don't think they would warn us if they wanted to get close enough to someone like Begin to put a knife into him?"

"Probably not. But the choice of Shakespeare is intriguing. The Bible is the most quoted source in every Western language, and if you were going to write a warning about Tisha B'Av, you ought to find appropriate sources there."

"So Shakespeare may be part of the message?" Eleazar asked.

"Yes. Not that that's much help." Paul hesitated.

"Unless it's the political nature of the themes. Brutus betrayed Caesar because he thought Caesar had betrayed them all, had betrayed the cause. Like Nahum Eckstein."

"Paul, you are confusing your fields of study."

"I guess so."

"Can you think of anything else?"

"Some obvious things. The use of upper case. I assume the use of upper case was the same in all versions."

"Identical," Eleazar assured him.

"Well, it sure doesn't seem random. Capital U's are not the easiest letter to come by in the Jerusalem *Post*."

"Not that hard. We took a survey. United States. United Nations. UPI. USSR. Not hard at all. In fact, the capital G was much harder to locate."

"I would not have thought that. But the principle is the same. Some of these letters are a lot less common in the average newspaper than others, and some of these rare upper-case letters are used. That supports the notion that the precise choice of letters is meaningful. One other thing: in the first two warnings the first letter was capitalized; here it was not, suggesting again that the use of capitals to start a sentence or as the first letter of a proper noun was not just done to conform to the rules of good grammar."

"So the letters mean something. But what?"

"Who knows? More work for a computer."

"More Gematria?" Eleazar asked.

"No. Gemátria only works with individual words or names. But maybe each one should be looked at separately." He stopped for a minute and wrote:

BAHITAV
JIO
GUNBTROS

"It could be three separate Gematric—if that is the word—messages."

"We'll let you work on that."

"Not me. My son."

"Your son, then."

Paul then noticed something he'd missed before. "The letters are different, aren't they?"

"You are becoming an excellent detective."

Paul ignored the compliment. "It's still newsprint, but the typeset is different. You see it more in some of the lower cases, but it's different. It's no longer the Jerusalem *Post*."

"No, he's switched to the *International Herald Tribune*. Why would he do that?"

"To find the right letters," Paul guessed.

"No, the same letters were available in the Jerusalem *Post*. We checked that out."

"I don't know, then."

"Neither do we."

"Unless . . ." Paul suggested, "he wanted to get the baseball scores. American sports news gets much better coverage in the *Herald Tribune*."

The students and residents brought Paul up-to-date on the half-dozen patients he was following with them. Mrs. Fahoum was still improving. The Ara-A had done the trick. Amoz Tabezi was about to be discharged. It was definite that he had Jakob-Creutzfeldt disease and that they had no miracle drugs to cure him. Mrs. Yousuf was stable. The weakness caused by her Guillain-Barré syndrome had not progressed further. Mrs. Sassoon had not yet had her myelogram but it would be done in a day or two. Radiology was trying hard to catch up. Several of the radiologists were in Lebanon. Mrs. Leah Gandel, the young woman who had become so sick right after she had given birth to a child, had had no more seizures. There had been no further progression of any neurological problems. She had been completely stable for forty-eight hours. Any further worsening was very unlikely. The major unanswered question was whether or not she would start to improve.

The students presented two new patients. John told him about a man with confusion from alcoholism and cirrhosis of the liver, and he, in turn, told them all about Beethoven and his death from cirrhosis of the liver. Then Yuri presented a woman with hysterical paralysis of the left arm, an arm that became useless because of psychological reasons. Paul told them about Sigmund Freud and Joseph Breuer and Anna O. And that Breuer had been a great physician who had also made major contributions to our understanding of the eighth cranial nerve and that Anna O had been his patient, not Freud's, and that she was a real person, Bertha Pappenheim, and that she had been a feminist activist in Berlin until the early thirties, and then . . . The last part of his story he didn't have to tell. Not here.

Throughout it all, Dalia Avni said nothing. She sat silently in the back of the conference room alone, seemingly ostracized, as if any contact with her would spread some sort of deadly plague.

Rounds were over and everyone rushed out except Paul and Dalia. They both stayed and somehow knew that the other one would also stay. How had he ever found her attractive? She was too skinny, too angular.

When she spoke, the quiet conviction in her tone reminded him of Carolyn, of how she had sounded when she had told him that she would be willing to serve in the IDF. The same restrained conviction. "I did not kill Mr. Cohen."

"I never said you killed him."

"No. Well, in any case, I never wrote that order."

"Professor Schiff has the order sheet. You initialed it."

"I did not do that." Her tone was more defiant now. Defiant and hostile. Not like Carolyn at all.

He wanted to believe her, but he couldn't. Avram had the order sheet. There couldn't be any mistake. Or could there?

If tissue samples could disappear and respirators become unplugged, why couldn't orders just somehow materialize on a chart?

No reason at all.

"Dalia, I want to believe you."

"It would be a lot nicer if you did."

"I guess I just don't know you well enough."

Even his semisupport had helped. She looked less isolated and less agitated as she went off to do her work.

Paul was happy to get out of the hospital, away from its problems and off by himself. He was becoming fond of the Armenian quarter, the smallest and least busy of all of the quarters of the Old City. He had always thought of it as a place to walk through to get somewhere else. It was now the place he headed for.

The Library of St. Thoros was one of the least-visited

spots in the entire Armenian quarter. When he got to the
door and gave them the card Sarkis had given him, he
received a warm welcome. Nothing was too good for
him. He had the entire library at his disposal. Room after
room lined with books from ceiling to floor. Many were
in Armenian, but many were in other languages, and the
card catalog was in Armenian and English. He was left
on his own.

Paul knew that he would have to learn a great deal
more about the early history of the Christians and the
various Christian churches to deal with Julian. He knew
that, but somehow he had never pictured himself sitting
in a library of the Armenian Catholic Church surrounded
by books on ecclesiastic history. In a way, he was thank-
ful that so many of the books were in Armenian or classical Greek or other languages that he was unable to read.
There were so many that he could easily spend four or
five years just getting background, and he had less than
two months to do all his research. He was becoming more
and more aware that even these two months were not
entirely at his disposal.

Where should he start?

He studied the early Christian community in Aelia
Capitolina and read about Saint Helena, the mother of
Constantine the Great. She had come to Palestine in 326
to find the holy sites and to erect great churches on the
exact sites where the events of the life and death of Jesus
had occurred.

What had it been like to be living in Aelia Capitolina
when she came here? It must have still been a pagan city.

Saint Helena tried to change that. She came to visit the
holy places and to build churches. The Bishop of Jerusalem brought her to Golgotha. It was now within the
city limits, near Hadrian's forum. It was buried under a
temple dedicated to Aphrodite. Saint Helena gave the orders and the pagan temple was torn down and a great
basilica of the Holy Sepulcher was begun.

From that time on, Christians began to flock to Jerusalem. They came from all corners of the empire. Most
came to visit the shrines, to walk in the footsteps of Jesus. Others came to stay, to live their lives in the city of
Jesus.

That gave them another reason to oppose the Third

Temple. Julian was not only going to give the Jews the Temple, he was going to give them the entire city. By that time most of Jerusalem belonged to the Christians. It had become their home; their lives were tied up in it. Religion was one thing. Taking away their homes was something else.

For the next several days, Paul spent as much time as he could manage buried in the St. Thoros library. Finally he was able to work his way up to the year 363. Work on the Temple had actually begun.

The first step had been the removal of some earlier foundations that were still standing on the Mount. Paul was not sure which foundations these were. Some Christian historians claimed that these were the sole remnants of the Second Temple, seeing irony in the fact that the Jews themselves were helping to carry out Jesus' prophecy to the last letter. Most Christians believed that this prophecy had long been fulfilled and that Jesus did not need the help of those who had rejected him.

It was more likely that these remnants were from the temple that Hadrian had had hastily put up two hundred years earlier on the exact spot where the Second Temple had stood. It had been a minor temple dedicated to one of a long list of deities in an unimportant Roman town. Like many such temples, it had fallen into ruin.

Then the work on the Temple itself began. The Third Temple.

It went on through what we would now call April and May. Then the miracle happened.

The earth under the building site suddenly opened up as if torn apart by the hand of God. Great tongues of fire, great flaming balls, issued forth, enveloping everything and everyone. They swirled about Temple Mount and then formed into one sheet of flame that flew up into the late-evening sky above Jerusalem, broke into two parts, and formed a great fiery cross that illuminated the sky for hours.

Under the crack in the Mount where the fire had burst forth, workmen found a mysterious cave, and inside the cave they found a glowing pillar. On the pillar, illuminated by the light of the cross, they found an open copy of the Gospel according to Saint John. It must have been there waiting for this moment of revelation since the time of creation.

The cross burned brightly. It stretched from the Mount of Olives to the newly finished basilica built over the site of the Resurrection. Every footstep that Jesus had walked in that final journey shone brightly.

Crosses suddenly appeared on the clothes of everyone who was in the city that night—Christian, Jew, and pagan alike. Those on the Jews and pagans were black. Those on the Christians were white.

Jerusalem was no longer Aelia Capitolina. It was once again Jerusalem—not the Jerusalem it had once been, but nonetheless Jerusalem.

Fortunately, even without Paul's participation, other events moved forward.

The package arrived at the Armed Forces Institute of Pathology. William MacNeal carefully examined each paraffin block and personally cut off the small sections they would need and rewrapped the rest of the blocks. He then called the embassy. They had been expecting his call. A courier would be on his way immediately. In less than eighteen hours the package was hand-delivered to the Department of Pathology at Maimonides Hospital, to Yitzak Cohen.

Yitzak personally inspected each of the blocks. He divided each of them into two relatively equal halves. One of each pair he placed inside a blue pouch carrying the official seal of the State of Israel. The other he kept. He handed the blue pouch to one of the three men standing in the hall outside the pathology laboratory, who handcuffed it to his wrist and left. The other two stayed. As soon as Dr. Cohen left the laboratory, one went inside while the other remained in the hall. The tissue blocks would not disappear this time.

Like Paul Richardson, Rivkah Geller spent several hours each day working by herself. It was now after five and she was alone in her own laboratory. The technicians had all gone home for the day. She had always been more at home in her lab than anywhere else, more than with patients, more than in her own apartment. Working alone in the lab when everyone else had gone home, she could be herself. She could putter on her own, work on new ideas, new problems. She never understood how people could give up working in the laboratory. Most of her colleagues had given it up. They let their technicians do it all. Not Rivkah Geller. And certainly not on this project.

She removed the samples from the deep freeze. There were four samples of different body fluids. She checked each label and recorded it in the large notebook on the desk in front of her. There were seven samples of different organs or tissues. She recorded each of these, labeling each with the same name of the organ and autopsy number. She did the same for the samples of hair and fingernails. With a sharp scalpel she cut each of the samples of tissue into four approximately equal parts and put each part into a separate vial which she then labeled and put into the deep freeze. She then used a tweezers to separate the hairs and fingernails into three samples of each. These too she carefully labeled and put away. By the time she had done these tasks, the first four samples had melted. This allowed her to easily pour parts of each flask into other small vials, which she then labeled and froze. Next she wrote out an outline of the exact procedures she would follow, listing each and every step. That alone took her almost an hour. It took her another twenty minutes to review the outline. She was satisfied. The biochemical procedures should be able to detect the Pickwick poisons. It would be a bit harder than most such processes, since she didn't have samples of the exact poison she was looking for, but the government had sent her small amounts of four other closely related compounds: P970, P974, P975, and P976. P973 never really existed except on the drawing boards. The chemical was far too unstable.

Each of these had some structural similarity to the missing toxins. Using them, she would be able to discover how the missing compounds would show up in her detection setup. She had the latest equipment, both thin-layer liquid chromatography and mass spectroscopy. With enough work and luck she would be able to detect and identify even the smallest amounts of such poisons, if they were there. She'd need some normal tissue samples to work with to get started. She'd find them if—

She heard a noise. She was usually alone in the building when she worked this late. It must be one of the security men, unless . . . She listened again, heard nothing, and returned to work.

Paul was not certain how to get started. He needed some answers, and so far had not gotten very many. However, the atmosphere was not exactly right for a cross-examination. He and Chaim Abramowitz were in a café in the Jewish quarter of the Old City having coffee, listening to the sounds of the children playing and the construction crews working and the tourists being tourists, and lingering and saying nothing substantive. He could not continue to merely skirt the issues. "Chaim," he began, "could you tell me how a respirator in an ICU could manage to become unplugged without anyone noticing it?"

Slowly, carefully, Chaim went over the events of that day. He spoke as if he were selecting each and every word, not as if he had anything to hide from Paul, but more to be certain that he described exactly what he had seen and not seen. Chaim had been there himself. It had been one of those terrible, chaotic days when everything goes wrong at once. It was one of those days that can happen only in an ICU—but, thank God, only every once in a while. "You've never seen our ICU, have you?"

"Not yet."

"It's a nice facility. We have fourteen beds and all fourteen are always filled. There are seven separate rooms built around a central nursing and monitoring area with two beds in each of the rooms. Each of the rooms has only three walls, and the front facing the central area is open except for curtains. We usually remember to pull the curtain during an arrest."

"Did you that day?"

"Most likely. But I can't swear to it." Chaim went on with his narrative. "Anyway, it was a ghastly morning. One patient, a thirty-six-year-old guy, had been admitted with a myocardial infarction. He'd already arrested twice over the previous night and both times we had managed to resuscitate him. At five-thirty he finally seemed stable. We were all so damned beat. Then the bottom fell out. One patient started to vomit blood and went into shock.

Another patient, an older woman who had chronic respiratory failure, chose that moment to have an arrest. While most of us were trying to get her heart started, the first patient arrested again. I spent over twenty minutes pumping on his chest.

"By the time things had quieted down, the woman who had arrested was dead, the first guy had again been successfully resuscitated, and the third catastrophe had stopped bleeding and was out of shock. And the respirator was unplugged. No one had seen Nahum Eckstein since four A.M."

"Why not?"

"He just wasn't that sick."

"Not that sick?"

"Look, he couldn't breathe, but he was on a respirator for that. His blood gases were fine. His oxygen level was normal; so was his carbon-dioxide level. So everything was fine. He had no cardiac diseases. He wasn't even being monitored anymore. He was probably the most stable patient in the whole unit."

"So with all that chaos, nobody saw him between four o'clock and six forty five?"

Chaim just shook his head. "Not that we know of, at least."

"Who found him?"

"The nurse assigned to his unit. We have four nurses for fourteen patients on that shift. She'd been tied up with the first cardiac patient and then the bleeder. She found him and called me over."

"What did he look like?"

"Dead. His pupils were fixed and dilated. There was no response to anything."

"Who could have walked in?"

"Anyone. It's a public hospital. We don't have any special security unless we have a patient who needs it, like Begin. Anybody could have walked in."

"Anybody?" Paul was not sure he believed what he had just heard.

"Yes, anybody," Chaim repeated. "And not just Jews. We have Arabs as patients, doctors, employees of all sorts. We are not running a tight-security institution. Anyone who really wanted to could have walked right into our ICU."

Paul thought for a moment and then asked one last question.

"Could it have been an accident? Or just plain old-fashioned negligence?"

"Negligence?" It was clear that Chaim was insulted by the question. It was all right for someone to kill a patient in his ICU, but God forbid that someone should suggest that his personnel had been negligent.

"I'm not making any accusations. It might have been possible that someone accidentally left the respirator's alarm system turned off and then found him dead and didn't know what to do and panicked and pulled out the plug."

"None of my nurses could have made a mistake like that."

"Did you or anyone else check to see if the alarm was still on?"

"No. There was no reason to."

Paul paid the bill and followed Abramowitz out of the café. They walked out and found themselves in front of one of the many construction sites within the reborn Jewish quarter. Like men the world over, the two of them forgot some of their concerns and just watched.

"I watched them build the Hancock Center."

"When were you in Chicago?" Paul asked.

" 'Sixty-eight."

"Oh," Paul replied in a tone that was far more judgmental than he would have liked it to be.

"You're right. I wasn't there to watch construction, I came for the convention." Chaim hesitated.

"Don't tell me you were going to push LSD into Lake Michigan."

"No. But only because we didn't have enough to waste. Don't look so surprised. I was a real radical and activist. I still am."

"Peace Now."

"More or less."

"You must have . . . disliked Eckstein."

"I detested him. He stood for everything in Israel that I am against. But I didn't pull the plug."

"No, you just didn't resuscitate him."

"He was dead. His pupils were fixed and dilated. He . . . I don't have to explain that to you, Paul."

Paul nodded. He needed no further explanation. He had already heard too much. All he needed was some overage Yippie. He stared at the workman loading a wheelbarrow as hard as he could.

"It's not like watching back in the U.S.," Chaim said. "No?"

"No," Chaim echoed Paul's reply. "Here we have much less mechanization. Fewer great pile drivers. No great towering cranes. In the Old City we only build up four, five, maybe six stories. No great topping-off of a hundred-story skyscraper. But it's more exciting here."

Paul just let Chaim continue his monologue. "You never know what you are going to find. Here, come with me." He led Paul a short distance, less than two hundred yards, across two small streets to a newly finished building.

"When they dug here to build a shopping center, they ran into the Cardo."

"The Cardo. I know the Cardo. The Cardo was the main street of Byzantine Jerusalem, a broad avenue of columns leading straight to the Church of the Holy Sepulcher. It's on the sixth-century mosaic map of Jerusalem."

"And there it is ."

Twenty feet below street level, incorporated into the new building, Paul could see Byzantine paving stones, the broken columns that had once lined this broad thoroughfare.

"There," Chaim said, pointing toward another set of large rough-cut stones, "that is part of the wall Hezekiah built to defend Jerusalem from the Assyrians. We are at the corner of the Cardo and Hezekiah's wall. It may not be State and Madison, but it has a hell of a lot more history."

Paul left the Cardo behind him. He walked from the new quiet street of the Jewish quarter to the noise, crowds, and smells of the Arab market, called the shuk, and then onto another quiet street, in the Christian quarter, a broader street than the stone-paved lanes of the Jewish quarter, and there, across from the Lutheran Church of the Redeemer, he entered the shop of Sarkis Boyajian and was quickly shown upstairs.

As soon as the tea was served, Sarkis as a good host began the conversation.

"Tell me, Paul, have you made any progress?"

Paul reviewed what he had learned and Sarkis said nothing until he had completed his story. He was a more polite listener than Paul.

"So it was a miracle."

"That is what they would have you believe."

"And you do not believe in miracles?"

"I believe in miracles. I believe in Mount Sinai, in the parting of the Red Sea—"

"Ah! You believe in Jewish miracles."

"I . . ." Paul began to answer and then stopped himself. "No, not just Jewish miracles. But to accept this miracle, as such, I would have to accept a miracle in which God chose Christianity over Judaism."

"Why?"

"Why!"

"Yes. Why? Perhaps the miracle was necessary to retain rabbinical Judaism as opposed to Judaism of the Temple with all of its trappings and sacrifices and so forth."

"I'd never thought of that."

"Not only is a miracle in the eye of the beholder as an event, but its meaning, its interpretation, also depends on the prejudices of the observer. The same event can result in the good being called early to heaven and the wicked being visited by premature destruction. All in the same miracle, and which ones were good and which wicked may differ from believer to believer." The Armenian hardly waited for Paul to absorb what he had said before he went ahead. "Well, where do you start now?"

"The pagan version."

"Hellenes, Paul, not pagans. If you want to understand what they felt and saw, you must understand them. They believed themselves to be the representatives of Hellenism—man's greatest civilization—the tradition of Homer, of Socrates, of Pericles, of Alexander, and their multitude of gods."

"I'll try to remember that."

"Is there any particular reason why you have chosen to take on the Hellene version next?"

"Fewer religious prejudices."

"Are you sure?"

"The Christians and the Jews were both so close to this issue. To the pagans it was just another temple, another nationalistic cult with Yahweh as the Zeus of Mount Moriah. What was one temple more or less to them? One god more or less? Nothing. But to the Jews, it was their Temple. To the Christians it was an affront."

"Was it that simple? Consider. It was more than just the Temple. It was a promise of the homeland. Not all Hellenes would have liked that, certainly not those living in Aelia Capitolina, who would also have been displaced by returning Jews rebuilding Jerusalem. And not all Christians would have been opposed. In the second century, yes. In the fourth, no. And the Jews? Would their views have been so unanimous?"

There was a knock on the door. It was his son. He needed his opinion on a number of stones. It was time for Paul to excuse himself. Mr. Boyajian wrote a name on his business card and gave it to Paul.

Abu Sadeh
17 David Street

"He is a Christian Arab with some very rare books. A private library that has been in his family for generations. He may help you."

Paul had one more stop to make before dinner. Eleazar Danin, as always, seemed pleased to see him. Eleazar asked him about his daughter and about his son. No, Paul admitted, Joshua had not come up with any more names. He was too busy reading to play Gematria. What was he reading? Leon Uris' *Exodus*. Eleazar had read it. He had not found it very exciting. Joshua could hardly put it down. Perhaps it was different if you have been there and lived through it all. Eleazar knew people who had been on the *Exodus*. He had once been in prison in Acre. He knew people who had been executed in Jerusalem for their underground activities, only a few blocks from where they were now sitting. He had friends who had died running the blockade of Jerusalem.

Somehow, they never got around to talking about what Paul wanted to discuss. He wanted to get Eleazar's feedback on who might have actually pulled the plug, but each time, Eleazar got sidetracked. Each question brought on a story, an anecdote. It was like sitting through his own rounds. Enough was enough.

"Could it have been an Arab who killed Nahum Eckstein?" Paul could not have asked it any more flatly than that.

"A terrorist? Of course, that is most likely."

"No, not a terrorist."

"Not a terrorist?"

"No, an Israeli Arab, a good citizen."

"Why would you suspect one of them?"

"They have reasons to distrust the Guardians, to hate them, in fact."

"That is true."

"And easy access to the ICU."

"So did I."

"What?"

"I could have walked into that ICU. I didn't, but I could have."

"I suppose so," Paul agreed. He didn't need this.

"I've been in the ICU before."

"But why would you?"

"For any number of reasons. The same ones as your friends. And some others. The reason doesn't really matter. In this country, politics is life itself. More than life, it's our survival. It's not a game. Once every four years we don't just get together and vote against someone. It's part of each of us. There's always a reason to want to eliminate the thorns like Eckstein. There is one big difference between me and Chaim and Rivkah and the rest."

"You weren't there."

"No, not that."

"What, then?"

"I've killed before. As a terrorist. I was a member of the Stern Gang in 'forty-seven. I was in prison in Acre. I was scheduled to be executed. We broke out. But I forgot, you read *Exodus*." He stopped. Perhaps he had gone too far. "Paul."

"Yes."

"Stop playing detective. This is not a game. Do what you were asked to do."

"And no more?"

"And no more."

"Should I do any less?"

"No."

"But any one of them could have been there when it happened."

"That is true. So they have motive and opportunity, but, my dear friend, such accusations would not be fair to the six hundred thousand members of the underground who suffered so terribly under British rule and yet somehow managed to survive."

"Six hundred thousand?" Paul was astounded by the figure. "There could not have been anywhere near that many. A few thousand? Maybe. But not six hundred thousand."

"Paul, you must be wrong."

"How could—?"

"There are, you know, some two hundred thousand friendly Israeli Arabs."

"Yes."

"And each and every one of them I ever met has told me how he personally saved at least three Jewish terrorists from the British."

This time they met in the King David Hotel and had dinner there. From where they sat on the balcony, they could see the illuminated western wall of Jerusalem from Jaffa Gate to Mount Zion. For twenty years Jordanian snipers had sat there randomly shooting whenever they pleased. A decade later, PLO descendants had tried the same trick from bases in Lebanon, using rockets instead of rifles—a measure of progress made by the terrorists in the last two decades. The choice of the King David had been Joshua's, and as soon as Paul and Rivkah sat down, Paul knew he had made a mistake. Joshua had been reading *Exodus* all week, fifty or more pages a day. And they had discussed it at every meal: his majesty's Jewish forces in Cyprus over breakfast, the UN vote on partition over dinner, the bombing of the King David Hotel when they said good night. In the book Kitty and Ari had come here to eat. So had Eva Marie Saint and Paul Newman in the movie. But Rivkah Geller was not Eva Marie Saint and he certainly was not Paul Newman and they were not there to discuss the founding of Israel and romance.

Rivkah immediately sensed his distress. They talked of easy things.

The war. The capture in Lebanon of three of the terrorists who had helped murder the Israel Olympic team in Munich in 1972. Was he interested in going to a concert in the Roman Theater in Caesarea? No. A play? No. A play in English? They were doing a Wolf Mankowitz play, *The Irish Hebrew Lesson*. No. Or *The Fantasticks?* No. Perhaps Joshua would like to . . . No.

"Paul, what's wrong?"

"I came here once, on a night likè this, with Bobbie . . ."

It all came out. He had not talked to anyone about what it meant to be here the first time without her. He told Rivkah about things that the two of them had done here together, then about Bobbie herself. He noticed when she put her hand on top of his, and he did not pull his away.

He took her arm as they walked out to her car. It was still early. They both had more work to do at the hospital. Perhaps they might go to the theater the next week and see *The Fantasticks*.

Paul certainly had not planned to spend his summer reading about Guillain-Barré. He'd never liked that subject. G.B. involved the nerves, not the brain. The nerves bored him. If only he were at home with his own books and his own reprint file and a library he knew. But he wasn't at home so he had to do the best he could. He knew there would be a lot to read, since it was a subject he had avoided as much as possible over the years.

At least he knew where to start. As soon as he got into the library, he went to the card file and found the reference he was looking for.

He carefully copied down the reference numbers. His next job was to find the two volumes in the stacks. It took him only a few minutes. He took the books back into the library and sat down at a large desk in the corner of the room. From here he could both study and look out on the Judean Hills. He made two sets of notes. The first consisted of facts on G.B. itself. Some were things he already knew, other things he had not known, or at least had not known well enough. The second was a list of references; original papers he would need to find.

By the time he had heard Hassan Rashem call his name and looked up to see the first-year resident standing across the table from him, he'd taken two pages of notes and had made a list of twenty-seven original articles to find and read, including two in French.

"Dr. Richardson, I hate to bother you."

"It's okay."

"I'm on call tonight and the attendings have all gone home," Hassan began to explain.

"What time is it?"

"Ten, a little after in fact. Everybody else has gone and I remembered seeing you here about an hour ago and I hoped you'd still be here to see Mrs. Fahoum with me."

As they walked up to the Neurology floor, Hassan brought Paul up-to-date on what had been happening to the patient. She had been diagnosed as having encephalitis caused by herpes simplex. Had they done a brain biopsy? No. No brain biopsy and there had not been time to grow out the virus in tissue culture, but the immunofluorescent antibody studies had pretty much confirmed the diagnosis. She had been put on Arabinoside-A and gotten much better.

"How much better?" Paul asked. One problem with being a visiting professor instead of the treating physician was that you didn't see each patient every day. When you did that, you didn't have to ask such questions. But here, as a guest, he saw only the patients they wanted him to see, and then only when they wanted him to see them.

"According to her family—"

"Her family is here too?" Paul asked in surprise.

"Sure."

"You mean they came down from Lebanon too?"

"Of course." Was there a trace of pride in his voice?

"Things like that never get into *Time* magazine. Arafat on the cover, yet. But such simple human decency—that will never get into a single one of our news magazines," Paul thought aloud. "What did the family say?"

"To them she seemed normal. A bit tired, of course. But she wasn't paranoid anymore and she knew them all and could talk about being back home and knew about the wedding in their family that was to take place next month."

"So what happened today?"

"She suddenly went back into coma. I went over her again. I don't know what's wrong with her."

Paul and Hassan spent half an hour with the patient. When they were done, they both knew what was wrong. As a complication of her encephalitis she was having continuous seizures, a problem called status epilepticus, or epileptic state. She needed more anticonvulsant medications.

Paul waited while Hassan wrote out the orders. Dilantin—eighteen mgs. for each kilogram of body weight. She weighed fifty-six kilograms. One thousand milligrams. Intravenously, over one hour. If that didn't work, they would have to add some phenobarbital.

The two neurologists walked side by side out to the bus stop and waited together for a cab to come by. It was too late for the last bus. It was a typically clear, bright, cool summer night in the Judean Hills.

"I'm glad you are chairman of the committee."

Paul was both surprised and puzzled by Hassan's remark, which came out more like an announcement. Before Paul could answer, the young Arab went on.

"At first I wasn't. We all—"

"All?"

"Yes. All of us Arabs working here. We figured it was either a whitewash or—what is the correct phrase?—a packed jury. We knew you were an old friend of Professor Schiff's and probably a dedicated Zionist. So you would give the committee international stature and the aura of impartiality and then you would blame us."

"Us?"

"Us. Arabs. Palestinians. Israeli Arabs born and living here as citizens—citizens second class." Paul had no chance to respond. "We figured you would just put your okay on whatever the powers-that-be wanted and pick out one of us—me, for instance. I was in the ICU that morning. We had two patients there. He was alive when I saw him. I was with our other patient—."

"You don't have to give me any alibi, Hassan."

"No? Probably not. But I was there that morning. Our other patient was even less stable than Eckstein. I was with her. By the time I got back to him, Professor Abramowitz was pronouncing him dead."

"So why did you change your mind about me?"

"Mrs. Fahoum is Muslim. Many people from her village belong to the PLO and yet you cared enough to come see her with me. You really care what happens to her."

"Of course."

"So many American Jews I meet seem to lump all of us together and worry only about Jews here."

"Look, Hassan. First of all, I come from a country that is only two percent Jewish. Most of my patients are not Jews. A patient is a patient—period. Regardless of anything else. You know that."

"Of course. But your interest, your attitude. You really wanted to help her."

"Yes."

"An Arab."

"Yes. Here comes a cab."

"I think we can trust you. You believe in truth and in doing what is right."

"Look, I've got to go. I want to talk to you more on this."

"Come visit me and my family in Abu Gosh."

When Paul got home, the emptiness of the small house hit him.

There was no one to talk to.

No one to share the excitement of Hassan's diagnosis.

No one to tell about the Third Temple.

No one to ask about Rivkah.

It was too late to bother Jonathan and Pat.

Carolyn and Joshua were both asleep.

He put on a cassette tape and listened to the New World Symphony. Bobbie had loved it. And he only halfheartedly looked at his reading notes.

For the second time the source was the *International Herald Tribune*. Once again, three copies of each letter were carefully cut out.

An n.

An o.

A W.

An F.

An a.

An i.

An r.
An h.
Another i.
A pair of p's.
An upper-case O.
An L.
A Y.
A T.
Another a.
Another o.
A U.
A second r.
A second n.
A second u, but lower-case.
A p.
A second T, again upper-case.
Another i.
Another a.
A second l, not capitalized this time.
Another h.
A fourth o, this one lower-case.
A third U, upper-case.
A third r.
A D.
A fourth r.
A fourth a.
A second w, this one lower-case.
An s.
Yet another a.
A fourth p.
An a, the sixth, all lower-case.
A C.
An e.

noW Fair hippOLYTa oUr nupTial hoUr Draws apaCe

9

Once again, his conversation with Avram Schiff was not going as Paul had planned it.

He had wanted to talk about Dalia Avni. They had to do something. Today she had again sat through rounds and said virtually nothing to him. Rounds, he admitted, had not been exciting. Mrs. Fahoum was still having her seizures and none of the other patients had made much progress. The myelogram had finally proven that Mrs. Sassoon had a spinal-cord cyst, but by the time they had seen the myelogram they had talked about her diagnosis so often that the myelogram had become more of a confirmation of a known fact than the discovery of a new diagnosis. And through it all Dalia had just sat quietly and stared at him impassively. Avram, however, wanted to talk about something else. "When are you finally going to come here to live permanently, Paul?"

"Who knows?"

"Why the debate? It is the perfect time to move your two children here."

"You don't really need me here."

"We need everyone."

"You know what I mean. You have enough neurologists. You don't need another one."

"That's not true. Anyone could use a neurologist and teacher like you."

"Perhaps, but here I could not do what I do best. As you know, I specialize in rather uncommon disorders. I'm the only one in Chicago who is really expert on such things. I draw my patients from a population of over ten million people—even more, since people fly in from all over. Here I wouldn't have such a luxury. I wouldn't be able to do my kind of research; there just aren't enough patients here."

"So. You'd do something else."

"I'm not sure I could teach in Hebrew."

"Come on, Paul. When Romain came here he could neither read nor speak Hebrew. He'd come from a totally assimilated French family. He knew French and English. That was all. Now he can't even speak French."

"Can't?"

"Can't or won't—ever since he learned what the French people and the Vichy government did to help the Nazis to 'solve' the problem of the French Jews. All of his family was rounded up, not by the S.S., but by the French police. Such a well-kept secret. England may have known what the Nazis were doing and said nothing. And your country did the same. But Vichy was in some ways worse than the Nazis. Once Romain found out, he could no longer speak French. None of us really knew what they had done until the mid-fifties. Romain was here then. He was almost crushed. He was so proud of his French heritage, and in part still is—"

"I know. He traces his descent to Charcot."

"That's all that remains of the first thirty-four years of his life, his life before he came here. He gave the rest of his life to us and occasionally he reminisces about the war and the blitz but never about anything else."

It was time for Paul to find out what he wanted to know. "Avram. What are you going to do about Dalia Avni?"

"Nothing."

"Nothing!"

"That is right, nothing."

"But why?"

"She was telling you the truth. She did not sign an order for morphine for her patient, Zalman Cohen. She countersigned an order for morphine for another patient, a Mr. Solomon Cohen. Somehow the order got into the wrong chart."

"How?"

"That we are trying to discover. But Dr. Avni is innocent. Zalman Cohen did not die from anything Dalia Avni did."

"No, from something someone else did."

"Yes, the negligence was not hers."

"If it was negligence," Paul reminded him.

Paul only wished that it could be that simple. At home,

he would have just shrugged his shoulders and accepted it. Mistakes did happen, even fatal ones. Whenever there were two Smiths or a pair of Joneses on the same floor, one of them would get the wrong X ray taken or be given the incorrect medicine. Here the only difference was that the common names were Cohen and Levi. That didn't make it any more sinister.

Paul wanted very much for it to have been an error. Just another simple instance of inadvertent malpractice. That was better than political assassination. Tightening of procedures might prevent the repetition of an error. Nothing would stop the unending spiral of politically motivated murders. At least nothing that they could do. That would be beyond the control of mere physicians. But somehow it was too simple, too pat, too easy. There had been two deaths, two very unexpected deaths of two politically active and controversial people. Two deaths under mysterious circumstances. One he was investigating. One Avram had investigated and . . . whitewashed? Perhaps. Well, if they thought he was going to do the same, they were mistaken. Very mistaken.

Paul was getting angry, but perhaps he was reacting prematurely. After all, Avram had not completed his investigation. Not yet, at least.

Paul spent three hours that afternoon trying to read about Julian. It was difficult to really get a feel for Julian. Was he that contradictory, or was it the sources that were the problem? On the one side were the pagans—no, Hellenes—and on the other, the Christians.

He read and reread.

It was difficult to concentrate. There were other, more important problems. Not just Nahum Eckstein, but Zalman Cohen. It was a brilliant way to kill someone, almost foolproof, giving him the wrong medicine. Something that would kill him because he had emphysema, but would not have killed the other patient. Whoever did that had to be a physician or someone who had a lot of training in medicine. Everyone he knew around here had enough knowledge to have done it.

Paul thought for a moment and then he recognized it. Hippolyta had been a character in only one Shakespearean play. "It's from *A Midsummer Night's Dream.*"

"But what does it mean?" Eleazar asked.

"The time of the event."

"The nuptial hour?"

"No, I don't think so. More likely the nighttime, the time of the Dream itself. It makes sense that way. The first warning told us that something would happen and on what day. Whoever the hell is choosing these messages is smart. He knows that Tisha B'Av is a day of mourning. You can't get married on Tisha B'Av. Hell, you can't get married for three whole weeks from the seventeenth of Tammuz, when the Babylonians first broke down the outer walls of Jerusalem, through the ninth of Av. There is no nuptial hour on Tisha B'Av. But the twenty-four hours from sundown has its parts: evening, night, morning, afternoon. Whatever is planned, it's going to take place during that midsummer night."

"During the observation. That makes sense."

"The way I would analyze—" Paul stopped himself. "Just listen to me. You're the pro in this field, not me."

"No, no. Go on. Sometimes it is helpful to have a nonprofessional's impressions."

"Well, the way I look at it, each message must tell us something new. The first we've already talked about. The second must have given us the location, the place . . ."

"Or the means."

"Possibly, but I think the third, 'A plague on both your houses', gives us the means."

"Or perhaps the place."

"The place?"

"Sure. At two houses, at two separate places," Eleazar explained.

Paul reflected for only a moment and then said, "You may be right. Jericho is two places. The old archeologic sites and the modern village."

"That is assuming, of course, that the second one really means Jericho."

"Assuming! I hate making assumptions. Whenever I do that I get burned. Maybe this guy's smarter than we all are." Paul's conjecture was not a pleasant one for either of them.

"No, not smarter," Eleazar corrected him. "It's just

that he knows what he is planning and we don't. I'm sure he must be sending those messages to tell us something. He wants us to know something."

"But what?"

"Aye, there's the rub."

"You've been reading again."

"Yes. We've had to give up trying to analyze the individual letters. There are just too many of them now. The number of combinations is too great. So instead of reading through the computer printouts, I'm reading Shakespeare. He reads better."

Once again it was Jonathan's turn to stand guard at the gate. And once again after dinner Paul walked down to join him. Much of the time they just leaned on the closed gate of the moshav peering down the dark road. It was another cool, clear night. The army remained poised outside of Beirut. Each day Arafat said something different. Each day there were some shells and rockets which ignored the cease-fire. Each day some Israelis got orders from the army. The call-ups were being extended. Each man would be on active duty for forty-five days, not thirty. Israel was preparing to be in Lebanon for a long time. Perhaps the entire winter. The Judean sky was full of stars. Jonathan's submachine gun was hanging from his shoulder.

"Did you ever hear of Zalman Cohen?" Paul asked.

"I don't think so. Why?"

"He died at the hospital."

"Was he a patient?"

"Yes."

"Patients do die."

"He was murdered."

"Are you sure?"

"Yes. No. I don't know." With that definitive introduction, Paul told Jonathan all he knew, including his own lingering doubts.

"So you're still worried that Dr. Avni did it intentionally?"

"I'm not sure."

"Or perhaps one of the Arabs? Like Rashem?"

"Maybe. Or maybe it was all a setup."

"By whom?" Jonathan asked.

"Anyone who was sick and tired of his reactionary antics."

"Even the government?"

"Why not?"

"Begin is no Nixon."

"So Begin wasn't involved. Everything doesn't have to start at the top."

"Then who?" Jonathan persisted.

"I don't know."

"What did Avram Schiff tell you?"

"That it was a mistake."

"Paul, leave it at that. You don't really believe that this was all done intentionally, do you?"

"I guess not." He didn't feel like arguing. He had hoped that Jonathan could act as a sounding board for his own thoughts. It had been a foolish hope.

The two friends walked in silence. Their quiet was disturbed by a sharp crack in the distance, then three more in rapid succession, then total quiet. The first could have been a car backfiring. The other three were rifle shots from a hilltop Arab village. Jonathan led the way back to the gate area and made three phone calls. Within minutes, some dozen or more armed men in teams of two were patrolling the borders of Neve Ilan.

Paul and Jonathan stayed by the gate peering out into the darkness.

"I know two people who were in the ICU when Nahum Eckstein died, but one, at least, had no motive," Paul said.

"Who was that?"

"Chaim Abramowitz."

"I'm sure I know him. He's a cardiologist, isn't he?"

"Yes," Paul answered.

"You're wrong about him having no motive. He had a damn good reason to hate Nahum Eckstein."

"He did?" Paul was surprised.

"You remember two years ago when the Arabs in Hebron massacred some of the Jews living there as they came out of Friday night services?"

"Yes, I remember reading about it."

"Here we did more than read about it. Especially Chaim. His son was one of the victims."

"God—but what has that got to do with Nahum Eckstein?"

"He was the one who talked Chaim's son into going to Hebron to live. To maintain a Jewish presence near the burial place of Abraham, Isaac, and Jacob."

So Paul knew two people with both opportunity and motive.

The card Sarkis had given him worked the same magic in the noise of the Arab market as it had in the quiet of the Library of St. Thoros. Paul found the right shop, just a few steps beyond the vegetable market, just where the Crusader Hall ended. The first leather shop on the left.

His host led him through the shop, up some stairs, and back to his left. He was sure he was now on top of the vegetable market, in a room built above the Crusader structure. The brickwork here was not Norman. It was more recent, no more than three hundred years old. The room had no furniture, just a Persian rug on the floor, some pillows, and shelves with row after row of books.

He was to treat this library as if it were his own.

Did he prefer coffee or tea?

After the tea arrived, Paul was left alone to work.

They had what he wanted. The complete works of Julian the Philosopher. He started at the beginning of the three volumes. It was another project that would take him more than one morning to finish.

The meeting of the committee that afternoon was shorter than any of the previous meetings. Rivkah Geller gave her report. She had found no evidence of any of the common toxins. No heavy metals like lead or mercury. No metalloids such as thallium or arsenic. No organic solvents. No pesticides. No herbicides. She told the group that she was still investigating the unlikely possibility that he had gotten some very unusual toxins which were hard to measure. She was working on the technique with samples of blood, and spinal fluid from other patients with neurologic disorders. Nothing was said about the type of toxin and the possible source. Nothing was said and nothing was asked.

No one had anything else to add so Paul closed the meeting.

As she left, Rivkah asked Paul if he still wanted to see *The Fantasticks*. It was being given at the Hilton the next night at nine-thirty. He declined her invitation, telling her that he was not interested in seeing it again. That was not the reason. The question was whether or not he was ready to see her again. Or any woman, for that matter. That was a question he was not prepared to face. Saying no was the easiest out.

Late each afternoon the 85 bus carried Paul past Abu Gosh, but tonight was different from all other nights. Hassan Rashem was at the bus stop. Paul waited until the villagers had gotten off and then jumped down to meet Hassan. They walked back up the road together, to the Caravan Inn, a roadside café with its signs for Marlboro cigarettes, Avis Rent-a-Cars, and Pepsi-Cola. Like all the buildings in this town, it was made of beige Jerusalem limestone which took on a pink hue in the morning and a golden one in the evening. It was just five and the gold was coming out with the first hint of the evening breeze.

They sat on the patio overlooking the village. It was hard to tell which buildings were old and which were new. They were all built in the same style, of the same stones, perched on both sides of the narrow valley below them.

The statue of Mary from her perch at Kiryat Yearim was looking down from above them.

"Professor Richardson—"

"Not 'Professor,' Hassan. We are not in the hospital and even there I much prefer 'Dr.' to 'Professor.' Here 'Paul' would be better, but the choice is yours."

"Dr. Richardson." It was what Hassan felt most comfortable with and Paul did not want to push the issue so he said nothing more. "You see that house there just to the right of the minaret."

Paul looked where Hassan was pointing. "The one with the washed-out blue dome?"

"No, the one just behind it."

"Yes, I see it. It's a large house with two sets of windows facing us."

"That was the house of my uncle and . . ." Here Hassan paused. "It was in that house that my uncle hid

Menachem Begin and other members of the Irgun from the British in 'forty-seven and 'forty-eight.

"We hated the British as much as you did and wanted them out as much as you did.

"This has always been an independent village. Even when the Turks came here, they left us alone. But we did not love them. Nor the British. Nor the Jordanians. They were all outsiders.

"The British," he continued, "of course, never understood that Jews and Muslims did not have to hate each other, so they never even looked here.

"My uncle is dead now, so that is now the house of my cousin, my uncle's only son. My uncle's son is a second-class citizen of Israel, as we all are. We are all considered security risks. I have more trouble traveling through Israel as an Arab than I do elsewhere as an Israeli."

"It is not all bad. Had this ended up as part of Jordan, you would not have had a university education."

"That is true."

"Nor be a doctor."

"That is also true," Hassan said, and then he changed the subject. "All this land once belonged to Abu Gosh. Even Neve Ilan, where you are now living."

"And we bought it."

"Yes, for nothing."

"But we did buy it. Who else ever bought land here? No one. Everyone else just took it, and you know that."

Hassan did know that.

Paul didn't wait for a bus, but walked up the road to Neve Ilan.

All this land once belonged to Abu Gosh. Were they worried about losing more land? Had they felt threatened by Nahum Eckstein? Had Hassan acted as their agent and pulled the plug? Such suspicions were unfair. But to whom? To Hassan? To friendly Arabs? And the six hundred thousand Jews they had saved? Those six hundred thousand did not exist. They never had. It had been a bad joke, a sick joke with a message. A message that implied that Arabs who claimed to have saved Jews were not to be believed. But some Arabs had saved Jews. That was a fact. Just as some Germans had saved Jews. Even a few Austrians had. Not all Germans were Nazis. And not all

Arabs were terrorists. Or anti-Israel. But which were which? That truly was the rub.

Which were which?

And how could he tell?

And did he care enough to bother trying?

That was the only question he could answer. He cared enough to try to tell the difference. Or was he just too naive to understand the world?

Just as they were finishing dinner, Carolyn called. She had changed her plans. She would not be home for Shabbat. She wanted to spend her free weekend with her friend's cousin near the Golan Heights. Paul was pleased. He was happy for her. She would be in Jerusalem for Tisha B'Av. The night before, she had slept on the Lebanese border at Kiryat Shemona. They had all slept in a bomb shelter. It hadn't been necessary, since the PLO rockets were gone, but they all wanted to do it to see what it must have been like. Perhaps no one would ever have to sleep in a bomb shelter again.

One night in a bomb shelter could be a sobering experience. It was for Paul. His bomb shelter was not on the Lebanese border, but in the basement of the Jerusalem Hilton, a bomb shelter that was called the Little Theater, but was a bomb shelter nonetheless. He took Joshua there to see *The Fantasticks*. Joshua loved the show. Paul did not. But he was able to buy a *Herald Tribune*. The White Sox were doing better. They had somehow managed to win three straight.

There were no lights on when they got home.

No sounds except theirs.

"Dad, will we always miss Mom this much?"

"I'm afraid so."

"Will it always hurt this much?"

"I hope not."

He studied the sports section once again. Victories were always worth at least one rereading. The pitching staff seemed to be putting it all together, especially Dotson and Burns and some guy named Hoyt. The infield still had its problems. Oh for the days of Fox and Aparicio. For the first time all summer Paul wanted to go to Comiskey Park on a Sunday afternoon and see a ball game. Or a double-header. They don't play double-headers anymore, he reminded himself.

For once Paul had nowhere he had to go. He could spend the entire day at Neve Ilan. There would be no rounds. No visits to Jerusalem. Instead, he would stay at home and get some reading done and even clean up a bit.

Had Toynbee ever mopped a floor?

Or Hercule Poirot?

Or Charcot?

The place was a mess. It was starting to resemble his office in Chicago. The buffet and the coffee table were both covered with Xerox copies of articles. Everywhere were piles of articles and stacks of books, books borrowed from the various libraries in and around Jerusalem, books from the Neurology Department at Hadassah, books from the History Department at Hebrew University, books purchased from used-book stores, and even some old treasured possessions personally loaned to Paul. They were all spread out within easy reach of the one lounge chair he always sat in, arranged in order, not by subject or by author, but by their likelihood of being really necessary.

As Paul read on, he began to understand Julian the man. Julian was an anachronism, a classic pagan born a few decades too late. He believed in ritual and sacrifices. The last thing Paul read before lunch was Julian's letter to Oribasius. Oribasius. That was a name that Paul already knew. He had not only heard of Oribasius, he had actually even read some of his writings. Oribasius had been a great physician, perhaps the greatest of all Byzantine physicians. He had also been a close friend of Julian's, his adviser, and the interpreter of his dreams. Had Oribasius bothered to record the events of his lifetime? Had this pagan friend of the Apostate left any record of what he had seen in Jerusalem? One more source to try to find somewhere in Jerusalem.

While Romain Bernhard and his colleagues were operating on Mrs. Sassoon, Rivkah Geller was working on another problem, the detection of Pickwick poisons in body fluids. What seemed to be a simple, straightforward task when she had outlined it was turning out to be much more complex.

She had to know whether Nahum Eckstein had been

poisoned or not—and whether someone had poisoned him with either of the two missing poisons. Had her leak in security somehow caused his death? Had her carelessness led to this? She should have been more careful. She had known that David was becoming more and more reactionary in his ideas. Yet, in bed, at night, it had been impossible to censor every word, especially after they had made love and she felt so warm and open. It had always been then that he seemed most interested in her work. And she had told him whatever he asked. She never understood why he had been so interested in the Pickwick Project. She hadn't worked on it in years, and the project had been scrubbed. It had failed. She should have been more suspicious. Had David given that information to someone else? David had been dead now for four . . . no, five years. When had she told him? When she already knew that their life together was over? It was near the end. In bed. Always in bed. Even then they still made love. And at times, he was so ardent, so tender, so . . . insistent. It must have been near the end.

She did all the work on the samples from Nahum Eckstein's body herself. She felt safer that way. If no one knew what she was doing or where, it would be difficult for anyone to sabotage her work. She had not told anyone what she was doing except the security people, of course, and Paul Richardson. Why him? Was it because he should know as chairman of the committee? No. It was not just that. He was an outsider and a good listener. He was strong, incisive, and yet, so vulnerable. . . .

She had four toxins to work with: P970, P974, P975 and P976.

She began the first step, the fairly simple one of proving that the method she had devised could detect the presence of these poisons in the very small concentrations that would be found in the tissues of a poisoned patient.

After several trials, the method seemed to be working. The machine gave its results by drawing a long graph. Each chemical appeared at a specific place on that graph; the more of the chemical that was present, the higher the line went at that point. She had calculated where each of the four toxins should register on that graph and she had been right. There were four peaks. And each was in the correct spot.

The missing two would appear on the same graph. The first, 972 would show up between 970 and 974, and the other, 971, between 975 and 976, but closer to 975. She had done enough for one day.

Now all she needed was some blood samples from patients to work with and some spinal fluid, and she would be able to find the answer. To clear herself and the Guardians or find them guilty. She heard a noise again. Someone was in the hall.

She became very tense. She was alone. All they had to do was eliminate her. She was the only chemist who knew this process.

No chemist . . . no answer. No proof.

David would not have hesitated.

She listened.

The voice called her name.

She relaxed. It was a voice she knew. The voice of the security guard. She was safe.

Or was she?

David had once worked as a security guard.

After lunch Paul received a package from Arnold Chiari. It contained twenty-three articles. Twenty were about Guillain-Barré syndrome, the other three on Julian.

He spent the next several hours trying to get through them all. But he was interrupted twice, first by a phone call from Avram Schiff. They had found out exactly what had happened to Zalman Cohen. A tragic error. Both the regular head nurse and the medication nurse had been in the north that week. All the floors were shorthanded. Nurses were working double shifts and cross-covering on unfamiliar units. Dalia Avni had signed the order as a favor for one of the nurses. It was a routine preoperative order for morphine. It had been for another Mr. Cohen, a Mr. Solomon Cohen. It had been a verbal order, and since it was for morphine, a doctor had to sign it. Things like that often happened. But somehow, the order was written on a blank order sheet which was then taken to the nursing station and stamped with Zalman Cohen's name and hospital number and put on his chart. Then it was recorded and a copy was put on the medication sheet to assure his getting the injection on time. It had all been done most efficiently.

It was not murder, Paul thought as he hung up the phone. There was no evidence of a conspiracy and Dalia Avni was off the hook. That meant that whoever pulled the plug on Eckstein had not also killed Zalman Cohen. So he didn't have to find someone with two motives. One motive was sufficient. Like the one Chaim Abramowitz had? Or Hassan Rashem? Or Rivkah Geller?

The second interruption was much more welcome. Joshua had finished planting the new flowers and demanded a series of backgammon games—or Shesh-besh as he now called it. Joshua won four games to two. The same margin by which the Sox had lost the series in 'fifty-nine.

Of course the loss of a World Series was not always just bad luck or lack of talent. Sometimes it was a conspiracy.

That had been in 1919. This was 1982.

What about the nurse who put the order in the wrong chart?

She was substituting for someone else.

What was her usual assignment?

The ICU?

Dalia wasn't the killer, but that didn't mean it had not been a murder. The solution of a murder goes from murder to clues and motives to murderer. Not vice versa.

Paul finally went to bed. He had trouble falling asleep. His mind kept returning to two patients he'd never really known.

Nahum Eckstein.

Zalman Cohen.

And one woman he had met: Rivkah Geller. If she could prove that Nahum Eckstein was poisoned, then it would all tie together. Perhaps the respirator had been unplugged to prevent anyone from proving he had been poisoned. An ordinary autopsy would have found nothing. Perhaps the murderer had even hoped to avoid an autopsy. The Orthodox considered autopsies a desecration.

And perhaps Zalman Cohen knew about the poisoning or the murder, and perhaps Rivkah was already in danger. And . . .

10

For the first time in years, Paul overslept. At least he had a good excuse. Chamseen. The desert wind. Suddenly the Mediterranean breezes had been displaced by a hot desert wind. The temperature rose. The humidity decreased to practically nothing and the hot wind pervaded everything. Arab countries understand the chamseen and the irrational, often violent behavior it can elicit. Their laws classify it as a mitigating circumstance. So do their work schedules. Israel tries to be too Western for that, so life just goes on.

Paul and Joshua both felt the difference. Carolyn was in the north, in an air-conditioned bus. Fortunately, the news from north of the border was good. The cease-fire was holding. No PLO infractions. No Syrian infractions. It was probably more a matter of comfort than commitment. Arabs had never liked to fight during chamseen.

Paul noticed the changes as he commuted into the city. There were fewer soldiers to be seen at mustering points along the highway. The traffic was heavier. The security less. The second, outer checkpoint on the main road into Jerusalem was now gone, so that Paul's 85 bus had to shift around only one roadblock. On the bus Paul could now pick out the familiar faces of the daily commuters. Their features had changed. It was not just familiarity which had altered them. They were softer, the jaws and muscles more relaxed, especially the women's. Perhaps their husbands were home. Or their lovers. Or their fathers and their brothers. Or their sons. Back from the north. Home or not, the shooting had stopped. There would be no more dying for now. Despite the discomfort of chamseen, their world had become a better and a safer place.

The pace of life in Jerusalem picked up. There were

159

more tourists. Mostly Americans. More shops were open. Construction work was going full swing. The PLO threats to other Arabs had not ceased, but very few workmen could afford to stay home week after week out of fear of such reprisals. They returned to work first as a trickle and then as a flood. Life was returning to normal. American teenagers could be seen everywhere. They, like the Richardsons, had come despite the war.

Paul stopped on his way to the hospital to see Eleazar Danin.

Neither of them had anything really new to say about the warnings. But that had not been what Paul had wanted to talk about. He had wanted to talk about Nahum Eckstein and about his committee and also about Zalman Cohen. Something did not smell right to him. This was not Denmark and the source might not be rotten, but it was at least overripe. Too many members of the committee had ties to Nahum Eckstein.

"Who?" Eleazar asked.

Paul was sure Eleazar knew the answer as well as he did. Better, in fact. "Two, at least."

Eleazar ignored the qualifying phrase. "Which two?"

"Chaim Abramowitz and Rivkah Geller."

"Ah, yes. The grieving father and the wounded lover. But, Paul, and you must forgive me here, as I am not a physician but just a simple . . ."

"Consultant."

"Yes, consultant. Are those two not logical members of the committee?"

"Yes, they are."

"They will do a good job."

"It still seems odd to me."

"Something rotten in the state of Denmark."

"Yes."

"But what, Paul? What exactly are you afraid of?"

"A cover-up."

"What kind of a cover-up?"

"Let's say someone killed Nahum Eckstein. These two might well have done it themselves, or at least they might have wanted to murder him. So what would they care if the murderer gets off free? The easiest way to assure that would be to prove that he wasn't even murdered."

"I will not concede that there is any cover-up, but perhaps, Paul, it might be better just to let things be."

"Let things be!"

"Paul. Listen. Less than three weeks ago, four terrorists in London shot our ambassador, and the next day we're at war. What if Nahum Eckstein was killed by the same terrorist group, or worse, by some less radical Arab group right here in the middle of Jerusalem?"

"So?"

"We do not need a rash of retribution. This is not Belfast."

"No, it isn't."

"And we don't want it to become one. And besides, one member of your committee would not permit such a cover-up."

"Who?"

"Professor Bernhard."

"Bernhard?"

"Yes, he's to the right of the Guardians. He will not allow any whitewash. Don't get me wrong. He's not an activist, but his heart is with those who are."

"That may not be true."

"What do you mean?"

Paul tried to put it all into words. He started with what Avram Schiff had told him. Perhaps Eckstein had been poisoned by some right-wing extremists and then killed to prevent the poison being detected. And perhaps Zalman Cohen had known about it, and perhaps as part of the right wing, Bernhard would try to cover things up.

"Paul, stop. You are getting carried away."

"Perhaps."

"Look. If you don't believe what Avram told you, investigate it. Go talk to the nurses."

Paul thought he might just do that.

When he got to the hospital for rounds, he discovered that the pace of life in the hospital had also changed. There were more nurses. More personnel at every level. Work was getting done faster, better, and more accurately. He wondered if Zalman Cohen should be listed as a casualty of war. One more Israeli dying in an attempt to free Israel of Arab terrorism.

Mrs. Fahoum was still in coma. The additional doses of anticonvulsants they had given her the night before had made no difference. She had therapeutic levels of three different anticonvulsants and she was still having seizures one right after another.

She was no longer on the Neurology floor, having been moved to the ICU to allow closer monitoring and more intensive nursing care. In the ICU there was one nurse for each two-bed unit, with extra floaters available now that there was less need for nurses in Lebanon. Mrs. Fahoum was in a room with another comatose patient; both were on respirators and cardiac monitors.

Paul, the residents, and the students stood at her bedside watching as the technician attached the EEG machine. As soon as the voltage switch was turned on, all eight pens which had been tracing flat lines suddenly burst into a continuous flurry of vertical movement. Up and down they went, fifteen to twenty times each second, resulting in a series of rapid, sharp individual spikes one right after another.

Continuous seizures.

Status.

Even the two students recognized it.

The technician turned off the machine and began to detach the electrodes, but Paul stopped her. He knew what the next step was and they would have to have her attached to the EEG machine to do it. Fortunately the patient was already in the ICU and on a respirator.

Seizures were caused by uncontrolled electrical discharges of the brain. They could stop the seizures by stopping all of the brain's electrical activity. This could be done by using an anesthetic agent and putting the patient into a very deep coma. A coma so deep that all brain activity stopped—a coma with a flat EEG, like the EEG of someone who was brain dead.

"Isn't that dangerous?" Yuri asked.

"Not as dangerous as uncontrolled status," Dr. Richardson told them.

"But a flat EEG," Yuri continued, not entirely convinced, "doesn't that mean that the brain is dead?"

"No. A flat EEG is only one of the criteria for a dead brain, and that requires a flat EEG not due to drugs or toxins. If it's due to drugs or toxins, it may well be reversible. Look, she is already on the respirator, so we're breathing for her. Her brain isn't really functioning in a useful way. She's in deep coma. We won't hurt her, and the odds are good it will help. When we let the brain functions start again, the seizures usually do not return.''

It took them forty minutes, and when they were done, Mrs. Fahoum was no longer in *status epilepticus*. Her EEG no longer showed any seizures at all.

It was flat.

Like the EEG of someone who was dead.

It was only her respiration that kept her alive.

Her heart beat on its own.

But without her brain, she could not breathe.

It was the machine that did that.

Unless . . . Paul didn't want to think about that.

''We'll keep it flat for several hours,'' Paul said.

''What will happen then?''

''We'll have to wait and see. With any luck at all, the seizures won't come back.''

There was no time to go over any of the new patients. The students had a meeting to attend and the residents had other work to do. So did Paul.

He did manage to say a few words to Dalia Avni. It was not a very graceful apology, but it was an apology nonetheless and she appreciated it. No other professor had ever apologized to her.

''There was something I wanted to ask you,'' he went on.

''What's that, Dr. Richardson?''

''About that order.''

''What about that order?''

''Look. I know you didn't write it. I already apologized. Calm down.''

''Okay.''

''Was it just an error?''

''What do you mean? What else could it have been? We're so overworked here. People are working double, even triple shifts sometimes. I know that nurse. He's good. He'd been on for twenty-four hours.''

''I didn't know that,'' Paul replied. He also didn't know that the nurse in question was a male. He'd assumed just the opposite. It was another reminder that this was not Chicago.

''No one does. He had covered one shift for his sister, whose husband was back from Lebanon for twelve measly hours. He's a great nurse. He's beside himself. He made a mistake. Can't you forget it? There's nothing else to worry about. I've got to go.''

Dalia was probably right. People made mistakes. Even nurses. They did in Chicago. And they did in Israel too, especially at times like this. As Paul watched Dalia leave proudly with her head held high, he realized how much of a woman she was.

He was left by himself in the ICU. He had never been there before. It was much like every other modern ICU he had seen, a model of planned efficiency in a world of unscheduled chaos. So many patients died in ICU's. Who would be bothered by one more? If the plug had been replaced before Nahum Eckstein had been found, who would have ever known what had happened?

Chaim was at the nursing station, writing orders. Should he say something?

"It's quite a unit you have here."

"Thank you. We're proud of it. Our record is very good. Are you here to investigate?"

"No. I saw Mrs. Fahoum."

"Is she still in status?"

Paul explained his plan for her treatment and then asked, "Why didn't you tell me about Eckstein and your son?"

"Why should I have? What difference does it make?"

"Don't you think it might influence your opinion?" Paul answered.

"No."

"No?"

"Will the fact that Mrs. Fahoum is an Arab whose family may be dedicated to pushing us into the sea make you treat her any differently?" Chaim asked.

"No."

"It's the same with me. What happened is over. My medical opinions will not be influenced."

As he left, Paul remembered that he hadn't gotten the name of the nurse from Dalia. It probably didn't matter.

He spent the next couple of hours back in the St. Thoros library reading and taking notes. He had moved on from Julian to Oribasius, the court physician to Julian, and his friend and adviser. He had accompanied Julian on his final campaign against the Persians and had attempted to treat Julian after the emperor had been fatally wounded.

When Julian died, paganism died with him, but Oribasius lived on to a ripe old age as an honored physician and a writer. His memoirs had apparently been written specifically for one Eunapius of Sardis, for him to use for his now-lost history.

Eunapius of Sardis was used by all subsequent historians as their main source—Ammianus, Zosimus, even Gibbon. From Oribasius to Eunapius to Zosimus. Another source to be chased down. What had begun as an emotional issue had become an intellectual challange.

It is unlikely that Paul would have gained any reassurance by watching another newspaper being systematically cut up.

One lower-case a.

One lower-case b.

One C, a capital.

Two D's, both capitals.

Five E's, two upper-case and three lower-case.

Two lower-case f's.

One upper-case G.

Two lower-case h's.

Five I's, just like the E's, two upper-case and three lower-case.

A single capital K.

A single small letter l.

Three lower-case m's.

Five N's like the I's and E's, two upper-case and three lower-case.

Eight O's, five of which were capitals.

No P's or Q's.

Five R's with the usual distribution.

Six S's, five of which were lower-case.

Five T's, again two and three.

Four U's, three upper, one lower.

Two capital W's.

Two small y's.

No X's.

No Z's.

This time the process was not repeated two more times. Instead all the letters were arranged and glued onto a single sheet of plain white paper. There was no copy for the Jerusalem *Post*, no copy for the mayor of Jerusalem, Teddy Kollek, just one for Eleazar Danin.

The first step was to prove that she could detect the various poisons; not just in water but in the human fluids where they could cause harm—blood and spinal fluid. This was done by taking the actual fluids, adding the poisons, allowing them to mix together, and then attempting to detect the poisons.

Thanks to Avram Schiff and his residents, Rivkah had as much blood and spinal fluid as she needed. She started with the blood samples. Each sample had the patient's name and diagnosis. Each sample had already been centrifuged, so she merely poured the plasma off. She divided each sample into two parts and added known amounts of Pickwick toxins to one of each pair.

40 nanograms of #970
20 nanograms of #974
10 nanograms of #975
10 nanograms of #976

Then she ran both samples from each patient. If the process worked, the regular sample would have no peaks on the results graph, while the test sample which contained the poisons would have four peaks and each of them would be just where her calculations had predicted.

She watched as the results came out.

Sassoon—Diagnosis syringomyelia
Blood sample: No peaks
Blood plus toxins: Four peaks
827
398
219
201

The peaks were in the right places on the graph and their sizes correlated with the amount of each poison she had added.

The whole process worked again in the sample named 'Fahoum.'' There was no interference from the various drugs circulating in her blood.

She went on to the next sample.

> Yousuf—Diagnosis facial diplegia
> Blood sample: One peak
> Blood plus toxins: Five peaks
>   814
>   103
>   412
>   216
>   208

Five peaks. Dr. Geller checked the results again. The first peak corresponded with 970, the third with 974, the fourth with 975, the last with 976. These four were as they should be. In the right places. And in the right amounts. The other one, the second one, was wrong. It was in the wrong place. A location where none of the toxins she had added would show up. The reading was low, only 103. A very low concentration. Five nanograms or so. Perhaps it was not really there but merely a blip caused by some different drug that this patient was taking, or perhaps it was just an error. She would have to check it over again.

Rivkah Geller was not the only one whose time was occupied by the remains of Nahum Eckstein. Professor Yitzak Cohen spent the week studying the slides that had been prepared from the tissue samples hand-carried back from Bethesda to Maimonides Hospital.

He started at the top of the brain and worked his way down. The brain itself looked normal. It took two days, but he was satisfied. Nothing was abnormal in any of the slides, just what he had expected.

The brain stem, the area that controlled respiration, was next.

It too was normal.

Next came the spinal cord. It was normal.

All that was left was the nerves, the tiny filaments that carried the messages from the brain to the muscles.

* * *

Paul split his time between teaching and learning. In general, he enjoyed the former much more than the latter.

After they had gone over two new patients, one with Tourette's syndrome and one with muscular dystrophy, John Haddad brought him up-to-date on Mrs. Yousuf. Her facial weakness was rapidly improving. The most likely diagnosis was still Guillain-Barré syndrome. Since she was so much better, the precise diagnosis no longer made very much difference. She was to be discharged in a day or two. Had she lived in Israel, where follow-up was easier, they would have already sent her home.

Yuri had news of Mrs. Sassoon. She was feeling well. The surgery had gone well. She had a syrinx, which they had drained. She felt her hand was stronger.

When he ran into Romain Bernhard that day after rounds, the neurosurgeon said nothing about Mrs. Sassoon. Instead they spoke about the war, which Bernhard carefully called the Peace for the Galilee Operation. Bernhard distrusted Philip Habib, the U.S. negotiator. He would give the PLO too much. They deserved nothing. They had been killing Israelis for over a generation. To say nothing of their seven-year rape of Lebanon, Paul thought to himself. Professor Bernhard had said nothing about that.

"Was Vincent a great teacher?"

Bernhard stared at Paul intently before answering. It was as if it had been so long ago and so far away that it took a massive effort to recall the vaguest memory, much less any of the details. When it finally came, his answer was short and soft. "Yes."

It seemed to Paul that there was much more he wanted to say and perhaps even needed to say.

"But . . . ?" Paul prodded him.

"He . . . he . . . was not a real friend." Bernhard stopped as if he needed to catch his breath.

"To you personally?"

"No, to us."

"To the residents?" Paul knew that that was not the "us" that Bernhard had meant. It was a much more significant "us." He wanted to hear Bernhard say it. He wasn't sure why he felt that he had to goad him on, but he did.

"What do you mean?"

"Nothing. Let us speak of more pleasant things."

"Such as?"

"Babinski. Charcot. There were such stories about them. Such legends. I was brought up on those legends."

Bernhard talked on and Paul listened. He had heard most of the tales before. They were part of the folklore of neurology. But never told with such passion or such an air of nostalgia. This was a different Bernhard, not the older man he had become, but the younger man he had been. Avram was right. He was a man worthy of their concern and assistance.

The problem with Paul's research was that he found too many sources, too many ancient historians. The number of important documents increased geometrically. And somehow, thanks in part to Sarkis and his connections, Paul located virtually all of them. Zosimus had told the whole story. Julian had appealed directly to the Jewish people to support his project. So, it had been his project, his rebuilding of the Temple, not the Jews'.

Julian's declaration that the time had come for Jews to return to their native land to rebuild the Temple evoked a wave of enthusiasm throughout the entire Diaspora.

Julian created a Jewish authority to levy taxes. He revoked Hadrian's edict forbidding Jews to enter Jerusalem, and no longer could Jews enter Jerusalem only on Tisha B'Av. Soon the city would again be Jerusalem, not Aelia Capitolina.

Jews began to arrive in Jerusalem. Building materials were collected. Silver tools were prepared: no iron could touch the altar. The rebuilding started.

Julian left for Persia, hoping to offer his victory sacrifice to the most High God in the new Temple as part of his triumphant return.

Then came the fire. The earth trembled and great balls of fire erupted.

Other events took place during the week as Philip Habib, the special U.S. envoy, shuttled between the PLO, the Syrians, the Lebanese, and the Israelis. The pathway toward a just solution was tedious.

In the Judean Hills, justice moved very quickly. Two automatic weapons were found in a village just beyond

Neve Ilan. The guns had been found during a house-to-house search, hidden in the basement of an old stone hut. The Arab family who lived in the house claimed that the guns were not theirs. They had never seen them. They must have been left there years before by the previous inhabitants. The guns had been fired recently. Within forty-five minutes a heavy army truck arrived. All of the family's possessions were loaded into the truck and the family members were put into a small bus. The van and bus drove to the Allenby Bridge and the family and the belongings were escorted out of Israel and into Jordan. There was one more empty house on the gray side of the green line. In Israel, chamseen was not an acceptable excuse for such activities.

Paul and Rivkah had dinner together once again that week, on a Saturday night, when Shabbat was over. They ate in a French restaurant, Chez Simon. Paul had eaten there before, a fact he did not remember until he sat down and recognized a painting that Bobbie hated. He rather liked it.

He told her about his children, then about Julian, then about himself and his life in Chicago, and then more about Bobbie.

She told him about her life, especially about David, about his involvement with reactionary movements in Israel, about his scars from the Holocaust, about his bad dreams, about the insistent, intense, yet tender way he made love.

They both seemed embarrassed by this, but laughed nervously and studied the dessert menu.

Paul was disturbed by the intimacy of her story, but when she told him of the end of their love and David's repeated questions about her work, he understood why she had told him so many details. He had to feel what she felt. What she still felt. How she hated David for it, how she hated herself for letting him use her mind and her body. And also, Paul realized, how she hated the Guardians for what they had done to David.

During coffee, they held hands across the narrow table. It was yet another routine intimacy which disturbed Paul. He did not know what to do or say.

"I have eaten here before."

"I know."

"How?"

"The way you look at that painting."

"Was it that obvious?"

"Yes. Paul, if you really wanted to get away from memories, why did you come here?"

He still held her hand. "I don't know. Maybe I needed to get away from the one set to deal with another."

"Next time, we will go somewhere peaceful and without memories."

"Where's that?" he asked.

"My place. It will have no memories at all for you."

"For you?"

"No. It's a new apartment. I have only lived there for three years. No painful memories for either of us."

There was no place like that for Paul. He took his memories with him.

This time she did not leave Paul off at the Central Bus station but instead drove him all the way to Neve Ilan. Paul tried hard not to think about her or relate to her, so he talked about his two children and she listened, wishing that he did not feel a need to use them to protect himself from her. It was only as she drove off and he felt her threat recede that he thought of another threat, one that also hung over her. He had meant to tell her about Zalman Cohen. Perhaps she too was at risk as long as she was studying the Pickwick toxins. Perhaps the paranoia of a besieged Israel surrounded by her enemies and chastised by her friends was rubbing off on him. Rivkah knew more about the Guardians than he did. She could probably look after herself. She had for years.

It must have been after one o'clock in the morning when Jonathan woke him up. There was a phone call for him at the office. It was Hassan. Hassan didn't like to bother Dr. Richardson at home, at night, but the prolonged coma hadn't worked. Mrs. Fahoum was again having continuous seizures. They were going to do a brain biopsy on her in the morning. Hassan wondered if Dr. Richardson had any more ideas. Paul did. He would borrow a car and go back to the hospital.

Paul was not the only one who lost sleep that night. Eleazar had received the fifth message. Once again it had come by mail, postmarked Jerusalem.

NOW IS ThE WINter Of oUr DisCOntent
maDe GlORioUs sUmmEr by this Sun of
yOrk

He looked at all five messages spread out on his desk:

BewAre tHe nInTh of AV

JerIchO

a plaGUe oN BoTh youR hOuseS

noW Fair hippOLYTa oUr
nupTial hoUr Draws apaCe

The winter of our discontent. It was from *Richard III*. What did winter have to do with Tisha B'Av, or the sun of York with Jericho? Why was the message so much longer? Why did it contain so many capital letters? What would be GlORioUs about a sUmmEr disaster on the nInTh of AV?

11

"A pneumoencephalogram!" Hassan had certainly not been expecting that solution. "I've never seen a pneumo."

"It's strange, you're less than twenty years my junior and you've never seen a pneumo, much less done one. I've done dozens of them. Dozens and dozens. Now they are just a part of history, replaced by the CAT scan."

The two physicians watched as the succession of spikes continued unabated from all eight pens of the electroencephalograph. "Do you know how the pneumo was invented?" Paul asked.

Hassan shook his head. "Not really."

"It was a by-product of World War One. A soldier had been wounded, shot in the head. He was alive, awake, alert. They X-rayed his head. The cavities of his brain were filled with air. They could see the outline of his brain. It was a simple step to introduce air without employing a gunshot. It revolutionized neurosurgery.

"It's an old trick," Paul explained, "but sometimes it works. You do a pneumo and the seizures stop. Somehow the air changes something in the brain and the seizures go away." Paul had seen it work, once. It was simple to do. First you did a spinal tap. As the spinal fluid came out, you replaced it with air. In order to make sure that the air got up to the brain, the patient's head had to be elevated. Paul went over it step by step and then the two of them went to work.

They positioned Mrs. Fahoum on her side. Hassan cleaned her back, took a spinal needle, and carefully eased it into her spinal-fluid space. The fluid was clear and colorless.

Next they shifted her into a seated position. Dr. Richardson supported her head and shoulder as a nurse draped the comatose patient's legs over the side of the bed.

Then came the pneumo itself. Following Paul's instructions, Hassan drew ten cc's of air into a syringe and injected it into the spinal needle and then waited as ten cc's of spinal fluid dripped out.

He repeated the procedure and then he repeated it again.

Five times. Fifty cc's. The spikes were slowing down.

Eight times. Eighty cc's. The spikes were gone.

Twelve times. One hundred and twenty cc's. The total capacity of the spinal-fluid space. They had replaced all the spinal fluid with air. They took out the needle and put Mrs. Fahoum back in bed. The seizures had stopped. They had stopped before. Only time would tell whether or not they would return this time.

The repeat testing of blood from Mrs. Yousuf gave the same results: an extra blip, one more peak than Rivkah Geller had expected to find. Altogether, she had looked at the blood from seventeen patients, and only in the blood of this one patient, Mrs. Yousuf, who carried the diagnosis of facial diplegia, had she detected an extra peak.

The next step was to examine the spinal fluid samples. This was the real test. A toxin in the blood might not be able to cross the blood brain barrier which is there to protect the brain from many poisons. If the poison couldn't do that, it couldn't get into the brain itself, or the spinal cord, or even the nerve roots, and therefore could not cause any neurologic disease. A toxin within the spinal fluid had already gotten there. Analysis of the spinal fluid was the real bottom line for this project.

She had spinal fluid samples from four patients. She used the same procedures to study these that she had used to examine the blood samples, and she got the same results. Mrs. Yousuf once again had an added peak of thirty nanograms in the spinal fluid. That meant that there was much more of whatever was causing the peak in the spinal fluid than there had been in the blood.

She rechecked Mrs. Yousuf's diagnosis. Facial diplegia. That was merely a description of bilateral facial weakness. Rivkah wondered what the true diagnosis was. What had caused this patient's facial diplegia? Had they known? What had happened to her? Did this added blip mean anything? She didn't have enough spinal fluid to run it over again. And she had checked only four spinal-fluid samples altogether, so it was hard to tell if this result really meant anything. She needed more samples from more patients. Maybe she could also get another from Mrs. Yousuf.

She wanted to repeat the analysis one more time.

And not find an extra peak.

That extra peak was between the locations on the graph for #970 and #974. It was not precisely where she had calculated that the missing #973 would show up, but not far enough away to ignore. She'd try to obtain another sample and try again. Maybe it would just go away.

Despite having only two hours' sleep, Paul caught his usual bus. He was not so sleepy that he didn't realize that the bus fare had gone up twenty-two percent overnight. The telephone tokens had not gone up yet. He should have put his money in bus tickets.

At the Central Bus Station he picked up a Jerusalem *Post*. There had been some shelling in Lebanon, nothing serious. No one had been killed on either side or even seriously wounded. Beirut was now completely surrounded. It was only a matter of time. Internally, divisiveness was increasing. More and more Peace Now members were calling for a pullback all the way to the forty-kilometer line. More and louder voices were calling for the total destruction and annihilation of the PLO, or at least the dethroning of Arafat. It was probably the healthy expression of a free democracy at work, but it was hard to appreciate at the moment.

Back home, the Space Shuttle had been launched. It was raining at Wimbledon, postponing the tennis matches for a day. The World Cup soccer series was still plodding on. It seemed to last longer than the NBA playoffs. And he could not find any news about his White Sox. No news was undoubtedly better than the real news.

Eleazar had a new message to show him.

Paul recognized it immediately. After all, he had just reread it.

"*Richard III*," Paul said. "The opening speech."

"Very good. Your college professor of Shakespeare would be proud. But, my friend, what does it mean?"

"That's not so easy." Paul considered it for a minute. "It probably wasn't chosen just so he could find the right letters for his message in that one speech."

"What message? As far as we can tell, the letters have no obvious meaning," Eleazar reminded him.

"Not yet. I would guess that the meaning depends upon our having all the letters."

"That, unfortunately, is most probably true."

"Since there's no limitation on the number of lines he can use, or for that matter the number of messages, the choice of a quote can't be based entirely on what letters are in the quotation. This opening speech must have been chosen because it would be easily recognized as *Richard III*. So we are left with the simple task of figuring out what *Richard III* means." Paul paused but Eleazar said nothing, so he went on. "I guess to most people the one thing it means is the two little boys, the two princes who were killed in the Tower by order of Richard III, at least according to Shakespeare. The murder of the two boys, both so young and innocent, is the first thing people associate with Richard."

"But what's that mean to us?" Danin asked.

"Two."

"Two?"

"Two. Two targets. Two objects. Two houses. Two places. Two locations. Two people. Two. A related pair. The two tablets of the law. Abbott and Costello. Amos and Andy. The two remaining tribes. Fibber McGee and . . ."

Paul stopped. He had said enough. Now Eleazar had to worry about two targets, not just one. Paul himself already had more than enough to worry about.

There were both new patients to see and old patients to keep up with. Mrs. Yousuf had been sent back to Lebanon. Her face was all but back to normal.

Mrs. Sassoon's right arm was definitely better. Both the patient and her physicians were pleased.

Mrs. Fahoum was beginning to wake up. She responded to her name. She moved all four extremities. She followed simple commands—if they were given in Arabic.

There was one new patient the group wanted to discuss

with Paul. The problem was one of management, not diagnosis. The patient was named Tarshish and he had severe myasthenia gravis. He'd had the disease for a dozen years and he'd been on every medicine in the book. And he was still very weak. They had decided to put him on steroids. Paul led them in a discussion of myasthenia. The weakness was thought to be due to the production of abnormal antibodies that attached to the muscles and prevented the nerves from delivering their messages to the muscles. Steroids somehow cut down the production of the antibodies.

That was the logic.

Fewer antibodies meant less weakness.

Would the steroids work?

Only time would tell.

Just as rounds were ending, Rivkah Geller called and asked Hassan Rashem about Mrs. Yousuf. Dr. Geller told him that she had been concerned about the diagnosis. So had they, Hassan told her. He went on to explain Mrs. Yousuf's entire course and reported that she had gone home virtually normal after ten days of observation.

That was all that Rivkah had to know. She thanked him and hung up. She was relieved by what she had been told. The extra blip she had found in Mrs. Yousuf's spinal fluid hadn't meant anything. It had not been a trace of a Pickwick poison. All the neurologic problems those poisons had caused had lasted far longer than ten days. The animals they had studied had all died or had stayed weak for the rest of their lives. None of them had just gotten a little sick and then in a few weeks recovered.

As the members of the committee entered the conference room, Yitzak Cohen handed each of them a set of typed notes listing each tissue region. All fifty-three sets of slides were listed, and following each, there was a brief description of the findings.

At the end of the table there was a portable screen and on the table an arc lamp for projecting tissue slides onto the screen. Once they all sat down, Dr. Cohen stood next to the projector. The other five doctors sat on either side of the table as close to the screen as possible. The rabbi sat at the opposite end of the table by himself.

At a signal from Paul, Avram Schiff flicked off the light

and Yitzak Cohen began projecting the slides. Since two of the doctors, Chaim Abramowitz and Rivkah Geller, were not used to looking at brain tissue, he started at the beginning.

"This is a sample of the left frontal lobe treated with a cell stain to bring out the details of the nerve cells themselves. Here we can see the regular architectural arrangement of the six layers of the cortex. The architecture is well-preserved." He switched to a higher power. "At this magnification you can see the details of the individual neurons, which are all well-preserved and . . ."

How strange it all was, Paul thought, sitting here in a room with at least two people who wanted Nahum Eckstein dead, or at least were not sorry to see him dead. Sitting here with them, trying to find out what had killed him.

Paul had to remind himself that that was really his task. What killed Nahum. Not who.

The brain was normal. Next came the brain stem with its variety of intricately organized substructures, miniature organs serving different functions: eye movement, balance, swallowing, blood pressure, respiration, breathing. Yitzak showed them each area.

Paul could not ignore the question of who. What if it were someone in this very room? Chaim or Rivkah? If it were Rivkah, why was she concerned about those Pickwick poisons? Or was that merely a cover?

Had David been a good lover?

Was Rivkah?

Did he really want to know?

The brain stem was intact. The respiratory center was normal. It was able to send out its messages to the nerves, which would then initiate respiration. But, Paul reminded himself, at one time in the ICU Nahum Eckstein had not been able to trigger the respirator. Why not?

As if in answer to Paul's unasked question, Yitzak began another explanation, again aimed primarily at the two nonneurologists:

"In order to figure out why the patient was unable to breathe, we have to look at two more regions: the spinal cord and the nerve roots."

Yitzak showed them the nucleus of the phrenic nerve, the nerve of the diaphragm. At lower power the cells looked a little pale. At high power the details of the individual cells were blurred. The material in each nucleus seemed a bit clumped and irregular. The cells themselves looked pale and a little shrunken. But none of the cells looked dead. They all looked functional. The changes did not seem to be enough to cause total lack of function, unless the organs which controlled the metabolism of each cell were poisoned. They were doing special electron microscopy of these cells to rule out that possibility. But as far as he could tell, from analysis of the nucleus of the nerve to the diaphragm, it looked as if this part of the nervous system was working.

The rest of the nerve centers in the spinal cord looked the same. A little pale, a little shrunken. Not normal, but probably not abnormal enough. These too would be studied by electron microscopy.

The last set of slides was of the nerve roots as they left the spinal cord. First they looked at the mid-cervical root, C-5, the root which travels to the diaphragm. For contrast, Yitzak showed a normal C-5 root with its tightly packed bundles of myelin-covered nerve fibers. Then the C-5 root of Nahum Eckstein. The fibers were swollen and distorted. The myelin was fractured. The bundles were no longer tightly packed. It was hard to tell whether any of the fibers were intact. If they were totally disrupted, they could never have repaired themselves. Detailed electron microscopic studies might help. The other nerve roots looked the same, up and down the cord. Nahum Eckstein could not breathe. He could not talk. He could not move anything. All the nerve roots had been involved.

The nerve roots were the usual site of pathology in Guillain-Barré syndrome. But as far as Paul could remember, they never looked this bad in Guillain-Barré.

It had taken three hours. Everyone was tired, even Rabbi Levi. As a final step, Yitzak gave a complete set of slides to Romain Bernhard and each of the neurologists. Each set included slides of the spinal cord and the nerve roots. Each of them could study the set at their own leisure. If they had any.

When the meeting was over, Avram stopped to talk to Paul. Now that the war was winding down, there was not as much need for Paul's skill in teaching. Instead of three times a week, he should make rounds only once or twice each week.

They had told Joshua the same thing that morning at the moshav. It was a bit humbling for Paul to discover that he was as expendable as an extra thirteen-year-old who had volunteered to plant seedlings for free.

They did talk a bit about the war. Avram was not as careful as Romain had been to always refer to it as the Peace for Galilee Operation. But his political views were similar. He too would not give an inch. Even if the army had to stay in Lebanon all winter.

Wasn't he concerned that they might get trapped in the quagmire of internecine war?

No. The Lebanese had been killing each other for a thousand years. When Israel got the PLO and Syrians out, they could once again continue that tradition without outside interference.

Paul wanted to ask if it was his own experience in the Holocaust that made Avram so callous. But he didn't. Instead he asked about Chaim Abramowitz.

To Avram it was easy to see how Chaim could be misled into being a peacenik. He, like Paul, had grown up safe and protected. Avram was more experienced. He knew better. He would not let anyone destroy Israel. And only Israel really knew what actions she had to take to protect herself.

Paul was becoming tired of the reality of everyday strife here. No one talked about last night's ball game or who was sleeping with whom on the soaps. Or down the block. Life was easier back home.

Perhaps it would be better, Paul realized, if he taught less at the hospital. That would leave him more time to read and study and do what he had to do. There was one more problem to be solved. "I'd like to talk to that nurse," he said.

"Which nurse?"

"The one who put the orders into the wrong chart," Paul explained, even though he was certain that any explanation was superfluous.

"You can't," he was informed.

"Why not?" By now Paul was angry. He was being treated like a child. "Can't an outsider try to find out what really happened? Or is this the Israeli version of Watergate?"

"Paul! Stop it!" Avram too was angry. "That's not it and you know it."

"Then why can't I talk to him?"

"Because he's not here."

"A convenient vacation, I suppose."

"If you still consider Lebanon a vacation spot. Most of us don't."

Paul felt like a foolish child. He wanted to run and hide in the corner. The need for nurses in Lebanon had to be enormous. And being there was no vacation. "Tell me one thing. Did he work in the ICU?"

"No! The O.R. He's a scrub nurse in the operating rooms. Hell, half the scrub nurses in the country are up in Lebanon."

Avram didn't have to explain to Paul why they were all needed up there. The news every day made that clear.

Paul spent one last day among the pagans.

Ammianus and Zosimus both described the great balls of fire coming from a cave below the foundation.

Several workmen were burned. In other reports they were killed. According to Gregory, the workmen were Jews who had returned to what they thought was to again be their homeland. Zosimus didn't define them by religion or country of origin.

The undertaking stopped. Why it was stopped was unclear. Who had ordered the work stoppage? Certainly not Julian. He was somewhere in Mesopotamia leading his legions against the Persians.

Rufinus elaborated on the story. He recorded how Cyril, the bishop at Aelia Capitolina, foretold the miracle. To the exact day. To the exact hour. To the exact minute. Even few Christians really believed in the predictability of true miracles. A predictable miracle was an apparent contradiction. A miracle was just that because it went against all expectations. And against all predictions. Unless God had spoken directly to Cyril announcing his intentions. Even Cyril had never made that claim. He just knew, to the exact minute.

Arson by miracle. Miracle by arson. It all depended on whose ox was gored, whose temple was destroyed.

Oribasius had been in Mesopotamia with Julian. Julian

knew the work had stopped and had written back to his overseer in Jerusalem in order to get it started again.

It had been important to Julian that the work on the Temple proceed. He was going to celebrate his victory there. On the altar of the Most High God. He understood the Jews. They would never revolt against him. They would join him against their common enemies: the Christians.

Oribasius dismissed such rumors of a miracle as no more than Christian propaganda, like Constantine's Sign of the Cross.

That night, after a full day of reading history, Paul met Rivkah outside her laboratory and she drove them to her apartment. Paul had arranged for Joshua to sleep at his aunt's. That meant that he had no curfew, no reason to hurry home.

Rivkah's apartment was on the top floor of a six-story building, with a balcony that looked down on the Old City.

They sat on the balcony and had a drink and watched the setting sun. It was another of those layered sunsets, as the haze of Tel Aviv acted as a prism to the rays of the sun. Chamseen was over. A cool breeze filled the entire city.

They talked about Jerusalem and the changes they had both seen over the years. How much cleaner the city was now. And more crowded. And how the standard of goods and services had seemingly improved over the three years since he had last been there. They talked of safe topics. The war. The PLO. The fate of Arafat. And of Beirut. That subject just could not be avoided.

She then showed him her apartment. The artwork struck him. It was obviously chosen with care and understanding by someone who knew what she liked. No postimpressionist French prints, no abstract expressionism, no pop art. Just Israeli art, and all scenes of the country. Mostly of Jerusalem. There were several by Nachum Gutman, a couple of Jossi Sterns, and one brilliant oil by Reuven Rubin. Paul fell in love with it. It was pure early Rubin, of sun-baked Jerusalem seen from the Mount of Olives, without a trace of the Chagall influence which often pervaded his later works.

It was that Rubin hanging above the large double bed that Paul would always remember.

After dinner, they again sat on the terrace, sipping coffee, looking out over the city, and listening to Mozart.

She knew she would be the one who would have to ask, so she did. "Shall we go and look at the Rubin again?"

Paul nodded and they walked into the bedroom arm in arm.

In the bedroom they kissed each other. At first merely gingerly, then tenderly, then needfully. It was Rivkah who let go of him and stepped back to start to step out of her dress.

"Wait."

"Don't you want to make love?"

"Of course I do, but I want to undress you."

She stopped. "No man has ever undressed me." It was not a complaint, just a statement of fact.

"One will. Tonight." Another statement of fact.

He took his time removing her clothes, and kissed each of her breasts longingly before he began to slip out of his own clothes. Once they were both naked and face-to-face below the Rubin oil, things began to happen at a faster pace. Much too fast. It had been so long. He entered her too soon. He was sure she wasn't ready. He was done much too quickly, too suddenly.

She held him tightly to her breasts.

"Don't worry, Paul. It will be fine."

And it was.

She waited just long enough and then kissed him, with her tongue nervously reaching into his mouth as her hand trailed down to his groin.

It was better.

This time he did not finish before they had begun. It was difficult not to think about the last time he had made love. He had to try not to.

Paul wondered which of them had gone longer without making love. He thought about how well he might measure up to her other lovers, to David. Was he still the standard by which she judged all others? He studied the Rubin oil. He even thought about Nahum Eckstein. Anything not to remember. It worked. They finished together.

"Paul, that was good."

No comparisons, an absolute. It had also been good for him. More than just good, in fact, but he couldn't tell her.

Instead he said he had to go home to be with Joshua. She offered to drive him. No, it would be better to take a taxi, even if the taxi rates had just gone up twenty percent. He raced home. He had not panicked, merely fled.

Rivkah wondered if he would return.

Paul knew he would.

As the week wore on, Paul made another visit to Sarkis Boyajian to tell him what he had learned. The old man sat quietly sipping tea throughout Paul's entire recitation. Paul told his story as a single unified narrative, putting all of the bits and pieces from the different sources into one tightly knit whole. He used all the sources, Christians and Hellenes, anti-Julian and pro-Julian, but especially the pagans, the eyewitnesses who had lived through the reign of Julian, who had been in the Middle East with Julian, and whose stories had been relayed by Oribasius. It came out as a tale of Christian sabotage of a joint pagan-Jewish project.

Sarkis said nothing until Paul finished. "Perhaps the most impressive strands of this entire fabric which you have so carefully woven for me are the two points of agreement between Christians and Hellenes."

"What two points?"

"Are they so obvious that even the storyteller has missed them?"

Paul thought for a moment. "I guess so. The stories seem fairly contradictory to me."

"They are contradictory. Diametrically opposed, in fact. But they agree on the issues over which they disagree."

Paul said nothing.

"Paul, you are investigating an event which took place in a small backwater of the vast Roman Empire sixteen hundred years ago. Jerusalem was a small village, not even a provincial capital. It was not even Jerusalem. No emperor had been here in over two hundred years. You told me much of this story two weeks ago. Julian started to rebuild the Jewish Temple and a fire from a cave below the foundations erupted and destroyed the building site."

"You're right."

"Yes. It's obvious, isn't it? But is it of great significance? Of course. These two sides who hated each other, who were engaged in a life-or-death struggle against one another, corroborate each other on two basic points.''

''The Temple. Julian did try to build it. And the fire.''

''Yes. The fire. Julian's minions started the construction and something dramatic, cataclysmic, perhaps even miraculous, brought it to an unexpected halt. So you are not dealing with a nonevent, a rumor, a legend. Something did happen on the Temple Mount in 363. Something sudden, something final. Was it a miracle?''

Paul just listened. He wished he knew the answer.

''Or was it an act of man?'' Sarkis paused to let the two possibilities sink in. ''Why do you think Oribasius and Eunapius rejected the idea of a miracle or an act of one of the gods? After all, Hellenes were firm believers in gods directly interfering in the day-to-day lives of people. More so than Jews or Christians. They were brought up on Homer, not Moses. They knew that gods could interfere anytime they wanted to.''

''True.''

''Miracles, divinations, were everyday events. The Hellenes told the future by reading the entrails of a sheep. They believed in omens, in auguries, in gods bothering with their affairs. But this event, great balls of fire from the bowels of the earth, this they are sure was not a miracle, not due to any god. Why?''

''I don't know.''

''Put yourself in their place. For god or gods to interfere, you had to fulfill a couple of conditions—''

''Motive,'' Paul interrupted Sarkis.

''Yes. Today we would call it motive. Did any god care enough to do something?''

''I can think of at least three.''

''What three?''

''Apollo. Hadrian had rededicated the Temple Mount to Apollo. In rebuilding the Temple, the Temple of Apollo was being desecrated. Some pagan sources say Apollo had been angered and that he himself destroyed the shrine as a warning, an omen to Julian not to bring back the old sacrifices.''

''Hellene historians would have accepted Apollo as a source of divine interference,'' Sarkis said.

''True. Even Oribasius. When Julian went against the gods, he recorded such things. He never tried to whitewash his friend.''

''The other two are, I assume, the God of the Christians and the Most High God of the Jews,'' Sarkis Boyajian went on.

''Yes.''

''Three suspects, then,'' the older man summarized.

''Each with a motive.''

''But motive alone is not enough, is it, Paul?''

''No. You need motive and opportunity.''

''Opportunity is certainly not an issue here. Gods, by definition, have the opportunity.''

Paul chuckled.

''But there is one other thing, Paul. As in any criminal investigation.''

Paul thought for a moment. ''Motive, opportunity . . . evidence. That's it. Evidence.''

''Or more precisely in this case, lack of evidence. Gods leave *no* evidence. Men leave evidence. There is no evidence of the parting of the Red Sea. No evidence of the Resurrection. No evidence of a cause of the fire at the Temple of Artemis at Ephesus which announced the birth of Alexander of Macedon. Gods neither create evidence nor leave it behind.''

''I think I see where you're going. Since Oribasius never even considered the possibility of a miracle, there must have been evidence of a manmade event.''

''Yes. To Oribasius it was never a question of whether this had been done by men or gods. Men were the culprits. The only question was who. Not if, who. To be that sure, he must have seen the evidence.''

''The army, or the remnants of it, including Oribasius, were in Jerusalem sometime later in 363 on the return from Persia,'' Paul said.

''So Oribasius was here and he saw the evidence himself. To him the answer must have been obvious. The Christians had done it. They had opposed everything that Julian had done. Besides, the Temple was a direct attack upon them. It was a carefully orchestrated project which would have made a prophecy of Jesus' false. The ancients, both Christians and Hellenes, had a great belief in prophecy. Not just in moral prophecy, like the great prophets of Judaism, but in the prophecy of day-to-day events. To make Jesus a false prophet was to remove his claim to divinity.''

"If we are to believe Oribasius," Paul said, "and he was a firsthand witness, we must apply the same criterion to men that we applied to the gods."

"I agree."

"The Christians had the motive," Paul pursued his own point. "But did they have the opportunity? Would they have access to the Temple Mount? As potential saboteurs, would they not have been excluded by the Romans? And by the Jews? Could they have found this cave and started the fire there?"

"Those are all good questions. And I must say, the point you make is a strong one. If it was a fire from a cave below the foundation, whoever started it must have known about the cave. Most Christians were outsiders, like us. We came here in 301, but we knew nothing of the Temple Mount. We shunned it. It was a refuse dump. Only the Minims, the Judeo-Christians, would have known about the cave—those few Jewish converts who still observed the rituals of Judaism but accepted Jesus as the Messiah. They would have had the knowledge and the opportunity to pass as Jews."

The Jewish converts were one more subject Paul would have to pursue.

It was Shabbat again. Another week had gone by.

The binocular microscope Paul had borrowed was set up on the kitchen table. Services were over and he sat by himself and pored over the set of slides that Yitzak Cohen had given him at the last meeting of the committee. He carefully scanned each of the slides at low power, and then studied selected sections at higher magnification. He methodically went through each and every slide, each section of the cord, each nerve root. The roots were severely disrupted. There were few, if any, normal remnants of nerve fibers. Could Eckstein have recovered? Who could tell for sure? Not Paul.

Was Rivkah home? Was she alone too? He called her and asked her if she wanted to get together on Monday night. She did. He hung up. Could she have pulled that plug? Could she still be carrying an old grudge? As far as he knew, she hadn't even been in the hospital that morning.

12

Sunday was the fourth of July. Back home it was a holiday. Picnics. Family outings. Double-headers. Here it was the start of yet another week of work. Paul didn't even know what team his White Sox were scheduled to play. There were some differences from the previous Sunday. The news had become more expensive. Israel's unending spiral of inflation, fueled by the taxes to support the effort in Lebanon, had taken its toll. The Jerusalem *Post* had gone up twenty percent, from ten to twelve shekels per day. To Paul, the increase was not serious. He lived in a world of dollars, not shekels, and each day the shekel decreased in value. For him the price went up only eighteen percent. By the end of the week the shekel would go down another three or four percent. He hoped the added price would include added coverage of sports.

Despite its increased cost, the news had a peculiar sameness about it. The Israeli Defense Force remained poised around Beirut, waiting to see what would happen. Arafat remained intransigent. The Europeans were still loudly condemning Israel, especially France. The Arab states remained relatively silent; the solutions were as elusive as ever.

In Israel itself all was quiet. No terrorism, but a brief mention was made of increased security needs. Everyone should be more cautious than ever. Paul doubted that that was a manifestation of paranoia.

Connors had beaten McEnroe at Wimbledon and the Space Shuttle *Columbia* had landed safely. It had been a good day for Americans. There was no mention of the White Sox.

The week had one noticeable difference about it. Early on Sunday morning Joshua left for a four-day camping trip to the Negev, leaving Paul on his own. As soon as the bus pulled out of Neve Ilan, Paul went into the hospital for a meeting with Yitzak Cohen. Somehow, Paul left the meeting both dissatisfied and disturbed. Dissatisfied because Cohen, the neuropathologist in charge of the case, had, as far as Paul could tell, no imagination. Yitzak was a classical pathologist, trained in the old school. Paul should have known from Yitzak's C.V. He was careful, compulsive, and thorough. Whatever was on the slides, he would find it. He would describe it. He would analyze it. He would catalog it, classify it, define it, cell by cell, fiber by fiber. But if something was not there, it was not his worry. Yet, to make the decision, they were going to have to have some imagination; some creative thinking was going to be necessary. Could Nahum Eckstein have survived? Paul had a feeling that merely counting nerve fibers would not answer that question. That was where he needed help, and Yitzak Cohen offered him no such help.

And to make matters worse, Yitzak had a motive. A darn good one. "I never met Nahum Eckstein," he carefully told Paul, "but my family knew his family. We knew them for six generations, dating back to my great-great-great-great-grandfather, a rabbi of unsurpassed learning. He left Poland and came to Jerusalem to live and teach. No one lived outside the walls of the Old City then. He started a yeshiva. All of the great teachers of this yeshiva came from the two families. Over the decades the yeshiva split into two factions. The disputes became more bitter. Then came the great split over a major issue. The two families no longer spoke to one another. The hatred grew. My family was driven out."

"When was that?"

"We left in 1927, the year I was born."

"Where did you go?"

"Poland," he said, and then added almost as an afterthought, "Only I survived."

Another story that had not been revealed on the C.V. All that that document had recorded of the first twenty years of Yitzak Cohen's life was that he had been born in Jerusalem in 1927 and that he had entered Hebrew University in 1948. A few details had been omitted. What Rivkah Geller had said to Paul about C.V.'s was absolutely true: those facts that really mattered about a person could not be discovered by reading his C.V.

"Certainly the Ecksteins didn't know what would happen."

"Of course not. No one did. They just hounded us out of our homes."

A family feud. Did that give Yitzak a motive? "What was the great issue?" Paul asked.

"Whether all of Jerusalem was one walled city for ritual purposes or not. My grandfather believed that the Jews in the New City were within the walls. They said 'No.' He was of course right. It is all one city. They survived."

The meeting was over. Paul remembered that Yitzak had been in the hospital that morning performing an autopsy. He doubted if either grandfather would have approved of that. Yitzak had been there, a mere one hundred yards away, so he had had the opportunity.

And a motive. A family feud, with the loss of his family thrown in for good measure. A longstanding feud like the Capulets and Montagues. Verona had been lucky. It had only two factions. Jerusalem always had more than that.

A plague on both your houses.

Paul spent the rest of the day reading in various libraries, both official and private, and then took the bus back to Neve Ilan. As soon as the bus left him off, he knew he did not want to be there. He wanted to be in Jerusalem. Not inside the wall. On French Hill, overlooking the Wall. He packed a small overnight bag, mostly taking things he wanted to read, and took the next bus in.

Rivkah was happy to see him and even happier to see his overnight bag.

When they made love that night, Paul did not have to think of other things to keep his mind from wandering. He thought of making love with this one particular woman. It was she that he felt. It was she that he saw even when he closed his eyes.

Could Rivkah tell the difference too? To Paul, it was like day and night. Yet was the physical act that different? Was he any more tender? Was he any more considerate? Was it better for her? He wanted to ask her, but he couldn't. It was strange. He could share this with her, but he couldn't ask a simple question about their love-making. It was often this way. It had been so with Bobbie once. The memory did not distress him. All of a sudden he could safely think of both Bobbie and Rivkah and not be threatened. He looked at his watch. It was five in the morning. The sun would soon be rising out of the wilderness of the Judean desert. He watched Rivkah sleep. He had never before made love to a woman who did not shave under her arms. At that moment, he knew he loved her. Not in the way he loved Bobbie, but he did love her. He woke her gently with a kiss and again they made love. And he was confident that this time she recognized the difference.

He stayed with her the next two nights.

During the days, she worked at the hospital and he did his work. Mostly he visited Sarkis and sat with him and read a bit and talked a bit. A peaceful idyll in the midst of tensions.

Each night Paul and Rivkah made love. Was it only three nights? They were both comfortable with it. No anxiety. No hurried fumbling. A rightness that was outside of time, devoid of comparison, isolated from memories.

He would watch her sleep and knew that she was beautiful. Had she always been? Or was she a woman whose beauty peaked late in life? Her breasts were still high, her nipples small and light pink.

When he told her she was beautiful, she merely laughed self-consciously. He told her that he had never made love to a woman who didn't shave under her arms.

Did he want her to?

No.

Was he sure?

Yes.

They talked of the first time they had each made love and laughed at themselves.

They did not talk of other times.

When she told Paul that she had recognized the difference between the first time and now, it was not as a question. It was an observation. He made no answer. He just held her and cried for a minute. No more.

On Wednesday morning, she dropped him off to see Eleazar Danin and then drove on to the hospital.

Another message had arrived:

aLaS PoOr YoricK I kNEW
hIm hoRatIo a FeLlOw of
inFinite jESt

Paul did not have to look at the other five messages spread out on Eleazar's desk. He knew them by heart. Which letters were capitalized. Which were cut from the Jerusalem *Post*. Which from the *Herald Tribune*, like this one. Which plays they were from. *Julius Caesar, Romeo and Juliet, A Midsummer Night's Dream, Richard III*, and now *Hamlet*. He knew that any questions about paper, envelopes, stamps, paste, or ink were useless.

Paul remembered his list of groups of suspects, the differential diagnosis of a murder.

1. PLO
2. Moderate Arabs
3. Guardians of the City
4. Jewish radicals
5. Christian fanatics
6. Main-line middle-of-the-road Israelis

Didn't the same list also apply here?

Not quite. Main-line middle-of-the-road Israelis did not resort to terrorism.

Nor did moderate Arabs.

What good was the list?

They didn't need a list of the political factions that could foster violence. They needed names. Specific names. Not vague categories. It wasn't the same as medicine. In medicine the individual bacteria which killed the patient didn't have a first name. It was time for ideas, not vague generalizations. "In this scene, Yorick is represented by his skull, thrown up from the grave by the gravediggers."

"You remember your *Hamlet* well."

"A skull," Paul mused. " 'Golgotha' means 'skull.' So does 'Calvary.' They are the same word. Greek and Latin."

"Then why 'both'? There is only one church on Golgatha.

"Today it's only one chuch. But it wasn't always that way. In the first few centuries after Saint Helena there were two separate churches. One over the Sepulcher and one over Golgotha."

"Perhaps. Terrorism against a Christian site to show the Christian world that we as Jews don't protect their holy sites. Perhaps to bring pressure for making Jerusalem an international city on the way to making it an Arab city once again." Paul could see that Eleazar Danin had not even considered the possibility that a Christian site might be the target.

"It would be an easy site to attack on Tisha B'Av. The Old City will be full of soldiers and police protecting the Wall and people walking to and from the Wall." Eleazar got up and went to a map of the Old City. "Here, look. This is where the troops will be. On the walls surrounding the entire city we will have soldiers every five feet." As he talked, his fingers traced out the bright thick red lines on the wall map. "The main pathways to the Wall will also be lined with armed men. From Jaffa Gate down David Street to the Wall, or around the Armenian quarter and the Jewish quarter. In from Dung Gate. Not from Damascus Gate. And not from New Gate through the Christian quarter. Jews never go that way to get to the Wall. Not on Tisha B'Av." He pointed to a domelike structure on the map. "Here it is. The Church of the Holy Sepulcher."

"You will have no special troops anywhere near it," Paul said as he studied the map.

"Correction. We wouldn't have. Now we have to and we will."

"Where will you get the extra troops?"

"That is not our problem. Every man's a soldier. A few more will be on duty that night. Where to get them is the easy part. Where to place them is what's hard."

"It will probably be better duty than sitting in a tank somewhere in Lebanon. And safer."

Eleazar began drawing new lines on the map. All of the Christian sites in Jerusalem were fair game. The Via Dolorosa. Eleazar studied his map and drew a new red line from Lion's Gate to the Holy Sepulcher, past the

Pool of Bethesda, past the Stations of the Cross. Then he walked over to map of the Mount of Olives, and again began drawing in red. Gethsemane. The Church of Pater Noster. Each holy site on that holy mountainside was touched by a thick red line.

Many Jews who had expected to spend Tisha B'Av at home in Safed, Eilat, or Beersheba would now spend the twenty-four hours in Jerusalem protecting a Christian site. They did it every Christmas, every Easter. Now they would do it on the ninth of Av.

As he got to the door, Paul stopped. He had remembered one more thing.

"Gertrude."

"Who?"

"Hamlet's mother, Gertrude. Gertrude and Hamlet's Uncle Claudius killed Hamlet's father by pouring poison into his ear while he slept."

"Back to poison again."

"Yes. And," Paul added, 'they did it while he slept."

"Wait a moment, Paul, and I will walk out with you. I have to go to the mayor's office. A meeting, you know."

Paul nodded. He knew too much about official meetings, although perhaps his were not exactly the same as Eleazar's.

They walked downstairs together and strolled down to Jaffa Road. Eleazar turned left toward Mayor Kollek's office and Paul turned right to get to Zion Square, the heart of Jerusalem's tourist and shopping district.

"Shalom," Eleazar said.

"L'hit," Paul replied. Until next time. He looked at his watch. It was twenty-seven past two.

The street was bustling with chatter and activity. It was hard to believe that a war was going on. At least it wasn't very much of a shooting war anymore. No one was being killed. Each day meant only a few casualties. Men were being returned home. Even some of the doctors. And the nurses.

That nurse!

Why had he been sent to Lebanon now, when the shooting had all but stopped? That made no sense. Then why?

Paul turned to ask Eleazar.

Neither of them had taken more than a few steps.

Paul knew immediately what the noise was.

It was a shot.

Not a car backfiring.

There were more shots.

Coming one right after another.

Not a string of firecrackers, even though it was the fourth of July, a legal holiday back home.

More shots.

This couldn't be happening here.

This wasn't Lebanon.

Or Belfast.

It was Jerusalem.

Not here.

Not now! It wasn't the ninth of Av.

Screams.

Paul stood and listened.

People were falling to the sidewalk.

Paul watched.

A car window shattered in front of him.

Not here.

Bullets smacked against the buildings.

Others pierced the cars.

Not on Jaffa Road.

Not to him.

It was just a dream.

It was happening around him.

Behind him, the large plate-glass window of the T-shirt store exploded. A piece of glass struck him in the shoulder.

"Paul."

More shots.

"Down!"

Three young Arabs with automatic weapons were running up the street toward Zion Square, firing.

A steady stream of small explosions filled the air.

People were lying all over the street.

Rat-a-tat-tat . . . rat-a-tat-tat.

The beat was getting louder.

He could hardly hear the crying.

Only the whistling bullets and the screams of terror.

"Get down!"

More shots.

Someone else was shooting, right next to him.

The head of one of the Arabs splattered. He fell. Adding another body to the dozens already scattered about.

Another stopped and took aim, directly at Paul.

Something heavy slammed into Paul's legs. It was a body. He was thrown to the street.

Windows were exploding all around him.

Another body fell on top of him, blood spurting out of one of its arms, bright red arterial blood. It was an Israeli soldier. A boy. No more than eighteen years old. Two years older than Carolyn.

"Paul."

It was Eleazar.

He was the body that had thrown a perfect rolling block into Paul, saving his life.

"Paul, are you okay?"

"Yes. Thanks to you."

More shots.

Eleazar disengaged himself and grabbed the submachine gun which was now lying next to them. He crawled forward until he reached a parked car with shattered windows and half a dozen bullet holes in the hood. He crouched behind the car and looked toward the square. Bodies were strewn everywhere. Some were trying to crawl toward cover, others couldn't.

Paul was no longer frozen, no longer an observer, an outsider. The young soldier was bleeding. Arterial blood was squirting out of his right arm, spilling his life out over the sidewalk and over Paul.

Automatically Paul loosened his own belt and pulled it out of his pants. The spurting was less forceful, more rapid. The boy had obviously lost a heck of a lot of blood. His pulse was getting faster as his blood pressure was falling. He was going into shock. Paul put his belt around the soldier's arm, above the gaping hole. He had to stop the bleeding completely. Otherwise the young Israeli would die. Yet another victim of terrorism.

He pulled it tight, as tight as he could. The spurts stopped. Paul carefully worked his way out from under the patient.

Was the soldier wounded elsewhere?

He was covered with blood.

So was Paul.

A shot.

A series of shots.

A burst from in front of Paul, from Eleazar.

Moans.

Screams.

Crying.

Sirens.

The unmistakable rumble of heavy trucks.

The squeal of tires.

Rat-a-tat-tat.

Brakes.

Shouted orders.

The sounds of men in heavy boots. Paul saw them. They were coming down the street behind him, heading toward Jaffa Road.

More Israeli soldiers were coming up Jaffa Road from the direction of the Old City.

Others were now advancing from King George Street. Behind them roadblocks were being thrown up.

Soldiers were converging on Zion Square from three different directions.

The shooting stopped.

The only sounds now were the heavy footsteps of the running paratroopers.

And the crying.

And the moans of the wounded.

The soldier was not in shock.

His pulse was thready and weak but he was awake and alive.

Paul saw the name on his uniform.

Teller.

He knew some Tellers.

Was the soldier related? Probably. The world of Jews was very small.

A group of medics came down the street, a few seconds behind the paratroopers.

"Arterial bleeding," Paul said. "Right radial artery. He's lost a lot of blood. I had to use a tourniquet."

"How long?"

"It's only been on for a minute or so," Paul replied.

"Good. We'll take over," the other physician said, already starting an I.V. "Stretcher! Plasma! Notify the surgical team that they have a radial bleeder!"

The moans continued.

The soldiers were going door to door, shop to shop.
The crying continued.
A murmur of voices could be heard building up.
There were other injured people to be examined.
More army physicians ran by Paul.
"You okay?"
It was Eleazar again.
"Yes."
"You're covered with blood."
"It's not mine." He paused. "Thanks to you."
Three shots.
They came from a souvenir shop across the street. He
had shopped there once. With Bobbie. So many years
ago.
The street was quiet. As quiet as death.
An unreal quiet.
His neck hurt.
No one moved.
Four paratroopers came out of the shop dragging two
Arabs. One was struggling. The other was dead.
It was over. Paul looked at his watch.
Two-thirty-three.
Less than six minutes had passed.
In another three minutes the army medical teams had
gotten all of the wounded onto stretchers and into am-
bulances and on their way to the hospitals. There was
nothing else for Paul to do there. He looked around for
Eleazar, but he was nowhere in sight.
Paul needed a clean shirt so he could get to the hospital
and make rounds. He walked into the T-shirt shop. They
looked like they could use the business. It was only when
he changed his shirt that he realized that some of the
blood was his. A piece of glass from the shop window
had cut him in the shoulder. It was only a superficial
wound, a red badge of belonging.
A few Band Aids from one of the medics took care of
it.
He kept his bloodstained shirt as a souvenir, and started
for the hospital.
Joshua.
Carolyn.
Both names hit him at once.
Where were they?

Where had they been?

Were they safe?

The answers came back to him.

They were not even in Jerusalem.

And certainly nowhere near Jaffa Road.

They were far away and safe.

Could he be sure? In a crazy place like this, where people get shot in the street? He had been right. Making lists of groups with different political motives for their violence didn't do much good. To prevent the violence, names were needed. Not labels, but specific names.

In contrast to the events which filled the rest of their consciousness, most of the news on rounds was quite good. Even Mrs. Fahoum was doing well. Her seizures had stopped. Leah Gandel, the young woman who had had a stroke following delivery of a child, had been transferred to the rehabilitation center. There was no longer any need to keep her on acute service with a full nursing staff to watch her receive physical therapy.

Moshe Tarshish, the man with myasthenia, had now been on prednisone for several days. For the first two days he had been, if anything, weaker. Now he was a bit stronger. He could swallow better. His breathing was stronger. No one was sure why steroids worked, but fortunately they did, even without that knowledge.

John had also seen Avi Mashir, the young girl with Sydenham's chorea, the day before in the outpatient clinic. They had not been able to see any abnormal movements at all. No one even mentioned Mrs. Yousuf, who was back in Lebanon, not to be seen again. There would be no routine follow-ups of Mrs. Yousuf.

Rivkah Geller continued her search for the Pickwick poisons.

She had more samples than she had wanted. Maybe even more than she needed. She even had 120 cc's of spinal fluid from a patient named Fahoum; that was enough to run a dozen different recovery studies on the same spinal fluid and then run them over again and still have fluid left over.

And that was just what she did. She had to be absolutely sure of her methods before she studied the few cc's she had of Nahum Eckstein's blood and spinal fluid. That could never be replaced.

When she was done, she had studied eleven new non-neurologic disease controls. None had any peaks of their own. In all eleven, the toxins came out just as they did in the Fahoum fluid. Same size. Same place. Same recovery. The methods were working perfectly.

The five o'clock news was dominated by the terrorist attack which had struck the heart of Jerusalem.

No Israelis had been killed. Twenty-seven had been injured, most by bullets, some by flying glass. Nine were in serious condition. Four were critical.

The attack had been staged by three Arab terrorists. Two were dead. One was in custody. All three were from Silwan.

Silwan was hardly a stone's throw from Jerusalem, at the southeastern corner of the city, across the valley from the original city built by King David himself. It had been taken from Jordan in the Six-Day War. It was rife with PLO sympathizers.

All three of the terrorists had been members of the PLO.

The PLO took full credit for the attack. Arafat proclaimed that no Jew would ever again be safe, not even in the streets of Jerusalem.

No one but Israel condemned the PLO.

It was difficult for an experienced clinician like Paul to diagnose the Israeli response as paranoid.

13

Paul got off the bus. His overnight bag was slung over his shoulder. Joshua was already back from his trip to the Negev. He was playing catch with Dalia Avni. This time Paul recognized her figure without any difficulty. Considering her schedule as a resident, she must have come directly from the hospital to Neve Ilan.

Joshua saw his father and ran to him. They hugged and kissed. Joshua was bubbling over with excitement. The trip had been the greatest. They had camped out in the Negev like bedouins. And today they had been in Jerusalem. They had explored Solomon's Quarry. It was called that because Solomon had used stone from there to build the Temple. The real Temple! Had Paul ever been there? He of course had. But not for years. Joshua loved it. It was great. A giant cave right under the Old City. Did Paul know that it was also called Zedakiah's Tunnel? That was because King Zedakiah had escaped from the Babylonians by using it. That entrance had disappeared long ago. He wanted to go back. Could they go together? They could.

"Dad," Joshua continued. The change in his voice would have been obvious to a casual observer, and Paul was certainly not that. The excitement of a thirteen-year-old boy had become the dark concern of a young adult. "Did you hear what happened at Kikar Zion today?"

He had.

"That's right in the middle of Jerusalem."

"I know."

"You weren't there, were you?"

"No, of course not."

"You do go there a lot."

"Sometimes, yes, but today I . . . was at the hospital."

201

"Thank God. That's a lot safer place."

Dalia sensed that she was intruding on their privacy and put down the glove and began walking up the road.

"Dalia, don't run off," Paul called after her.

"I . . . " She hesitated.

"Didn't you come by to see me?"

"Yes, in part."

"Tell me why." He and Joshua stood with their arms around each other's shoulders.

"Another time, Dr. Richardson."

"No, stay. We'll all go in the house and have some juice."

It was only then that Joshua saw the overnight bag that Paul was carrying. Paul hoped that he didn't understand the significance. Joshua was only thirteen. When he had been that age Paul hadn't known about such things.

Or about terrorism.

"Well, do you like my new T-shirt?" Paul asked, figuring that that was a safe topic. It was a Snoopy T-shirt proclaiming the beagle's love of Jerusalem.

Joshua had seen better. "It's okay," he admitted.

"I made rounds in it."

"At the hospital?"

"Where else?"

"Wow!" That he liked.

After they had finished their juice and Joshua had told them both about the Negev again and gone out to see his aunt, Dalia told Paul why she had come by. He had been wrong.

"What about this time?"

"Goethe," she explained.

"Goethe?" he asked. Then he remembered. On rounds he had taught them that the first description of aphasia had been written by Goethe and not by a physician, much less a neurologist.

"Goethe didn't write the first description of aphasia. It was written in Babylonia during the exile. I'm surprised you never noticed it. It's in a prayer we say every day."

Paul still didn't know what she was getting at.

"We're supposed to say it after each meal. It just struck me today. Loss of speech and loss of the fine use of the right hand just like a stroke."

He knew. " 'If I forget thee, O Jerusalem, let my right hand lose its cunning and . . . ' " He hesitated.

" 'Let my tongue cleave to the roof of my mouth,' " Dalia said, completing the quote.

"My God, you're right. It is a perfect description of a patient with a stroke and paralysis and speech loss, written by a Jewish exile over two thousand years ago. I never made the connection before. As far as I know, no one has. Why don't you write it up? There's a meeting in Puerto Rico sometime this winter on the history of medicine. You should submit it. I have the address somewhere."

She wasn't interested in that, but she had wanted to tell him about it.

They were both silent and their silence was awkward.

"I couldn't tell Joshua," Paul said firmly.

"He doesn't have to know."

"You know?"

"I guessed. So did some of the others. We live in a very small world. You were seen."

"I have nothing to hide."

"Of course not."

The quiet was not as awkward now.

"She is a special person," Dalia began.

"She?"

"Professor Geller."

"What do . . . ?"

"You should be . . . happy that you and she are . . . I mean . . . ah . . . "

Her embarrassment was obvious.

"That's not what I meant."

"It's not?"

"No. I was talking about the shooting at Kikar Zion. I was there."

"Oh, God."

"That's why I came to the hospital in a T-shirt. My shirt was covered with blood."

"Oh, God. Don't tell him. Don't tell Joshua. I'm sorry. You were right. I had no business . . . I . . . "

On Thursday he woke up to the news that the arms the Israelis had captured in Lebanon were on display at the fairgrounds in Tel Aviv. Some of them, that is. There was not enough room to show them all. There was no admission charge. It was the eighth of July. that made it also the seventeenth day of the Jewish month of Tamuz. That was the last day there had ever been sacrifices at the Temple. That was one thing to thank the Romans for.

Eleven Israelis injured in the shooting at Kikár Zion remained hospitalized. Three remained critical. The one corporal whose arm had been damaged severely was off the critical list. that had to be the young soldier who had fallen on Paul. The surgeons had repaired his torn artery during a six-hour procedure and saved his arm and his life. He was now expected to recover completely. One of the other wounded Israelis, a young woman who had been shot in the chest, had died.

Such circumstances did occasionally occur in hospitals, Paul reflected.

In Silwan, members of a special unit of the Israel Defense Force had located the houses of the families of the three terrorists. The families had been moved out and the houses blown up.

No lives were lost.

No injuries.

No torn arteries.

No chest wounds.

Three more displaced Palestinian families.

It was not enough. They should have been sown over with salt.

A systematic search of Silwan was continuing. If any weapons were found, the homes would be blown up.

West Germany and Italy had won the big soccer games. They would meet in the World Cup finals on Sunday.

American ships were standing off Beirut to take the PLO out.

To where?

No one was sure. No Arab country was willing to take them. Not Jordan. They had been there before. Jordan was Palestine. It was the other half of the British Palestine Mandate. Most of what had been Palestine was Jordan. Jordan had thrown the PLO out. That's why they were in Lebanon.

The Arab states were all willing to give them arms and to fuel their hatred. Arms but not homes.

Brezhnev had warned Reagan to stay out of the Israel-

Lebanon conflict. That was as good a way as any to assure American involvement.

While Paul was lingering over the news, Rivkah Geller was in her laboratory working on the problem of the Pickwick poisons. She had received samples from eight patients with various neurological diagnoses. Their diseases involved different parts of the nervous system. That was precisely what she needed. If the extra blip she had found was the result of damage to part of the brain or spinal cord and not the cause, some of these samples would have that same blip.

It took her the better part of the day to do all of the work. When she was done she had found nothing. Damage to the brain or spinal cord by itself did not result in any new peaks on the graphs that resembled any of the Pickwick poisons. No added blips.

Tomorrow she would run Rabbi Eckstein's spinal fluid and then she would know.

Of all the meetings with the individual members of the select committee, it was the meeting with Rabbi Levi that Paul had looked forward to with least enthusiasm. It was not the rabbi's Orthodox beliefs that made him uncomfortable, but their lack of a common ground in nonreligious matters. They could not debate nerve-root pathology, discuss toxic neuropathies, or reflect on the legacy of Charcot. They were separated by more than their common religion.

Rabbi Aaron Levi was not uncomfortable. "You are interested in the Third Temple, I am told."

"Yes, the attempt to rebuild the Temple by Julian the—"

Rabbi Levi waved off Paul's reply as if it were a fly, a small insignificant fly, a gnat of no meaning. "The Third Temple remains what it had been for over nineteen hundred years. A dream. An unfulfilled prophecy. But we are a patient people, we will wait some more."

This was not the Third Temple Paul was seeking. A Temple of marble columns and limestone blocks. Blocks quarried out of the Judean Hills, and cedars brought down from Lebanon. This was a different Temple, a Temple that had sustained the dreams of Jews for two thousand years.

"Julian could not build the Temple. Nor could you. Nor I. I, of course, would never even entertain such thoughts. Only the Messiah, may the All-merciful hasten his arrival, can build the Third Temple."

"But now that we have Temple Mount, couldn't we—?" Paul began.

"Of course not. We have neither the right nor the knowledge. Only the Messiah can rebuild the Temple."

"I am well aware of that tradition, but that was not always the tradition. The first exiles did not wait for any messiah. When Cyrus let them return, they built the Second Temple. Cyrus was not that different from Julian. And we, at least, are Jews."

Rabbi Levi knew enough not to pursue an argument based on tradition with one who rejected part of tradition. Yet Paul Richardson was not totally lost. "The Jews who never went into exile in Babylonia and continued living here knew many things we do not know."

"Such as?" Paul asked.

"Where to put the Temple. Traces of Solomon's Temple were still there. They knew where the Holy of Holies had been. We do not know that. We, who are observant, do not go onto Temple Mount lest we tread on the site of the Holy of Holies."

Paul knew this was true. It had been true for centuries. For how long? When the Arabs conquered Jerusalem, the Jews put a synagogue on Temple Mount. A synagogue was not the Temple, but still they must have known where the Holy of Holies was or they wouldn't have gone up. It was there until the Crusades. The children of Ishmael were kinder to Jerusalem's Jews than the followers of Jesus, and much less vicious.

"They also knew who the Cohenim, the priests, were."

"We still have Cohens."

"But are they really of the priestly tribe? Can they trace their descent from the days of the Temple? No, of course not. We have no true priests. No Cohen Hagadol. No high priest."

That was the truth and Paul knew it. He also knew another reason. Biblical Judaism had been a sacrificial religion, and no one wanted to resurrect such an anachronism in the twentieth century.

"In some other ways," the rabbi continued as if teaching a class of youngsters, "we are well-prepared. We have the plans. We understand them fully. If the Messiah appears, and may the Holy One, blessed be His name, hasten the day of his arrival, we are ready. The plans are there in the last nine sections of Ezekiel. Once we know the exact location, we can start. Once He reveals the exact location and tells us who will be the Cohen Hagadol, we are ready. We know every detail of every Temple ritual, of each sacrifice."

Paul had been wrong. It was the same Third Temple.

As he was leaving the conference room, Paul saw Eleazar Danin. What was . . . ?

"Paul."

"Eleazar."

"You saved that boy's life."

"And you saved mine."

"Perhaps. It's all in a day's work for me. But what you did—"

"Was," Paul interrupted, "all in a day's work for me. We do different things."

"Not so different, perhaps."

Paul shook his head slowly, in agreement.

"It's not over. Far from it. Be careful. You aren't safe. Don't go wandering alone around the countryside."

How had he known that?

"Or even in the Arab quarter after dark. Stay out of East Jerusalem."

"Okay."

"Paul. We have heard a lot of rumblings. This may be just the beginning. Shalom."

"Wait. Was that just a general warning?" Eleazar said nothing. "You know what I mean. Do you tell that to everyone or just me?"

Eleazar merely shrugged his shoulders ambiguously, like a medical student who wasn't quite sure of an answer.

Paul had to go. He was late for rounds. He was probably taking it all too personally. He was not used to being shot at. "You are warning me directly, aren't you?" Paul asked angrily.

Again Eleazar said nothing.

"Why?"

"I hear many things."

"I'll bet you do," Paul replied. "Well, I'm not going to resign from the committee. And I won't whitewash anyone."

"If you are not going to give in, then you must be careful."

"Is that all you have to say?"

"It's all I can say."

Paul left to make rounds without saying another word. Everyone was already waiting for him.

Moshe Tarshish was much worse. His myasthenia had deteriorated rapidly. The steroids were not working.

"How bad is he, John?"

"He can't swallow liquids anymore, so we have him on an I.V. and he's having severe trouble breathing."

"How's his cough reflex?"

John shrugged.

It was Hassan who answered. "It's almost completely absent."

The concern was obvious both in the tone of Paul's voice and in the look on his face. "That makes him a real setup for pneumonia. He's bedridden with poor respiration, lousy swallowing, and can hardly cough to protect himself. John, what would you do?"

"I'm not sure."

"Yes, you are. Think for a minute. If you had that much trouble breathing, what would you want us to do for you?"

"Put me on a respirator."

"Right. Hassan?"

"It's already been arranged. He's being transferred to the ICU"—he looked at his watch—"in about twenty minutes. And once there, he'll be intubated and put on a respirator."

"Very good. What else do you have in store for him, since the steroids aren't doing any damn good?"

Again it was the chief resident who answered Paul's

inquiry. "Plasmapheresis. Professor Schiff came by earlier this morning and he decided to try plasmapheresis."

If he couldn't make all the decisions, he could still teach. "Dalia, what's plasmapheresis?"

"It's sort of like exchange transfusion," she said slowly. Then, faster, "Only different."

"That's as clear as mud. Could you try to explain it a bit better? Take your time."

"I know that you take a patient's blood and run it through a machine . . ."

"Have you ever seen one?"

Dalia shook her head. Hassan filled in the answer.

"We only have one machine and it's only been in use for about five months. I doubt if many of the residents have ever seen it."

Paul nodded. "What does the machine do with the blood?"

It was still Dalia's turn. "It leaves the blood cells but takes away the proteins. It removes the plasma and puts in other plasma."

"Absolutely right. New plasma for old. Now, Yuri, why would that help Mr. Tarshish?"

Yuri Aharoni didn't know.

Nor did John Haddad.

Dalia wasn't sure but she took a stab at it. "Every patient with myasthenia is making antibodies against his own muscle. So these antibodies must travel in the blood as protein. If we get rid of all of his plasma, we'll get rid of whatever antibodies are still in his blood."

"That's right. Now, what will that do for him?"

"It should keep him from getting any worse, since there won't be any new antibodies to attack his muscles."

"In fact," Paul added to end the lesson, "it might also help make him better. There is a balance of sorts among antibodies. When there are no more left in his blood, some may well come off his muscles to keep his balance and he might get stronger."

It was only on the bus ride back to Neve Ilan that he realized that his morning meeting with the rabbi had not been so bad. At least the rabbi had not revealed a personal reason for possibly eliminating the late Rabbi Eckstein, of somewhat tarnished memory. All told, there were seven members of the committee and two of them had motives. Yitzak and Chaim. Two out of seven. .286. Not a bad batting average. No, it was three. Three out of seven. .429. Better even than Hornsby's single-season record. Three: Yitzak, Chaim, and Rivkah.

Had he made love to a murderess? No, he hadn't. That was preposterous. Or was it?

Three out of seven.

He could eliminate himself. He hadn't even been in Israel when it happened. Three out of six. An even .500. And two of them were in the hospital when it happened.

So was Hassan.

Hassan had a motive. One Paul understood all too well.

Did anyone else? Avram? The rabbi? This was getting him nowhere.

No matter what Danin said, he was going to see it through. They couldn't scare him off.

Or could they? He did have a responsibility to his two kids. He was all they had left.

It could not have been Rivkah. She could not have killed anyone. He had forgotten to stop by her lab to ask her over for Shabbat dinner.

When he called her, it turned out to be as much an apology as an invitation. She could come for dinner, but not stay over. Not with Joshua there.

He was embarrassed and angry.

She was neither.

She would be glad to come under any circumstances. She ended their conversation by telling him to stay well and to be careful. They both hung up. He had forgotten to ask her about her work on the Pickwick poisons.

Eleazar's crisp warning came back to him: "It's not over yet. You aren't safe."

Had he meant Paul as a Jew or Dr. Paul Richardson?

No one was trying to kill him.

Of course, they had shot at him, but not specifically him.

Just at him as a random victim.

He shouldn't take it personally.

It wasn't a personal matter.

Did Corporal Teller take it personally?

Paul was damn sure he did.

* * *

Paul stayed at home on Friday. He cleaned house and went shopping. He spent the whole day with Joshua, avoiding the complex issues of both the fourth and twentieth centuries.

Yitzak Cohen worked all day Friday. He had started the next step. Electron microscopy magnified the object being studied up to one hundred thousand times by using electrons rather than beams of light. With this, he could see inside each cell and study each part. All week long they had been using the electron microscope to take pictures of Nahum Eckstein's nerve roots.

Yitzak must have had at least five hundred electron micrographic photographs in front of him, all labeled the same: "N. E. Nerve roots."

It was also difficult for Rivkah Geller to escape from her world. The sample labeled "5742-87" contained twelve cubic centimeters of spinal fluid. She divided it into six samples of two cc's each. There was enough to carry out three separate runs. She took the first two samples, put the other vials back into the locked refrigerator, and then took an aliquot portion of Mrs. Fahoum's spinal fluid. She added small amounts of the four Pickwick toxins to the samples from Mrs. Fahoum and took one of the two labeled "N.E."

She followed what had become her usual routine and recorded the amounts of the substances added to the other two tubes. Then she put the three samples into the thin-layer liquid chromatograph, sat down, and watched the pen as it traced a record of the results on the roll of graph paper.

On the sample from Mrs. Fahoum, the peaks came out one at a time. The first peak measured 817, the second 403, the third 223, the fourth 189.

Excellent recovery.

No false positives.

Just the way it should be.

Next was the one labeled "N.E. Sample One; Recovery Sample." To this one she had added known amounts of the four poisons, as she had to the sample from Mrs. Fahoum.

The peaks came out one at a time:

911
542
271

They were all running a bit too high. They shouldn't be any higher than Mrs. Fahoum's. She had added the same amounts of each toxin to both samples. Maybe she should turn down the sensitivity.

147

No, the last one was a bit low and a few centimeters early. It wasn't the last one. There was one more: 223.

911
542
271
147
223

Five blips. Five peaks. Five toxins?

She had put in four. Was the fifth some of the missing toxin? Were her worst fears coming true?

She checked her figures: 970 was 104 points too high; 974 was 139 points too high; 975 was only 48 points too high, but still too high; 976 was pretty much within range—34 points high, but the Fahoum sample had run a bit low.

The other sample measured 147 points. The results were too high. Was it all just lab errors, a series of false results? Or was there something in Nahum Eckstein's spinal fluid that made things read too high?

Or was that just imagination?

It was just where the missing poison should be, right between 975 and 976. A little closer to 976 than she had calculated, but in the right range.

The next test was on "N. E. Sample Two; Tissue Blank." This one had no added poisons. It should just be a flat line.

As Rivkah watched the graph being drawn, that is what she saw. A long flat line.

A long straight flat line with one peak: 157.

One peak just about where it should have been, to be one of the missing toxins.

Just where it shouldn't have been.

She would have to work on that another time if she wasn't going to be late for dinner, and she certainly didn't want to be late. Why had Paul been so uncomfortable? She knew about his children and would respect their feelings and his.

Should she tell him about her discovery? No, that could wait until she was absolutely certain. Or until they were alone together.

But that was how she had made the first mistake. In bed with a lover. She had to shut down the equipment and leave. Tonight he would not be her lover.

The difference was not a radical one but it was a true departure from form. Some of the cuttings were whole words; others, groups of letters; and then, only when easier, more convenient, there were single letters. As soon as he cut something out, he pasted it on the plain sheet of paper.

He started with a whole word: but.

A letter s.

A word—OF—from a headline.

A letter t.

A word: what.

Another word: light.

A group of letters: thr.

A pair of individual capital letters: U and Y.

A lower case o.

And an upper case N.

Two more upper-case letters: DE.

A lower-case r.

A word: wind.

An upper case O

A w.

A word: breaks.

Then: It.

And: is.

A t.

An H.

A pair in upper case: E, E, cut from a different headline.

The last three-fourths of past: ast.
A word: an.
A capital D.
A series of letters: j, U, l, i, E, t, i, s.
A word: the
Three letters: S, u, N.
He looked at his watch. He'd finished in time. He would make it to the post office with time to spare before the early Shabbat closing.

Dinner was a disaster.
Pat and Jonathan liked Rivkah. She was warm and charming. Their children were not impressed, one way or the other.
Joshua hated her.
Paul had been so careful. He introduced her as a colleague. He was polite, precise. He didn't hug her. He didn't kiss her. He didn't put his arm around her. He sat opposite her at dinner.
Joshua hated her.
When they were alone together later Paul waited for Joshua to say something and Joshua did. There were no tears. Bitterness, but no tears.
"I don't want a new mother."
"Rivkah doesn't want—"
Joshua didn't let Paul finish. "Neither does Carolyn."
"How does—"
"She's too old for you."
"Too old—"
"You should go with someone younger."
"Younger?"
"Yes. Someone who won't want to replace Mom. Someone like Dalia."
Paul was angry but stopped before he said anything, and hugged his son. They both had tears in their eyes now, and not from anger.

14

The following Sunday morning was the beginning of a work week which promised to be even more hectic than the one just completed. According to the early-morning news, almost all of the Arab laborers in Israel had returned to work. Now that the PLO had turned its attention back to its traditional enemies, there seemed to be less anger directed at fellow Arabs. There were no more hand grenades being cast at buses full of Arabs in Gaza, no more threats of fratricide for collaboration with the enemy.

The bus stop at Neve Ilan was more crowded than usual. Three more men from the moshav had been called to active duty in the Israel Defense Force; two for thirty-five days each, one for a mere two weeks. Quiet, prolonged embraces were exchanged, then it was onto the bus. Perhaps there would be a twenty-four hour pass or two.

On Jaffa Road, glaziers were putting new windows into place. The battered cars had been either driven or towed away. The fragments of broken glass had all been swept away. Some bullet-chipped bricks and a few bloodstains were all the physical evidence that remained. Those and the indelible memories.

Rounds were started where Paul felt most useful, at the bedside of a sick patient. They were in the ICU, at the bedside of Moshe Tarshish. Mr. Tarshish was on a respirator. Was it the same one that Rabbi Eckstein had been on? Paul looked around. He could see four other respirators. That made the odds four to one against. What difference did that make? Respirators didn't unplug themselves.

Paul examined Mr. Tarshish carefully. He found generalized weakness, manifest as weakness of the eye muscles and other muscles of his face.

They all watched as two technicians wheeled in another machine and placed it next to the respirators and plugged it in. The large white box had more dials than an EEG machine. Inside this white box, Moshe Tarshish's plasma would be exchanged. His blood would flow out of the one tube now being attached to a vein in his left arm, through the machine, and back through another tube into his right arm. His red blood cells would leave his body and return unchanged. His white cells would leave, traverse the white box, and come back unscathed. His plasma, however, would be exchanged for plasma from normal donors. In this way the antibodies which were attacking his muscles would be slowly but surely filtered out. In a period of three hours about one-half of the circulating antibodies would be removed. Fifty percent each day. How many more would his body manufacture each day? How many would come off the muscles? And how quickly? Only time would tell—time and one plasmapheresis session each day.

They went from the ICU back to the Neurology conference room.

Mrs. Fahoum remained seizure-free. She could remember everything that had happened before she got sick and could now remember new events. At lunchtime she could tell them what she had had for breakfast. At dinnertime she could remember both lunch and breakfast, although not perfectly. But each day she was getting better. Next week she would go back home, back to southern Lebanon.

She was not, Paul was told, Lebanese. She was a Palestinian refugee, living in southern Lebanon and wondering what her future would be like now that she had been given back her health.

Rivkah Geller's new week began in the same way the previous week had ended, studying the spinal-fluid samples. Over the one-day weekend, when she was not thinking about Paul and Joshua and Joshua's obvious dislike of her, she had gone over this project in her mind from beginning to end.

She hoped Paul hadn't been hurt by Joshua's response.

She hadn't. She didn't want to replace his mother. Or did she? She stopped herself. She had not allowed herself to consider that possibility. Would the Richardsons move here? It was a nice fantasy. Much better than being obsessed about Pickwick poisons and remembering David. He seemed further away than ever.

She had worked it out Saturday night. There was one more step to be completed, one final step. Or was it final?

This simple biochemical determination of levels was becoming more complex, each step led to another. It was like most research, you were never really through. There was always something else you could do, something else to eliminate, some other possibility to control for, but eventually you had to draw the line. So far, it had gone well. The method worked. Normals were normal. Patients with neurologic diseases were virtually all normal. Rabbi Eckstein had not been normal. His spinal fluid had a peak of seven nanograms in the region where Pickwick 971 would appear.

He must have been poisoned. Unless his specific disease caused a false positive reading. This was the last question she had to answer. The other neurologic diseases had involved other parts of the nervous system. The brain itself. The spinal cord. The cerebellum. Eckstein's disease had involved only the nerves. Perhaps the injured nerves themselves produced some substance which caused the false result. She had to be one hundred percent sure. She had to study samples from patients with diseases of the nerves. After all, that one patient with facial diplegia, involvement of just two nerves, had had a false positive reading. It had been in a different spot, to be sure, but in the general range. It was possible that different neuropathies resulted in different false positives—one of which could masquerade as 971.

She had no idea how Neurology ever got all those samples as quickly as it had, but she was very happy to have them.

Six samples from patients with diseases of the nerves.

The process began again. A tissue blank, a recovery sample, a Fahoum control.

When she was done, three out of the six samples had

registered an added peak and all of them were in the 972
spot, like Nahum Eckstein's. Fifty percent!

One-half of the patients with diseases of the nerves had
a 972 spike. Why had Nahum Eckstein fallen in that fifty
percent? Luck? Random chance? Good luck? Bad luck?
Maybe he really fell into the other fifty percent and had
been given 972. That was possible, wasn't it?

She restudied the list.

When she included Nahum Eckstein, it was four out of
seven. Over fifty percent. It was the diseased nerves that
caused the blip, not any poison. Half of the patients with
diseased nerves had the same extra peak on the graph.
And none of them could have been poisoned. She felt as
if a great weight had been removed from her shoulders.
She wanted to tell Paul, but he had already left for the
day and she didn't want to bother him at home.

Hassan was not at the bus stop waiting for Paul when
he got off at Abu Gosh this time. There was a group of
Arab children waiting for their fathers, two dust-covered
construction workers returning from rebuilding the new
Jewish quarter of Jerusalem. Paul watched as the noisy
group crossed the street behind the bus and entered the
narrow winding streets of the town. He could hear the
high-pitched, excited voices long after he lost sight of
them.

He was not sure what he should do. The next bus was
not due for an hour and a half. He walked back up the
road to the Caravan and sat on the open patio overlooking
the golden-tan bricks and domes of Abu Gosh.

He ordered a Pepsi. A rare treat in Israel. Pepsi long
ago had caved in to Arab pressure and stopped selling in
Israel. But they sold to Jordan, and the Jordanian distrib-
utors supplied East Jerusalem and even some of West
Jerusalem, and some Arab stores and restaurants.

He should have ordered a Coke. Coca-Cola never gave
in to the Arab boycott. Only in Israel does your choice
of soft drink have political significance.

He counted the domes.

He counted the minarets.

He ordered a second Pepsi.

He still had over an hour to wait for the next bus.

He recognized the dome of Hassan's house. He was

sure he could find it even in that unfamiliar maze of streets. He sipped his second Pepsi.

"Professor Richardson." It was a familiar voice.

Not friendly but familiar.

"You seem surprised, Hassan. You shouldn't be. I did say I would come back soon."

"Why didn't you tell me?"

"Sit down. Have a Coke or something."

Hassan's order was apolitical. Coffee.

Neither the professor nor the student knew where to start.

"I was not sure I would be comfortable. Or . . . even welcome. When I got on the bus, I figured I would stop by and just say hello, but when I got off here, I wasn't so sure."

"You know my house." It was more a statement than a question.

"Yes. I recognized it. I'm even sure I could find it from here."

"You are always welcome. Friends are always welcome in an Arab home."

"And strangers?"

"Of course."

"Which am I? A friend or a stranger—an outsider whom you welcome only because of your traditions?" He didn't give the young Arab time to answer. "My traditions are different. It's not just that I am a Jew. I'm an American. I neither give nor take friendship lightly." He stopped to order some coffee and resumed again. "I didn't know that Mrs. Fahoum was a Palestinian." Paul was not sure why he had said that.

"Would that have made any difference to you?" Hassan asked.

"No . . . yes. Yes, it would have."

"Would you have treated her any differently?"

"No, of course not."

"Would you have come that day?"

"I would have come if she had been Mrs. Yassir Arafat. I would have felt differently. But I would have come. And I would have done everything I did. But I would not have felt the same."

"Why? I am a Palestinian Arab as much as she is. In

'forty-eight, her family left. Mine stayed. What's the difference?''

"The difference? Palestinians. Refugees. Jews should always be sensitive to the problems of refugees. We've been refugees for twenty-five hundred years.'' Paul tried to explain, but made little headway. It made little sense to Hassan. To Hassan, Israel created most of the problem; to Paul, the Arabs.

"Professor Richardson, even you must admit this was all our land.''

"But they left," Paul reminded him. "Of their own free will.''

"Because of the Israeli victory.''

"And Arab propaganda that the Jews would kill and rape and pillage,'' Paul added.

"Yes.''

"So they chose voluntarily to leave, right?''

"Yes,'' Hassan admitted.

"And the neighboring countries took them in.''

"Yes,'' Hassan agreed.

"As fellow Arabs.''

"Yes.''

"They welcomed the strangers into their midst as Arabs should.''

"Yes, sir.''

"And then kept them strangers in their midst. They gave them no land. No rights. No homes. They kept them refugees. Well, we have refugees too, but we don't keep them as strangers. We call them brother and give them citizenship. A Jewish refugee in nineteen-forty-eight has now been a citizen of Israel for over thirty years. His children are sabras. An Arab refugee is still that. Not a brother. Not a citizen. A political football bounced out of Jordan into Lebanon. Fuel to fire the flame of hatred. Would I have felt differently? You're damn right I would have. Not about her as a patient, but about her as a political fact which I can do nothing about and which may someday destroy this land. Hassan, Israel saved her life. The least the Arabs can do is give her some land she can call her own.''

Paul walked back to the moshav alone.

He was a single solitary figure, in the twilight, on a quiet road cutting through the Judean Hills from Abu

Gosh to Neve Ilan. The road was only a few hundred paces from the old green line.

Suddenly two phrases came to his mind uninvited. They were more like two warnings.

"It's not over yet. Far from it."

"Don't go wandering around the countryside alone."

Paul had said that he wouldn't, but here he was all by himself on a lonely country road, a few hundred yards from the old Green Line. The sun was setting and he was suddenly very chilly. He started to walk more quickly. There was really nothing to worry about. No one wanted to kill him. Then why had they shot at him? Merely because he was there? Now he was here. It wasn't very comforting. There were so many rocks a terrorist could hide behind in order to pick him off. He was an easy target. His eyes scanned the hillsides, from one rock to the next, from an olive tree to an old stone fence.

Honk.

Paul heard the shrill blast of the horn and dove into the hillside, landing on his injured shoulder and ripping yet another shirt in the process.

The brakes squeaked and the taxi swerved briefly and then continued down the road at seventy miles an hour.

Paul sat up, rubbed his shoulder, and took a deep breath. No one was trying to kill him. But he might get killed. Business as usual. Each year more Israelis were killed in auto accidents than in war and terrorism combined. The hell with the terrorists. The Israelis were a greater threat. That was what Eleazar had said, and he hadn't been referring to the drivers. "If you aren't going to give in, then you must be careful." Paul had assumed he was referring to Arab terrorists. But Eleazar had not specified Arabs. The night air suddenly got much colder.

Paul and Joshua had dinner together by themselves and took advantage of their privacy to talk of important things. The White Sox. They were still in third place and still struggling. They were even having trouble defeating hapless Minnesota. Was it the pitching or the defense? From the brief line scores in the *Herald Tribune*, it was impossible to tell.

After dinner, Joshua went next door to watch the World Cup and Paul returned to the fourth century accompanied by some Beethoven. To Julian, the Jews were just another nation, and each nation had a right to its own god. More than a right, an obligation. Julian wrote to Hillel II, the head of all Palestinian Jewry, outlining his entire plan.

How had the patriarch Hillel and the Sanhedrin responded? Was this a turning point? A return to past glory? A revival? Would Jerusalem once again be the capital of Judea? No longer Aelia Capitolina?

But could Julian be trusted? Was he really interested in the welfare of a Jewish state? And what would happen after Julian? Emperors came and went at a startling pace.

The Third Temple would also change the power structure. There would once again be a High Priest of the Temple, a Cohen Hagadol, the leader of all Judiasm. Would that be good for the Jews? Or would it all crumble again when the climate changed?

It would not be good for Hillel. The House of Hillel was not of priestly descent. Priestly authority and with it political power would go to someone else. And so would the money; the tax on all Jews throughout the Roman Empire would go to the Temple, to the new High Priest.

Hillel was a loyal Jew, dedicated to his religion. He wouldn't have opposed the Temple solely for personal reasons. A pagan rebuilding Jerusalem was bad enough. A pagan attempting to rebuild the Temple in a sea of hostile Christians was far worse; it was dangerous. The entire project hung on the life of one man, Julian. No emperor lived forever. Hillel knew that most Roman emperors didn't last too long. It would be like putting all your eggs in one thin, fragile basket. A dangerous gamble at best. More likely betting your life savings on the White Sox to win it all. It could happen. It had twice. But don't bet on it. The Sox were the team that had thrown the World Series in 1919.

15

Eleazar was standing in front of a map of part of the Old City. He did not look up when Paul walked in but merely grunted a "Shalom." Paul recognized the map. It showed the Temple Mount and the adjacent areas. "I have been giving your problem some thought," Eleazar said.

"Have you reached any conclusions?"

"As a matter of fact, I have."

"That's great." Paul hesitated in order to allow Eleazar to divulge his thoughts, but Eleazar said nothing as he continued to study the map. "Would you like to share them with me?"

Eleazar chuckled and turned toward Paul. "No one had any personal motives," he said.

Personal motives? Who could have a personal motive for building a Temple? Or for destroying one that wasn't even open for business yet?

"It had to be political" Eleazar continued.

Political? Julian had no political enemies. There were no false pretenders. There were political usurpers waiting in the wings. There always were in Rome. But in 363 there were no hints of revolt anywhere in the empire. "Are you sure it had to be political?" Paul asked.

"What else?"

"What else? Religious," Paul suggested.

Eleazar looked quizzically at Paul for a moment. "Religious? Religion and politics are so intermingled here it's almost the same thing."

"But the Christians."

"What Christian would have wanted to kill Eckstein?"

"Oh, God, I thought you were talking about Julian and the Third Temple."

"Paul, I am not a historian. Remember, you're the

223

professor, not me. I was talking about Rabbi Eckstein's untimely death.''

''So I finally figured out.''

''There were no jealous husbands. No estranged lovers. No revengeful business partners. His life was exactly what we know about from reading the newspaper. No skeletons in his personal closet.''

''Which leaves us with . . .''

''Arab fanatics or perhaps some fanatic within his own organization who thought he was not radical enough.'' Yet Paul knew differently. People had personal motives. Chaim Abramowitz. Or was the loss of his son in Hebron really a political matter? Or Yitzak Cohen. The loss of one's entire family was certainly more personal than political.

Was the defection of David from Rivkah's bed to the Guardians a personal or a political loss? It all depended on your perspective. Eleazar might consider it political. Most Israelis would. Here religion, politics, and survival merged and became inseparable. For Israelis politics had become a way of life, were life itself. Few Americans took politics that seriously. Paul was beginning to understand that difference. It was a mere short-range rocket trip from Lebanon to the heart of Israel.

It all had to matter. Each issue. Each inch of land. Each life. The life of Chaim's son, of Rivkah's David.

Yet there were also personal issues, very personal, and Rivkah at least was certainly not primarily a political animal. Romain Bernhard, on the other hand, was, and his motive was also political. So was Hassan's. Could Yitzak's vengeance be called political? Had the Hatfields ever tried to outvote the McCoys? Was not the Capulet-Montague feud political? And religious? Somehow it didn't help. Whether he considered the motives to be personal or political, they were still there. They didn't disappear.

As Paul continued to stare at the map, lost in his own thoughts, Eleazar brought out the latest message.

but sOFt what light thrU YoNDEr windOw breaks
It is tHE East anD jUliEt is the SuN

Paul had little to add. The lines were from *Romeo and Juliet*. Maybe they merely meant what they said. The break of day. Sunrise on Tisha B'Av.

"Fortunately," Paul said as he got up to leave, "I don't have to solve the murder of Nahum Eckstein. Only the mystery of his death. Even if we decide he was killed, I don't have to find out who committed the murder."

"Are you sure?"

"Of course," Paul said automatically. It had been a strange question, especially coming from Eleazar. Paul accepted it at its face value. "I am not going to give in."

"I never thought that you would."

That was all that Eleazar said. Paul had the distinct impression that the "consultant" wanted to tell him something more. Perhaps he couldn't. Was it just another vague warning that the other man was unable to get out? Or something more specific? The silence became awkward for both of them. It was time to leave.

"L'hit," Paul said.

"Yes, L'hit," came the reply.

Jaffa Road was as busy as ever.

The bloodstains were hardly visible. Paul could just make out the outline of the spots left by the corporal who had fallen on top of him. Had some of that blood been his own? He touched his shoulder proudly.

Jaffa Road reminded him of the shopping streets of the Chicago of his youth, a series of personally owned and managed small stores. Real stores, not franchises.

No McDonald's. He bought a piece of pizza.

No Baskin-Robbins. And some freshly squeezed orange juice.

No Waldenbooks. He stopped in Steinmatzky's and picked up a *Herald Trib*. The Sox had won. It would be a good day.

Avram had asked Paul to stop by before he made rounds. He had to ask a favor of him. The war of nerves was still going on. There were still thousands and thousands of Israelis within Lebanon, waiting, hoping. Today the cease-fire was in place, but they had to be prepared. Doctors were still being rotated back and forth. Avram had just been there on an inspection tour. If Paul could take over the service completely, they could send another of their doctors north.

Of course he could. What did it involve? Making

rounds every day. But only for a week. The next week, Paul would be free: to work on the final report of the committee. He had somehow lost track of time. It surprised him that there were only two weeks left until the report was due. That also meant that it was only two weeks until Tisha B'Av.

He had so much else he wanted to do. Still, he was glad to do whatever he could to help out.

Paul asked if the operating-room nurse was still in Lebanon. He was. Avram also told Paul about the curious nature of the war in the north. The Israeli troops were being greeted as liberators by most of the population, yet Israel was being castigated publicly by both enemies and friends alike. Avram could not understand the former. He hoped that events would help to unify the country. The doves were only a small minority. And not so long ago, the country had been even more divided because of Yamit. He had been there. He had seen it himself. Religious fanatics, Jews dressed all in black, slapping Israeli soldiers. The same Jews who did not have to serve in the army could attack it.

"I thought everyone had to serve."

"No, the ultraorthodox who study are exempt."

"You mean guys like Eckstein and his supporters can go around piously causing trouble with the Arabs and not have to go in the army?"

"That's right."

"Some people must hate that."

"Only every mother with a son in the army. Every wife with a husband. Every child."

"I get the point."

Paul had to leave. It was time to make rounds. He walked over to the Neurology ward by himself. The conversation with Avram disturbed him. He liked to think of Israel as the promised land, not as a struggling democracy divided against itself.

Had one of those divisive problems led to the death of Rabbi Eckstein?

Had some bereaved mother who had lost a son done it?

Eckstein had lost his own sons. His sons had not dodged the draft. Did that make him a traitor to his own cause?

Abram had volunteered to be in Yamit at the end. Why? There were some things that had to be done.

Paul had asked him what had happened at Yamit.

The protesters had been removed and the town had been given back to Egypt. But not as Yamit. As Israel had found it. Not as a prospering agricultural village, but as a piece of desert.

Each tree had been uprooted, each building either moved or torn down, each road destroyed.

Yamit was once again part of the Sinai Desert and of Egypt.

Not one stone had been left standing upon another.

Teaching rounds went by quickly. Mr. Tarshish had had a total of two sessions of plasmapheresis. His weakness had not progressed. His eye movements were a little bit better. His breathing was no different. He was still in the ICU. He was still on a respirator.

The only new patient admitted over the weekend was a seventy-year-old woman named Goldstein with a severe stroke resulting in right-sided weakness and total loss of speech. Complete aphasia. He taught them a little more about the history of aphasia. How Broca, whose name was now associated with total—or Broca's—aphasia, had not been the first one to show that the left side of the brain controlled both the right arm and leg and also speech. That critical association had first been made by nineteenth-century phrenologists—charlatans who felt the bumps on people's skulls. Who had written the first description of aphasia? He wasn't sure. He asked Dalia to comment on this, hoping she would tell them the interpretation she had told him last week. Once again she surprised him.

"It may be in the First Book of the Maccabees," she told them. "There is a description there that may be of aphasia. It happened to Alcinus. He was the high priest who wanted to Hellenize our people and our religion. Alcinus ordered that the wall of the inner court of the sanctuary should be torn down. Then he himself began to pull down the words of the prophet and was struck with palsy."

"Which side?" Paul asked. "Right or left?"

Dalia didn't know. The text didn't say. "All it says is 'palsy.' All we know is that he had a palsy and his mouth stopped and could no longer speak or give orders. Shortly afterward, he died.''

"Palsy and inability to speak" Paul said. "That certainly sounds like it could be a stroke with aphasia. You should write them both up.''

Only Dalia knew what he meant when he said "both," and she just nodded and sat back in her quiet way.

The committee meeting that day seemed to go on forever. Yitzak Cohen showed over a hundred slides of electron-micrographs. His conclusion? Typical severe Guillain-Barré. Would Rabbi Eckstein have survived? He wasn't sure. He had sent copies of the slides to two outside consultants. The reports would be back in less than two weeks, just before Tisha B'Av.

Rivkah gave them a preliminary report of her findings. She would review her methods and the results once more before she gave her final report. So far she had not found anything unusual except in a patient who had facial weakness and recovered. She was certain that that had not been meaningful. These poisons didn't cause just a little bit of disease.

Again, the cutting was a mixture of single letters, sets of two, three or four letters, and a couple of words. The source was different, however: the slick pages of *Time* magazine had been substituted for the cheap newsprint of the Jerusalem *Post* or the *Herald Tribune*.

He started with a word: the.

A pair of letters: ki.

Two single capital letters: N and G.

Then four single letters: s, A, b, E.

A set of two: gg.

An upper case A.

A lower-case r.

A lower-case n.

Two more capital letters: O and W.

A pair: th.

Three in upper case: E, P, and L.

A second a.

An upper-case Y.

A word: is.

A four-letter word, cut from a headline—all upper case:
DONE.

>   the kiNGs A bEggar
>   nOW thE PLaY is DONE

One copy.
Pasted, folded, stuffed, stamped, addressed, and mailed.
Now the play was about to begin.

It had been Rivkah's suggestion. Instead of a fancy dinner, they should go to the annual Jerusalem Art Fair and have a falafel or shawrma and eat while they wandered among the exhibits. The Art Fair was held in what had once been No-Man's-Land, the northern branch of the Valley of Hinnon, which cut between the western wall of the Old City and the New City. Thirty centuries ago, Canaanites had sacrificed children here. Thirty years ago, Jordanian sharpshooters had taken potshots at children playing in the valley. Now it was strung with lanterns and crowded with food sellers and displays of watercolors, jewelry, rugs, sculpture, oil paintings and even macramé.

While many considered falafel to be the national food of Israel, Paul had never developed a taste for deep-fried balls of ground-up chick-peas. He preferred the Israeli version of gyros, made of turkey and called shawrma. So did Rivkah.

Hand in hand, they enjoyed the cool evening. They each bought a picture, a watercolor of Jerusalem by Ben Avram. Rivkah chose one of a quiet street in the Old City dominated by a glimpse of the golden tip of the Dome of the Rock. Paul chose one of the western wall. It was his first picture that was without old memories.

"Rivkah."

Paul immediately recognized the voice. He did not have to turn to see who it was.

"Elie," she replied.

Eleazar and Rivkah knew each other.

Rivkah and Elie hugged warmly.

They knew each other well.

"I didn't know you two were . . . friends," Paul said by way of greeting.

Eleazar chuckled. "It's nothing to be jealous of. We are old friends."

"Oh."

"We worked together on a security committee for the rebuilding of Hadassah Hospital on Mount Scopus."

"I see," Paul said.

"We had met before that, of course," Eleazar added.

"Of course."

"Jerusalem is a small town," Rivkah said. "Everyone knows everyone else."

That was what Dalia had said.

"And his or her private . . . affairs," Paul added.

"That is my business," Eleazar reminded him.

"Come on, you two." With that Rivkah placed herself between them and took their arms. It was her aim to bring them together, not separate them. "Let's look at the leather goods. I need a purse."

Arm in arm, the three of them walked down the Valley of Hinnon to pick out a purse for Rivkah. She disengaged herself to fondle the merchandise. She needed a large dark purse. She inspected a black one that Paul thought was much too large.

"I suppose that Dean Ben Zvi is also an old friend," Paul said half-sarcastically.

"He was on the same committee," Eleazar replied.

The small brown one was also nice.

Had Eleazar helped select the members of his committee? Paul somehow had had the idea that the dean had done that all by himself, naive American that he was. No one had ever told him who had done the choosing. And he had never asked.

Rivkah asked them which purse she should get.

Paul had no idea.

"Both," Eleazar said, and with that he bid them good night. He had work to do.

Paul understood. The work of a consultant in security was never done.

Afterward, the two of them went to Rivkah's apartment.

He wanted to ask her how much Eleazar knew.

She kissed him.

How much she had told him.

She hugged him.

When he had become involved.

She pressed against him urgently.

Converstion was not on her mind. Nor on his. Once again Paul undressed her. Awkward fumbling and anxiety were now long past, replaced by a subdued wonder and excitement.

It was well after one when she drove him back through the Judean Hills to Neve Ilan. It all happened so suddenly that neither of them realized it was happening until it was almost too late. Rivkah drove slowly. She was in no hurry to say good night to him. Cars passed them in a steady stream. One after another.

The road was dark.

And narrow.

And winding through the hillsides.

More and more cars raced past them. Paul's hand was resting on her thigh. On the naked skin of her upper thigh, moving back and forth softly and unhurriedly over the softness of her upper thigh.

More cars whizzed by.

Then one pulled up next to their car and swerved toward them.

Paul yelled.

Rivkah slammed on her brakes.

The car skidded to the right.

Onto the narrow shoulder—above a sixty- or seventy-foot drop.

The other car lurched forward and disappeared into the darkness of the Judean Hills.

"Asshole," Paul said.

"Damn," she said. "I shouldn't have let you distract me so. I almost got us killed."

Her heart was pounding so hard that her breasts were quivering with each beat.

Paul's heart was also pounding.

It had been a close call.

Had they been distracted? He was skeptical. The hills were not safe. Not for him. Should he warn her? It was not her problem. Besides, he could be wrong. Why worry her? "Let me distract you some more," he suggested.

After all, his hand was still underneath her skirt and they were already off the road.

It was nearly two in the morning when they got back to Neve Ilan. They kissed and exchanged pictures: he now had the street scene and she the western wall. It was now a street scene with new memories. He could feel her warm body pressed against him as he held her and kissed her again. She was naked beneath her thin dress. Was Joshua asleep? He was a sound sleeper. Paul could feel his own urgency reappearing. It surprised him. As they kissed again, Paul saw Joshua's head appear in his window, watching them. He was not asleep. Paul's urgency disappeared. Rivkah understood. They said good night.

Paul went into Joshua's room. He was pretending to be asleep. Paul sat on the bed and started to talk to his son. There was no anger in his mood or his voice. No frustration.

"She doesn't want to be your mother."

Joshua opened his eyes. Even in the dark, Paul knew there were tears there.

"Nor take me away from you."

Paul could hear his son fighting back the tears.

"I don't like her."

"Why?"

"She is too much . . . like . . ."

"Mom?" It was a suggestion made softly.

The answer came slowly. "I like Dalia."

"Dr. Avni?"

"Yes. She told me to call her Dalia. She came by again to play catch with me. We talked. She's fun. She is taking me to the Rockefeller Museum on Thursday. She has the afternoon off. Come with us, Dad."

"Maybe, but if you have this date with a pretty girl, I shouldn't butt in."

"Dad!"

They both laughed.

"Come with us."

"Okay," Paul said. Dalia was closer in age to Joshua than she was to him, and somehow she had reached Joshua and his needs. Better than Paul had. And certainly better than Rivkah. Rivkah's interest was not in his children. He was glad of that.

"I told her about Dr. Geller."

"You what?"

"I'm sorry, Dad. Don't be mad at me."

"That's all right."

"That's what she said."

"What?"

"That it's all right. That you weren't leaving me or trying to replace Mom."

"She's right."

"I know, but still . . ."

Mr. Tarshish was significantly improved. He was off his respirator. His speech was more distinct, less slurred. His swallowing was much better. Strength was returning to his arms and legs. They would watch him in the ICU for another day or two, and then bring him back to the Neurology floor.

The non-war in Lebanon was off the front pages. Iran had invaded Iraq, giving the UN and the U.S. something else to worry about. And Israel too. The Ayatollah had announced that conquering Iraq was the first step in regaining Jerusalem for the Arabs. Of course only Israel was concerned enough about that motive to devote any news time or space to it. Paul was certain that no American newspaper would carry the story. And it certainly would not make the evening news on any of the networks.

The Israel Defense Force remained in place around Beirut. The brief incursion was assuming the same temporary air as the Soviet move into Afghanistan.

Paul was happy to leave the Jerusalem of 1982 and move back in his imagination to a less personally threatening era. Julian was disappointed by the cool reception his project received from the patriarch Hillel and the Sanhedrin. But Julian was a shrewd politician. He knew what to do. He appealed directly to the people, to the community of Jews scattered throughout the empire. They would support the new Temple. The special tax on Jews would now go to rebuilding the Temple.

Then Julian set out for Persia, and the building began. Disaster struck. Or was it disaster?

An earthquake. A fire. Destruction. Cyril, the Bishop of Jerusalem, had foretold the event several days before it occurred.

Was it arson? Or was it an earthquake?

One thing bothered Paul. Why had the Jews not even hinted at arson, nor even accused the minions of Cyril? Was it because Julian had died so soon afterward? Jovian became the emperor. Christianity was truly triumphant, and the destruction of the Temple became a Christian legend. It was best to leave Christian legends unscathed and make no mention at all of the Third-Temple. Accusations that the Christians had sabotaged the construction would have been very dangerous, like accusing the Nazis of burning down the Reichstadt.

It was getting late. Joshua wasn't home yet. There was no need to worry. He was perfectly safe. He must be watching the late show on Jordanian TV, an old American movie with Arabic subtitles and free propaganda.

It was time for a change.

Paul took out the reprints of papers he had brought home from the library.

The first two he just threw on a pile on the buffet far from his chair. It was much easier to request a paper and have someone make a Xerox copy of it for you than to actually read it. And once you had a copy, which you carefully kept in your permanent file, you must know what it said. Why else would you keep it?

The third paper was different. He didn't carelessly disregard it. He devoured it, word by word, illustration by illustration, especially the electron micrographs.

He pulled out the pictures Yitzak Cohen had passed out. They were just like the ones in the article. And these patients had all died. So had Rabbi Eckstein. They had not died because someone had pulled the plug, but dead was dead.

What would their nerve roots have looked like if they had recovered? Could they have recovered? Or did they just remain paralyzed until they got pneumonia, the friend of the debilitated patient, and died?

Would the rabbi have recovered?

He read on.

There it was, the micrograph he needed to see—the nerve root from a patient with severe Guillain-Barré, who had recovered, and died years later. Had her Guillain-Barré syndrome been as severe as Eckstein's? He checked the case report. The patient had been on a respirator for more than six weeks. She'd had pneumonia twice. But thanks to antibiotics, she had recovered, to die three years later of . . . he checked carefully. A heart attack.

Paul looked intently at the illustration. The roots had been devastated and the patient had lived, and the roots had repaired themselves.

As devastated as Rabbi Eckstein's? Probably.

She'd needed a respirator for six weeks.

But then again, how could he be sure?

Had the respirator been on automatic or assist? The report didn't say. They never did. How could you ever be sure?

If a patient died and you saw his roots, how did you know if he would have recovered if pneumonia hadn't killed him?

If he recovered, how did you know what they would have looked like if he had died?

It was catch-22—only more so.

Somebody pulled the plug. Who?

Hassan had been there. Hassan, an Israeli Arab, must have hated Rabbi Eckstein. Hassan had asked Paul if he would have acted differently if he had known that Mrs. Fahoum was a Palestinian.

Of course he wouldn't have. That was a reflex answer. Was it true? Wasn't he more likely to go back to the hospital at two in the morning for a sick rabbi than a ghetto junkie? You tried not to, but . . .

Hassan. Motive. Opportunity.

Hell, anyone in a white coat had the opportunity. Security was not much better at Maimonides than it was in Chicago.

Chaim Abramowitz. He was in the unit then. He was an American sports fan. Maybe he switched from the Jerusalem *Post* to the *Herald Tribune* to check out the sports results.

He might as well be suspicious of Rivkah. Shakespeare had said it best. "Hell hath no fury like a woman scorned." Rivkah. Paul just didn't believe she could do it. And besides, she was working so hard on those samples. If she had killed Eckstein, why would she go through all of this? As an elaborate cover-up?

Not Rivkah. Could a woman give herself as selflessly

as she had and be a murderess? He hated the obvious answer.

Chaim; perhaps.

Romain; perhaps. Israel was his entire life. Would he hesitate to kill if he thought that that life was truly threatened? Wasn't that self-defense?

Yitzak; why not? He had one hell of a good reason to hate the entire Eckstein clan.

Hassan; a definite possibility which needed no explaining.

Even Avram must have hated Eckstein after Yamit. Enough to kill him? Why not?

Maybe they took a page from Agatha Christie and each one pulled the plug partway out until it finally fell out by its own weight.

Not Rivkah. Of course she had been very protective of the samples. Yitzak had sent the slides and micrographs out for second opinions. She insisted on doing it all herself. Could that activity be a smokescreen? Maybe her friend was still in the Guardians and was the one who had killed Nahum Eckstein.

That would make her an accessory after the fact. Unless she was in the hospital that morning.

Someone else should check those samples.

She could have been there that morning. Chaim was. Romain Bernhard was in the hospital getting ready for surgery. Yitzak was there starting an autopsy. Avram always got in by six-thirty. That had been his routine for years.

The whole damn committee could have been there. Except Rabbi Levi.

Any one of them. . . .

Eleazar opened the letter without any excitement and only some curiosity. It was much as one opens a bank statement, curious to know whether the bank agrees with one's own records, but without fear. Eleazar didn't even use a letter opener to help preserve the envelope. Whether or not he preserved it made no difference. It would be untraceable.

As always, it contained a single sheet of plain white paper.

the kiNGs A bEggar
nOW thE PLaY is DONE

He immediately picked up his copy of Shakespeare and
began flipping the pages. It took him some time. It wasn't
from a history. Nor one of the great tragedies. One of
the comedies perhaps? A closing couplet. That was easy
to check.
All's Well That Ends Well. Not quite the closing couplet, but close enough. The first line of the Epilogue:

The King's a beggar, now the play is done.
All is well ended if this suite be won,
That you express content; which we will pay
With strife to please you, day exceeding day
Ours be your patience then and yours our parts:
Your gentle hands lead us and take our hearts.

EXEUNT OMNES

"Now the play is done." The last message. There
would be no more. He spread them out on his desk. Eight
obscure notes, signifying something. But what?

Sarkis Boyajian sipped his tea and listened.
Paul's tea got cold in his glass as he spoke, almost
without a stop, not hurriedly, not excitedly, but contin-
uously. He recited the history of the Third Temple from
the viewpoint of the House of Hille—the Jewish version.
His usual flair for telling a story, his enthusiasm for
his subject, his drive to get his point across, were all
missing.
"There are several things which I don't understand,
Paul. Aspects, some of which, I am sure, are also discon-
certing to you," Sarkis said when Paul was through.
"Such as?" It was almost a challenge on Paul's part,
as if a pet but insecure thesis were being attacked. Did
he have a vested interest in this version?
Sarkis seemingly ignored Paul's tone, and went on.
"You tell me it as if it had to be sabotage."
"Yes."
"Why? Is there any proof?"
"No."

"Then why are you merely rejecting a miracle out of hand? Because it favored Christians, not Jews?"

"No, of course not." He was more excited now. "Hillel said it was a miracle which was part of God's promise to his people."

"But you don't believe what he said. Why do you reject the hypothesis?"

"Sabotage is more logical, more likely," Paul answered firmly.

"Miracles are never logical or likely. If they were, they wouldn't be miracles."

"Nor predictable." It was more of a challenge than an answer.

"Unless God has announced them beforehand. The Ten Plagues, for instance."

"But Cyril never claimed that God had spoken to him, announced the miracle to him. Yet he made the prediction, so he must have known beforehand, on his own, that it would happen. He knew what would occur and when it would happen. He must have planned it or at least been aware of the plan."

Sarkis nodded slowly.

"And it wasn't the first time. The Temple of Apollo outside of Antioch burned down just as Julian was to reintroduce ritual sacrifices. Unless of course you want to suggest a succession of miraculous fires."

It was getting more difficult, but Sarkis continued to ignore Paul's sarcasm and bitterness. "You are convinced it was sabotage?"

"Yes."

"Done by Christians?"

"Absolutely." Defiance replaced mere sarcasm.

"Which Christians?"

"Cyril."

"Not very likely."

"Why not?"

"Let us assume you are correct. Cyril knew beforehand and announced the upcoming miracle. What would have happened?"

"I'm not sure."

"Paul, you are no fool. When a government receives a threat, what does it do? Don't forget, Julian was a Roman emperor, not the elected representative of some weak government. He was a strong emperor. His local governors had total power, total authority, and were expected to use it. Public opinion was not a factor. No one worried what the UN might do.''

"I doubt if the Romans would have done anything directly to Cyril.''

"Why not?''

"It wasn't Julian's style. He believed that persecution resulted in martyrs, and the last thing Julian wanted was more Christian martyrs, more saints. His attacks were more subtle. Anyway, the church was already quite strong. The Nazis rarely attacked bishops. Even the Communists hesitate. Close observation. House arrest, maybe. Nothing more.''

"And the construction site?'' When Paul said nothing, Sarkis asked again more directly, "What would the Romans have done on the Temple Mount at the threatened site?''

A slow, measured answer. "Increased security. Guards. The Moorish cavalry stationed at Aelia Capitolina would have been alerted.''

"Were they?''

"No . . .''

"Why not?''

"The prediction was never made public.''

"Correct, Paul. In fact, was it ever made before the miracle, or was it merely made in retrospect by Cyril, as a form of self-aggrandizement?''

"We have his letter.''

"We have a fifth- or sixth-century copy of his letter in Syriac. And what is it? A copy of an undated letter which described both the prediction and the event.'' Sarkis continued to press his point. "So we can't be sure if Cyril really made the prediction of an impending miracle.''

"You cannot dismiss the parallel with the Temple of Apollo.''

"I don't, but that is only one incident, and we have no proof how that fire started. Now, Paul, if it was sabotage, where were the firebombs—naptha, I presume . . .''

Paul nodded his agreement.

"Where were they planted?'' Sarkis didn't wait for an answer. "Somewhere in the hidden recesses below the

Temple Mount, below the site of the Temple of Solomon.
'The bowels of the earth' was your phrase, I think.''

Again a nod.

"But Christians did not visit the Temple Mount; they
used it as a garbage heap. Only one group of Christians,
the Judeo-Christians, the Minims, would have been able
to hide a firebomb in the bowels of the earth below the
Temple Mount. If you want to blame the Christians, it
would have to be the Minims, not Cyril and the mainline
Christians.''

"It's not that I want to blame the Christians . . .''

"Isn't it?''

"No.''

"Are you sure?'' Sarkis asked.

"Certainly,'' Paul answered.

"I too have read Hillel. He did not blame the Christians. He never even mentioned them. If the Christians
did it, why did Hillel say nothing?''

"It's part of our tradition. We didn't blame the Babylonians for destroying the First Temple, or the Romans
for the Second. Our transgressions were the cause.''

"Paul. Think a minute. Of course the destruction of
the two temples was because God allowed it, but the
Babylonians and the Romans are clearly labeled as evil-
doers who will eventually fall. Here we have no mention
of the Christians at all, and furthermore—''

"It's a miracle, not a tragedy.''

"Hillel was as self-serving as Cyril,'' Sarkis went on.
"God's destroying the Temple may or may not have been
good for the Jews, but it was good for the House of Hillel. It showed that their position and attitude were right.''

"But only if God did it, not the Christians.''

"Paul, I am surprised. Perhaps I should not be. You
are looking through eyes which have read sixteen hundred years more of European history. The Crusades. Tor-
quemada. Blood libels. You once read a fourth-century
statement about the diseases of Christians to me. Do you
remember it?''

"Yes. All diseases of Christians are due to demons.''

"Do you believe it?'' the older man asked.

"No,'' the physician responded. "Of course not. All
diseases are not due to demons.''

"Nor are all the troubles of Jews due to Christians.''

It was late. Paul had to hurry to meet Joshua. He wanted to leave. He was sick of tea.

"One more thing, Paul. Not all Jews were opposed to the Temple. Some had to be excited by the prospect. Find out something about them."

The most direct way to get to the Rockefeller Museum was by going through the Arab quarter of the Old City. Paul could walk around, outside the old walls, but it would take too long. It was a fairly straightforward route through the Arab quarter—down David Street into the Shuk, a right turn just past the corn dealer, and then up a broad shopping street to Damascus Gate.

It was crowded all the way. The streets were filled with Arabs and Israelis. It was perfectly safe. He felt relieved as soon as he got through the gate.

When Paul got to the Rockefeller Museum, a virtual fortress opposite the northeastern corner of the wall of the Old City, Dalia and Joshua were seated on the low wall out front, waiting for him. The museum had been used by the Jordanians as a fortress, and Israeli paratroopers had had to storm it in 1967. Its walls were pockmarked, traces of a disease more deadly than smallpox, one for which there was no cure and no vaccine.

Once inside, they started with the temporary exhibit of toys and games of the ancient world, which included modern tabletop versions of the old games waiting to be played.

They played and played, especially the mill game. It was the same game that had been found cut into the Roman roadway on the Way of the Cross, the Via Dolorosa, the same game the Roman soldiers had played less than a thousand meters from here during that one Crucifixion, and undoubtedly others that went unrecorded.

Joshua learned quickly. He defeated Paul four games to one. Dalia was better. Paul left them when they were tied two games to two and went to look at the permanent collection.

Even here, he could not get away from his work. Without really trying, he found two busts of Julian, both bearded. He hadn't brought his camera, so he couldn't take a picture, but he copied the inscriptions from one.

It was four-thirty, and the museum was closing. Dalia

and Joshua were still at it. Dalia was ahead, so Paul declared her to be the winner.

Dalia suggested they might take a look at Solomon's Quarry. It was still open. Joshua asked if they could, the three of them. Of course, if Dalia had the time. She did.

The Quarry reminded Paul of walking into a long, deep cavernous movie theater, like the old Shore Theater on Seventy-fifth Street. He had gone there each Saturday afternoon for years. There he had first met Frankenstein alongside Abbott and Costello, and Basil Rathbone and Nigel Bruce and the other black-and-white heroes of his youth.

Once inside, Dalia and Joshua ran ahead, leaving Paul to wander on his own. For a moment he lost track of them. Then he saw them, deep in the cave, hand in hand like a pair of kids.

Two busts. Why? Someone here must have liked Julian. Who? Pagans? No. Christians? Certainly not. Jews? Julian was treated well in most Jewish sources, as a just philosopher-king. Some Jews must have liked him, supported him, wanted the Temple. Sarkis was right. He would have to pursue this.

The show was over. The lights flashed off and on. It was time to go home. Paul wandered back up the deep incline past numerous branching tunnels, still recalling the old Shore Theater. Now it was no more, no more Sherlock Holmes, no more Thin Man, no more Sam Spade. Hammett. Hammett had changed it all. He gave murder back to murderers, to real killers, not to lords and ladies.

To real killers. It is murderers who commit murder, the Machine Gun Kelleys, the Al Capones, not the Rivkah Gellers of the world. Nor the Chaim Abramowitzes, nor the Yitzak Cohens, nor the Hassan Rashems, but real murderers.

Some Arab must have pulled that plug, someone who hated Jews and not for mere religious reasons, someone threatened by a Jewish presence in Jerusalem, in the West Bank. Some Arab. Some Palestinian. That still left Hassan. It always came back to that.

Why couldn't it have been a disgruntled Jew, a fanatic Jew terrorist? We are always our worst enemies. We have found the enemy and they are us.

While they waited for a bus, Joshua went to get a soft ice cream and Paul tried to thank Dalia for her kindness. She said it was nothing. She liked Joshua and she too had lost her mother. A hand grenade had been thrown under a bus. Here, that simple fact was as much a part of life as drunk drivers in the U.S. Would it ever end?

The doctor who saw Mrs. Yousuf at the border clinic was not the same doctor who had seen her before. He was not a neurologist. He was not an internist. He was not a specialist of any kind.

He had lived and practiced in the south, in Beersheba, ever since he finished his medical training in 1955. His smattering of Arabic was helpful, but her accent was different from the bedouin tones he was used to, more lilting. Her slurred speech did not make it any easier.

He talked to her for several minutes, did a brief examination, reread her old chart, then wrote his brief note.

> Thirty-six-year-old Palestinian Arab woman. Usual good health until earlier this year, when she developed weakness of her face bilaterally. Came across Fence, then was admitted to Maimonides and discharged two weeks later much improved. Diagnosis: Guillain-Barré syndrome.
>
> Returns now because of recurrence of facial weakness for last three days. Now has marked facial weakness. Also complains of walking difficulty. Her feet are weak on exam. She has difficulty lifting them to walk. Her reflexes are absent at the ankles but active elsewhere.
>
> Plan: Readmit to Maimonides Hospital.
> Status: Emergency

When Rivkah Geller came for Shabbat dinner again, Joshua did not rebuff her. He was open and talked to her. If anything, it was Paul who was distant, as if Joshua's distrust had somehow rubbed off on him.

16

Paul selected a quiet spot in the back of the library at Maimonides Hospital. He surrounded himself with the books and articles he wanted, organized them into appropriate piles, and began to read a subject as removed as possible from the political complexities of what was now his world.

In many circles, Julian's declaration had evoked a wave of wild enthusiasm. The news spread quickly throughout the Diaspora. Ephraim, a Syrian Jew living in Syria, described how his fellow Jews were seized by a frenzy, rejoiced, and blew the shofar. Rufinus, the pagan of Italy, noted that the Jews there expected the prophets to come back and the Messiah to follow quickly.

Hillel of course had not been the average Jew. He was the patriarch living in Tiberius, spending his life studying and teaching, not scratching for a living among the gentiles. He could not be detached, skeptical. But what about the average Jews scattered throughout the empire? The Jews of Rome, of Gaul, of Britannia? What would they have done?

Perhaps they would have responded like modern Jews who sent money to help build the fourth sanctuary. They could have started the first Jewish National Fund.

Would they really have responded in that way? Paul rejected his hypothesis. A fourth-century attempt at fundraising seemed to be too much of an anachronism. They must have responded differently.

How many would have felt the call to return to Zion, to go to Jerusalem to help rebuild the Temple? There were no national borders to cross, no exit visas to apply for, no petty bureaucrats to frustrate them. Jerusalem, like Rome, was a city within the empire. How many went? How could he tell? There were not accurate numbers. No real data.

As he was collecting his papers to leave, Paul realized that someone was looking over his shoulder. He turned around quickly. It was Chaim Abramowitz. How long had he been standing there? And why had he been standing there saying nothing? Why had he not said hello? Or anything? "Shalom," Paul said. It was a greeting that fit the occasion, meaning hello, good-bye, and peace.

Chaim returned his greeting using the same Hebrew word. "I see you've deserted Guillain-Barré syndrome for the fourth century."

So Chaim had been there long enough to see exactly what Paul was reading. And he had been curious enough to find out.

"That," Chaim continued, "is a good choice."

"It's not a choice," Paul replied, "merely a change of pace."

Chaim nodded and disappeared into the stacks.

Neither of them had bothered to say shalom again.

Had Chaim's remark been a harmless observation? A mild form of criticism? A rebuke?

Or a warning?

Suddenly Paul missed being in Chicago. Most comments there were just that—comments. There were observations, an occasional criticism, rarely a rebuke, and never a warning.

On his way out of the hospital, Paul stopped by to see Avram. Avram was glad he had come by. He had wanted to talk to Paul, not about rounds or neurology, but about the committee. "Tell me, Paul, how do you like the rest of our committee?"

Our committee. Something about the way Avram said that disturbed Paul. Had Eleazar and Avram helped the dean pick the committee? Had they in fact told him whom to select? And whom not to select, including Paul Richardson, visiting Zionist? Or Paul Richardson, visiting native American with an advanced degree in guillibility? "I have mixed feelings," Paul answered.

"Mixed? In what way?"

"Only four of us know anything at all about neurologic diseases. Yitzak is good. He knows neuropathology, but like all neuropathologists, he can only describe what he sees. He can't tell us anything about things he doesn't see. He has no imagination. You and I are both clinicians. We both know neuropathology. Not as well as Yitzak, but we're used to looking at clinical data and making guesses. Good guesses. We're good at it.''

''Certainly. We've had a lot of experience guessing.''

''It's more than just experience. Hell, Romain Bernhard has had more experience than I have, and yet he is not a good guesser.''

''No, he isn't.''

''And he's arrogant and—''

''Don't, Paul. I know Romain and his faults. God knows I know them. We spend a lot of time protecting him clinically. But he has given Israel so much over the years and he is a great technician.''

''Chaim, I presume, is a good cardiologist, but he knows nothing about neurology. Nor does Rivkah. Aside from pharmacology and toxicology, her background is very limited. Once she has proved Nahum Eckstein wasn't poisoned, she'll be out of her field. So that leaves you and me.''

''And Rabbi Levi,'' Avram added. ''Don't forget Rabbi Levi.''

''Come on, Avram. We can't let Rabbi Levi make our decisions for us. He knows nothing about medicine. Eckstein's death is not a theological problem. I actually like Rabbi Levi. I have learned something from him, but this matter is not in his field.''

''The problem with you, Paul, is that you believe in the separation of medicine and religion. You are too American. Separation of church and state. Separation of church and science. Such separations don't work here. This is not the South Side of Chicago, after all. This is Jerusalem.''

Paul seemed unconvinced. ''That is not the only problem with the select committee.''

''What else?''

''Except for you and me and the Rabbi, all the others, as far as I can tell, had reasons to want Eckstein dead. Or at least not to care if he died.''

''Don't leave me off your list of suspects.''

''You?''

''Yes. I am not unhappy that he is dead. Anyone who

organized what happened at Yamit and tried to destroy the fabric of this country—''

''But could you have killed him?''

''Could I or did I?''

''Could you have?''

''After Yamit, no, I don't think so. After all, what is done is done. Before, to prevent it . . . who knows? That is a much more complex issue. But one cannot relive the past. We have become good guessers in part by not reliving the past. You realize, that Romain is right?''

''In what way?''

''We are wasting our time. Nahum Eckstein would not have recovered. Pulling his plug made no difference. It was a misguided act. An accident, perhaps. Intentional, perhaps. It makes no difference. Opening up that can of worms would undoubtedly cause more problems than it would resolve.''

''How can you be sure of that?''

''How can you not, Paul? Any other decision is too complicated.''

''Come on, Avram. This isn't a game we're playing.''

Or was it? It was very late. They were getting nowhere. For whatever reason, Avram believed it was best to let sleeping dogs lie. It was over and done. Reopening the case would not help Rabbi Eckstein. Giving the terrorists more publicity wouldn't help anyone. Giving the Guardians more fuel for their hatred wouldn't help either.

Maybe Avram was right.

''Who picked the committee?''

It was Paul's parting question and it had the effect that Paul had expected but not wanted.

''Why . . . ah . . . the dean, of course,'' Avram replied awkwardly.

''Are you certain of that?'' Paul insisted.

''What difference does it make?''

''None, I suppose. But I sure would like to know.''

''The dean.''

''With appropriate consultations?''

''Of course.''

What else could he have expected?

* * *

the kiNGs A bEggar
nOW thE PLaY is DONE

Paul could think of little to add to what Eleazar already knew. It was obviously the last warning.

All's Well That Ends Well.

Was it really a pun? Did "well" have two meanings? Were they back to poisoning the water supply? It had to be something dramatic. Why not poisoning the water? The ninth of Av was only a partial fast day. Even the most religious Jews would drink fluids after lunchtime. But whatever it was, it was scheduled to occur at sunrise.

Jerusalem hadn't depended on a well for centuries.

Eight warnings.

Six direct quotes.

Six plays.

Two weeks.

Two weeks to Tisha B'Av.

The game of musical chairs went on.

The Lebanese government officially announced once and for all that the PLO had to leave Lebanon.

Yassir Arafat said the PLO would only leave Lebanon to go south into Israel.

The U.S. said that the Arab states had to find a home for the PLO.

Syria said fine, but not in their country. Saudi Arabia voiced the same sentiment. Iran and Iraq were too busy fighting to say anything. Jordan also said nothing, hoping that the world would forget that three-quarters of what had once been Palestine, the home of the displaced Palestinians, was now within the borders of Jordan.

Elsewhere it was business as usual. In England, eighteen-year-old Richard Charlesworth cut forty-three minutes off the record by swimming the English Channel from France to England in eight hours, fifty-two minutes. In Geneva, the head of the Iranian delegation to the United Nations Human Rights Committee failed to answer the charges of mass executions in Iran. At home the National League won the All Star Game four to one.

Carleton Fisk, the lone White Sox player on the American League team, went hitless in two trips to the plate.

One more twenty-eight-year-old father of two was called up from Neve Ilan and sent to Lebanon. He and his family lived in the house next to the Richardsons'. Joshua had baby-sat there a couple of times. They were peace-loving Jews who had come to Israel from South Africa because they detested injustice even more than violence. And now he, like thousands of other Israelis, was heading north into the war zone for at least forty-five days.

There was a new patient at the hospital, or rather, a readmitted patient, Mrs. Yousuf. John brought Paul up-to-date. When she had been discharged, she still had some mild facial weakness, with just a little slurring of her speech. By the time she had been home for a week, she was back to normal. All went well for another two weeks. Then her face got weak again. Her speech became slurred. She had difficulty swallowing and began to drag her feet. The weakness was progressing rapidly. Now she had generalized weakness with loss of all her reflexes.

"What has she got, John?"

"Everyone seems to think she has some sort of Guillain-Barré syndrome."

"What kind, Hassan?"

"Recurrent, relapsing."

"Meaning?"

"More than one attack."

"What do you do for such patients?"

"Steroids."

"Why?"

"I don't know. But they seem to help these patients."

"I couldn't have explained it better myself. We don't know why, but steroids help these patients. What did you do?"

It was Dalia who answered this question. "We put her on a hundred milligrams of prednisone each day, and we are carefully monitoring her respiration. If the steroids work well, she may not need a respirator, but if she progresses much more . . ."

"Sometimes on steroids, patients get worse before they

get better." Paul hoped it was just a warning, not a prophecy. Mrs. Yousuf too might need a bed in the overcrowded ICU.

The track record of G.B. patients in the ICU wasn't very good.

Of course, she was an Arab, not a Jewish reactionary who was too reactionary for many and not reactionary enough for the rest.

There was only one item on the agenda: Professor Geller's final report.

She had prepared a complete report, replete with detailed slides of all her data. She began with a thorough description of her approach and techniques, with no mention at all of the specific Pickwick poisons. Paul had to admit it was a masterful performance, a masterpiece of evasion combined with detailed data.

He watched the rest of the committee. Rabbi Levi, as always, sat by himself. If he was not praying, he was at least meditating. He rarely if ever bothered to look up.

Chaim Abramowitz was busily taking notes. Why? Was this just a way of maintaining concentration. Toxicology was foreign to him. Or were the notes for someone else? Had Chaim run into him in the library by accident? Had his words been a warning? Chaim had been there in the ICU that morning.

Avram, his mind made up, was reading through his mail. He had been in the hospital that morning. He could have gone to the ICU without being noticed. Rabbi Eckstein was his patient. If he had been seen at the respirator, no one would have thought anything of it, or remembered it.

Romain Bernhard just sat as if oblivious of all the data around him. His mind was closed. His decision had been made. He believed that Eckstein had become too soft, that he had deserted the cause, and that that cause was better off without Rabbi Nahum Eckstein. That meant that the rabbi had just died. Patients did that. Bernhard had operated that morning. He was in the hospital. He was a frequent visitor to the ICU. He, too, could come and go unnoticed, unremarked upon, unremembered. Was that why his mind was already closed? His mind was often closed, as if neuroscience had stopped in 1945, as if life had stopped then. Other than Israel, the Holocaust had stopped everything for him. Would that make him want to kill Nahum Eckstein? Was Eckstein a threat to his Israel?

Yitzak Cohen was not taking any notes. Was his mind already made up too? The lights went out and Professor Geller began to show her slides. They followed one another in rapid succession. Yitzak, at least, didn't wander in and out of the ICU each day. He might have been seen. Moreover, he might have been noticed and remembered.

The slides were over, the light turned on. No toxicity. No toxin. No poison. Guillain-Barré, not a Pickwick poison.

As soon as tea was brought in, Paul knew the format had changed. It was his turn to sit back and sip and listen. Sarkis, who usually spoke slowly, carefully selecting each word and phrase, began at what was, for him, a breakneck pace.

"Many years ago, probably before you were even born . . . yes, it was in 1935, and you were born in . . ."

"Nineteen-thirty-seven."

"Yes, 'thirty-seven. Well, in 1935 I was just beginning to try to locate and read all of the old documents, books, scrolls, and fragments that I could find in Jerusalem. I was in a unique position. It was not just my background as far as education, but also my own personal background. My family had then, and still has now, a reputation for fairness and honesty, not only among our own people, but among other Christians and even non-Christians, both Muslims and Jews. Many people opened their doors to me. Doors that then and now are often closed to most, and some doors which no longer exist.

"Behind one of those doors, in the old Jewish quarter, in the house of a rabbi of sainted memory, I ran across a group of fragments written in Arabic by a Jew. I am sure that does not seem strange to you. Jews living in Arab countries have written in Arabic for the last thirteen hundred years.

"But these fragments were different. They were in an archaic form of Arabic, a form that was used before the time of the Prophet. The original must have been one of the oldest of all such documents. The fragments were

copies done, according to the scribe, in the Muslim year
372, about the middle of the tenth century. This copyist
was apparently an archivist who, like monks in Europe
at the same time, was concerned with preserving old
writings. This anonymous scribe tried very hard to make
an identical copy, but the original was already in very
bad shape. Whole passages were missing. Others were
damaged so badly that they could not be read at all. Or
perhaps only a few words could be made out.

"When I read this some forty-seven years ago, I didn't
understand its meaning. I knew it was important. It was
one of the oldest examples of Arabic writing known. I
wanted the rabbi to have it published so that the great
scholars could study it. He refused to allow that. In fact,
he once told me that if it were not for his reverence for
the original author, he would have burned it long ago."

"What happened to it?"

"The rabbi got his wish. Not in a way he wanted, but
he got it nonetheless. In 1948, when the Jews in the old
quarter were finally beaten and the few surviving men
straggled out of the Old City, they could only take a few
things with them. Some old Torahs. I can still picture
him walking out through our quarter. It was safer than
being marched through the Arab mobs. He had a Torah
on his shoulder. His head was unbowed. And his lips
moved constantly, saying a psalm, 'If I forget thee, O
Jerusalem . . .' "

For the first time he stopped for a sip of tea. "It was
a time of great turmoil, massive confusion, hatred, and
mistrust. I wanted more than anything to save the rest of
his collection. He had so many old and wonderful and
rare books.

"As soon as I could, I went to his house. It was too
late. The Arab Legion had razed it. They had carefully
taken out all of the books and burned them. All the sa-
cred scrolls. All the commentaries . . . everything.

"If only I had gone there sooner . . .' "

Paul decided to say nothing, and in a moment the older
man began anew.

"Fortunately, I am a man of bad habits. Many bad
habits. Some of which are at times very fortunate. I have
never learned to study without taking notes, making a
record, and I never throw anything away. Last week,

something struck a chord. The mind works in such strange ways. You are a specialist in that. Perhaps someday you will explain it to me. So I began to search for my old notes. I am not well-organized, but I did find them. My notes are in Armenian, in a private sort of shorthand. They would be unintelligible to anyone else. I read them over. They may mean something to you. I think it is best if I read them to you.

"There were five old fragments and some marginal notes by the Arabic scribe. The first fragment was the largest and was in the best condition."

Paul was as surprised by the delay, the first real halt in the long monologue, as he had been by its initiation. Sarkis quickly drank his entire glass of tea and picked up the old worn covered notebook sitting on his desk. He turned on his desk light and began to read:

> "I am a wanderer. I was born a wanderer and although I have now lived here for over eighteen years, I will die as a wanderer. I was born into a family of wanderers, into a race of wanderers. Not all men are homeless. Not all men spend their lives moving from place to place. Nowhere at home. Nowhere at peace. Always a stranger. Yet easily adapting to each new environment. Never sinking into the background. Never becoming the background. I did not learn that this peculiar fate of ours was meant to be for at least all of my lifetime, until much of it was past. I am not yet sure that I understand why. But when he . . ."

"Here is a space and a note by the scribe . . . he apparently didn't understand the word, which he felt was a borrowed word from some other language. He used the word 'Prophet' instead."

> "But when the Prophet, may the Holy One, Blessed be His Name, hasten the day of His arrival, when the Prophet comes, then and only then will we understand His ways. For now and until then, it is enough to know His laws."

"It wasn't a Prophet," Paul interjected.

"Of course not. That I even knew then. Ancient Arabic before Mohammed had no word for 'Messiah.' They had no concept of a Messiah. That concept was quite unique to Judaism. So our original author—"

"Was a Jew. A Jew living in an Arab land. Who wandered there late in his life."

"Yes. And our scribe?" Sarkis asked Paul.

"A Muslim Arab who lived after Mohammed the Prophet and assumed that the translated Hebrew word 'Messiah' meant 'Prophet.' That certainly helps to date the original, doesn't it?"

"Yes. But let us go on." The old Armenian seemed even more anxious than his listener.

> "For forty-eight years I have been a wanderer. Forced to live without ever again tasting the one home I could have called my own. I used to think it would have been better to have never tasted it at all. For sweetness that has rotted and become bitter is harsher than that which is naturally bitter. But I was wrong. One taste, however brief, however bitter, however unhappy, is more than any one man, than this man, ever deserved. May the Holy One, Blessed be His Name, continue to grant such blessings to other undeserving souls.
>
> According to my father's reckoning, it is now the year 341."

"There was a marginal note by the scribe here. Since he copied the document in the year 372, he couldn't understand what precise year the author really meant. He knew that it did not mean the real year 341, three hundred and forty-one years after the Hijirah. That had been just thirty years earlier."

"No, it couldn't mean that," Paul said.

"Our poor scribe was an uneducated man of letters. A copyist without much knowledge. To him, all dates began with Mohammed's migration from Mecca to Medina, the starting point of the Muslim era. But it couldn't have been that."

"No, of course not," Paul agreed. "The Hijirah was

in 622, and archaic Arabic had disappeared long before that. So what calendar was it?"

"I gave that a great deal of thought then, and came to no conclusion. There were several choices. The writer was clearly, as you will see, from the Roman world. He spent much of his life in the eastern part of the empire, and on its eastern borders. What are our choices?"

"It can be a pure Roman calendar dating back to the founding of Rome, in 753 B.C. The one-thousand year celebration was in 248," Paul said.

Sarkis nodded in agreement.

"It can't be in Hebrew, dating back to the Creation, and it can't be the Christian calendar because 341 only existed in retrospect."

"That too is where I originally left it." Sarkis looked at his notes. The sun had set. No more light was coming in through the window. Paul knew that he would have to leave soon. There were limits to how much he could impose on the hospitality of Sarkis' family. "There is an apparent break in the original text. The scribe left a space. There is no way to tell if this was a missing sentence, a paragraph, or more. Then he resumed in the middle of a thought."

> "Such events should be recorded. My children and my children's children must be strengthened by such knowledge. It will not decrease the bitterness of their lives, but it may keep them from making the same mistakes that I made. False dreams and false hopes. May they profit from my story and not be misled. Someday there may even be false Messiahs. May they not be misled. May their good deeds . . .

"Again, another break. And then it resumes." Tisha B'Av has come to signify the end of good things, the destruction of that which is holy and right. It also denotes the beginning of bad times. The destruction of Solomon's temple and the beginning of the exile in Babylonia date from the same moment in history. Every Jew knows this now, and will always know it, if he is truly a Jew. Given a choice, a Jew will never begin a journey on Tisha B'Av."

Like Columbus, Paul thought to himself, and wondered anew.

"My journey began on Tisha B'Av. The day of the destruction. Long before I was born."

"That's it."

"What?"

"The date."

Sarkis listened.

"It began long before he was born. It was a calendar dating back to the beginning of the exile, to Tisha B'Av of the year 70. That makes it 411."

"Yes, that is what recently occurred to me. When I first read it, I had no idea what Tisha B'Av really meant, no true understanding. Until we began meeting together, I had not thought about this document since I first read it, except in 'forty-eight, when I tried to save it. But then I just thought of its significance as a document, not as a history."

"Four-eleven, forty-eight years after Julian. He must have lived at the time of the building of the Third Temple."

"Yes. Let me read just a bit more. It is getting late. My eyes are tired."

For the first time Paul noticed a slight stoop in Sarkis' shoulders, some strain on his face, but the fire in his eyes was still bright. It was not his eyes that were giving out. Paul had been so busy listening, he had not noticed the voice become softer, more quivery.

"Let me see. 'I am now dying. I will never reach my four score and ten. My breath is too short. I must sleep on many pillows. My legs are thick. If I push on my ankle, I leave a mark. . . .' "

"Amazing. A clinical description of heart failure written in 411."

Sarkis ignored his remark. He needed to finish the fragment.

"Here the scribe had to put together the broken sentences, lost words. But the sense is that he was then sixty-six years old. One sentence was preserved. 'It all happened in a few months, when I was eighteen.' "

"Eighteen!"

"Yes."

"That would be 363!"

"The year of—"

"The Temple! Julian's Temple!" Paul exclaimed. He wanted to hear the rest of it right then and there. But it was too late. He had to leave. The two men embraced warmly. They had together discovered something that neither of them would have discovered alone. It was one of those rare moments. They both savored it. Delaying the final details would prolong the joy of this discovery.

On his way out of the jewelry shop, Paul was totally preoccupied recalling the exact words that Sarkis had read to him. He opened the door into Muristani Road by reflex and ran right into someone.

"Excuse me," Paul said reflexively, forgetting to use his Hebrew.

"It's okay," a voice replied. "But you should watch where you walk, Paul."

Paul! It was Chaim. Chaim Abramowitz. What was he doing here? He should be in the hospital saving lives or something.

"I'm looking for a gift for my wife," Chaim said, answering the unasked question. "It's her birthday, but I'll never tell which one. This is the best place to get gold jewelry in all of Jerusalem."

Paul nodded rather automatically. He wanted to get back to 411. The manuscript had been written in the year 411, and the event had happened 48 years earlier. In the year 363.

The year of the Third Temple.

Paul's excitement should have carried over, but it didn't.

It wasn't that anything went wrong that evening, because nothing did.

Paul and Rivkah went out to dinner. They went to Taj, the Iranian restaurant where they had gone the first time. Once again, they sat below a portrait of the shah and drank Carmel Grenache Rosé and ate lamb.

Then they went to her apartment and made love. Slowly, caringly, tenderly, well.

They both knew something had changed, but neither of them said anything. Some things are best left unsaid.

Rivkah drove him home, a twenty-minute drive through the Judean Hills.

"I did not kill Nahum Ekstein," he began.

"I never said you did."

"I could have. I was in the hospital that day. I always get up early."

"I noticed that."

"Not just when I am in bed with you. But every morning. I was there in the hospital. I knew he was in the ICU and I hated him. It is not that I couldn't have killed him. I have killed before. In 'forty-eight. I was only fourteen then. But I killed people and I could kill again if I had to. I just didn't."

Joshua was up.

Paul could see his head in the window. Paul kissed Rivkah good night.

Joshua watched. When Paul came in, Joshua did not pretend to be asleep. He hugged his father and had something to show him—the mill game, a copy of the original game they sold at the museum. Dalia had bought it and given it to him.

Paul and Joshua played.

They played a World Series. Best four out of seven.

Joshua won. Four games to one.

Paul, like the White Sox, had problems with his defense.

17

Nine o'clock. Paul had taken the early bus to be sure he got to Maimonides on time to start rounds earlier than usual, and now he sat and waited in the Neurology conference room while the students and residents straggled in. Hassan had been there when he arrived, but after a cordial greeting, neither of them said anything. Hassan buried himself in a book, *Models of Human Neurological Diseases*, while Paul took out his small notebook and reviewed some of his own notes. They were nowhere as thorough as Sarkis' old notes. Sarkis had been so much more compulsive. He would have made a good—no, a great—neurologist.

Models of Human Neurological Diseases? The library here didn't have a copy. Hassan must have ordered his own through the bookstore when Paul had mentioned the book to him. That must have been four weeks ago or more, around the time when he first visited Abu Gosh. They had even talked about Hassan's possibly spending a year or two in Paul's lab. Was Hassan still interested? Abu Gosh was only a mile from Neve Ilan, yet so far away, separated by religion, language, culture, and distrust. At times the two communities were held together by mutual dislike for someone else, but left to their own devices, they went their own ways. Separate and . . . unequal. Whose fault was that? Ours? Theirs? Both? Did Hassan still want to come to Chicago and again be surrounded by Jews? Did Paul want him there?

Dalia Avni and the two students arrived together. It was Dalia who spoke. "We're sorry we're late, Dr. Richardson. But we have so many patients that rounds took much longer than usual."

"No explanation needed. Catch your breath and tell me what's going on."

It was a series of disasters, patients with strokes who had developed pneumonia, patients with seizures who were continuing to have seizures, a patient with Parkinson's disease who had fallen and broken a hip.

It had been a day when everything had gone wrong.

Like that morning in the ICU, Paul mused as he listened to the recitation of problems. Virtually everything that could have gone awry obviously had.

What else could have gone wrong? The answer was almost too obvious.

Mrs. Yousuf.

Paul was almost afraid to listen, as if their telling her story in some way made her worse. It was merely that old magical thinking. If the doctor doesn't biopsy my lump and prove it's cancer, then it's not cancer and it will go away. I'm better off not going to see my doctor because only he can give me cancer. How many women had died because of such thinking? Patients were not the only ones who were that superstitious. Don't say it and maybe it will go away. Say it, and it won't. John said it.

"She's much worse."

"In what ways?"

"Every way, Professor Richardson. She can't swallow, so we have her on I.V.'s. She can barely move her arms and legs. She can barely open her eyes, and when she does, she can hardly move her eyes. Her breathing is getting weaker."

"Sounds like she needs to be on a respirator."

"That's what we thought. But . . ."

"No room in the inn."

"That's right. There's no room in the ICU. We have two patients there already. They both have severe pneumonia," Dalia explained.

It was Hassan who challenged them all. "We do have one option, sir. We can bring one of our old stroke patients down here and put Mrs. Yousuf up there. She is younger. The ICU should be used for younger patients who will live much longer if we save them."

Hassan's voice was bitter, his attitude aggressive and challenging. It was as if this was an argument he had had before. Paul began to answer abruptly, almost reflexively. Then he stopped himself and started cautiously. It seemed as if everyone else suddenly faded into the background, leaving the two of them in the center of the stage, in the center of the ring.

"I . . . don't . . . think . . . that's what we should do."

"Why not?"

"It is all a matter of prognosis," he began.

"What is her prognosis?" Hassan asked him.

"It is not just a question of her prognosis."

"What is her prognosis, Professor?" Hassan persisted.

"I'm not completely sure."

"Would it be better with a respirator?"

"Certainly," Paul conceded.

"Then . . . ?"

"Hassan, it's not that black-and-white and you know it."

"I do?"

"Yes, you do. Hell, if we bring either one of those patients with pneumonia down here now, it's like signing a death certificate. And they'll make significant recoveries if we can cure their pneumonias."

"That seems unlikely."

Paul ignored that jab and went on. "Mrs. Yousuf, on the other hand, we don't know whether we can help her or not."

"We can usually do a lot for relapsing G.B." Another jab. "They do well on steroids." A series of jabs. "That would make her prognosis good, wouldn't it?" A right cross.

"We're not sure what she has. We don't know what her prognosis is." Head down, and keep those arms up.

"I see. When you don't know the prognosis, you assume it's bad. The classic American method. Guilty until proven innocent."

Hit back. "Let's keep nationalities out of this. I don't know Mrs. Yousuf's prognosis. I can't assume it's better than the other two patients'. If we keep them alive, we can help them. Mrs. Yousuf?" With that, Paul just shrugged his shoulders. His rally was working. The tide had swung. Momentum was on his side.

"And she is an Arab." A right hook. A real haymaker.

Paul understood now. It was an old argument. Hassan

must have had it before, probably many times, over many patients.

"While the others," Hassan continued, "are . . ."

He didn't say it.

Even unsaid it was a knockout blow.

Or was it?

Was he right? Was it the disease or the patient?

"That's not the issue, Dr. Rashem, and we both know it." Paul, as Professor Richardson, had ended the discussion. "Dr. Avni, is there a new patient?"

There was, and Yuri told her story. A young woman named Castel. She was twenty-eight years old. Her problem had started when she was twenty-two and woke up one morning and couldn't see out of her right eye.

That was all Paul needed today.

"She went to her family physician. He looked in her eye and said her eye looked normal and that she would get better, and she did in about two months."

Of course she did. They always do the first time.

"What's that called John?" Paul began.

"What?"

"She looks out of her eye and can't see anything, and the doctor looks in and he can't see anything either. It looks normal to him. What's that called?"

"Neuritis."

"What kind?"

"Optic."

"No. What kind?" Slow down. It's not their fault. Never blame the witnesses. Go slower, softer. "No. Optic neuritis means swelling of the optic nerve itself. It can cause loss of vision in one eye, but the back of the eye is swollen, not normal. Here her eye was normal-looking. That's called . . ."

John looked more relaxed. The atmosphere was less hostile. He remembered the right word. "Retrobulbar neuritis."

"Give that man a cigar or something. Retrobulbar neuritis. Swelling retro, or in back of the eye. The doctor can't see it and the eye looks normal. Retrobulbar neuritis. What's that a sign of, John?"

"I'm not sure."

"Yuri?"

"Multiple sclerosis."

"M.S. How often. Does anyone know?"

Dalia answered. "No one knows for sure. But if you follow patients for a long time after an episode of retrobulbar neuritis, for fifteen years or so, about one-third end up with multiple sclerosis."

M.S. All they needed today was another patient they couldn't help. Maybe they should all have gone into O.B. Paul nodded to Yuri and went on with the story. They hadn't had to wait fifteen years to make a diagnosis on Mrs. Castel. At age twenty-two she had had an episode of double vision and a drunken gait. Ataxia. Her vision came back. Her walking never returned to normal. The next year, another episode of near-blindness in the right eye, with only partial recovery. Two years later, more trouble walking. Again partial recovery. Each attack took its toll, left its mark. Everything that could possibly go wrong had—weakness and numbness of her right hand, trouble controlling her bladder, slurred speech, head bobbing, double vision, more walking difficulty.

Paul hardly heard the rest of the presentation. She had received a dozen courses of steroids, all to no avail. She was admitted for plasmapheresis.

"Tell me, Yuri, why plasmapheresis?"

"As I understand it, in M.S. the patient is making antibodies against his own brain, so you use the plasmapheresis to remove the abnormal proteins, just like we did in Mr. Tarshish."

"Except there are two differences." At this the residents perked up, even Hassan. "Two differences. One is the source of the abnormal proteins. In myasthenia, the abnormal proteins are made by white blood cells outside the brain, and the protein is in the plasma and easy to get to. In M.S., the abnormal proteins are made inside the brain. You find abnormal antibodies in ninety-five percent of the patients, but only in the spinal fluid, not the plasma. That's the first difference. In myasthenia, the antibodies are in the plasma. In M.S. they are in the spinal fluid.

"The second difference is more significant. In myasthenia, plasmapheresis works very well. We're still not sure how much it helps in M.S. Some patients do seem to respond, but others don't."

* * *

Paul hurried to get to the jewelry shop on Muristani Road. The street was quiet, there were no friends to bump into. He hadn't thought about that since it happened. Bumping into Chaim twice in one day was a coincidence. He hadn't bumped into him since. Was Chaim being more careful?

No. Those were merely coincidences.

Coincidences did happen, even in Israel.

Their second session began as the first had ended. Paul sat and drank tea. Sarkis read. "This next part has some very sketchy portions. Apparently the original was in very poor condition and our scribe had a great deal of difficulty piecing things together. At times, my notes are also very fragmentary. I am afraid I cannot recall whether the original was as disjointed as my scribblings. It was all so long ago," he said more than half-apologetically. "I can remember being in the house. I can remember studying the documents. I remember knowing they were important. I recall my feelings, but I cannot recall the exact words. Maybe I am getting too old."

"No. There are other explanations."

"There are?"

"Yes. It was almost fifty years ago."

"I remember other things from that long ago, other important—"

"Yes. But even though you knew this was important, you didn't know why, so you had nothing to peg your memory to." Paul began in the style of an authority on the brain explaining some facet of neurological science to a neophyte. "There was no event, no philosophy, no history to tie it to. That makes recall much more difficult." By the time the explanation was over, it was no longer an objective opinion. Had Sarkis also noticed the difference?

It was dark in the room and the only lights played mostly on the desk. Paul could not see Sarkis' face hidden in the shadows, so he couldn't judge the effect of his words.

Sarkis looked down at his notes and began reading them. " 'Our entire family left. We were not there that day. We left two days before. Many died. Some stayed. We all left.' "

"That must be leaving Jerusalem, or at least Judea," Paul said.

"Yes. I would agree. But when?"

"The year 70. Two days before Tisha B'Av. Two days before Titus destroyed the Second Temple." Paul couldn't see his friend's response but was sure he agreed. The story had started when Rome crushed the First Revolt.

"The next part is less fragmentary, but I am sure it is not in the correct place. The scribe himself made no comments. He had put them in the order in which I took my notes, but this must have originally come later."

"The port was still busy. Trade was still good. Ships came and went from throughout the empire, carrying goods from the far corners of the empire and beyond. Lead and tin brought from . . . Britain . . . and was loaded onto ships for Ostia, Constantinople . . ."

"That helps date it."

"Yes."

"Constantinople was renamed in the year 323. Before that it had been Byzantium. That confirms our date a bit."

"Yes, but it could be much later. Constantinople did not become Istanbul until 1453." Sarkis stared once again at his notebook. "Then there is an obvious break and my notes go on."

"Dyes. Our business for well over two hundred years. We collect pigments from Spain, from some cousins: malachite, vermillion, azurite, ochre. Dyes for the finest of clothes. Carmine, not just Spanish carmine, but the finest carmine from Anatolia. No cheap dyes. No indigo. No saffron. No madder. And sometimes we do get the royal purple of Tyre. Made by crushing the rotting shells of thousands upon thousands of shellfish. More costly than silk or amber or lapis."

"Then came a very different segment, very hard to be sure of. The scribe put it here, I think, because it also mentioned Tyre. 'First they went north beyond the din of revolt. Tyre. We were not welcome. We have never been welcome there. . . . Some to Antioch. Some to Duras Europas.'

"Exactly what the 'some' refers to is unclear. The scribe felt it meant some of the rare dyes of Tyre, but I think this refers to something else."

"The family's personal exodus from Israel. The beginning of their exile, their diaspora. First they went to Tyre, but then the family split up, some going to Antioch, some to Dura Europas. Both were major trade centers," Paul said.

"Precisely. So that this is really a history of the family beginning in the year 70. The rest reads like a Cook's tour of the Mediterranean world: Cappadocia, Commagene, Byzantium, Knossos, Piraeus, Ostia."

"Where did they end up?"

"I think the next part answers that. 'We trade the dye to the great landowners in the interior, as far away as Trier and Paris.' "

"Somewhere in southern France."

"Yes, probably a great port."

"Narbonne," Paul guessed.

"Or Nimes, but somewhere in Gaul. Now we come to the most important part, from your viewpoint. This fragment was relatively well-preserved."

"I was only eighteen when I heard of the proclamation. My father was afraid. My uncles were distressed. I was excited. More than excited. I knew I had to respond personally. Warnings of false Messiahs meant nothing to me at that age."

"Again, the word used isn't 'Messiah,' but I have taken the liberty of using the term which I am sure is correct. 'When the second decree came down, changing the tax on us. I knew I had to go.' When I first read this, I was mystified. I had no idea, but now it is so obvious."

Paul agreed but said nothing. The first proclamation had to be Julian's announcement that he would rebuild the Temple. A true false Messiah. The second proclamation was the decree that the tax on Jews would not go to the patriarchs of the House of Hillel, but to the construction of the Temple. It is not surprising that a non-Jew would not immediately grasp the story. There had been no mention of Jerusalem yet, no mention of Julian.

Sarkis continued:

"The fastest way possible was not fast enough. It was going to happen without me if I didn't hurry. My father opposed my leaving. So did my uncles. I took the next boat to Ostia, then to Cyprus, where we had family, and on to Tyre. So close and yet so far. Tyre to Caesarea. I was almost there. When I got there, it was too late. False Messiahs, false promises, false predictions."

"Clearly something was missing here. The scribe left a long space. No comment, just a long space. Then the next paragraphs are again intact."

Barely started and it was over with, never to be restarted. It had been stopped before it was truly under way, by a miracle. The bishop called it a miracle. Even patriarch called it a miracle. The ways of God are stranger now than they were.

I was angry. It was as if God's miracle were directed against me personally. I was only eighteen then. I was so young, I was idealistic. I still believed in purity. That did not last long. Who had seen the miracle? The cross in the sky? On the chests of nonbelievers? No Jews that I talked to, no pagans. It had happened only two weeks earlier, but no one had actually seen it.

I stayed there to see what would happen to our false Messiah. The stories changed. Witnesses appeared. Cyril's prediction became known. No one had ever heard it when I arrived. Two weeks later, I knew a hundred men who had heard him say it, and two hundred who had seen the crosses. All of them were Christians.

Had miracles always been thus? Was it better to live after a miracle was over and believe in it without questioning? Had people seen the burning bush? Had the Red Sea parted? Was it a miracle? Or merely an earthquake? Was it . . .

"There this part ends. I am tired. We will meet again soon."

Tired? How could Sarkis be tired at a time like this? They had to finish it. Paul began to say something. He couldn't. Starkis looked exhausted. He must have been working too hard. Had he looked that tired when Paul came in? Paul couldn't remember. He had been too excited to notice much of anything.

Or was Sarkis ill? Not Sarkis. He was like an eternal verity. He would go on forever. Paul knew it was not true, but he still wanted to believe it. It was time to leave.

Paul's excitement was growing, but so was his sense of caution.

He looked before he opened the door into Muristani Road. There was no one in the doorway.

And no one in the road. How comforting was a deserted street in the Armenian quarter? He'd rather have seen the usual crowd of faces. Armenians. Jews. Arabs. Or would he?

When the phone began to ring, it was already five-forty-five and she usually left the hospital no later than five-fifteen. Five rings. Seven. Whoever it was really wanted to get through. Eight. Nine. She gave up and answered it.

"Professor Geller."

"Professor, it's Hassan Rashem, the chief resident from Neurology. Mrs. Yousuf is back at the hospital."

Mrs. Yousuf. It was a name she could not immediately place.

"We sent you some blood and spinal fluid of hers several weeks ago."

There had been so many samples. She couldn't place one with the name Yousuf. "She had facial diplegia."

She was beginning to remember.

"And you asked for some more samples."

She remembered.

"But she went home before we could get any more blood or spinal fluid for you."

It seemed an age ago, but it had only been three weeks—three weeks of concentrated effort and worry, three weeks to prove nothing, to disprove nothing.

Despite the lack of replies, Dr. Rashem continued the conversation.

"She is back in the hospital. At first, her face got stronger, back to normal, but now she's worse again."

There was nothing she could do about that.

"We're not sure what's wrong with her. She may have relapsing Guillain-Barré."

Guillain-Barré. Why was he calling her? She was no expert on Guillain-Barré. Avram Schiff knew much more than she did. So did Paul Richardson. Especially Paul.

"Then I remembered you wanted more spinal fluid from her and I wondered if that was because you had found something."

She had found something. But she had found something in many of the patients with nerve disease. Nahum Eckstein included. She began to answer, "Yes, I did."

"What was it?"

"We were working on a new method, but it didn't work out."

That was all she could say.

"A method for what?"

Was it his persistence that angered her? He was very persistent, but no more than another doctor with a sick patient whose disease he didn't understand.

"Professor Geller . . ."

"Yes, Dr. Rashem."

"Is there anything you can tell me about my patient?"

The method worked and was specific, but she couldn't tell him that. It was not his concern. It was done and over and had nothing to do with Mrs. Yousuf. She didn't want to think about it anymore.

"We were looking for a method for . . ." she began slowly, "Toxins. Pesticides. Mrs. . . . what did you say her name was?"

"Yousuf."

"Yes, Yousuf. Her samples were positive, but it turned out that finding didn't mean anything. We got positive results in other patients with a variety of different disorders. Diabetic neuropathy. Guillain-Barré. All sorts of conditions as long as the nerve roots were involved."

"That wouldn't help us very much. We already know she has root disease. It's too bad we collected more samples for you—'' thank God she wouldn't have to study them— ''we were hoping you could help us.''

She couldn't.

''But if she had the exact same abnormality as all those other patients . . .''

The exact same. An extra peak between 975 and 976. Just like . . . She no longer heard Dr. Rashem. The peak had been in a different location. Earlier. Between 970 and 971. It was different. Maybe it meant something. Maybe it wasn't nonspecific. Where could she have gotten some poison? Rivkah never wanted to think about the Pickwick Project again. Neither of the missing poisons should have been precisely at that spot. Unless she had made an error in her calculations. Or in the assumptions on which her calculations were based.

''Well,'' Dr. Rashem concluded, ''I'm sorry I bothered—''

''Dr. Rashem.''

''Yes.''

''How sick is she?''

''Very sick. She has generalized weakness and she's getting worse.''

For a moment neither of them said anything. Then Professor Geller spoke. ''I'm not sure I'll be able to be of any help at all, but I'll take a look . . .''

''Thank you.''

''Where are the samples now?''

''I have them.''

She looked at her watch. Being a few more minutes late wouldn't do any harm.

''Do you know where my laboratory is?''

''Yes.''

''Can you bring the samples to me now?''

''Yes. I'm on my way.''

As soon as he delivered the samples, she carefully labeled them and locked them in the freezer.

Tomorrow she would start again. Luckily she had not discarded the standards or the control samples. It couldn't be a Pickwick poison. The disease those caused didn't improve and then get worse. Unless . . .

That night, at home, Paul ignored Julian and Nahum Eckstein equally. He and Joshua hosted a major mill-game tournament. Paul was eliminated in the first round. Pat beat Joshua in the finals.

Carolyn called. She was coming home for Shabbat. The three of them would be together again. They had all missed being together.

The news of the rest of the world was rather depressing. No progress was reported in the various diplomatic efforts.

In the little town of Bethlehem, in Manger Square, a young Israeli had been shopping with his two young sons, buying cucumbers, and was shot in the head by an Arab terrorist. He was dead when he hit the ground. No respirator for him. No ICU.

The Arab terrorist was a teenager, no more than sixteen or seventeen years old. He had calmly walked up to the Israeli in the middle of the marketplace, taken out a pistol, and with a single shot had blown the top of his head off.

Paul had been to Bethlehem. He had shopped there with Carolyn and Joshua. Not for cucumbers, but for dates and olives. Bethlehem was closer to Jerusalem than Neve Ilan was.

The Arab murderer was no older than Carolyn. He had disappeared into the crowd. Would he strike again?

The war between Iran and Iraq remained a stalemate as judged by the conflicting claims of total victory by each side. Paul wished them both continued success.

European nations who depended on Arab oil but claimed at the same time to be friends of Israel demanded that Israel recognize the PLO. It was a necessary step toward peace.

Eight people were killed and fifty-one maimed by two bombs planted in central London parks by members of the Irish Republican Army.

No one demanded that Britain recognize the IRA.

Another half-dozen articles had arrived in the library. Paul hid there to escape from pneumonia, M.S., Arabs, and G.B. syndrome. He found refuge in the purity of history. God couldn't change history. Only historians could do that.

The Minims were Jewish converts to Christianity, the original backbone of Christianity. All twelve Apostles had been Jews, not just Judas. Then Paul had opened the religion. Generation after generation, Jewish Christians became rarer and rarer. By the end of the second century, there were none. None at all.

The meaning was clear. By 363, there were no Christians in Jerusalem who really knew Judaism and the Temple Mount. They couldn't have gotten into the secret chambers below the construction site. They wouldn't have known enough about the Temple Mount to have known about such rooms—

Once again Paul sensed someone looking over his shoulder. This time it was Hassan.

"I finished the book. I learned a great deal from it. But it is now seven years old. Can you give me some more recent references?"

"Yes." Paul tore a sheet of paper off his writting pad and began to write. He started with Jenner and Marsden. Before long Hassan had a list of over twenty papers to read.

Somehow Hassan's presence behind his back had not been as threatening as Chaim's. That had to be his imagination and not reality. If only the world were that simple.

As expected, there had been no more messages. Eight in all. One more and they would have had a full ball club. There were no more maps of Jericho on the wall, just Jerusalem. The location of the security forces was clearly marked out. The number of colored pins was impressive, as was the diversity of the colors. Paul didn't know what each of the different colors represented. It wasn't really his business. He was sure, or at least fairly sure, that Eleazar would have explained it to him if he asked, but he didn't.

Only one site would be important. The issue was to find that one location, to know beforehand, to prevent tragedy. Where would it be?

On that question, Eleazar had no new information.

"It's all there, I'm sure."

"So are we, Paul. But it's a big leap from our scattered data, our iambic hints, to knowledge. There is nothing else for us to do but scatter our forces wherever we think something might happen."

"There must be an answer. We're just too close to see it. We must step back and look again. Change our perspective."

"Do you want to see the messages again?" Eleazar asked.

"God, no. I know them by heart. I've looked at them until I'm blue in the face."

"So have we."

Paul walked to the map of the Temple Mount. It was drawn from above, showing details of the Dome of the Rock, El Aksa, the stairs down to the sealed Golden Gate, the footbath where the faithful washed their feet so that when they removed their shoes to stand on holy ground, they would not track dirt upon it. The tradition that went back to Moses and the burning bush, when God had told Moses to remove his sandals since the ground he was walking on was holy.

Paul studied the map in silence. It showed every stone, every pathway. Nothing. Only the things he had walked over himself so many times. And touched and felt and smelled.

"Eleazar, are there any maps of the understructure of the Temple Mount?"

"The understructure?"

"Yes, showing the foundations of the present buildings and the older buildings, the supports for Herod's Wall?"

"No, only for the southern tip. El Aksa. Not for the rest."

"Why not?"

"The knowledge doesn't exist. The Muslims have never been great archeologists, and we cannot go digging around up there. Neither they nor our Chief Rabbinate would allow it."

Paul's response seemed strange to Eleazar. "We know as little as the fourth-century Christians."

When Eleazar asked him for an explanation, Paul brought him up-to-date on his historical project.

"You are very involved for a man who came here for a vacation."

"A sabbatical."

"A sabbatical is a time of rest."

"Supposedly."

"Instead you are working on three very different problems."

"More than three."

"More? Let me see. You have your, shall we say, inquest."

"Yes."

"And your historical research."

"Yes."

"And our little security problem." Paul merely nodded. "What else keeps you busy?"

"The medical problems of half a dozen patients."

"Yes. Your teaching. I had forgotten. All that variety must be a lot of fun."

Some fun.

So many papers had collected on Guillain-Barré syndrome that he could no longer ignore them. The pile was getting higher every day. Not as high as an elephant's eye, but much too high to ignore any longer.

He put on a tape. He wanted something he could sing along with, not just hum, but actually sing. A musical would do.

There was a knock on the door. He had a phone call. Good, while he was at the office answering that one, he'd call the hospital.

It was Carolyn. She would be in Jerusalem for Tisha B'Av, but not at the Wall. Her group was having a special service in Solomon's Quarry.

"Solomon's Quarry?"

"Sure, Dad. It's more authentic. That's where the stones for the original Temple came from. Not just Herod's Wall, Dad, but Solomon's Temple."

"Well, I'll be at the Wall. Tradition, you know?"

"I know. We'll be in the cave all night."

"Good." At least she would be away from the action. "You're not angry I won't be with you like we'd planned?"

"Of course not." In fact he was relieved. You couldn't poison a quarry.

"Anyway, we're going to be through at about eight o'clock, so I'll come to the Wall and then we can break fast together, after noon."

"That'll be great. See you on Shabbat."

As soon as Carolyn hung up, Paul called Maimonides and paged the Neurology resident on call. He was relieved when a female voice answered. It was Dalia. Not Hassan. Thank God. He told her that he had reconsidered. Mrs. Yousuf should be in the ICU.

She already was. A bed had opened up unexpectedly earlier that evening.

Paul didn't ask how that had happened. He knew. Unexpected openings in the ICU were always bad news for someone.

No, she told him, it had not been one of their patients.

Teaching rounds started on time. Mrs. Castel was to start on her plasmapheresis tomorrow, as soon as the machine was available. It was as hard to get on the plasmapheresis schedule as it was to get into the ICU. There were more candidates than there was time in a day to run them. Mrs. Yousuf, now in the ICU, could no longer breathe by herself. Their diagnosis was severe Guillain-Barré. She was on a respirator and maximal doses of steroids. The record of Neurology patients in the ICU wasn't very good, and they all knew it. The last one with G.B. had died. "Is her respirator on assist or automatic?" Paul asked. It was his first question of the morning, and caught everyone by surprise.

It was Hassan Rashem who answered, "Assist."

That was a relief. That was the way it should be in G.B. Now, if they were lucky and the steroids started to work, and she didn't get pneumonia, and her machine didn't somehow get unplugged, she should do okay.

Whoever pulled the other plug was still . . .

Paul pulled himself out of his train of thought. They were talking about another patient already. Like Scarlett, he'd worry about Mrs. Yousuf later.

Rivkah Geller had not done any work on the Pickwick poisons in over a week, but she remembered each and every step.

She took out the samples.

Mrs. Yousuf.

She had both blood and spinal fluid.

She took out the four Pickwick toxins and set up the runs.

She decided to run the plasma first. She began with the control, four measured amounts of toxin. She waited. The method worked perfectly. The readings were lower than in spinal fluid, but the plasma proteins did that. The toxins attached themselves to the proteins and that lowered the results. The poisons actually did harm because they attached themselves to the proteins.

Next she ran the plasma from the patient—Yousuf. Just as before, there was an extra peak between 970 and 974, where no known peak should appear. She ran the spinal fluid. There were six peaks. One was small, 197. That was about ten nanograms. Ten nanograms of nonspecific response. It was located between 975 and 976; just where it had been in Rabbi Eckstein and all those other patients with root disease. Relapsing G.B. was a disease of the nerve roots. Mrs. Yousuf didn't have classic G.B., but she did have a disease of her nerve roots.

It was the other peak that bothered Rivkah Geller: 972.

Forty-five nanograms. That was enough to kill a horse. More than enough to kill a woman. But what was it? It was in the wrong spot to be one of the poisons.

Or was it?

She checked her calculations.

She had made an error.

It was in the right place.

It was just where 972 would show up.

It was one of the Pickwick poisons.

One of the missing poisons.

Mrs. Yousuf had been poisoned.

Not once.

Twice.

Where had she gotten it? Where? And how?

Rivkah wondered what she should do next. She ought to tell Mrs. Yousuf's doctors, but what difference would it make? Maybe they could do something. Where had she gotten that stuff? Where? Why? From whom? That was the real question. Yousuf. An Arab name. Where was she from? There were Arabs from all parts of Israel. Rivkah had to tell her physicians. Dr. Rashem? No, that would take too much explaining. Avram Schiff? No, that would also take too much explaining.

Paul Richardson. It was easier to call him. She called the moshav and got him on the phone. Where to start?

"Paul."

"Hello, Rivkah."

Where to start?

"Paul. Do you know a patient named Yousuf?"

"Yes."

"Where is she from?"

"Lebanon, Why?"

For a moment Rivkah didn't answer. Her mind was racing through all the possibilities. Had they done more work on Pickwick than just testing the poisons on animals? No, she couldn't believe that. No, the poisons had been stolen. That had to be it.

"Why?" Paul asked again.

There was no holding back. "I've found evidence of a Pickwick poison in her."

"What?"

"I've studied her and she's got high levels of a poison. One of the missing ones, Number 972, and she's got very high levels. She had a low level before, and I didn't think it meant anything, but now . . ."

"And that poison would cause a severe G.B. syndrome?" He knew the answer but he asked anyway. The correlation of the levels and the severity of Mrs. Yousuf's disease made the relationship obvious.

"Yes."

"But where . . . ?"

"I have no idea."

"What can you tell me about the poison?"

"Not much else except that it is tightly bound to protein."

"Too tightly to come off with dialysis?" Dialysis was often used to remove poisons. After all, that's what the kidneys did and what dialysis did for patients with kidney failure, remove toxins. Perhaps it could help Mrs. Yousuf.

"I'm afraid it's much too tight for that."

Paul had no other good ideas.

He asked Rivkah whom else she was going to tell.

"Eleazar."

He should have anticipated that. At least she'd called him first.

It was difficult for Paul to get to sleep. He kept worrying about Mrs. Yousuf. A Lebanese woman had been poisoned with a Pickwick poison, a poison that was so tightly bound to her own proteins that they couldn't get it out of her body by dialysis. The steroids she had been put on sure as hell wouldn't do any good. If there was nothing they could do, she'd probably be better off if someone actually pulled the plug. Life on a respirator was not exactly the good life. Where the hell had she gotten poisoned?

That was obvious. In Lebanon, But who put it there?

The Israelis? No.

There were some missing poisons. Maybe the PLO had stolen this poison and they were using it to kill each other.

Paul did not want to believe that it was Israelis. Or the Guardians.

It was not his problem.

He'd worry about something else.

There had to be some way to help Mrs. Yousuf. There was no way to help Rabbi Eckstein anymore.

Mrs. Yousef . . . poisoned with a protein-bound poison . . . you couldn't get rid of the poison without getting rid of the proteins.

That was it. Get rid of the proteins.

The poison was too tightly bound for dialysis.

Plasmapheresis. It was the perfect solution.

If they couldn't dialyze the poison out of her body, they could take it out with plasmapheresis.

Another call to the hospital. This time he hoped Hassan was on call.

He wasn't.

18

The fact that Hassan was not on call cost Paul some time. All told, he had to make nine phone calls. Thank God the phone in the office didn't require tokens. He never would have found that many at twelve o'clock at night. While the operator paged the Neurology resident on call, he tried to piece together a story. He would have to bowdlerize it.

The resident on call was Dalia. The story came out in an awkward, halting, fragmented way, but the message was clear. Mrs. Yousuf needed plasmapheresis. Plasmapheresis? Yes. Why? Because she had been poisoned. With what? Some sort of organic pesticide. No, he didn't know exactly what pesticide. Yes, he was sure. Where had she gotten exposed to the stuff? In Lebanon, in all probability. How? How should he know? How could he be so certain of his diagnosis? Professor Geller had detected the toxin by a new method she was studying.

If it was an organic toxin, why couldn't they just dialyze her? The toxin was too tightly bound by proteins to come out with dialysis. It had to be plasmapheresis. She was Professor Schiff's patient. Dr. Richardson had better call him at home. Dalia gave him the number.

Avram Schiff was home. Once again Paul told the same story. Once again he answered the same questions. Another censored rendition.

In the end Avram agreed. She needed plasmapheresis. Paul should call Dr. Avni so that she could order it.

Two down.

Dalia Avni. She was pleased that Professor Schiff had agreed. Now there was only one more problem. What was that? The hospital had only approved the use of plasmapheresis in two neurological disorders: myasthenia and M.S. Dalia was fairly confident that they would agree to

279

do it on Mrs. Yousuf. But it would probably be best if Dr. Richardson called Dr. Nathan. Dr. Nathan? Dr. Nathan was in charge of the plasmapheresis program. Yes, she had his phone number.

Three down. One to go.

Dr. Nathan was at home. He knew who Professor Richardson was. Paul told him that he had a patient who needed plasmapheresis. For what? The same old story. The same old refrain. Okay, he would do it. There was only one little problem. What was that? No time. In order to add a patient to their schedule, they would have to drop a patient, a Neurology patient. Professor Richardson should talk to the Neurology resident.

Four down. How many to go?

Dalia Avni. The only patient they had who might be taken off the schedule was Mrs. Castel, the woman with M.S. She was a patient of Professor Schiff's. Maybe Dr. Richardson . . .

Avram Schiff. But she had been admitted specifically for plasmapheresis. It probably wouldn't help her. It usually didn't help in M.S. Would it help Mrs. Yousuf? Who knew? Avram agreed to the switch. Paul had better call Dalia.

Dalia. Good. Could Dr. Richardson let Dr. Nathan know?

Nathan. Fine. Could Dr. Richardson inform the chief resident so she could be started today?

Chief Resident Hassan Rashem. Another explanation. And more questions. Asked more aggressively. And then agreement. The plasmapheresis would start as soon as possible.

In the seventy-fifth reported infraction of the cease-fire, four PLO terrorists left Syrian-controlled East Lebanon, infiltrated the Israeli lines, ambushed a small convoy, and killed five Israelis before they were themselves killed.

For the first time, Vartan Boyajian did more than nod when Paul walked through the shop. Paul was almost startled when Sarkis' son said something. His voice was much deeper than his father's. It was also stronger and colder.

"Professor."

"Yes, Mr. Boyajian."

"My father is not young anymore."

"I know . . ."

"He is over eighty."

"I . . ."

"He tires more easily than he used to." The son did not wait for any response. It was obvious that he didn't care that Paul was a physician, and equally obvious that Paul's degree of understanding was not of interest to him. Paul felt like a small child being admonished for playing baseball too hard with his grandfather.

He stood and listened, his hands folded behind his back.

"He is still well. But we want to be sure he stays well. He and my mother will be married fifty-two years in the spring."

When he stopped, Paul nodded and went upstairs. Sarkis was at his desk. For the first time, his shoulders seemed a bit stooped, yet his eyes were as bright as ever, his movements as rapid, his voice as precise.

"I think we should begin right away. There was a great deal of material. I have spent several days trying to piece it together. It is still puzzling to me. I look at my notes. I can still picture the manuscript, the room, but not all of the original words. There was a time when I could."

"That's over forty—"

"Posh! At one time, I would have remembered it. I am getting old."

That was the second time today someone had said that. First Vartan, now Sarkis. Had it originally come from the son or the father? "Sarkis, I am a neurologist, you know."

"Yes. So?"

"Your mind is not getting old."

"Don't humor me."

"I'm not."

"Paul, let us not waste time. The problem is complex enough without our draining our energies on self-evident trivialities." He paused for a brief moment. Paul knew better than to interrupt. "The original must have been very fragmented. Our poor scribe had a hard time, and

of course some of his work is missing, and my notes are
less complete, less . . .''

''Compulsive.''

''I prefer the term 'comprehensive.' But in either case,
they are not as good as they should have been. I wish I
could remember why. Was I hurried? I doubt it. Was I
confused? Yes. I still am. Was that all? The rabbi was no
help. That I remember, as clearly as the fire that burned
his treasures. Old gold can be melted, not destroyed.
Words are worth so much more, and yet are so much
more fragile. So easily destroyed by those who do not
even understand them. The lifework of a great philosopher can be burned to warm the feet of one tired shep-
herd, or worse, to vent the spleen of an illiterate or hateful
victor.''

''We are both used to that.''

''What a world. We have to get used to the destruction
of truths.'' His voice changed, but he never paused. ''The
rabbi I recall. He and I talked about this part. All he
would say was that it was a disgrace. No, that wasn't his
word. His word was 'shonda.' ''

''That's Yiddish for 'shame,' 'disgrace.' ''

''Yes. As I look back, I think he even tried to hinder
my understanding of this section. Strange. He was always
so tender, so kind. He would never have understood his
son.''

''His son?''

''Nahum Eckstein.''

''Nahum? Rabbi Eckstein?''

''Yes. He died just before you got here.''

''I know that. I . . .'' Paul stopped himself. What more
should he say?

''His father died just after 1948. He would not have
understood. We must get on with it.''

The old man opened the second of his old cardboard-
covered spiral notebooks and began to read his notes. ''I
would read these to you, but they make no sense. They
are filled with phrases like this: 'Why did they have to
do it?' Or, 'With that one act, all is lost.' 'What Nebu-
chadnezzar could not do, or Titus . . . ' 'Gone forever,
and we did it.' Then there are briefer fragments like 'Holy
of Holies,' and that is all that can be understood. The
rest is merely a salad of words and phrases. A word here,

a word there. No sense. Even the scribe recorded that at times he changed the order, and at others, he just had bits and pieces and he did not know the order. Phrases also appear: 'Temple of Solomon,' 'Ark of the Covenant,' 'Manna from Heaven.' Then we come to the last two parts. These are better preserved, and my notes can be read and understood.''

Paul listened. It told of some forty years of wandering. Was it merely a symbolic forty years derived from the forty years in the desert, or a real forty years like the forty years between the last two Sox pennants? Forty years of wandering to end up in Medina among the descendants of Ishmael. God had not yet kept his promise to them. They were not yet a great people. Just wait, Paul thought. They got more than mere greatness. Glory and oil.

"This fragment ends here. I am getting a bit tired.''

"I know, I must leave. I have to get to the hospital for my rounds.''

"There is just one more thing. The scribe made a marginal comment that many Jews of Medina were with the forces of Allah that captured Jerusalem in 638. He wondered if perhaps some descendants of the wanderer came home then with this document.''

"After an exile of over two hundred years?''

"It would explain how these Arabic fragments written in Medina got back here.''

"A strangely Jewish path leading always to Jerusalem. But what happened in that middle segment?''

"I don't know, Paul.''

Nor did Paul.

Muristani Road was not deserted when Paul left the jewelry shop. Yet it was not so crowded that Paul could not have noticed the two men who followed him down the road at a safe distance. They were both in their twenties, slim and dark. They looked like just another pair of unemployed Arabs.

It was his last teaching session and it did not go well. The news from the ICU, like the reports from Lebanon, was far from good. Mrs. Yousuf was still there, still on a respirator, on her first day of plasmapheresis, and was no better. No worse, but certainly no better. She still triggered the respirator, but patients with G.B. always did. Except Rabbi Eckstein, Paul thought to himself.

So much for the ICU.

There were two new patients. Paul discussed them both at length but no one seemed very enthusiastic. Were they too overworked to relax and enjoy learning? Or was it him?

The teacher set the tone, not the students. And he was fed up with so many things. He thought he had left that all outside the conference room, but he was too close to judge his own responses.

He said good-bye to them all and reminded them to stop by if they were ever in his part of the world. He would stop by from time to time to see how "his" patients were doing.

Paul wondered if he should stop by and say something to Avram. He probably should. He was going off the service. What was protocol? Was it up to him to thank Avram for letting him teach? Or was it up to Professor Schiff to come down and thank him for all his teaching?

It was most likely the latter, but what difference did it make? He wasn't a stickler for protocol, and moreover, he wasn't up to seeing Avram Schiff any more than he had to. He'd see him at the last meeting of the select committee, and bid him a farewell there, and thank him for everything.

Each member received a copy of the report done by Dr. MacNeal at the Armed Forces Institute of Pathology in Bethesda. He had studied the samples of tissue that Yitzak Cohen had sent to him. Yitzak stood next to the projector with slides and asked if there were any questions.

Paul had read the report. It said what Yitzak had said. Severe devastation. No more, no less. No messages could have gotten out of the brain system. No respiration. No movement of any muscles. Would he have recovered? That seemed to be beyond pathology. A question of philosophy or theory.

Romain Bernhard wanted them to vote on the cause of death. Determining the cause of death was not a democratic process. The committee was stacked. Paul pulled rank. He was the chairman. He knew how everyone felt.

He appointed himself as a committee of one to write the final report. They would meet again the day after Tisha B'Av and vote on it.

Yes, they could get together and put together an alternate report, and with that he left, avoiding everyone on the way out.

He left behind a great deal of commotion, more hushed conversations than any of the previous six meetings. They could write whatever they wanted, but he was going to write a truthful, unbiased report.

They could vote it down, but they were going to listen to him; at least once.

Shabbat dinner went well.

Carolyn was glad to be home, if only for one night. She was happy to see everyone, even Dr. Geller. Joshua had told her all about Dr. Geller. Carolyn was having a great summer. She told them of her adventures. It was wonderful to hear her laugh.

After dinner, there was no mill-game tournament, no T.V. Everyone just sat and talked.

At eleven, Rivkah excused herself. It was time for her to go. She had a long drive home and it was late. Paul walked her to the car.

"Your children are wonderful."

"Tonight."

"No, always." She paused. There were so many things they had not said.

She seemed to ramble. She talked about her lack of knowledge in neurology, her failure to find any poison in Rabbi Eckstein. She asked about Mrs. Yousuf. No better. Well, the poison, whatever it was, was tightly bound, so it might take some time to get it out of the brain. Such high levels. She talked about her other experiences with strange toxins, about the strange twists in their lives that had brought them together in this strange inquest. Why didn't she get to her point? This was all interesting, but that wasn't why she had to see him. Patience, Paul, he reminded himself.

"You know who Garcia d'Orta was?" she asked him.

"Yes, certainly."

"I knew you would. He was brilliant. He wrote the first book on medicinal drugs after ancient times. A Portuguese physician living in Goa. He lived and worked there most of his life.'' She stared at Paul and asked him a question. "Do you know that Garcia d'Orta was Jewish?''

"No.''

"Not many people do. It was suppressed during his life and afterward. He was a crypto-Jew who practiced Judaism in secret to escape the Inquisition. That is why he left Portugal and lived in India. Then, twenty years after his death, the Inquisition condemned him, and his body was exhumed and burnt.''

"Impressive. Such craziness.''

"That is what I wanted to tell you.''

"Why?''

"I will not exhume Nahum Eckstein. He is dead and buried, and it is better that way.''

"But . . .'' Paul stopped himself. He said no more. Neither of them did.

He watched her start her car and drive down the hilltop.

There were so many stars in the sky, more than in Highland Park. He would have appreciated them more, but the night breeze was chilly.

That night, he again had trouble sleeping.

The committee.

Some committee. Most of them were happy that Nahum Eckstein was dead. Was that why they had been chosen?

Had they been picked to give the right answer?

Was he just a rubber stamp? The frosting on the cake? Merely there to give some credence to a put-up job?

Rivkah had said so much. She was not going to exhume Nahum Eckstein. No witch hunts for her. No Inquisition. Even her choice of terms was peculiar. To compare what they were doing with the Inquisition. If she didn't want to know, why had she gone through that whole business about the poisons? Paul had never heard of them. He wouldn't have worried about finding traces of something he didn't know existed. Was it all a sham? Did she go through that for effect, so the final written report would look so thorough, so complete? Even the most suspicious would be satisfied. Hell, had she even done the work?

He was imagining enemies everywhere. He had become overtly paranoid. Next he'd probably imagine that people were following him. And he'd be convinced that they really were. After that he'd start surrounding his bed with wadded-up newspapers so no one could sneak up on him.

Mrs. Yousuf.

Where had that poison come from? Israel?

The real Israel? The government? Or the army?

Had those missing poisons actually been stolen? Or conveniently misplaced?

Was that story of the theft of the poisons a pure fabrication?

Or had they been stolen?

And by whom?

The PLO?

The Guardians?

Some other bunch of lunatics?

Israel had no shortage of those.

Or had someone else synthesized the same damn poison?

Why not?

If Israel could do it, why not the U.S. ?

The CIA?

Russia?

Israel?

Us or them?

But which us?

And they had all been in the hospital that morning. All of them.

Chaim.

Romain.

Rivkah.

Yitzak.

Avram.

All but the rabbi.

Including Hassan. He had been there too.

Was it all a cover-up?

Chaim Abramowitz was in the ICU that morning. He was the perfect one to have choreographed it all. And he had been spying on Paul.

Bernhard was a man who lived on outdated skills and pride, on transplanted chauvinism. His mind had been made up before the first committee meeting.

Maybe everyone else's had too, and he just hadn't been smart enough to see through the charade.

And Rabbi Levi, who'd sat quietly at each meeting, saying nothing? Was he a Madame Defarge who never learned to knit?

And that nurse. Could he have been in the ICU that morning? He was an O.R. nurse, not an ICU nurse. That hadn't stopped him from mixing up the orders on Zalman Cohen. And he was somewhere in Lebanon now.

Tisha B'Av was only four days off.

Four days.

Had he set the alarm? He could just see the clock radio across the room: 6:56. If he had set it, it would go off in four minutes. Should he get up and turn it off so it wouldn't disturb Joshua and Carolyn?

Outside the window, a few noises of awakening could be heard. Muffled, far-off voices, a few barks, a baby crying, a car starting. He had set the alarm; the news started.

Using a coordinated effort which included planes, tanks, and artillery, Israel had shelled Syrian positions along a forty-kilometer front in response to continued infractions of the cease-fire. Following two and a half hours of continuous firing, Israel announced a new cease-fire with the reminder that she took a dim view of any infractions. In London a prominent Israeli neurosurgeon examined Shlomo Argov and expressed the hope that the injured ambassador would soon be able to return to Israel.

"Two submachine guns were found last night in the village of Abu Gosh." It came like a lightning bolt. The staccato voice delivered the story with no emotion. Paul hung on each word. Two Russian-made machine guns, suspected to be the weapons used in the fatal attack on bus 65, in which two or more unknown assailants had fired on the commuter bus, killing two, including an unborn child, had been found by Israel security forces in the same building in Abu Gosh where Prime Minister Menachem Begin had once hidden from the British during the Mandate. No suspects had been arrested. Several were being questioned. The area had been cordoned off.

That was all. With no change in inflection the next story began: "At the UN today . . ." Paul shut off the radio. That house belonged to Hassan's cousin. Maybe Paul wasn't so paranoid.

How had they gotten the Russian weapons? Via Syria? From fellow Arabs? Was Hassan involved?

Hassan had acted more withdrawn lately. Was it something at the hospital, or did he know that discovery was likely?

Machine-gunning a bus wasn't as subtle as pulling a plug.

Both were effective.

Sarkis looked less tired. Perhaps morning meetings were easier on him than starting later in the day.

The last segment had been found intact by the Arabian scribe. It had been easy to copy and the notes were complete. Sarkis read it word for word:

> "Let it be known from generation to generation, so that no rumors of false miracles will grace our enemies, so that neither undeserving friends nor despising idolaters can gain by their lies. The truth is simple. It was an act of God, as is everything an act of His will, but not a miracle which favored one people over another. It was a great earthquake which devastated much of the region. Let him who is in doubt travel sixty miles east, seventy miles south; there he will find the evidence. Tell this story as a mitzvah, that it may help someday reunite our people. That is our story."

"That's all?"

"That is everything, Paul."

"What really happened?" Paul asked.

"Will we ever know?"

"That's a cop-out. He really believed that the Jews themselves, the patriarchs, did it, that they sabotaged the Temple, but he couldn't tell the world. Why? What could have been so terrible? That they caused some deaths? No, it had to be more than that. But what?"

"I do not know," Sarkis said.

"And that's all? I can't stop there. There must be someplace more to go."

"The rabbi kept another manuscript next to this one.

It is now lost. I searched for it, but it was burnt in the fire."

"Do you have notes?"

"In my foolishness I didn't think it was necessary."

"Not . . . !"

"You see, it was a common book. The Book of Eze-kiel. It was old but not handwritten. Printed in the early eighteenth or late seventeenth century, I guess, published in Safed. A small edition, quite rare. He told me that the one explained the other."

"And it's lost?"

"Not altogether. There are two other copies of the same edition."

"Where?"

"One is in Constantinople." Sarkis, like a few Eastern Christians, still preferred that name to Istanbul. Jews never called Jerusalem Aelia Capitolina. Maybe they were right.

"Constantinople. The Coded Ezekiel!"

"Paul, what do you know about that?"

"The Parker Mission. In 1911. You were here then."

"Yes, I was a boy. I was just ten years old. The first we knew of it were the riots when the Muslims discov-ered that some Christian infidels had been digging under the Dome of the Rock. They rampaged through Jerusa-lem. No Christian was safe outside. I remember hiding inside our cathedral. A cousin of mine was not so lucky; he was beaten badly."

"They were looking on the Temple Mount for the trea-sures of Solomon's Temple, and they used a Coded Eze-kiel from Constantinople as their guide. But I thought it was all a hoax. I never knew . . ."

"Much of it was a hoax, I'm sure. Montague Parker was just an out-and-out adventurer, and the Swede, Ju-velius, who discovered the Coded Ezekiel, was a char-latan. But they both insisted it had something to do with the understructure of the Temple Mount, and . . ."

"And whoever set the fire had to know about that."

"Precisely."

"But I can't go to Constantinople," Paul complained.

"There is another copy here."

"Where?"

"In a small Greek library connected with the Church

of the Holy Sepulcher. It is under the control of a Father Dimitrios. I have, unfortunately, known him for over forty years. He is a man of only two virtues. He is dedicated to preserving books; not reading them, but assuring their survival.''

"We can't all be scholars."

"His other virtue is more obvious. He is a Cypriot and therefore hates the Turks. We should be close, he and I. We live in the same city, pray to the same God, have lived through the same disasters and privations, and hate the same people.

"I know I should not hate them, but it is hard to forget the Holocaust. Yet we two are not close. He is an arrogant man who cares only about preserving books, not spreading their truth. But I will speak to him for you and arrange for you to study the book. Tell me, Paul, how did you know about the Parker Mission?''

"I probably know something about it that you don't know.''

"What?"

"Who supported it,'' Paul said rather smugly.

"Who?"

"Chicagoans, the Armour family. They have done better things with their money recently.''

"Such as?"

"They support a chair in Neurology at our medical school.''

19

In ten minutes, all had been arranged with one phone call. Professor Richardson was most welcome to come to the Church of the Holy Sepulcher and read the book. Paul didn't need a second invitation. He thanked Sarkis warmly and hurried across Jerusalem. He once again did not see the two young men who followed him through the Shuk.

The twelfth-century facade of the church had always struck Paul as rather cold and drab. Today it seemed much warmer. Not quite friendly but at least it was non-hostile. That was also the most he could say for the man who was waiting just inside the door to greet him amidst the incense and the flickering lights of oil lamps and candles. Father Dimitrios' masklike face hardly moved under his flowing white beard as he returned Paul's greeting with a short grunt. No, he spoke no English and absolutely no Hebrew. That surprised Paul. The man had been living in Israel for fifteen years. Even Arabs who lived in Jerusalem spoke at least some Hebrew. But not Father Dimitrios. Did Paul speak any Greek? No. The priest shook his head. They settled on French, through which they could both barely struggle. Paul followed the massive black robes as they moved slowly yet powerfully across the church, creating the illusion of force, determination, fate. It was probably not an illusion.

They passed below the last three Stations of the Cross, through clouds of thick incense, across the rotunda, and through a small door. Paul could barely keep pace up a narrow staircase which barely allowed the massive girth of the Greek father to ascend. The father stopped outside an ancient wooden door. Once Paul caught up to him, he opened the door. Only then did Father Dimitrios' face show some emotion. He would bring the book to Professor Richardson and the professor could examine it inside this room.

No, the professor could not just rummage through the library.

What a thought; it verged on heresy!

The professor should understand that he, Father Dimitrios, was allowing him to view the book as a favor to an old and trusted ally. He could take no notes. He could look at the book as often as he wanted.

The room was dark and barren, its walls adorned only by icons and a single carved wooden crucifix. There was a small desk against the wall under the crucifix, with a high-backed wooden chair facing it. The only source of light was a naked sixty-watt bulb hanging on a cord above the writing desk.

Paul recalled that Dimitrios had described this visit as a favor for an old ally. Who were the father's new allies? Certainly not the State of Israel or most of its citizens. Did Father Dimitrios realize that Paul was a Jew, despite his Anglo-Saxon-sounding name and his friendship with an Armenian?

The father came back in without knocking and gave the small, well-worn, leatherbound book to Paul. When he was done for the day, the professor should leave the book on the desk and, yes, he could come back as often as he wished. The book would be there waiting on that desk until the professor was done with it. And may Our Lord, Jesus, bless his mission.

He didn't know. Sarkis had not told him. Had that been an act of omission? Or of commission?

The door closed with a hushed thud, and Paul sat at the old, narrow desk.

The old man's memory had not failed him. It was not just a published version of the traditional Book of Ezekiel. It was not the usual Hebrew manuscript written without vowels. This was published with vowels, and with the trope signs, the series of notations which appeared just above the individual letters and conveyed the melody of the traditional chant that went with each line. They served much the same purpose as traditional notes, but each had its own shape, and each shape carried a specific musical meaning. Paul recognized the chant immediately. It was the same trope he had studied as a child, preparing for his bar mitzvah.

He chanted the first line:

> It happened during the thirteenth year, in the fourth month on the fifth of the month, as I was among the exiles by the River Kevar.

Chanting the words of the prophet in Hebrew inside the oldest church in Jerusalem was a sensation worth savoring, but his progress would be much too slow if he chanted his way from beginning to end. He was not here to pray, he was here to solve a riddle. There was not enough time to chant it all. Instead he began to read it as carefully as he could, word for word, as if he were proofreading one of his own manuscripts before submitting it to a journal.

Ezekiel ben Buzi had been an exile in Babylon, by the Euphrates, when the heavens opened up and he was shown visions of God and became a prophet.

For the next two hours Paul read the pronouncements of doom and destruction, Ezekiel's dirge for his people, and the final promise of rebirth, of return, of rebuilding the lost Temple.

He reread every word, and learned nothing. He found no code, no secret message. He spent three and a half hours, and learned nothing about his problem. He would have to compare this text with a standard text, to see what was changed, what was coded.

He put the book down, and as he left the room, he suddenly noticed how chilled he was. The cell, and that was precisely what the small room was, a monk's cell, had been cold and damp. His shoulders ached, his hands felt stiff. He would bring a sweater next time.

As he walked out of the church, the brightness and warmth of the sun surprised him. Inside that mammoth structure the outside world hardly existed. It was always dark and always cool. Paul stood in the courtyard and absorbed some of the warmth and reached in his pocket and put on his sunglasses. It was time to go. Once again he was too preoccupied to notice the same two young men, who once again fell in behind him.

Somehow he felt relieved to be in Eleazar Danin's office. It was warmer, lighter, and friendlier than the monk's cell. It wasn't just that the atmosphere was Jewish. The scattered piles of paper made him feel at home.

They never even talked about the Tisha B'Av warning. There was nothing new either of them had to say. They talked of Tisha B'Av itself and drank some coffee. Paul was going to be at the Wall, all night. It was something he had always wanted to do. Carolyn and Joshua would be in Solomon's Quarry. As would Eleazar. His son had wanted to spend the night with some friends of his who were here for the summer. They, like Paul's teenagers, were going to spend the night in Solomon's Quarry.

"They will be safer there," Paul commented.

"Everyone will be safe on Tisha B'Av," Eleazar replied.

"Come on, you can't guarantee that and you know it."

"We'll have more men in Jerusalem that night than we ever have had before."

"They still have the advantage."

"Yes. Only they know where they are going to strike. And precisely when. But we will stop them. We have to."

After a pause Eleazar added, "They will be safer in Solomon's Quarry."

Both men felt the need to change the subject, but what other subject was not equally sensitive to at least one of them? They did not talk about Mrs. Yousuf and the Pickwick poison that had somehow made its way into her body. Instead Paul asked about the submachine guns that had been found in Abu Gosh. Eleazar immediately understood.

"The resident at Maimonides, Hassan Rashem. You and he have become quite good friends."

How did he know that? And why? Why did he have to know that? It was getting chillier by the minute.

"He's a good boy."

A good boy! Paul said nothing. The condescending bastard!

"His cousin may be involved. We are not sure. But young Dr. Rashem has been cleared. He should already be back at the hospital."

Paul didn't know how to reply. He was out of his realm.

He was on foreign soil. It wasn't Chicago. Even Mayor Daley had not had such pervasive tentacles.

"I only told you this because I know you're concerned. And in view of everything else you've done, I suspect that you have a legitimate right to receive such information."

Right!

"The guns came from here."

Finally he could respond. "I thought they were Russian-made."

"They were. But they were ones we captured from the Egyptians in 'seventy-three. They'd been missing for several years. We never had been able to trace them. They disappeared from a depot. We thought some right-wing group like the Guardians of the City had them.

"By the way," Eleazar continued, "I talked to that nurse."

Paul did not have to ask which nurse. There was only one nurse to talk to, the operating-room nurse who had been sent to Lebanon. The one who could tie it all together.

"He swears that he put the orders in the correct chart."

"And you believed him?" The tone of Paul's words suggested that he did not.

"Yes."

That was it? A simple yes. "And I suppose that I'm supposed to believe you? And him?"

"You can call him yourself. He's back in Jerusalem. Talk to him." With that Eleazar wrote a number on a sheet of paper and handed it to Paul.

Paul stuffed it into his pocket. He might just do that. What good would it do? The nurse would tell Paul what he'd told Eleazar. If he could lie to Eleazar he could lie to Paul. Or, if it was Eleazar who had invented the lie, the nurse would say whatever he was told to say. This was not catch-22. It was every catch in the book all combined into one.

Paul had to change the subject. There had to be something else to discuss, not the select committee, not the report. Eleazar undoubtedly knew where everyone had been that fatal morning, who could have pulled the plug and who couldn't. Paul knew only one thing for sure: he himself could not have done it. Anyone else at the hospital could have.

They talked about the Third Temple. That was safe. He told Eleazar about his first reading of the Coded Ezekiel and Father Dimitrios.

"Does he know you're Jewish?"

"No, I don't think so."

"Don't tell him."

"Why not?" Paul asked.

"It will end your visits there quicker than if you offered to sodomize Dimitrios himself. He's an old anti-Semite, from a long line of Jew-hating and Jew-baiting Greek Orthodox priests. He was once implicated in supplying arms to terrorists, but we could prove nothing. Someday we will get him. If you want to break that code, say nothing."

"I'm not sure it's worth it."

"It will be."

How could he be so sure? Paul wondered to himself, but did not ask.

"Let me know what you find out. I'm enjoying your hunt."

Paul wished that he were enjoying his quest as much as Eleazar seemed to be.

Paul saw two young men standing across the street from Eleazar's office. They looked vaguely familiar. Where had he seen them before? He was terrible with names. But he usually remembered faces and could place where he had seen them. The hospital? That must be it. They probably worked as porters or something. "Shalom," Paul called to them.

"Salaam," they replied.

Arab porters, he decided. But why were they here? To spy on him? To watch him? To pursue him? He had to stop that. Not everyone in Jerusalem was involved. This was not the Watergate cover-up.

If anyone was involved, it was that nurse. He could have slipped into the ICU and pulled the plug on Eckstein. He had switched the orders and killed Zalman Cohen. And maybe he had poisoned Mrs. Yousuf.

Or had he?

What had Rivkah said?

Mrs. Yousuf had been poisoned twice. She had already

been poisoned when she was admitted to the hospital with facial diplegia. That meant that the nurse couldn't have poisoned her. Not the first time. He was in Jerusalem then, killing his other two victims. This was getting him nowhere.

He might as well suspect those two porters. Perhaps they had been sent to follow him. Paul turned around to look for them. They were not there. He was now imagining that people were following him. What next?

While he waited at the bus stop, he called the hospital to find out about the patients. He paged the Neurology resident on call. It was Dalia.

Mrs. Yousuf was no different. Four days in the ICU and three runs of plasmapheresis had made no difference at all. Questions of why, who, or where seemed less urgent when confronted by the frustration of having no solution at all, no matter who did it and no matter what the reason was.

Dalia had little more to add.

If it was not his week to help patients, perhaps it was his week to solve problems. It took him only two hours to translate the inscription he had copied at the Rockefeller Museum. Two hours and a very good Latin/English dictionary. The first two lines read: "Liberator of the Roman World" and "Restorer of the Temple."

The rest of the inscription consisted of other claims, from propagating liberty to defeating numerous barbarians. There was no mention of restoring Jerusalem to the Jews.

It had at least answered one question. Julian's own pronouncement, his own propaganda, proclaiming to one and all that he was rebuilding the Temple of the Most High God, made no mention of returning Jews to their land, or the land to the people.

So one more group of suspects went down the drain. The pagans had nothing to fear from the reconstructed Temple itself. Only if the Temple were part of a plan to give Jerusalem back to the Jews were they really threatened. And Julian had made no such claim. The pagans had no reason to sabotage the Temple.

Paul was now left with two tasks. The Coded Ezekiel and the final report. He was not sure which was more frustrating.

At home, surrounded by piles of papers, he shifted back and forth from subject to subject. He compared three different versions of Ezekiel word for word. They were identical. The Soncino had the easiest print to read. He would take it with him to the monk's cell. He shifted through the reprints, reading a paragraph here, a page there, looking at some illustrations, studying others. His part of the living room was beginning to look like a rabbit warren, or worse, like his office back at Austin Flint Medical Center.

He painfully began to type out the final report. He decided to do it chronologically, to give all the details as they had occurred. He would start at the very beginning, the onset of Rabbi Eckstein's first symptoms, and go through his entire hospital course, up to and including the pulled plug, and then cover each and every phase of the committee's work.

He knew the final decision. What was the official wording? Murder by person or persons unknown. The who was not his concern.

For the next two days he followed the same schedule—two sessions of typing divided by a trip to the Church of the Holy Sepulcher, to a small monk's cell, and the old leatherbound book lying on the old wooden desk underneath the bare light bulb and the ever-present crucifix.

He brought his Soncino text with him and started comparing the two word for word. Nothing was amiss. No code, no secret message revealed itself.

The next day he did it again, but found nothing more.

Then he went over it letter for letter, consonant for consonant, vowel for vowel. Two vowels didn't match, but that wasn't enough to make a message. Even the great cryptographers like Champollian and Sherlock Holmes could not have made much out of two lousy vowels.

The report was not going any better. He went through it step by step. History of present illness, physical examination, hospital course, autopsy findings, gross, microscopic, and electron-microscopic, even toxicology. There was no way to tell whether Eckstein might have recovered or not. The odds were against it. What were

they? Two to one? Ten to one? Fifty to one? A hundred?
Probably closer to one hundred than two. But there was
always that chance, and no one could rule that out. Not
Romain Bernhard or Avram Schiff or Rivkah Geller, or
the whole damn bunch of them. They could outvote him
and they undoubtedly would, but he would write what he
believed, no more and no less. Not one word less. In
less than a week, it would all be over.

After another trip to the sources of Christianity and
more frustration, Paul decided to visit Sarkis and tell him
he had failed.

Vartan was surprised to see him, and not entirely dis-
pleased. He sent him upstairs without any admonitions.

Sarkis was at his desk. His eyes were clear and quick
as ever, but the rest of him seemed tired. His years were
showing.

Paul told him his story and the old man listened. There
seemed to be nothing else to do. He was at a dead end.

"My young friend, you have forgotten a major principle when dealing with a matter of faith. You must always approach it properly. On Friday, make the proper
approach."

Sarkis was obviously tired, so Paul left without asking
him to explain his advice.

What the hell had he meant by the proper approach?
Sarkis always chose his words so carefully. He looked so
tired, so worn. He had aged ten years in less than two
weeks. Not his mind, not that wonderful intelligence, but
his body. You didn't have to be a great clinician to realize
that something was wrong.

The proper approach? The correct attitude? Maybe he
should wear a skullcap and prayer shawl while studying
the book. It would probably be the first time anyone had
ever done it in that room, or anywhere in that entire
building. Father Dimitrios would love it. He might do
it just to aggravate the good father, but not before he
broke the code.

The proper approach? What the hell was the proper
approach? As a pilgrim on a Friday afternoon, surrounded by other pilgrims, following a cross? It was
Tuesday and in two days it would be Tisha B'Av. He
would make his pilgrimage on the ninth of Av. And the

place would be the Western Wall, not the Church of the Holy Sepulcher.

Paul was done. The report of the select committee had been completed, down to the last detail. He had crossed all the T's and dotted all the I's. He had even typed out the final conclusion: 'CAUSE OF DEATH: anoxia due to an intentional act by person or persons unknown, who removed the plug of his respirator from the wall while he was still alive and potentially capable of recovering.'' As a compromise he had left out the phrase "premeditated murder.''

That done, he got a plastic laundry basket and started going through the stacks of papers. The ones on Guillain-Barré syndrome he threw out without a second look. The others he saved for a second review. With all the neurology papers culled out for early destruction, he went through the others one at a time. He got nothing from any of them. Histories of emperors, of wars, even of building the Temple. The Church of the Holy Sepulcher. The proper approach. There was only one proper approach and it was taken by pilgrims on Friday. The Via Dolorosa. The Way of the Cross. He would do it. In the morning. As early as he could. Stat.

He started at Lion's Gate. His back to the Mount of Olives and Mount Scopus, Paul entered the Arab quarter. He walked past the Pools of Bethesda and the Crusader Church of St. Anne down Al-Mujahideen Road, dodging donkey dung as he hurried to start. Then he was there, at the El Umariah School, the First Station of the Cross. Its courtyard had once been part of the Roman fortress named Antonia, where Pontius Pilate had conducted the judgment of Jesus, and it was there in the Antonia that Jewish rebels had made their last stand against Titus in the year 70. Now it was a government-supported school for Arab boys. Only in Jerusalem could that have come to pass.

Down the road some twenty paces and across the street, he stopped at the Church of the Flagellation. It had all taken place there over nineteen hundred years ago. Inside that church, in the basement, there was an ancient Roman street. The street. The actual Roman street.

He was on an Arab street. A crowded Arab street. Someone jostled him.

Paul turned, expecting the worst.

It was a young boy hurrying off to school. Paul watched him run down the street, bumping into more people than he missed. Paul thought he caught a glimpse of the two Arab porters. Then he wasn't sure. There were lots of young Arabs in the street. Often in pairs. And the pairs all looked alike.

Slim.

Dark.

Solemn.

Menacing.

Plotting.

His particular pair was not there.

Had they vanished into the Shuk?

Had they ever been there?

He had to get on.

Paul paid merely token homage to the next few Stations.

Three.

Four.

Five.

The Fifth Station, the Chapel of Simon of Cyrene, who was made to help bear the Cross. Across the street he recognized a familiar landmark, the Jerusalem Pottery Shop. Every other time he had taken the trip, he had been a tourist and had stopped in that shop to view its wonderful selection of enameled tiles. He did not even give it a second look.

Six.

Seven.

Eight.

Nine.

The Ninth Station. Paul was in a hurry, but he kept his pace appropriately slow and proper. He was not a Christian pilgrim, but he was a pilgrim nonetheless. He stopped where Jesus had fallen for the third time, now a doorway in a Coptic monastery.

Five more to go. The last five Stations were all inside the Church of the Holy Sepulcher, just a few steps from the narrow stairway. As soon as he entered the building the familiar smell of incense hit Paul's nostrils. In a few more minutes he would again be seated at the desk, below the crucifix, but he had to do it properly.

The Tenth Station, where Jesus was stripped of all his clothes except for a solitary loincloth.

The next three were all together on top of Golgotha. Up the stairs.

The Eleventh Station, the exact spot where Jesus was nailed to the Cross. Not through his hands, the way artists had depicted it for the last fifteen hundred years, but through his wrists like the image on the Shroud of Turin.

The Twelfth Station, where the agony of Jesus finally ended.

The Thirteenth Station: the lifeless body of Jesus taken down from the cross. The Pietà.

Three separate events which all took place on this one small hillock just outside Jerusalem. All demarcated in one small area, and in the minds and hearts of untold millions.

The last step in the drama took place at the base of the hill. Down the stairs and into the Rotunda.

There, in the middle of the Rotunda, laid out by Saint Helena, was the last Station, number fourteen, the Holy Sepulcher itself.

Paul edge his way through the low passageway to the Rock of the Tomb. He did not say a prayer. He did not light a candle. Neither would have been appropriate. He merely stood in silence and awe. Then, and only then, did he leave the trail of the Fourteen Stations, cross the Rotunda, and climb the staircase to the small room, which no longer seemed like a cell. He once again sat at the small desk and began to finger the worn leather binding of the precious book which lay directly below the crucifix. The book seemed different, as if it were something he had never seen before. Unconsciously he reached into his back pocket, pulled out his skullcap, and put it on his head.

He opened the book, not in order to scrutinize each letter, nor to examine each word. Not to find some extrinsic, hidden meaning which had eluded even the most mystical of cabalists, but to celebrate its real meaning.

He did not read it. He didn't have to. The trope markings were all there. He chanted the text, using the same melody, the same trope Jews had been using for as long as this building had been here. He chanted. He sang.

Sarkis had been right. This was the proper approach. Obscure messages be damned.

He sang louder. He began at the very beginning, with the dirgelike early chapters, bristling with doom and despair, made tolerable only by an unswerving faith in one God. He sang his way through the entire book, until he reached the vision of the New Temple. Not a Temple built by a pagan emperor, but one to be erected someday by the people of God.

There were no tempo markings. No metronome numbers. No accelerando. But Paul's pace quickened. There were times and places where such notations were superfluous. The New Temple. He stopped singing. He'd made a mistake.

Something was wrong. He had been following the trope markings with great care, but the melody had changed with an abrupt modulation, more Wagnerian than rabbinical. The trope must be wrong. They must be misprints.

He started to chant again. A real clinker. That one was absolutely unchantable. That word was never chanted with that trope. What a lousy job of proofreading. Even he proofread better than that, and he hated proofreading.

Another real clinker. Whoever had copied this was a first class idiot. Scribes who copied holy texts were professionals. So were the printers. Errors like this weren't supposed to happen. Just think if some poor kid had had to try to prepare for his bar mitzvah using this text. What a fiasco. What a shonda. It had probably happened to some scared thirteen-year-old. All because some careless jerk had not done his job correctly. Such a stupid . . . genius. A true genius.

What a brilliant code.

It wasn't in the letters.

The letters were all perfect.

You could read that book a thousand times and you'd find nothing.

You could read it.

You could study it.

You could memorize it.

And learn nothing

The code was in the melody. It was hidden as well as

the original purloined letter—right out in the open, right in front of his eyes. If he hadn't tried to sing it, he would never have found the code.

The code was in the errors of the trope. You had to know trope. Sarkis had been right. You had to approach it in the right way. No wonder the Parker Mission had failed. Valter Juvelius had not been Jewish. He could have been a great Hebrew scholar, a great gentile Hebrew scholar, but he would not have known how to chant Ezekiel. He could never have figured out its secret.

All Paul had to do was sing his way through and collect the clinkers.

It was real child's play—any well-educated thirteen-year-old bar-mitzvah boy could do it—and sheer genius.

Who could have done it?

And when?

He started at the top of the page on which he had noted the first mistake.

The first letter which had the wrong note above it was a Zayin. That had to be part of the message. Zayin. He took a pen and his pocket notebook and began to write. Zayin.

But was that the entire answer? Did Zayin stand for Zayin? Or did it represent some other letter? A Resh? Or an Aleph? Or a number? A two-step code?

Or Gematria?

This was Hebrew. And Ezekiel was a favorite of the mystics who had loved Gematria.

Zayin.

Twelve.

Joshua was so much better at Gematria than Paul was. Gematria was a game for mystics and twelve-year-olds. Paul was neither. And he did not believe that this was a game. Still . . .

It was simple. There was nothing to it.

A single letter.

He started again, past the first dissonant trope sign until he came to the second one.

Another letter. An Aleph this time. A silent letter, but with a vowel beneath it.

He recorded what he had found.

Two letters.

It was slow but it was progress.

He started where he had left it. It didn't sound right at all. The whole sentence seemed off tune. It was impossible for him to pick up a tune in the middle of a phrase and make it sound melodious. He was no Pavarotti. He wasn't even a Tony Bennett.

Back to the beginning.

Past Zayin.

Past Aleph.

He hit another one. He had three letters now. Or did he have three numbers? Or one number. After all, in Gematria, the numbers of each word were added together.

Twelve.

Six.

Five.

That made twenty-three.

Or L, F, and E. The twelfth, sixth, and fifth letters of the English alphabet. But Jewish mystics didn't use English. They used Hebrew and Yiddish.

What was the twelfth letter in the Yiddish alphabet?

That depended upon whether you were from Russia or Germany.

It couldn't be Yiddish.

Or Gematria.

It was a code.

A simple code.

Either that or he was lost.

He went on.

Finally the letters were no longer just letters.

If you had enough letters and they were in the right order, they formed words.

The first word. He had the first word. It was a noun. That made sense. Simplified Hebrew often started with a noun.

Gate.

Which gate?

Leading to what?

Leading from what?

Who knew?

Not Paul. At least not yet. But he would. He was sure of it. He could smell victory.

This was no Shakespearean acrostic. His letters were in order.

He started again.

They made words. Real words.

Back and forth.

Singing and writing. It was like the mirror image of composing.

The words began a phrase, an entire phrase.

From the gate.

He had to finish it. It was getting late. The church would close soon. This was not the place to stop.

A Taf.

Another Taf.

A Resh.

Taf, Taf, Resh.

That wasn't a word. At least not any word he knew. There were Hebrew words he didn't know, plenty of them. He should have brought his Hebrew dictionary with him.

Taf.

Taf.

Resh.

He could look it up when he got home. He didn't have time to waste. He could feel the minutes racing by.

Taf.

Taf.

Resh.

Once again he began chanting.

Taf.

Shin.

Five letters.

Taf, Taf, Resh, Taf, Shin.

It made no sense at all.

He'd translate it later.

Chant.

Chant and write.

It was a word he knew: From.

More than a word. A phrase.

From the gate.

Taf, Taf, Resh, Taf, Shin.

Another word: Steps. No: Paces.

Paces.

More letters.

Enough to be a word.

What was that word?

It wasn't a word. It didn't even look like a word. Paul stared at it. Perhaps part of the message was Gematria. These could be directions that used Gematria to convey the numbers. Why not? Was it one number or several?

He hated Gematria.

Numbers?

That was it.

It was a number.

But not a mystical number.

A Hebrew number.

Hebrew had no separate numerals. In Hebrew specific numerical values were given to certain numbers.

Not Gematria.

But real numbers in a real message.

Hebrew letters were also numbers. And not just in Gematria. Also in manuscripts, but they had different values than they did in Gematria.

Taf was four hundred.

Resh was two hundred.

Taf, Taf, Resh made one thousand.

Shin was three hundred.

Taf, Shin made seven hundred.

That was it.

From the gate, 1700 paces.

Now, if he only knew which gate. And which direction. It was only a start. The rest would come.

Champollian himself, the man who broke the code of the Rosetta Stone and translated hieroglyphics for the first time, couldn't have done it any better. Or any faster. The Rosetta Stone took him years. Paul had been at this for less than a week.

And he had less than half an hour left before the church would close for the day and he would have to stop. Thirty short minutes. And he had no idea how many more missounded notes were left. He had no way to predict.

It could be a couplet, or a synopsis of *Gone with the Wind*.

He went on.

Back and forth.

Letter by letter.

Until he had a word: Always.

A series of words: To the right.

The letters continued to pop out at him.

Miraculously they continued to form words.

And the words became phrases.

The right fork.

Phrases which made sense, which seemed to follow one another.

To the left 150 paces.

To the right 450 paces.

It was a simple, concise, logical set of directions.

A rope ladder.

It couldn't be much longer. He was almost at the end of the book. He had less than ten minutes left.

Two pages.

How many more phrases were there?

One more: The middle level.

And another: The room on the right.

One page left.

He chanted it as quickly as he could.

It was perfect.

Or had he gone too fast?

He had to double-check.

He had to double-check it all.

He started at the beginning.

He was half-humming, half-singing, half-shouting.

Thank God the door was thick.

He went through the entire fractured melody. It sounded as fragmented as that old four-record set of the complete atonal works of Anton Webern. But at least this made more sense. Or did it? He had to leave. He took one glance at his notes.

From the gate, 1700 paces.

Always to the right.

The right fork.

To the left, 150 paces.

To the right, 450 paces.

A rope ladder.

The middle level.

The room on the right.

It didn't make sense. At least not to Paul. No matter where you started on the Temple Mount, you couldn't go 1700 paces in the same direction, and certainly not 2150 paces. And that was what the directions called for. It was just impossible. Perhaps Eleazar could figure it out.

As he crossed the Rotunda for what he knew would be

the last time, he was still softly chanting to himself. He saw Father Dimitrios and began to walk over to him. The father might well be an anti-Semitic bastard, but Paul did want to thank him and tell him that he had completed his work, and would no longer need the book or the room.

Father Dimitrios saw him and gave him a shallow smile of recognition. It was no more than a brief flicker, and it was followed by a prolonged glare of pure hatred. All at once Paul knew why. He reached up and touched his yarmulke. Too damn bad. Paul smiled at the father, waved at him, and blew him a kiss.

From the gate, 1700 paces.
Always to the right.
The right fork.
To the left, 150 paces.
To the right, 450 paces.
A rope ladder.
The middle level.
The room on the right.

Eleazar carefully wrote out each step as if Paul had been dictating the results of his latest experiment to a skilled secretary for later transcription. Together the two of them tried to work out the solution on the map of the Temple Mount.

No matter what they did, it just didn't fit. There was no way to put those distances inside the Temple Mount. It was too damn small. Herod had not made it big enough. Or had Paul made a mistake? Perhaps 1700 was really 170, 150 was 15, 450 only 45. That way it might fit. That way you could start several places and stay within the Mount.

No, Paul was sure he was right.

It was 1700, not 170.

His dimensions were correct.

Then they had the wrong place.

The message said nothing about the Temple. Nothing at all.

Maybe it had nothing to do with the Temple Mount.

"What else could it be?" Paul asked.

Eleazar didn't know.

Neither did Paul.

But it didn't fit up there, on the top of God's Holy Mountain.

Paul finally brought their discussion to a close. "I have to get home," he announced.

"Any special reason?"

"They're showing a movie on the moshav tonight. I promised Joshua we would go together."

"What film?"

"*Cast a Giant Shadow.*"

"I don't know it."

"It's the story of Mickey Marcus, the American who came here in 'forty-eight and helped to organize the Israeli army. I'm surprised you never saw it."

"Why should I see it? I remember Mickey. Such a waste. He was a great help to us. He was the last person to die in the War of Independence. He died not far from where you live now. Shot by one of our own men because he had never had time to learn Hebrew. We all remember him." He paused. "Enjoy the movie."

"I will."

"And be careful."

"Careful?"

"The hills are still not entirely safe."

"I know Hebrew."

"Most of the danger is for those of us who know Hebrew."

It was another night without much sleep. He had a new puzzle, and he didn't get to work on it until late, until after he and Joshua returned home from the movie and talked at length about Mickey Marcus, the one great American hero of the 1948 war.

At least, Joshua reminded him, they knew Hebrew, and besides, the Judean Hills were safe now.

Paul said nothing. He had other problems to worry about.

Not Nahum Eckstein. That he had put aside.

Not Mrs. Yousuf. There was nothing more he could do to help her.

This was a pure exercise in problem-solving. No personalities were involved, no motives, no prejudices, no politics, just a complex puzzle. He went over it time after time. If he could solve this one simple problem, he could go home happy.

He went over it again.

From the gate, 1700 paces. It couldn't be 170, or 17, or 1.7. It had to be 1700. He was sure of it.

Always to the right.

The right fork.

To the left, 150 paces.

Which gate, Which entrance? The now closed Golden Gate? The present sloping entrance? The newly excavated Herodian stairway? What difference did it make? No matter which gateway you started at, you couldn't go 1700 paces without falling off, much less the required total of 2150 paces.

To the right, 450 paces.

A rope ladder.

The middle level.

The room on the right.

The instructions were perfectly clear. As the saying goes, "You can't get lost." The only problem was that Paul didn't know where the hell to start.

He read the eight short lines again. Maybe he had made a mistake. He ought to go back and check his results. Father Dimitrios would love to see him again.

He read his notes a third time. It didn't help in the least. When he finished, he had no more idea what it meant than he had had while he was sitting in that small chilly room chanting off-key.

Three tries and nothing. He had struck out.

20

From the window of the bus that was taking Paul and Joshua into Jerusalem, Abu Gosh seemed no more sinister to Paul than it ever had. It resembled every other quiet Arab village just waking up on a July morning with Ramadam just over. Were there still Arabs there waiting to kill Jews? To kill him? No. Eleazar couldn't have meant him specifically. Was Hassan back to work yet? What had happened to his cousin? He was a citizen; second-class or not, he was a citizen. A simple expeditious deportation across the Jordan River was not possible. The army could not just pick him up, bag and baggage, and toss him out. All they could do was try him and then put him in jail and throw away the key.

The patio of the Caravan Café was almost empty. Its bilingual sign for Pepsi-Cola hung motionless in the sunlight. Two lone Arabs were sitting at separate tables sipping their morning coffee. Paul looked at them more closely. They were not the pair of porters that had been trailing him, just two other Arabs. The floor of the restaurant was wet from its morning hosing. The other tables were not yet in service, their chairs still propped up against them. One lone waiter was outside helping the driver of a battered old Peugeot truck with East Jerusalem license plates unload several cases of Pepsi-Cola.

Nine Arabs got onto the bus. Paul recognized none of them. A few were in the midst of animated conversations with their friends. Were they discussing terrorism, or last night's sheshbesh game? Paul couldn't tell. He understood absolutely no Arabic. Others were quiet, reserved, inscrutable. What were they contemplating? Certainly not yesterday's baseball scores. An argument with their wives? Problems with their teenage sons, who were more concerned with motorcycles than Allah? Or were they going over their role in some terrorist plot? There was no evidence of hidden hatred on any of their faces, in any of their eyes. He had sat with Hassan and looked at that building where they found the guns used to shoot up this bus. The house of Hassan's cousin. He had suspected nothing. So much for the great diagnostician.

Judging people was not his forte. Hell, he had thought the committee would do an honest job.

That was yet another unsolved problem.

All he had wanted to do was solve three problems. That and do a little teaching. He had solved none of them. He did not know who had killed Nahum Eckstein. True, solving that mystery was not his official job, but that did not make his failure any less real. It was quite possible that Avram, Rivkah, and the rest already knew the answer and were covering up. The most efficient way to protect the guilty was to eliminate the crime.

He had no idea what the warnings really meant. Both your houses. What houses? Whose houses? That one at least was clearly not his problem. He derived no more comfort from that fact.

The Temple. He had broken the Code of Ezekiel and had learned nothing. What really happened to Julian's Temple? If that document was to be believed, Jews had destroyed it; but the very act was so horrid that no one could even whisper about it. What act? Certainly not destroying the Third Temple. Stopping Julian from building the Temple was not a terrible sacrilege. What else had happened there? He didn't even have a good guess. When in doubt, call it a miracle.

The Central Bus Station was crowded and noisy. The sound of the vendors selling hot bagelas, cold ice-cream bars, cold drinks, and newspapers in several languages could be easily heard above the din. Paul bought a *Herald Tribune*. He hadn't checked the American League standings in several days. He and Joshua looked anxiously. Sox fans never learn. He should have saved his money.

They had lunch on the terrace at the King David Hotel. Paul asked Joshua if he remembered the movie of *Exodus*. Of course he did, and the book. Joshua had liked the book better.

"In the movie, Paul Newman and Eva Marie Saint sat and had coffee while overlooking Jerusalem."

"I remember that."

"They were sitting here."

"Really?"

"Really."

"Far-out." Then Joshua said, "Didn't we come here once before? With Mom?"

"Yes."

"I thought I remembered it."

They spent the afternoon just wandering aimlessly through the Old City, through the Jaffa Gate, past the Imperial Hotel, down David Street. The coin store on David Street had a coin of Herod the Great that Joshua wanted, but the price was much too high. Paul stood in the doorway. Down the street he could see the Crusader Hall vegetable market above which he had spent several days reading. It was time to haggle. How much were they willing to pay for the coin? That was always a turn-off for Paul. Once they started bargaining, no matter how low the final price, Paul would know he had paid too much. And even Joshua knew that most of the coins in the Old City were fakes. Paul had been taken before, more than once.

They walked by the Church of the Holy Sepulcher into the Via Dolorosa to Jerusalem Pottery. Joshua bought three small round enamel plaques for his room at home and Paul bought a five-by-seven copy of the sixth-century mosaic map of Jerusalem from the floor of the Church at Madapa in Jordan. Someday he would like to visit that church. Perhaps he would in another era, in another incarnation. The map showed a barren Temple Mount, Herod's platform when it was in between temples. It also showed the other main features of the city: the Damascus Gate, the Cardo, the Holy Sepulcher. Paul also bought a round enamel showing the evil eye, the time-honored Middle Eastern amulet to ward off evil. He needed one for his office. It might even help him here. No. He had a better talisman. It was still in his wallet. The eighteen dollars that Mr. Greenberg had given him. It would assure his safety until he carried out the required act of charity. *Tzedaka.*

Paul felt safer; but once again he felt compelled to

scrutinize the street. His two friends were not there. At least he could not recognize them. The street was crowded. Did not all young Arab men look alike?

From there, they wandered down to the Armenian quarter, to Boyajian and Sons. Vartan was in the shop, behind the counter. For once he seemed genuinely happy to see Paul. Paul and Joshua looked through the gold Stars of David and picked one out for Joshua. Vartan weighed it and gave him a price. No debate, no haggling. Paul paid him exactly what he asked.

"My father enjoyed your visits."

"How is he?"

"Very tired. He is napping now, or you could visit with him."

"No. I don't want to disturb him. I will come back before I leave."

"You are leaving soon?"

"Next week."

"He will miss you."

"I will miss him."

"I am sorry if I seemed a bit harsh with you."

"It's okay."

"He is getting old."

There was nothing Paul could say in reply. He had become all too keenly aware of how much older Sarkis now looked. It was as if he had aged ten years in seven weeks. Time didn't work that way. Men were not like that. You didn't have to be a brilliant diagnostician to know that. He didn't want to think about it.

"I have something for your daughter, and for your son, and for you. I will put them together with the star." Vartan went into a small back room and returned in a moment with a small package.

"Thank you," Paul said.

"It's nothing. Stop back before you leave. To see my father."

Joshua couldn't wait, so they opened the package as soon as they turned the corner. It contained three small medieval Armenian silver coins, each set in gold, and on a gold chain. Two small ones for Carolyn and Joshua. A larger one for Paul. The gold backing of Paul's was inscribed:

Paul Richardson
Jerusalem 1982
In friendship
Sarkis

Paul put his on immediately. So did Joshua.

It was time to meet Carolyn. She would be waiting for them at the Damascus Gate, a twenty-minute walk from the Armenian quarter, right through the heart of the city and the heart of the Arab quarter, a short, safe stroll.

BewAre tHe nInTh of AV.

That was probably very good advice no matter what it really meant. It traditionally had been.

The Arab quarter was probably not the smart place to be just now. It was still the eighth of Av but in just an hour, Tisha B'Av, the ninth day of Av, would start with its celebration of the return of Jerusalem to the Jews. That was not something that would please very many Arabs.

Would it be dangerous to cut through the Arab quarter?

Perhaps.

Perhaps not.

It certainly wouldn't be tranquil.

There was an alternative. It was a bit longer but it was certainly more peaceful and probably—no, definitely— safer. They walked from the Armenian quarter to Jaffa Gate and then walked around outside the wall.

When they got to Damascus Gate, the most Arab of the city's major gateways, Carolyn was already there. So were Jonathan and Pat, along with their two children.

The four kids went off to Solomon's Quarry and the three adults walked back around the city to Jaffa Gate. They didn't even debate it. Jonathan led the way. It would have been much quicker to go through the Arab quarter. They didn't. It wasn't appropriate to approach the Wall from Damascus Gate, especially not on Tisha B'Av. Despite Eleazar's revised plan, which now called for some Israeli soldiers to be actually stationed within the Arab quarter, it was safer to avoid that area altogether. It was called preventive medicine. Besides, the exercise would do them all a lot of good.

They entered the Old City through Jaffa Gate and followed the throng past the Imperial Hotel and then right

onto the road which skirted first the Armenian quarter
and then the Jewish quarter, and there before them was
the Wall. The sun was setting. Night was almost upon
them. The new day was beginning, the ninth of Av. It
was a time to remember the First and Second Temples,
not the Third Temple of Julian.

At the guardpost, there was a wait to be searched and
frisked. Had the Romans done this to the Jews in Aelia
Capitolina? Each person was gone over briskly and efficiently, both by hand and with a metal detector. This was
not a night to take chances. A midsummer's night on
which the dream of Zionism could be tasted. That dream
should not become a nightmare.

    noW Fair hippOLYTa oUr
    nupTial hoUr Draws apaCe

Tisha B'Av was a time of mourning, a memorial for
all national disasters focused into one painful catharsis.
Now it had taken on a new meaning. Jerusalem was no
longer a prisoner. The Temple Mount was still crowned
by Muslim domes, but the Temple is ours, Paul thought.
The Wailing Wall should now be a site for more than
mere wailing.

They split up. They had no choice. The Wall itself is
governed according to Orthodox laws, and men and
women cannot pray together in Orthodox tradition. Both
Jonathan and Paul wanted to hear the Lamentations of
Jeremiah, at least once, down at the Wall itself. They
wanted to be close enough to hear the chants reverberate
off Herod's building blocks, to be able to touch the rocks
themselves, to feel their strength and purity. Yarmulkes
in place, they edged their way through the crowd. It was
as if every Jew in Jerusalem were there. Paul saw both
Avram and Chaim in the distance. He wondered who was
on call in the hospital.

This was Jerusalem.

Jerusalem the Holy.

What had the psalmist written in his exile?

    If I forget thee, O Jerusalem, let my right hand lose
    its cunning. If I do not remember thee, let my tongue

cleave to the roof of my mouth. If I set not Jerusalem
above my chiefest joy . . .

How could anyone forget Jerusalem? Any Jew, especially. Anyone who did deserved to have his right hand
lose its cunning. Dalia was right. It was a good description of a stroke, with only partial paralysis, resulting not
in severe weakness, but in a loss of fine motor control.
The psalmist was a good clinical observer. The victim
would be aphasic, without speech and without tongue
movement. Another good clinical observation. Dalia really should write that up as a formal paper.

They were inside the crowd now, surrounded by Jews.
There were no Arabs anywhere in sight. He was at home.
He was safe. He could feel the chanting. Each group of
men chanted together, using the melodies they had
learned from their fathers. Paul and Jonathan paused and
listened to the mournful Yemenite dirge. It was a strange,
Eastern melody, more Arabic than Jewish, at least to
Paul, who had been raised in a background dominated
by Western elements. It was a melody filled with the
sorrow of Jews barely surviving on the southern end of
Arabia and giving life to their grief that the Temple was
lost and that they themselves were also lost, a refrain
burned into their very souls by the parching sun of Arabia. The melody was as old as their exile. Was it as old
as the fragments Sarkis had read to him? Perhaps older.
No one knew.

Next they moved a few yards to another world, that of
the driving, relentless rhythms of medieval Morocco. Was
there anyone left in Morocco to sing this chant? Life had
been better for Jews in Morocco. Not great, but better
than the Arabian peninsula with its more fundamental
Muslims.

Neither of these was what they wanted to hear the most.

Jonathan and Paul continued pushing through the crowd
until they joined a group of men near the Wall. An old
man with a wrinkled face, withered by more than just
time, his left arm uncovered to reveal the number tat-
tooed there during the Holocaust, was chanting the words
of Jeremiah. It had its own sad trope, the European one
that Paul knew so well. The tears streamed down the old
man's cheeks. A younger man, perhaps his son, helped

steady him. He was almost in a trance. Which tragedy occasioned his tears? Was it only one? His voice was tremulous. It was frequently flat, and cracked many times. No one had ever chanted it more beautifully. Not Richard Tucker, not Jan Peerce. No cantor that Paul had ever heard.

"How desolate lies Jerusalem, that was once so full of people."

This was what Jerusalem, what Israel, was all about. The reborn Jerusalem was once again so full of people. The two old friends looked at each other. It was as if Jonathan knew exactly what Paul was thinking, and Paul knew exactly what Jonathan was feeling. This was why it was all worthwhile, why all the aggravations and inconveniences of the day-to-day struggle to get along were worth it, no matter how deeply they cut. And why the threats, both generic and personal, and even the losses were worth it too. Jews had not been able to be here like this for almost two thousand years, yet here they were. Here he was.

"Your prophets have misled you, with false and foolish visions."

False and foolish visions. Like the Third Temple. What difference did it make what happened then? Sarkis had been wrong, it wasn't worth knowing. At least not for Paul. Not anymore. Let some real historian try to figure it out. He was convinced he had not made any mistakes. It was seventeen hundred paces.

"We are as fatherless orphans: our mothers are as widows."

The voice cracked with almost every word. There was little melody left to follow, and no rhythm. It was as if it had been made suddenly atonal, but miraculously more beautiful. It wasn't like the wrong notes in Ezekiel.

What did those directions mean?

If he only knew where to start, then he would know where to find that ladder to climb down under Herod's platform.

"Restore our days as of old."

The old man collapsed into the arms of two young men, and the three of them made their way through the crowd to a chair.

The small group broke up, joined with other groups

chanting the same verses. All of the groups had at least the required ten men.

They listened to men who chanted the Hebrew with different pronunciations, different melodies, different accents; dark Jews from India, black Jews from Ethiopia, blond Jews from who knows where.

*"To what can I compare you,
To whom can I liken you,
O Jerusalem?"*

To no place.
To no one.

*"My maidens and my young men are fallen
by the sword."*

Without pity, murdered . . .
Murdered like Nahum Eckstein. Why had he been killed? That was someone else's problem.
"Restore our days as of old."
It was getting late. It was time to join Pat. They worked their way back out of the segregated praying area to the open courtyard.

Here the atmosphere was different. People were singing, groups were dancing. Old friends were greeting each other. Everyone seemed to be there, even Rivkah Geller. The two of them exchanged polite greetings, very polite greetings. There was no need to be so polite. "I have finished my report."

"So has Avram."

"Avram?"

"You know that we thought the committee should consider two."

"Avram!" he exploded. He knew they were preparing a report. He somehow had not expected that Avram, his old friend, would be the one to write it.

This was not the place. There must be something else to talk about. "The plasmapheresis on Mrs. Yousuf didn't do any good."

Rivkah was also more comfortable with the change of topics. "That's not surprising," she said. "Whatever the toxin is, it's very tightly bound to proteins. Whatever's already in the brain may be there permanently. And the levels were so high.''

A polite farewell and then back to Tisha B'Av.

More tumult. More joy. More chanting. More friends. More crowds. More dancing. More tears. So many Jews. For a brief instant Paul thought he saw the two Arab porters, but he couldn't have. So many Eastern Jews looked like Arabs.

The four kids were in Solomon's Quarry with the rest of the teenagers. They were safer there. No one would put a bomb there. How many people were really on duty? Paul wondered. Like the soldiers slouching at the bus stop with their nonchalant alertness. He had not paid much attention to the soldiers, but they were everywhere. The plaza was surrounded by armed men. He had been too preoccupied to notice them.

By two o'clock the crowd was noticeably thinner; there was much less background noise. Most of the women had left, since they were not obligated to pray all night. Pat had gone to a friend's to get a few hours' sleep. There were still dozens of individual groups gathered together. Some were still singing and dancing. Most were chanting slowly. The old man with one rolled-up sleeve was still there in the midst of some twenty men. Jonathan and Paul went down and listened to him once again.

As the crowd dwindled further, Paul recognized Yitzak Cohen. They're all here: Yitzak, Chaim, Avram, Rivkah. It was just like the ICU that morning when Rabbi Eckstein was killed. They had all been there. All of them, plus Hassan.

He was glad that his kids were in that cave, far away from any possible danger.

Where the hell did it start? The gate. What gate? The Gates of Hell.

He went over it from front to back. He knew the directions by heart:

From the gate, 1700 paces.

Always to the right.

The right fork.

To the left, 150 paces.

To the right, 450 paces.

A rope ladder.

The middle level.

The room on the right.

He could recite it back to front:

The room on the right.

The middle level.

A rope ladder.

To the right, 450 paces.

To the left, 150 paces.

The right fork.

Always to the right.

From the gate, 1700 paces.

In his mind he had a clear outline of the surface of the Temple Mount, as clear as any of the maps in Eleazar's office. Even if you went diagonally from corner to corner, 1700 paces put you in the middle of the Kidron Valley someplace.

It didn't make any difference, front to back or back to front, inside out or upside down. None of it made any difference. He had struck out again. What was the record for consecutive strikeouts? He had no idea. He'd look it up in the *Baseball Encyclopedia* when he got back home. Back to Chicago.

There had to be an answer.

It had to make sense. Somehow, some way. It just had to.

One last try.

Ass-backwards.

Or upside down.

Upside down! That was it. It had to be. It was so simple. It was so obvious. It was like every Agatha Christie novel he had ever read: you make a logical assumption, and you're lost. You don't have to, but you do, because it seems so damn logical.

The instructions didn't say to go down the ladder, they just mentioned the ladder. He had assumed you started at the top and went down to get under the site of the Temple. That was what Parker had done. He had dug down under the Dome of the Rock, and had found nothing. Juvelius had been a charlatan. He had not actually broken the code.

Upside down. Up the ladder from below the city. How did you get below the city? The answer was obvious. There was only one way to get beneath Jerusalem. Solomon's Quarry! King Zedekiah had escaped from Jerusalem that way, through the quarry. Paul had known that fact for years. Even Joshua knew it. How could he have not figured it out sooner?

Paul reached into his pocket for his ever-handy map of Jerusalem and opened it up. Jonathan gave him a puzzled look. Why read a map in the middle of Lamentations?

"The Lord has uprooted his Temple."

Not his. Julian's. And not the Lord.

He checked it out: 1700 paces, 150 paces, 450 paces. It might work. If you started at the opening of Solomon's Quarry and followed the instructions, you might end up under the Dome of the Rock, under Solomon's Temple.

That might be it. Not might, would. What other possibility was there? None. If he started at Damascus Gate and followed the directions, he would end up under Julian's construction site.

Paul should have been able to figure it all out much sooner. After all, according to tradition, King Zedekiah had escaped from Jerusalem through that tunnel. To do that, there had to be an opening somewhere inside the city walls. Tomorrow he would have to go there and check it out. He'd take a good flashlight. The old ladder would probably be gone. If he was right, this would be of great interest to archeologists. The maps of the quarry showed that it stopped far short of the Temple Mount.

Would he find a middle room there, a room below the site of the Temple, where someone had started a fire sixteen hundred years ago, arson that got out of hand and destroyed more than just a barely started construction project? But what?

Had it not been Tisha B'Av, he would have smiled to himself for his accomplishment.

He had broken the code and no one else had ever done it.

Not Parker and not Juvelius. Juvelius didn't know trope. He read Hebrew, he didn't chant it. He had never studied for a bar mitzvah.

No one.

How did he know that for sure?

Could someone else have broken the code?

Not Father Dimitrios. To break the code you had to know trope. To know trope you had to be Jewish. And the good father didn't let any Jews read that book, the anti-Semitic bastard. That was the only copy in Israel and it was carefully being kept from those who might have understood it.

There had been another copy.

Rabbi Eckstein's father had had it. He had kept it with the old Arabic manuscript. He knew they went together. He must have understood it, that the one explained the other, that it showed how the Jews had sabotaged Julian's attempt to build a temple.

If Rabbi Eckstein, the old rabbi, knew, then his son Nahum probably knew. That meant that the Guardians of the City knew. Nahum *was* the Guardians. So the Guardians knew how to get under the House of God. That knowledge hadn't meant much when the mouth of the quarry was inside Jordan. But now it was in Israel. It had been since 1967.

Nahum Eckstein was dead, but his disciples were not. And they knew how to get under the House of God. The houses. After all, there were two Houses of God on the Temple Mount now, the Dome of the Rock and El Aksa. Two Muslim houses of worship. Two houses. THE WARNING. Paul now understood them all.

"My God," he blurted out. They all looked at him. Jonathan shushed him.

"My God," he repeated more softly. " 'A plague on both your houses.' Both their houses. Both the Dome of the Rock and El Aksa. A bomb under the Temple Mount on Tisha B'Av, at sunup." Then, louder, "Jonathan, we haven't got much time."

"What?"

"We've got to get to the quarry."

"No, Paul, the kids are going to meet us here."

"Oh, my God, the kids! Our kids! All four of them. I'd almost forgotten them."

Paul began to run. The crowd was thin enough now that he could actually run. Jonathan started after him, and then quickened his pace in order to catch up. He had always been a better runner. It didn't take him long to overtake his friend.

Without breaking stride, Paul yelled to Jonathan, "What's the fastest way to Solomon's Quarry?"

"Through the Damascus Gate. By way of the Arab quarter. But why . . . ?"

"We have to get there," Paul pleaded. By now they had slowed down to a jog. "We have to."

"Why?"

"To save . . . our kids."

"Paul!"

"What?"

"Don't go through the Arab quarter now."

"Why not?"

"It won't be safe!"

"It'll be safer than going any other way."

"What?"

"A hell of a lot safer. There is no time . . . no time . . . and the kids . . ."

"Paul!"

"I have to hurry!"

21

Paul was running as quickly as he could. He didn't know the shortest route. All he was sure of was the general direction of his goal, the Damascus Gate. And the fact that he had to get there as quickly as he possibly could.

The quickest way had to be through the Arab quarter, the one part of the Old City he didn't know at all. You could get lost there in broad daylight with a good map. It had happened to him more than once. The quarter was a jumble of narrow, oppressive winding streets, full of blind alleys, cul-de-sacs, dead ends with who knew what waiting for a Jew lost in the middle of the night. The mazes he put rats through in his laboratory were infinitely easier and obviously safer. His own analogy was not a comforting thought; the rats all died at the end of each experiment, sacrificed for the sake of science.

But not on the ninth of Av.

Eleazar's warning came back to him. It wouldn't be safe. His own safety was not the major issue. The other warnings were more important.

The lights and safety of the area around the Western Wall were behind them. Paul's heart was pounding in his chest and his head, filling his senses, but he could hear Jonathan running next to him.

"Do you know which way to go?"

"No," Paul yelled between huffs.

"Here, up these stairs."

It was the entrance to the Wall from the Arab quarter. He had once walked down this stairway. It had been an easy descent. From where they were standing it looked like a mountain to him.

"Slow down."

Paul was too out of breath to answer.

"Pace yourself."

"" . . . huff . . . huff . . I . . . can't . . . ""

"You have to."

"I . . ."

"We'll get there faster."

They were now taking the stairs two at a time.

Paul's heart was pounding so fast he could no longer count its rate.

"Here!" Jonathan yelled, pointing to a small alleyway to their left. "I think."

By now they had left the well-lit, heavily guarded open square far behind them. They both hesitated. They had to catch their breath. The alley was there in front of them, inviting them, enticing them, seducing them. They had no choice. They looked at each other. Jonathan's eyes had a question in them. One look at Paul and he knew the answer. They had no choice. They each took one more deep breath and without a word plunged into the Arab quarter itself. The buildings pressed in on them from both sides, oppressing them as if the ancient structures themselves were part of a conspiracy to stop them from reaching the gate on time.

The alley turned abruptly to the left and split in two.

Which way?

Paul was sure he knew. He started to the right up a winding narrow street which was little more than a cobblestone path.

Jonathan knew. He started to the left up another narrow street.

In a few seconds they were separated by thick walls and darkness.

Paul stopped. He was alone.

Where was Jonathan?

"Jonathan!" he whispered loudly.

There was no reply.

He said his friend's name aloud.

Again there was no answer.

His own heartbeat was all he heard. It sounded like a series of cannon shots. He fought to catch his breath.

He listened as hard as he could.

He heard nothing.

No one else was on that street. Unless they were noiselessly sneaking up on him.

"Jonathan," he whispered again.

The walls were crushing in on him.

Should he go on alone or should he work his way back to find Jonathan? That would take time. He didn't have any time.

He stood still, frozen in time and place.

"Jonathan," he whispered loudly, hoarsely. He had caught his breath. His ears were no longer filled with the sounds of his own body. It was like going down West Madison in the middle of the night. This was Arab territory, a foreign enclave, an armed camp in the middle of Jerusalem. There were virtually no troops on guard here. The streets were deserted. No police. No Jews. No Arabs. That was wishful thinking. It was the Arab quarter. It was full of Arabs. They might not be on the street at five A.M., but they were there behind each doorway, each shuttered window. They should just stay there. The last thing he needed was to run into some Arabs, a few of Arafat's friends.

Where was Jonathan? Paul knew the quarter was full of terrorists. Why weren't they all up in Lebanon, out in the open? Why did they have to be here in Jerusalem? Just a few more of Hassan's cousins. Friendly Arabs. The only good Arab . . .

A footstep.

He heard a footstep. He was sure of it.

It had been behind him. Had someone been following him?

He turned as slowly and silently as he could and focused his entire consciousness on his senses.

He couldn't see anyone.

He listened.

A soft footstep.

Another.

Getting closer.

Even closer.

"Paul."

"Jonathan."

"You made the wrong turn."

"I did?"

"Yes. Follow me." With that, Jonathan began to jog back toward the fork in the road. The pathway was too narrow for them to run side by side. Paul followed the sound of his friend's steps. In half a minute they were back at the start of the narrow alley Paul had erroneously taken.

"This way," Jonathan announced, and slowed a bit to allow Paul to catch up. This street was just wide enough now to allow them to jog shoulder to shoulder.

Although they tried to run as softly as they could, the noise of their heavy strides echoed through the narrow street. As if by some prearranged signal, they simultaneously increased their pace. Paul had not run this fast in years, or this far. An occasional window opened and unseen eyes peered down at the two intruders. Was one of them making a phone call to warn others that there were strangers in their midst?

Jonathan led the way and Paul tried to explain it all to him as he struggled to keep up the pace.

The sounds of their heels on the pavement were like paired pistol shots. Both men kept listening for return shots, behind them, in front of them, to their right or to their left.

The silence was perfect for listening.

It was also eerie and terrifying.

Neither of them knew which was worse—the absence of any sound or the possibility that some other human noise might suddenly crash in on them.

Paul told Jonathan what he knew. He didn't have the time to explain how he knew it all. Or the breath.

There was a bomb deep inside Solomon's Quarry in an ancient hiding place. The bomb was big enough to destroy the Dome of the Rock. It was in the same room where other Jewish fanatics in the year 363 had put incendiary materials in order to destroy Julian's attempt to build the Third Temple. This time the objective was different, the temple of a different God, of Allah. But the fanaticism was not much different. There were some things that time didn't alter.

The streets were narrower now.

And darker.

A perfect place for a mugging, an ambush. Almost as good as inside the Damascus Gate itself.

"Who?" Jonathan asked.

"The Guardians."

"Those nuts?"

"Those nuts."

They had made so many turns and changed directions so often that Paul had no idea either where they were or which way they were running. Their pace had slackened to a mere trot. It had not been intentional on their part, although their footfalls were quieter that way. Their lack of conditioning had taken its toll. All they could do was jog.

They quit talking to save breath.

In the distance behind them they thought they heard other footsteps. It was hard to be certain. If they stopped and listened, they could be sure. That was the last thing either of them wanted to do.

They stopped abruptly.

There was a wall in front of them. A modern wall made of large clay bricks and concrete, fresh new concrete. It completely filled the street. Their way was blocked.

"Damn," Jonathan cursed. "This used to go though. At least I think it did."

Paul spun around and was about to start heading back when he became aware that there were noises coming up the street toward them.

Noises.

A voice.

Voices.

A flashlight.

Two flashlights.

Several voices. At least two. Maybe more.

Speaking softly. Paul couldn't understand the words. It was not a language he knew. Not Hebrew. The voices had to be speaking in Arabic.

That was it. The voices were speaking Arabic and getting closer.

Paul and Jonathan both instinctively backed up. The wall was ten feet high and its top was bristing with pieces of broken glass. They couldn't climb over it.

A dead end.

They had nowhere to go and they both knew it.

The voices were getting closer. There were at least three or four of them and they were no more than fifty feet away.

Forty feet.

Thirty feet.

Twenty-five.

Twenty.

The voices were no longer saying anything.

Twenty feet away.

They stopped moving forward. The two flashlights were shinning directly at them, one directly at Paul, the other at Jonathan, pinpointing them against the wall, making them perfect targets.

A voice, a strong masculine voice, called at them in Arabic. Neither of them understood.

They said nothing.

The same voice challenged them again. It was harsher, more demanding.

"Salaam," Jonathan said. Hello and peace. Like the Hebrew word "Shalom."

The voice laughed. So did the others.

An ominous laugh, a derisive laugh.

A laugh which bounced off the walls.

Thud.

A light suddenly came on inside one of the windows. It illuminated the alleyway so that Paul could see their attackers. He recognized two of them immediately.

The two Arab porters who had been following him for days.

Why had they followed him?

Why were they doing this?

A rock hit the wall above Paul's head.

And another.

Then the light went out.

The Arabs once more disappeared into darkness.

Then a rock hit Paul in the shoulder.

Another struck him in the thigh.

He and Jonathan could see them coming and there was no way to protect themselves.

It was not a barrage.

Just one or two stones at a time.

They were being stoned.

Stoned in Jerusalem. It was all very Biblical, but this was 1982 and he and Jonathan were being stoned in the streets of modern Jerusalem by Arabs. That made no sense at all. Arabs didn't stone the guilty. Jews did that.

Biblical Jews.

Or modern Jews following the letter of the law.

The law.

Guardians of the law.

Paul was no longer certain that the two porters were Arabs.

He heard Jonathan grunt as a stone hit him in the chest.

There was one thing they could do. They could throw the stones back.

Paul bent down and picked up a rock. It was about the size of a baseball. A lopsided, overweight, jagged baseball.

The flashlight made a good target.

A fastball. Right down the middle.

He heard it hit.

''Ow.''

Bull's-eye.

He had hit the guy with the flashlight. All those years spent in schoolyards throwing endless numbers of fastballs at targets painted on the walls were finally paying off.

The flashlight clanked against the pavement and went out.

Pop, thud, whack.

The Arabs were throwing the stones as fast as they could.

It became a fusillade of rocks, a series of wild salvos.

Thank God they had not grown up playing baseball.

The more quickly the chunks of rock came in, the more they seemed to miss their marks.

Paul and Jonathan took their time and fired their rocks one at a time, aiming at the one remaining flashlight. Paul stumbled—he had been hit in the forehead. It was only a glancing blow but it stunned him for a second.

He could feel the blood streaming down into his left eye.

Crash.

The second flashlight went out.

Jonathan had made a direct hit. He had always had great control.

Clank.

The flashlight struck the wall next to Paul's head.

Everything was dark.

Dark and quiet.

Paul crouched down to make himself as small a target

as he could. Considering his bulk, that wasn't an easy job.

The fusillade had slowed to a steady, staccato rhythm.

Paul held a stone tightly in his right hand. He'd throw it, if he only had a target he could see.

Thud.

Thud.

One after another, stones struck the wall behind them.

Thud.

"Agh." One hit Paul on his left shoulder.

Thud.

Bang!

That wasn't a stone. It was a shot, rifle shot.

Bang.

The stones stopped banging against the wall.

He was fine. The shots had missed him.

"Jonathan," Paul whispered. "Jonathan!" he called.

"I'm fine."

A voice shouted at them in Hebrew from the other end of the alley.

It was one of the soldiers stationed in the Arab quarter. It had to be.

Paul and Jonathan stood up and Jonathan shouted back at the unseen voice, identifying the two of them.

"Advance," came the answer.

They did as they were told.

As far as they could tell, they passed no one at all. The attackers had disappeared.

The Israeli was no more than nineteen, a boy, a uniformed soldier on duty who was saving their lives.

He shone his light on Paul's face. While Jonathan briefly told him what had happened to them and that they had to get to Solomon's Quarry, the soldier reached into his backpack, pulled out a small bandage, and dressed Paul's wound. Paul had all but forgotten about it.

The soldier told them the most direct way to the Damascus Gate. He couldn't go with them. He had to stay where he was. They were not the only Jews who might get lost in the Arab quarter.

They were off.

It wasn't far, just two turns and a short jog up the broad market street.

In less than three minutes they were at Damascus Gate.

They slowed down. They were almost home—almost but not quite. If they were going to run into any more trouble, it would be here inside the gate. They both realized it. It was the perfect spot for an ambush, or for random anti-Jewish violence. What Jew would wander there in the early hours, before dawn? Not one in his right mind, that was certain.

Their friends from the alley must have gone somewhere. They could be waiting for them inside the gate. Paul only then realized that he was still clutching a large stone in his right hand. So was Jonathan. He was glad they were. Those stones might come in handy.

They were walking now.

The Damascus Gate was a classic medieval gateway, built inside a twenty-five-foot-thick wall. The gate was really a zigzag track cut through the wall to prevent direct passage in or out of the city. It was a passageway with two right-angle turns.

The gate was dark. The ceiling light was out. They had to feel their way. First they had to walk into the gate then go to the left inside the wall itself. They had to walk about fifteen feet inside the pitch-black wall before they could turn right and get out into the roadway outside the city.

They were now walking very slowly.

This was the perfect place for a . . .

"Why?"

Paul was startled to hear Jonathan's voice pierce the quiet.

"Why?" Jonathan asked again.

"Revenge," Paul replied.

"Revenge for what?"

"The murder of Nahum Eckstein. They must believe an Arab pulled the plug, and they finally had had enough. The first letter came on the day of his funeral. Revenge on Tisha B'Av. It's a nice touch."

A few more steps and a right turn and they would be home free. They turned. They were safe. They were outside the city, the Demascus Gate behind them. The Arab quarter was behind them. Armed, uniformed soldiers were everywhere. Another forty yards and they would be at the quarry. Once they were there, they had to figure out exactly what to do. There were teenagers everywhere. Some were standing around talking. Others were lounging on the benches in front of the mouth of the cavern.

Paul saw a friend of Carolyn's.

"Hi, Dr. Richardson."

"Where's Carolyn?"

"Someplace inside with Joshua and her cousins."

"Damn."

They knew what to do. They had to go inside. Inside the tunnel. That was where the answer was—and the danger, and their children. All four of them.

22

As soon as they entered the broad mouth of the cave, they were stopped.

Security.

Metal detectors.

Frisking.

The search was exceedingly thorough. And too late.

Hell, whoever had planted the bomb could have come here on a quiet day long before the crowd had gathered. Before security had been beefed up. Before the first warning. Long before the ninth of Av. Before Av. All they had to do tonight was make a last-minute check, make sure everything was all right, and set the timer.

"Is Eleazar Danin in here?" Paul asked the guard.

"Who?"

"Danin. Eleazar Danin."

"I don't think I know him. Should I?"

"Of course. He's the . . . ah . . . consultant."

The young Israeli soldier shook his head. He didn't know what Paul was talking about.

They were waved past the security checkpoint and quickly entered the cavern. Paul was confident someone else had gone inside that same entrance long before, armed with a bomb.

It was chilly inside, and damp. This time he didn't reminisce about the movie theaters of his youth. They had to find Eleazar and the four kids. Only Eleazar would understand what he was worried about. They had to get to him.

Once inside, they started to look for their kids. Paul knew he should look for Eleazar first. That would be the smart thing to do. Sometimes smart didn't matter. Joshua. Carolyn. Where were they? And where were their cousins, Jonathan's kids? Adena and Aryeh were also somewhere inside the quarry.

It was just barely light enough to make out shapes. Neither of them was sure where to start. Neither of them knew his way around the quarry. They both scanned the crowd as best they could, trying to spot a familiar figure. It was just too damn dark. All they could see were shadows and outlines.

Not individuals.

Not faces.

Not the faces that they needed to see.

As if by mutual consent, they started to edge away from each other. It was the only plan that made any sense. Two vantage points were better than one. Paul moved toward the right of the cave, Jonathan toward the left. They had a better chance this way of finding some of the kids.

Paul kept looking back, trying to keep tabs on Jonathan. It was useless. After a few seconds Jonathan disappeared into the darkness.

Paul kept saying the four names over and over again.

Loud enough to be heard.

"Joshua."

"Carolyn."

"Adena."

"Aryeh."

Over and over again.

He wanted to shout them out. But it was a cave. His shout would just echo off the walls and become a sound without direction, a scream without a source.

"Joshua."

"Carolyn."

"Adena."

"Aryeh."

This was getting him nowhere but deeper into the void of darkness. He had no choice. He would shout out the four names. One at a time.

"Hi, Dad."

"Josh! Thank God."

"Dad, what's up?"

"Where's Carolyn? Where are Adena and Aryeh?"

"They're right here."

"Where?"

"Right around here someplace."

"Where?" Paul yelled.

"I don't know for sure."

"You have to."

"Why?"

"You have to get out of here."

"Why?"

"You just have to," he explained.

"Dad."

It was Carolyn. She was right behind them. Adena and Aryeh were with her. They were all chattering away and laughing.

"What are you doing here, Dad?" Carolyn asked.

"I came to get you."

"What happened to you?"

"To me?"

"To your forehead."

"Nothing."

This was getting them nowhere. They didn't have any time to waste. He still had to find Danin.

"Dad, what's wrong?" Carolyn asked.

Before Paul could answer her, Jonathan came running up to them. He had heard their muffled voices bouncing off the walls. At first he couldn't locate them, but then he had heard his son's high-pitched laughter fly right to his ears.

There was no time for explanations.

"Just go with Jonathan and get the hell out of here," Paul ordered.

"But services aren't over yet," Joshua complained.

"Josh, please. It's important. Do what I ask. Jonathan will explain it all to you. I have something I must do."

"But . . ." This time it was his daughter.

"Carolyn, please."

"Okay."

"And, Jonathan, when you get to the door, find out who is in charge and get everybody out. Tell them the whole story. It may be a hoax, but we can't take that chance. Too many nuts actually do plant bombs."

Paul didn't watch them leave. He had to find Eleazar Danin. He looked around but couldn't see Eleazar any more successfully than he had been able to see his own kids. And Eleazar's slender frame would be hard to recognize even ten feet away. The place seemed to be populated by teenagers with slender frames. The cave was not getting any lighter, and it was just too damn big.

Eleazar could be anywhere. Paul couldn't go through the entire place looking for him. It was too enormous for that. Paul asked another soldier. Again the soldier didn't know who Eleazar was. He tried asking a third soldier, and then a fourth. They knew nothing. How could they be expected to know anything? They were young reservists pressed into service for one long night in a dark cave. All they knew was that it was safer here than in Lebanon. Or was it? How could they be expected to know who Eleazar was? Not many people knew his real job, just the wrong ones, like the Guardians.

He was now about seventy-five paces from the entrance. It was pitch dark now, as dark as it had been in that alleyway, except for the small flashlights carried by the scattered adolescents.

As dark as the inside of Damascus Gate. He felt in his pocket. His penlight was there. Why hadn't he remembered it before? He always carried it, out of habit. As a neurologist he always carried a flashlight so that he could check a patient's pupils. Its light was very dim. The battery must have been almost burned out already.

Paul remembered the instructions: 1700 paces.

Always to the right. He was already toward the right.

He made his way to the right wall. He'd have to find it himself. Maybe he was wrong. He prayed that he was. Using the dim beam of his flashlight, he located the wall, and then, as the light began to flicker on and off, he used it intermittently to work his way along the wall.

He started counting. He guessed that he had started at about eighty. He couldn't be more than five or ten paces off.

Taf, Taf, Resh . . . Taf, Shin.

Seventeen hundred paces.

One hundred paces.

Two hundred paces.

By now there were fewer and fewer voices.

Three hundred paces

Three-fifty.

A rare voice, with only an occasional flashlight.

Four hundred.

He couldn't hear anyone else.

He couldn't see any other sources of light.

Four hundred and fifty.

His own flashlight was getting ever dimmer. He stayed as close to the wall as he could. The cave was cutting more deeply into the earth.

Five hundred.

Six hundred.

No more lights. No more teenagers. He no longer heard the melody of Lamentations.

Seven hundred paces. It was getting colder and damper.

The instructions were accurate. According to all the maps he had ever seen, the cave stopped about a hundred paces behind where he was. The maps were all wrong. The cave was still reaching further into the darkness. The right wall clearly extended far under the city.

He wished he had a stronger light. He was lucky he had any.

One thousand paces. He was now in a much narrower passage. He could sense that the walls were not more than four or five feet apart.

Twelve hundred.

Thirteen hundred.

Fourteen hundred.

Fifteen hundred. The walls were wet. The floor was getting very slippery.

He used his outstretched hand to follow the wall and help maintain his balance.

Sixteen hundred.

At sixteen-fifty he came to a fork in the passageway. Which way? Always to the right. He took the right fork. Another fifty paces. Seventeen hundred paces. The passage stopped dead. He could go no further in that direction. He shone what was left of his light on the side walls. The batteries were all but dead. He could go to his right or to his left.

To the left, 150 paces.

It took almost no time to navigate the narrow passageway.

Another cross passage.

Another decision made easy by the Coded Ezekiel.

By the decoded Ezekiel.

To the right, 450 paces.

One hundred paces.

Two hundred paces. The ceiling was getting lower.

Three hundred paces. He had to crouch.

The battery was dead.

He walked very slowly, touching one wall with his left hand and holding his right arm out in front of him.

Four hundred paces.

The ceiling was lower. He scraped his head. He had to bend forward to get through.

Time.

How much time was left?

Not that much.

He had to hurry. There might not be enough time to walk.

He started to jog, bent forward with his hands stretched out in front of his body in an attempt to protect himself from the unseen. The unknown.

His foot struck something. It was a small rock. His ankle turned and his body hurtled downward. He tried to catch himself but he couldn't. He went sprawling onto the ground, scuffing both hands.

Jogging was out. He had to be more cautious if he expected to get to wherever he was going. To find whatever was there. And whomever.

Walk.

He had to walk.

He'd be safe that way.

Or would he?

They had tried to stop him in the Arab quarter.

They could still be following him.

Or at least some of their playmates.

Some other Arabs.

He had to go on.

Where had he been?

Four hundred?

No, a bit more: 410.

He started again: 420 . . . 425 . . . 430. He had to go faster . . . 440 . . . 450.

He was there.

According to the secret message, he was there.

Where?

He needed a light. Matches? Did he have any? He searched his pockets. He had an old matchbook from some restaurant or other. It only had a couple of matches in it. He'd have to use them sparingly.

He lit one of his precious matches. He was in a chamber of some sort, about ten feet in diameter. There was a rope ladder against the wall opposite him, going up.

How high?

He couldn't tell.

He crossed over to it and peered up into the darkness above him.

So far, all of the directions had proven valid. He had done it.

He dropped the match. It had almost burnt his fingers. What he had to do next was obvious. The ladder was right there, less than two feet away from him.

Two feet from the answer.

He reached through the darkness and grabbed the ladder and pulled on it as hard as he could. It held.

The middle level.

How many levels were there?

There had to be at least three to have a middle one.

Three.

Or five.

Or more?

At least three.

Paul started climbing the rungs one at a time: one . . . two . . . three . . .

At fourteen he knew that he was at a new level. He could feel a ledge. He went up another two rungs, pulled out his matches, and lit one before he realized that it was his last.

He could see that he was in a narrow shaft, no more than three feet in diameter. It stretched up above him. He couldn't tell how far. The ledge was little more than a resting place and he had no time to rest. The match went out and he was once again left in total darkness. It didn't do any good to hang on that ladder, suspended in space. The answer was in the darkness above him.

Up he went.

Hand over hand.

Eighteen.

Nineteen.

Twenty rungs. He scraped his left elbow on the rough stone wall.

Twenty-five. The shaft was much narrower now.

Thirty. He was at a new level. He could sense the difference. His breath no longer bounced back at him. He could feel the edge of another ledge.

Matches.

He needed a match.

He didn't have any.

He reached out cautiously. It was more than just a thin ledge. He couldn't feel any wall.

Carefully he got off the ladder and onto the ledge. He took short, hesitant steps, working his way to the right.

He had no idea how big the room was. He counted his steps:

one . . . two . . . three.

He had to find the answer.

Were they still here?

The Guardians of the City.

Were they now waiting for him?

Had it been they who had attacked him, not Arabs, but Guardians in the guise of Arabs? Wolves hiding in the clothing of other wolves.

No. Not Jews. Arabs. If Jews could find this place, so could Arabs. They had controlled Jerusalem since the Crusades. They could have known about this secret passageway for a thousand years and just handed that information down from generation to generation.

Were they—

The bright light exploded in his eyes, completely blinding him. He could see nothing. The burning glare sent waves of fire into his brain, freezing him where he stood.

Two pairs of strong hands grabbed his arms, yanking them behind his back, all but tearing his shoulders from their moorings. He started to fall backward. That gaping hole was somewhere behind him. The sudden jab of a rifle barrel into the middle of his back broke his fall. Pain was attacking him from all directions. He was being pushed forward. The gun barrel was driving him into the blinding light.

They had been waiting for him.

Who?

Arabs?

The PLO.

No.

The Guardians of the City. That made more sense.

But who were they?

23

The light filled his brain.

It scorched its way from his retinas straight back to his occipital lobes, leaving nothing in its wake. General Sherman could not have been any more destructive. Paul screwed his eyes shut as hard as he could in a futile attempt to stave off its intensity. It didn't help much. Slowly he felt the searing power of the beacon begin to decrease. His eyes were still blind but his cheeks were no longer on fire. He was not yet in control of his senses. The pain from the viselike grips engulfing his arms was increasing. His arms were being forced further and further behind him. His shoulders were all but dislocated. So this was what the rack had felt like. No wonder so many Jews had converted. Where could he sign up?

His brain was wandering in an attempt to fight off the pain and retain consciousness.

The hard steel muzzle of the gun had forced its way through his back and was seemingly jutting out of his stomach, pointing at the overwhelming light. It must have missed his aorta. He was still standing. And his spinal cord. He wondered about his kidneys.

Poof.

The sudden noise sounded like an atomic explosion to Paul.

The light was out.

He could not see anything except two huge balls of fire dancing before his eyes. Two red balls. Like the balls of fire that had erupted from the bowels of the earth to destroy the Third Temple. Except these balls seemed to have arisen from his bowels.

They were green now.

Had the fire that had destroyed the Third Temple been this intense?

Would these balls find their way into heaven and form a cross?

They were now less intense and more orange than red.

Paul heard a voice. It was a voice he had heard before. Could it be the Arab voice of that man who had stoned him and Jonathan?

No. The voice was speaking in Hebrew.

It was the voice of someone he knew.

But whose?

He wasn't sure.

The balls continued to fade. They were orange-yellow now, with a few traces of blue, and they did not resemble crosses. Cyril had been a liar.

A voice said something to him, in English.

It was a man's voice. A man he knew.

The pain in his arm was receding. His shoulders were no longer being forced backward. No one was trying to make them meet behind his back. The gun was gone. They had not shot out the light by firing through him. They had merely turned off the light. Now he could concentrate on the voice. If only the lights would stop exploding in front of his eyes, then he could hear.

"Paul."

The voice seemed so friendly.

"Yes," Paul managed to say weakly.

"One of the real problems in this business is that once you set a trap, you can never be absolutely certain who will spring it."

It was Eleazar's voice.

Eleazar Danin.

He and his men were here. Somehow they had managed to get here first and catch him in their trap. The vises on his arms disappeared, leaving them hanging uselessly at his sides. Slowly Paul could feel the circulation beginning to find its way back into his arms and down to his hands. His fingers still felt cold but life was beginning to return to them. He could still feel the imprint of the hands that had imprisoned him. The middle of his back burned. It felt wet. He was sure that he was bleeding. His heart was pounding in his chest more than it had during his run through the Arab quarter. He was confident they could all hear it. But he was safe. Once he heard that familiar voice, he knew that he was safe. He began to catch his breath.

"I am actually glad to see you, my friend," the voice continued as if to reassure him.

Paul found his voice. "Boy, you sure have one hell of a way of greeting your friends."

"That welcoming committee was not designed for you, Paul. It was arranged for, how do you say it in your country, person or persons unknown. Had I known you were going to drop by, I would have greeted you differently. I realized that you might also figure it out and even show up here. I wanted to warn you, and even tried to do so, but when I called the moshav this morning, you had already left.

"It was actually you who solved it for us. You located the Coded Ezekiel and revealed its secrets, even though at the time you did not realize just exactly what you had done."

"You mean you knew all along that the code meant something."

"Not all the time. But for some time now we have been convinced that the two houses were the Dome of the Rock and El Aksa. They made the most sense."

"But when I suggested that they might be Christian sites, you seemed to take me seriously."

"And I did. In our business we can't take any chances. I didn't think you were right, but it was a possibility and I had to cover all the possibilities, no matter how remote. Besides, all that extra activity was a good cover."

"It sure fooled me. I didn't know which two houses until an hour ago."

Eleazar laughed. "We knew, or at least thought we knew. But we had no idea how. The top of the Temple Mount has been crawling with our people for the last ten days, but we found nothing, nothing at all. There is no way to get under those houses from the top. We were at a dead end. Then you came along with the solution."

Paul listened in silence as Eleazar continued his explanation. "I of course knew all about the Parker Mission and there have been rumors about the secret passages below Temple Mount since the days of the Babylonian conquest. And we knew about that Coded Ezekiel. We knew that there was one copy in Istanbul and one copy here. Several years ago we tried to get access to the one in Istanbul but were told that it had mysteriously disappeared. The only one here was unfortunately out of our reach. Father Dimitrios, as you know, is not exactly a friend of ours, and he, of course, would do nothing to make it easy for us. The Church of the Holy Sepulcher is a protected sanctuary. It is off-limits even to me. And these never seemed to be any urgency about the Coded Ezekiel and any possible underground rooms. It was more of an archeological concern than a security issue. We just let things drop. I had not thought about the Coded Ezekiel in years, and certainly never thought about it in connection with this problem.

"Then you came by with a strange tale of Jews getting under the Temple Mount some sixteen hundred years ago and your story had some connection to the Coded Ezekiel. It seemed almost providential. Then when you broke the code, it was almost too good to be true.

"As soon as you left my office, I knew the answer," Eleazar went on. "I understood that—"

"How the hell? I just figured it out."

"I had one great advantage over you. I knew you couldn't start on the top. So it was easy. I worked backwards. I started at the Dome of the Rock and went through all the steps starting from the end. I wound up just outside the city. Since it had to be something that went under the Temple Mount, the only reasonable starting place was Solomon's Quarry. You see, I knew from the very outset that the ladder had to go up, not down."

By now Paul felt completely alert. He looked around the room for the first time. It was a small room, no more than ten by fifteen feet at the most, and cut out of raw, barren rock which had never been smoothly finished. He was certain that there were archeologists who could analyze the way in which the walls had been cut and tell the type of tools used and exactly when the room had been cut out of the ground. Paul had no such expertise, but he did know history. It must have dated back to at least the Second Temple, more likely the First. That was how old the legends were.

The rough-cut walls were dirty, discolored. Blackened. They were covered with soot, old soot. Again Paul did not have the expertise to date the soot. Some Ph.D., using a device that could count carbon 14, could do that as easily as his kids could beat him at backgammon. But they wouldn't know what really happened here in 363.

"The fire did start here, Paul."

Once again Eleazar was a step ahead of him. "Are you sure?" Paul wondered out loud.

"This would be the right place," Eleazar began. "We are directly under the Dome of the Rock, and according to tradition, the Dome of the Rock is on the—"

"Exact spot where the First and the Second Temple stood, and where Julian's engineers would have started their construction of the Third Temple."

"We had our specialists go over the place earlier today. The fire dates back to around the fourth century. It was arson, set with naphtha. Once it started, it sent towering flames through the cracks in the ceiling of this room. There are also two smaller rooms on this same level that were engulfed by the fire. It must have made quite a sight."

"A miraculous one." Paul's arms hardly ached. His back no longer burned. His pulse rate was all but back to normal.

It must have happened pretty much as he had figured it out—he and the elder Rabbi Eckstein. Nahum Eckstein's father must have solved this riddle long ago. He knew the secret of the Coded Ezekiel and wanted it kept a secret. He would never have published the notes. He must have known what they meant. So old Rabbi Eckstein had known about these rooms. Paul was catching up with Eleazar now. The old rabbi knew, and so did his son and at least one of his son's followers. When Nahum was killed, they came here to set a bomb as an act of revenge.

Eleazar's voice stopped Paul's chain of associations. "They would have destroyed two-thirds of Temple Mount if we hadn't stopped them. The Dome of the Rock would have been utterly destroyed."

"Not one stone would have been left standing on another."

"What's that?"

Paul repeated the prophecy, originally attributed to Jesus.

"True."

"Didn't they care what harm that would do to the State of Israel?" Paul asked.

"Obviously not."

"Do you know who?"

"Yes."

"Did you catch any of them?"

"Yes."

"How?"

"Two of them came here today to make their final adjustments. They had enough explosives packed in here to blow off the top of the entire Temple Mount. We'd already removed all that. It was sort of an anticlimax. They were just two old men. They didn't even put up a fight." Paul nodded and Eleazar went on, "One of them was a friend of yours."

"Of mine?"

"Yes, a doctor."

"A . . ."

"From the hospital."

"Who?"

Eleazar ignored this last question. "Does it surprise you that it was someone from the hospital?"

"No." It didn't really surprise him. No one knew about the pulled plug except for a few people from the hospital. They had been very successful in covering up that fact. Someone from the hospital. Someone who had been there when it had happened and knew what had actually taken place.

"No," he repeated.

But which of his friends? He repeated the question. "Who?"

This time he got an answer.

"Romain Bernhard."

It was not the name he expected, but he was not really surprised. "That explains his attitude."

"What?" It was now Eleazar's turn to ask a question.

"His entire attitude on the committee."

Paul sorted through the images of the past seven weeks before he elaborated on his statement. "It was as if he had made up his mind before we ever got started. As far as he was concerned there was no need for us to go through a charade. I thought that was just his personality. But that wasn't it at all. It was a charade because he knew what had happened and knew that he was personally going to right the wrong. He didn't see any need for a fancy version of a coroner's jury. If you have already set the sentence, there is no need for such mere formalities. It was like Wonderland.''

"Not Wonderland," Eleazar corrected him. "Just the Promised Land. The problem is that it had been promised to too many different peoples.''

Paul remembered something that Bernhard had said. He had said that it was a good thing for Israel that Eckstein was dead. Why would Bernhard seek revenge on Eckstein's killers? Paul asked Eleazar.

"Paul," he replied, "that's not hard to understand. Think about it for a minute. From his point of view, Israel, his Israel, was better off without Eckstein. But in his Israel, no Arab could ever be allowed to carry out that judgment. A Jew—yes. An Arab—no. Never. So when Eckstein was killed, the killers had to be punished.''

Eleazar was right.

"Is your vision back to normal?''

"I think so.''

"Good. Come with me.''

The two of them walked into the adjacent room. It was smaller than the first room. It too was carved out of the same raw rock and its walls were marked by the same rough troughs that had never been trimmed. The style of rock cutting seemed identical to Paul. He was sure that this smaller room must have been cut out in the same era with identical tools. Even the black soot was the same, although it may have been thicker. Inside the room were piles of weapons—submachine guns, rifles, hand grenades—and boxes and boxes of amunition. That stuff had certainly not belonged to Julian. Or Cyril. Or Hillel.

"We ran into another friend of yours here today.''

Paul was startled by the announcement. Startled, but not surprised. He could not bring himself to ask the obvious question.

"Your good friend.''

"My good friend?'' What other good friend of his could know about this place? Only one. Sarkis. But it couldn't have been him. Anyone else. Not Sarkis. Who else knew? Paul was afraid to ask.

"Father Dimitrios."

Relief. Dismay. A sort of joy.

"He was not the fool he pretended to be. He learned the story of the Coded Ezekiel and after many years managed to get it deciphered. We are not sure yet who actually did it. Soon we shall know."

Paul did not want to know how Eleazar could be so sure that he would discover the answer to this question. "I don't understand why he let me read it."

"He really had very little choice. Sarkis knew that the book was there, and although Dimitrios was its custodian, the book was the property of the church and as such it came under the joint control of the three ruling religions. One of which I need not remind you is . . ."

"The Armenian Catholic Church."

"So he had no choice. Mr. Boyajian could have gone over his head. And besides, he didn't know that you were a Jew. Mr. Boyajian carefully made no mention of that. Only a Jew would be able to understand a code based on the trope."

"That last time when I was there, he saw me with my yarmulke on. It must have been quite a shock."

"He knew he was in trouble," Eleazar agreed.

"I thought there was more than just hatred in his eyes," Paul replied, thinking back on that last day in the church.

"He had used this place for years as a hiding place. He and his Arab playmates. Those guns were stolen at the same time as the ones we found in Abu Gosh."

For the first time that night, Paul knew that he had heard enough. It was all over. He didn't have to know any more.

"By the way, that resident . . ."

He was going to hear more whether he wanted to or not.

"Hassan Rashem."

"Yes, Rashem. That was the name. His family was not involved"

Paul was entirely drained.

"One more thing."

There couldn't be anything else.

"When Romain Bernhard was in England during the war with the Free French, he became an avid Shakespeare enthusiast."

He was on the other side of the looking glass.

* * *

Paul retraced his own steps. It took him far less time than it had before. Or at least it seemed to.

The quarry was empty now.

Jonathan and the four teenagers were waiting for him. They all greeted him anxiously.

"Were you in time?" Jonathan asked.

Paul nodded.

"What happened?" Jonathan continued.

"Not now," Paul answered. "I want to go back to the Wall."

"Good," Carolyn said. "That's where our friends are. They made everyone leave here and go to the Wall."

"Let's do just what they did," Paul said.

The six of them did not go through the Arab quarter, even though it was late in the morning and the quarter now represented no threat. It was still Tisha B'Av and they were going to the Wall. They took the long way. They walked west along the northern wall of the city. Then they headed south and entered the city through the Jaffa Gate. Once more they went to their right. Their way took them past the Armenian Cathedral of Saint James and then the Jewish Quarter. By the time they got back to the Wall the sun was rising over the Temple Mount.

As they walked, Paul told them about the bomb. He did not tell them that it had been planted by Romain Bernhard, just that there had been a bomb but that Elea-zar Danin had gotten there in time to prevent a tragedy.

Paul did tell them about the Coded Ezekial and how he'd solved the riddle, and he told them all about Father Dimitrios.

When he was done, Paul realized that he did not know all the answers.

Who had killed Zalman Cohen?

Bernhard?

The nurse? The operating-room nurse. A nurse who worked with surgeons every day, surgeons like Romain Bernhard?

Who had pulled the plug on Nahum Eckstein?

Certainly not Romain Bernhard.

And who were those two men who had followed him and tried to stone him and Jonathan?

Were they Arabs?

The crowd at the Wall was larger than it had been when he and Jonathan had made their run. Many of those who had gone home to get a few hours' sleep had found their way back. Others who had spent the evening elsewhere had come here for morning prayers. Some who had started at the Holocaust Service at Yad Vashem had come here. The other teenagers from the quarry were here. So was Pat.

They once again had to segregate themselves by sex. They had not had to do that in the quarry. Now, here, it seemed appropriate. The three women went to the right, the four men to the left. They walked all the way up to the Wall. It was the perfect time to feel the Wall, to touch it, to hear it. No two groups of people were at the same place in the service. Some were just starting morning prayers. Others were finishing. They were all reading Jeremiah. The beginning, the middle, the end. The different voices intermingled in no order, giving a touch of welcome disorder to their mourning.

"All her people . . . "

"Jerusalem is among them as one unclean . . . "

"Punish them, O Lord, according to the evil they have done . . . "

Jonathan saw a group of friends and he and Aryeh went to join them. Paul and his son followed, their arms around each other's shoulders.

It was Jonathan's voice that they heard starting the next recitation.

"How desolate lies Jerusalem . . . "

It had not turned out so badly after all. Paul had done something worthwhile. Perhaps he didn't know exactly what had happened here in 363. But he did know what did not happen in the year 1982. And he had in some way helped make sure that it did not happen. That was the ultimate goal of a physician, the prevention of disease. He had also done some good teaching and he had helped some patients. Not all of them; you were never able to do that, not in his field. He had helped some of them. Not poor Mrs. Yousuf. What had Rivkah Geller said about her levels of toxin? Over forty nanograms per cc in the spinal fluid. In the spinal fluid. Rivkah had said it ws in her spinal fluid, not in the blood. In the spinal fluid. The spinal fluid!

That was the reason the plasmapheresis didn't work. It wasn't that his idea had been wrong. They were just doing it in the wrong place. The poison wasn't in the blood. It was in her brain and in her spinal fluid. They had to get it out of her spinal fluid, not out of her blood.

How? There was no known way to do that. Not yet. But there might be one. It was just possible. He was certain that it had never been done before. He knew it would work. It had to.

He needed to get to a phone.

There had to be one at the security checkpoint. He found Jonathan and left Joshua with him. He would see them later. At home.

At the security station he told the guards who he was and told them that he needed to call the hospital. One of the guards dialed the phone for him.

He asked the operator to page the Neurology resident on call.

It was Hassan Rashem.

"Hassan."

"Yes."

"This is Paul Richardson."

"Yes, sir."

"Is Mrs. Yousuf still in the ICU?"

"No."

"She didn't die?"

"No. They just took her out of the ICU. They've given up on her. She starts her last plasmapheresis in about three hours."

"How is she?"

"Worse."

"In what way?"

"She can't even move her eyes."

"Where is she?"

"On Neurology."

"Good."

"Good! Don't you care either?"

"Hassan, I do care. I think I know how to save her life. I know why the damn plasmapheresis didn't work. We need some spinal fluid from healthy volunteers. It will save her life. I'm sure of it. We'll need at least one hundred cc's of it. You get started on that. I'll explain it all as soon as I can get a cab and get there.''

Now all he had to do was find a cab—on Tisha B'Av in Jerusalem.

Thank God for Arab cabdrivers who worked on Jewish holidays. No, thank Allah.

The explanation was fairly simple. The toxin, whatever it was, was protein-bound. Plasmapheresis had made no difference at all. The reason why it hadn't worked was that they had been removing the wrong proteins. The toxin wasn't glued to the plasma proteins. It had crossed the blood-brain barrier and attached itself to the proteins of the brain and the spinal fluid. Those were the proteins they had to get rid of. They would have to try spinal-fluid pheresis.

They needed normal spinal fluid in order to try it, just as you needed normal plasma to run plasmapheresis. The problem was that you couldn't just call the blood bank and order some normal spinal fluid. No one stocked normal spinal fluid. They needed at least one hundred cc's of spinal fluid for each run.

They needed volunteers to donate spinal fluid. So began the world's first spinal-fluid drive.

They got all the volunteers they needed: nurses, practical nurses, nurses' aides, medical students, residents, janitors, transporters—more than they needed to get started.

Paul, Hassan, and Dalia, who had just stopped by to check one of her patients, did all the spinal taps. They removed ten cc's from each volunteer. Altogether there were twenty-seven volunteers—270 cc's. Another thirty cc's and they could do three runs. The solution was so obvious that no one even thought to debate it. Dalia did the spinal tap on Hassan and he in turn did the taps on both Paul and Dalia.

They had enough for three separate two-hour runs. By that time they would know whether or not Paul's idea was going to work.

Once the spinal taps were all done and the machine had been primed with spinal fluid, Paul let Hassan take over. Paul had had it. He had to lie down. He was exhausted and was getting a headache. It must have been caused by the spinal tap. He never got headaches. Headaches were for patients. He found an examining table and stretched out for a few minutes.

It was almost three hours later when Hassan woke him up. The headache was gone.

"I think she may be better."

"Think?"

"I'm not sure. It's hard to be sure. I thought that Rabbi Eckstein was getting better too, but when Professor Schiff went over him, he was actually worse. I would like you to check Mrs. Yousuf with me."

Paul did as the resident requested. Hassan had been right: there was evidence of improvement. She couldn't move her arms or legs, nor breathe on her own, but she could open her eyes and could lift her head off the bed. It might not be much, but it was progress.

By the time they had completed the three treatments, there was no longer any question of subtle signs of possible improvement. Mrs. Yousuf was truly better. She opened her eyes. She moved her eyes. She lifted her head completely off the bed. She could move her arms and legs. Not normally, or with a great deal of power, but she could move them. She was even able to trigger the respirator. It was now turned to assist, not automatic. If things continued like this for another day or two, she could be taken off the respirator. Her life would no longer depend on a single thin electrical wire and a lone plug.

It was early in the evening and already dark. Paul was just too tired to take a bus to the Central Bus Station and then another bus to the bus stop on the highway and then either hope that one of the guards would pick him up or walk up the hill to the moshav. One of the hospital drivers saw him as he waited at the taxi stand. He was an Arab who had donated spinal fluid during the afternoon when they all knew that it would work and the calls had gone out for more volunteers so they would have enough spinal fluid for tomorrow's runs. The driver signaled for the doctor to get into the official hospital car and asked him where he lived.

They didn't say a single word to each other during the entire trip. It had not been such a bad day after all. He had figured out how to help a patient. He should have thought of it sooner, but at least he finally had figured it out. He hadn't been a pathologist this time, coming up with the right answer only when it was too damn late to do anyone any good. Now, if he could only be sure what had transpired in 363, he would be finished. The report. The warnings. Julian. Done. Finished.

Joshua and Carolyn had been in that cave. All he had left in this world.

Thank God the code had been figured out.

Joshua and Carolyn. And Aryeh and Adena.

He thought about their first days in Israel, about playing catch, about their trip to Kiryat Yearim, where David had danced before the Ark. Paul could still see Joshua's excitement. He could still feel it. This was what Judaism was all about. Joshua had actually been standing where King David had stood, where the Ark had rested. The Ark of the Covenant and the Ten Commandments it had contained.

Paul, too, had stood where the Ark had been.

And not just at Kiryat Yearim.

Under the Temple Mount. In that small side room.

It all came together. Joshua had been right all along. The prophet Jeremiah had not hidden the Ark on Mount Sinai. The Ark had been hidden in that room below the Temple. That legend had been more than a legend. The Ark had been hidden in the small room next to the one where the bomb had been put, in the room where Father Dimitrios had stashed the stolen arms.

And it had all happened once before.

In 363. The year of the Third Temple. The fire that had been planned to destroy Julian's foundation had been started in the bigger room, but it had gotten out of hand. Too much naphtha, maybe. Or too big a draft. The flames licked upward as they had been supposed to do, but they also found their way into the small hidden chamber and had set the Ark on Fire. The Ark of the Convenant. That was what those fragments were all about.

The Jews had themselves done what the Philistines had never done.

Nor the Babylonians.

Nor the Romans.

They themselves had destroyed the Ark.

But who knew what they had done even when it happened? Who knew the Ark was there?

Not all Jews, that was certain. Not the average Jew in the street. Only the select few.

The Guardians of the City?

The Guardians of the Ark? Or whatever they were called then.

And the story had to be suppressed in order to save the spirit of Judaism.

The Ark of the Covenant was gone forever.

The car stopped. They were at Neve Ilan. The Arab driver got out of the car and walked around and opened the door for Paul. Such formality was rare in Israel.

As soon as he got out of the car, the Arab put his arms around Paul and hugged him.

Paul slept for twelve hours. Twelve fitful hours. Too many questions were still unanswered. Rabbi Eckstein had been murdered by person or persons unknown. But by whom? By Arab or Arabs unknown. Maybe by one of Father Dimitrios' playmates. Eckstein knew about their storeroom. Had they discovered that and eliminated him?

How could he be so sure it had been done by an enemy of Israel?

He couldn't.

And why would they want to kill Zalman Cohen? He seemed to be spending more time bothering Israel than attacking the Arabs or their friends.

Sarkis' warning came back to him. "Not all the troubles of the Jews could be blamed on the Christians." What was true in the fourth century was still true today. Not all the troubles of Israel could be blamed on the Arabs.

It wasn't the Christians who burned down Julian's Temple.

The killer didn't have to be an Arab.

The Arabs weren't the only ones who thought they might be better off without Nahum Eckstein.

The government was embarrassed by him. They couldn't control him. He was causing a rift in relationships with Israel's allies. Maybe they would just quietly eliminate him. No real harm in that. What a miscalculation that might have been.

They could have done it.

That would explain the cover-up. A few well-placed phone calls. Had one of them gone to Rivkah? To Avram? To Yitzak Cohen? They probably hadn't had to call Romain Bernhard.

He had to talk to Eleazar.

He got through on his first call.

Eleazar was happy to hear from him. He congratulated Paul on his work of the previous day.

"Can I ask you a couple of questions?"

"Certainly, Paul."

Paul was not so sure. "You do owe me one," he reminded him. "A big one."

"Paul, if I can possibly answer your questions, I will."

Where to start?

Slowly. Not at the beginning, but with the easier question. Zalman Cohen. "Did the nurse switch those orders?"

Eleazar knew precisely what Paul was asking. "No."

"Then the nurse had nothing to do with it?"

"Not quite. The nurse was a friend of Romain's. He told Romain that Zalman was in the hospital. All three of them had been members of the same organization. Zalman knew about the hidden room. Zalman and Bernhard no longer viewed the world in the same way. Zalman didn't believe in terrorism by Israelis, so Bernhard was afraid Zalman might somehow stop him."

"So the nurse did nothing but tell a friend that another friend was in the hospital?"

"Not quite. He also stole the tissue samples. He didn't know precisely what had happened to Rabbi Eckstein. He suspected that it had been Romain. He knew Romain well enough to realize that Romain was becoming more and more bitter. The Arabs were the usual target of his hatred, but lately he had accused Eckstein of having betrayed their Israel. The two of them never discussed it. The nurse just decided to steal the slides on his own. To protect Bernhard, if necessary. As a nurse, he knew enough about medicine to know that without the tissue, no definite answer could ever be reached."

"He also didn't know that other samples had been sent to America."

"No."

Romain had known that. Everyone on the committee had.

"So the nurse wasn't in on it from the beginning," Paul said.

"Of course not."

"He merely relayed a fact to Bernhard, and Bernhard switched the orders."

"Yes."

It still didn't hang together.

What about those Arabs who had stoned him?

"They were not Arabs."

"They were Jews!" Paul realized. "Jews who spoke Arabic as a cover while attacking Jews in the Arab quarter."

"They were friends of Bernhard's. They had been ordered to follow you, and if you seemed to be getting in the way . . . "

Eleazar didn't have to explain that in any further detail.

"They did not know that we had already caught Bernhard. They were watching you."

"But why did Bernhard send the warnings? Certainly not because he wanted to be stopped."

"Consciously? No. But unconsciously? Who can be sure? He seemed relieved that we had stopped him. He was not defiant. He blurted out every detail. He seemed glad that he had not succeeded."

That still left one big question unanswered. And a couple of small ones.

The small ones first. "What did those capital letters mean?"

"I asked Romain, and he merely smiled."

"Why did he switch newspapers?"

"Convenience. He was at one of the hotels that caters to Americans. They have more *Herald Trib*s there than Jerusalem *Post*s."

And one big question.

"Was it an Arab who pulled the plug?

"We are not even sure—"

"Please, don't beat around the bush. If you are able to tell me, then tell me. If you aren't, then don't. But don't play games with me. I'm tired of games." He asked his question a second time. "Was it an Arab?"

"No."

"Then who was it?"

"I can't tell you that."

"Who?"

"Paul, be reasonable."

"Who?"

"I can't tell you."

"Was it someone I know?"

There was no answer.

"A friend of mine?"

"I guess so."

"Working for you?"

"Paul, let up. It doesn't make any difference."

"Working for you?"

Eleazar said nothing. Paul was sure he understood. That was all he needed to know.

"By the way," Eleazar added, "I hear that Mrs. Yousuf is doing just fine."

Mrs. Yousuf.

The Pickwick poisons.

Number 972.

He'd almost forgotten.

"The Guardians," Eleazar said. "They gave the poison to a Lebanese group that is fighting the PLO and told them it would help them capture PLO strongholds. That's why Bernhard tried to kill Rivkah."

"Rivkah?"

"He tried to force her off the road."

"I thought that was just a crazy Israeli driver."

"We are not all bad drivers."

"Or that it was aimed at me."

"No. That day Rivkah had mentioned finding the toxin in an Arab patient."

"So Romain tried to kill her too."

"Yes."

"Why just that once?" Paul asked.

"When Rivkah made her final report, she made no mention of that finding. He thought she'd forgotten it. Or at least believed it meant nothing."

Neither of them had any more to say. No polite farewells. Just simple good-byes.

Who had pulled the plug?

He had had only one friend at the hospital: Avram Schiff.

Avram had been there that morning.

So had they all. Chaim Abramowitz. And Romain Bernhard. That was how Bernhard knew what had happened immediately. Bernhard had not pulled the damn plug. But he knew it had been pulled, and assumed it had been done by some Arabs. So who did pull it?

Yitzak Cohen had been in the hospital, just down the hallway, doing an autopsy.

Rivkah had also been there.

Could she have done it?

She had killed once.

And she certainly was a friend.

Or at least had been one. Once. It seemed so long ago now. As far back as Bobbie. No, farther.

Then he remembered, and it all hung together for the first time.

Hassan had told Avram that Nahum Eckstein was getting better, that he was finally beginning to show the first signs of recovery. Hassan had examined the patient and had told his professor the results of that examination. Then Avram Schiff went over by the patient himself and told Hassan that he had made a mistake. After all, Hassan was only a second-year resident. Such mistakes were to be expected. He needed more experience.

Hassan had not made any mistake. He had been absolutely right. Rabbi Eckstein had turned the corner. He would recover. It might have taken six months or a year, but he would recover.

As long as the rabbi was dying, there was no need to kill him. Let nature take its own course. But once he began to improve, there was no chance that he would die without some assistance. Only Avram knew that the rabbi would live. He had even convinced Hassan that their patient was not improving.

The utter confusion in the ICU just made it easier. But scenes like that occurred every day. The plug was pulled during that one because Avram Schiff knew that he could no longer rely on nature. So he assisted it a little bit. It all made sense now, too much sense.

The Guardians were crazy.

In their own way they were as much of a threat to Israel as the PLO. They had to be stopped. What better way than to eliminate the one man who had held them together for so many years?

None.

But did anyone have that right? Did Avram? Had he even acted on his own? Or had he acted on some sort of higher authority? That was yet another question that Paul had wanted to ask.

So he had.

Eleazar's answer had not helped.

Paul never mentioned Avram's name. Nor did Eleazar. Avram was merely a mutual friend. A friend who had other friends in the highest places and who did favors for these friends every once in a while.

Small favors.

24

When Paul asked for quiet in order to start the meeting, it was just after one-forty-five. The entire committee was already seated around the conference table. That included Romain Bernhard, professor and chairman of the Department of Neurosurgery. Paul had seated himself at his usual place at the head of the long conference table. The others had grouped themselves in a cluster at the center of the table. Paul was not surprised that the chairs nearest him were not occupied. He was surprised that the chair at the other end of the table was not being used. For the first time, Rabbi Levi neither sat in his accustomed spot under the photograph of Chaim Weitzman nor occupied himself reading one of his well-worn books. He sat between Chaim Abramowitz and Rivkah Geller on the right side of the table. Directly across from them sat Romain Bernhard. Paul wanted to be surprised that Bernhard was there and not in some prison, but he wasn't. After all, Avram was there. Of course Avram had merely carried out a small favor for a friend. Perhaps Bernhard also had friends in high places. Were they different friends? Or the same friends? Romain Bernhard, Avram Schiff, and Yitzak Cohen, the three members of the committee who, like Paul, had recognized expertise in neurology, sat together. Even the seating arrangement had been carefully choreographed. Paul knew it would not be easy.

It was Avram whose words really opened the meeting. "Mr. Chairman."

Mr. Chairman. That short phrase reminded Paul of the cold, hostile formality of the Army-McCarthy hearing he had watched as a youth. It had turned out that McCarthy had been on trial and not the Army. Who was on trial here?

Paul articulated his answer slowly and accurately. The

tone of his reply reflected neither surprise nor anger at the cold formality of the words of his erstwhile friend of simpler times. He could be as frigid as they could be. "The chair recognizes Professor Schiff."

"Several of us have written a, shall we say, alternate report. You have, I think, already been made aware of this fact."

"That is correct."

"If it is acceptable to you as chairman, we would like to propose the following agenda. First, you will read your report; then I will read the alternate report; and then the committee will consider the two reports."

"The usual procedure, Professor Schiff, as I am sure you are well aware, is to discuss the"—he paused momentarily—"the . . . ah, *main* report first and vote on it before considering any alternate or secondary report."

"The chairman is well aware that we have not adopted any particular rules of order." It was hard for Paul to tell whether this was a reminder or a warning.

He hesitated before answering. "That is true."

"If you wish, Mr. Chairman, we could of course vote on our proposal. Right now. Then we will hear both reports."

No, Paul thought to himself. A vote was not necessary. Why go through the formality of a vote he knew he would only lose? He'd do that later.

Paul nodded his agreement and looked around the table. He wasn't quite sure what he was looking for. Disagreement? Support? There was certainly no evidence of any support. Each of the six faces at the table looked back at him without any sign of emotion. They emitted no more warmth than the formal state photographs staring down at him from the walls of the conference room. No more warmth and no more support. They were as frozen as a parkinsonian patient during an unsuccessful drug holiday.

Paul checked his watch: one-fifty-two. It was as if he couldn't even trust the clock on the opposite wall to tell him the correct time. He would read his report first; then Avram would read theirs.

He placed his hand-typed report on the table directly in front of him and began to read it aloud. This was worse than any single lecture he had given in his entire teaching career. It was worse than an eight-o'clock lecture delivered to a three-quarters-deserted lecture hall where half of the students who bothered to show up were reading the morning newspaper or finishing breakfast. It was worse than a one-o'clock lecture on an early summer's day in the old lecture hall before they put in the air conditioning and even the lecturer was tempted to take a nap. In every other lecture he had ever given, at least one person in the audience was interested enough in what he had to say to take some notes. Someone always had a tape recorder to take down his every word.

Here no one had a tape recorder.

Here no one took notes.

No one was reading a newspaper. No one looked like he or she might go to sleep, but no one was taking any notes at all. They were not going to debate his report, discuss it, modify it, amend it. They were merely going to vote it down. They had already composed their own version.

The committee had been transformed into a jury of six impassive judges. Six peers.

And they had told him that there was no cover-up. No, that was not what Eleazar Danin had said. He said there was no cover-up to protect Arab terrorists. What a sucker he had been. If it had been an Arab group, the government wouldn't have suppressed it. They would have broadcast it from the rooftops to help quiet the antiwar movement. This cover-up was to save themselves, to cover their own backsides.

It seemed much more like the trial of Josef K. than a scientific inquiry. Too bad Kafka had died of tuberculosis before he ever got to Palestine. He would have understood these proceedings much better than Paul did. How had he ever gotten suckered into this one? What had the dean said? All they wanted him to do was to lend them his name and his reputation. Not his mind or his body or his soul. Was that so much to ask?

Whether they liked it or not, his report covered the entire event. It started at the beginning and went through to the end. He had made the wrong analogy. It was more like *Alice in Wonderland* than Kafka. First the verdict, then the hearing. He hoped that his presentation would somehow remind each of them exactly what had transpired since that morning only eight weeks earlier.

He began with a recitation of the clinical course of Rabbi Nahum Eckstein's neurological problem. The rabbi had been Avram Schiff's patient, but the chairman of the Department of Neurology showed absolutely no interest in the history or the physical or the differential diagnosis or the day-to-day progress of his patient. He had hopefully shown more interest eight weeks ago.

Paul then described the tumult in the ICU and watched Chaim Abramowitz. The cardiologist made no response. Why had Paul expected that he would? Such an expectation on his part made no sense. Chaim had made no response in the ICU eight weeks earlier. He had done nothing but sign the death certificate. No CPR. Nothing.

Paul went on to describe the autopsy itself, and his inquiring gaze at Rabbi Levi brought no response. He had been able to elicit more recognition in previous meetings when the good rabbi had been buried in one of his books. At least then he got an occasional grunt or snort. Today he merited not so much as a cough.

Next he described Yitzak Cohen's final pathology report and Rivkah Geller's report on the toxicology. He looked at her. She didn't return his gaze. Had he at least reached her? She had reached him, more than either of them had recognized at the time.

My God. Had that also been part of the cover-up? No. It couldn't have been. Not that too. It had been too real, too warm. Or was he more of a sucker than he had ever realized?

Throughout it all, he never once looked directly at Romain Bernhard. There was no reason for him to. Bernhard was truly from the other side of the looking glass. Sentence first, then the trial. Hell, he'd gone Lewis Carroll one better. Execution first, then the verdict, and then the trial. He was crazier than the Queen and the Mad Hatter put together. Some wonderland, this Promised Land.

Romain had assumed that it had been done by Arabs. He hadn't known about Avram. Did he now?

Had any of them actually known who had done it?

Paul looked down at the last section of his report. It began with the categories of possible suspects that he had drawn up after the first meeting of the committee:

1. PLO
2. Moderate Arabs
3. Guardians of the City

4. Jewish radicals
5. Christian fanatics

None of them had done it. Or was that too simple? Had not all of them been at the root of the problem? Were they not all participants?

It was two-forty-seven by both his watch and the clock on the wall. All that was left was his final conclusion. For that, he didn't have to use a script. He now knew what he had to say. It was not what he had planned to do. Not what he had so logically considered and so pains-takingly outlined. It was only what he had to say. He turned his manuscript over and looked around the room one last time. Only this time he didn't look at his six colleagues. He looked instead at the portraits on the wall: Theodore Herzl, David Ben-Gurion, Golda Meir.

"Since there is ample evidence that the patient, Rabbi Nahum Eckstein, could not possibly have recovered, that his nervous system had suffered irreparable damage which made it impossible for him to breathe without total exter-nal support and which made his control of other vital func-tions precarious at best, it is the considered opinion of this select committee that the patient died of natural causes."

The second report was never read.

The report of the chairman was accepted unanimously without discussion and without any amendments.

The animosity was gone. He was no longer an outsider.

They all wanted to welcome him back home. The prod-igal son had returned to the Promised Land. Only he did not belong.

They each congratulated him and slapped him on the back. Rivkah hugged him. He could feel her hips press against his.

"Call me soon," she whispered in his ear. "I would like very much to see you again before you leave."

As soon as he could, he fled from the room, leaving the report on the table. Someone else could deliver it to the dean. That was one more person he did not want to see, one more task he did not want to perform.

He wondered if anyone would take the time to proof-read his report. For their sakes he hoped someone would. That way they could rewrite the conclusion so that it agreed with the one they had just adopted. That was their problem, not his.

He had done his job. They could not expect any more.

Paul made one last stop in the hospital. He wanted to see Mrs. Yousuf one last time to see for himself how well she was doing. Fortunately none of the Neurology residents or students were there. He did not have to talk to anyone. Not even the patient. Being unable to speak a word of Hebrew, she had become accustomed to people walking in and out without so much as a word of greeting. She was better. She was off the respirator. She was much stronger. Her reflexes were coming back.

He ought to stick to clinical neurology. At least there he wouldn't get himself burned. At least not very often.

Paul and his two kids spent their last few days as tourists. They did all the things outsiders did. Many Carolyn had done on her trip, but this time they did them together as a family. They even played at archeology one day by joining Dig for a Day in the original city built by David just south of Temple Mount.

Each day Paul continued to take part in the Israeli national obsession with the news. Four times each day he listened to the radio. Each morning he read the Jerusalem *Post* word for word, and each day he became more of a spectator than a participant, a spectator at a game between two teams neither of whom was the White Sox.

Some days there was shelling on Beirut. Some days not.

Some days the PLO said that it was willing to leave Beirut. Some days it announced that it was not.

The war between Iran and Iraq continued to boil. To most observers it seemed that both sides were losing. Both countries continued to threaten to broaden the war.

Some days the UN voted yet another cease-fire. Some days it did not. It made no appreciable difference.

In Israel, the antiwar movement was gaining momentum. Despite Israel's obvious supremacy in southern Lebanon, each day the conflict there dragged on, there was more controversy, more dissent. Perhaps it had been the right thing to do. Perhaps the political fabric was too fragile to tolerate Nahum Eckstein's brand of activism.

The PLO remained in Beirut, hiding behind the skirts of the Lebanese.

Slowly but surely Israel tightened the noose around Beirut.

Not so slowly, the White Sox slipped further and further behind in the pennant race.

The wave of terrorism within Israel slowed down to a mere trickle. A few rocks were thrown at a tourist bus as it went past Silwan. Nothing more. It was written up in *Time* magazine.

They went on two of Marti Isaacs' walking tours of the Old City. One took them all around the old Jewish quarter and its synagogues, many of which were still being rebuilt and repaired. Paul finally performed the act of charity that Mr. Greenberg had asked him to carry out just before they had left Chicago. Paul had delayed completing this act of tzedaka intentionally. After all, carrying that eighteen dollars in order to perform an act of charity for another person had assured his safety. Paul laughed to himself. Perhaps it had. He was a scientist, not a mystic, yet he wanted to believe that it had.

How long had Greenberg been his patient? Ten years. Three visits a year. At an average of twenty dollars a visit. Plus the eighteen dollars he was carrying. Paul made out a check for six hundred and eighteen dollars to help restore one of the synagogues destroyed by Hussein and his henchmen—Rabbi Eckstein's old synagogue.

For Paul it was hard to think about anything else. He was still obsessed by it all. He tried to talk to Pat about it. Her emotional instincts had always been better than his. She was no help. She understood what he had done and knew he had made the right decision. She would have done the same thing. There was no need for remorse, for self-recrimination.

But this was not just a question of right or wrong. It was not that simple. He had to talk to someone else. Jonathan, his oldest and in so many ways his closest friend even after all the years of separation, was there, but Jonathan Weiss could not help him. Paul was not certain that Jonathan would even understand that there was an issue. He was too close to the land. He had made his commitment and he was not about to reconsider it, not even for his friend.

Sarkis.

Why hadn't he gone to him immediately?

Sarkis Boyajian.

Paul knew why he had not talked to him. The answer was obvious. Sarkis was not a Jew: he was not one of us; therefore he was one of them. Lessons learned and relearned over thousands of years were not so easy to unlearn.

Sarkis.

Sometimes they can be overcome.

Sarkis was the only one who might be able to help him to dissect this reality. Sarkis knew about the subtle shadings of light which resulted when the sun passed through the kaleidoscope of Jerusalem and of the influence of such distortions on the faces of the Old City. Sarkis knew and he understood.

Once more, as he had promised, Paul made his way to the small jewelry shop with its all-but-barren windows. One more time he went upstairs to the darkened study.

He told Sarkis everything. It took the better part of two hours. The old man's weathered face seemed to age a couple of more years in that short span of time. His eyes were still bright but his movements had changed. They were fewer, more labored, slower. His shoulders had become stooped. From time to time he rested his elbows on the desk and settled his head into his open palm.

In the end, when Paul had finished, the two men were exhausted, both physically and emotionally.

"Paul, my dear friend, I cannot solve your problem. Only you can do that. You have done what you have done. Once done, it is over. It has become a part of the history of this troubled land. You must learn to live with history. You can no more change history than you can change people. You must learn to once again live with yourself." He did not wait for an answer, but continued on. "Paul, go home and go back to work."

"What other choice do I have?"

"I will miss you, Paul."

"And I too will miss you."

"You and I are supposed to be rational men, men whose lives are ruled by intellect, not by emotion. But you and I know that that is not possible. It is for some people, but not for us." The old man hesitated and then said what he had to say.

"You know that we will never see each other again."

"That's not—"

"Do not lie to me Paul. I am not a frightened patient in need of such well-meaning lies. I have lived a long life, and, I trust, a good one. I am at peace. I wish that you could also be at peace."

The room was quite dark. Paul could hardly see the deep folds of his friend's face as he tried to figure out exactly what to say.

Once again it was Sarkis who knew what to say. "We have both aged a great deal this summer. I, however, was older when it started, so perhaps I can still give you some advice."

Paul nodded and waited.

The voice was getting softer and slower. The words were still well-articulated and carefully chosen, but they were harder to hear.

"Put it all away. Put all your energy into something else. Bury yourself in other problems. There are many in this world. I am sure there are many unsolved riddles in neurology."

"We have more unanswered questions than answered ones."

"Then answer one, or at least exhaust yourself trying. For the next six months let all of this summer lie dormant. Do not think about Jerusalem. Do not even think about Julian. Then after six months come back to it and write your paper."

"I don't see what good it will do."

"Do it as a last favor for me."

Neither of them said any more. One simple embrace and the summer was over.

As the plane carrying Paul, Carolyn, Joshua, and three hundred and thirty-nine other passengers left Ben-Gurion International Airport, another, smaller plane carrying only one passenger landed at a military airport less than a dozen miles away. The passenger, transported in a modified hospital bed and attended by two doctors and three nurses, was Shlomo Argov. He was alive, conscious, able at times to say a few intelligible words, and he was back home.

EPILOGUE

Paul wanted to follow the advice Sarkis had given him and leave the events of the summer behind him, hoping that time and distance would together ameliorate some of the pain and restore his perspective.

At first he thought it would be easy. There was so much work to catch up on at the hospital, and Carolyn had to start applying for college. And the White Sox remained just enough in the pennant race to maintain his interest. But it didn't work out that way. The events of each week seemed to be designed as constant reminders of his recent past.

The International Peace-Keeping Force landed in Beirut.

The Christian President of Lebanon was assassinated.

The PLO left Beirut.

The International Force left Beirut.

Israeli troops moved into East Beirut.

The Sox ended up third, six games out of first. Not too bad. Carlton Fisk had played well and some of the young pitchers had had good seasons.

Christian forces entered two PLO camps and murdered several hundred Palestinians.

The world was horrified. How had Israel let that happen? Israel was again condemned. This time for a crime committed by Christians. That was a unique twist.

A new select committee was named in Israel to investigate possible Israeli involvement in the massacre.

The International Peace-Keeping Force returned to Lebanon.

Steve Kemp played out his option with the White Sox and signed with the Yankees.

The Sox spent 4.5 million dollars to sign a pitcher from Seattle named Floyd Bannister. All Paul could think about was Floyd's namesake Al who in three years with the Sox had demonstrated to everyone's satisfaction that there were four positions that he could not play.

The Russians closed off a tunnel in Afghanistan, murdering some two thousand civilians. The world said nothing.

Israeli troops spent the winter in Lebanon.

By the beginning of the year, some of the bad taste had disappeared. And then came the perfect time to get away and try to deal with it.

The paper which he had submitted for the meeting on history and medicine in February in Puerto Rico had been accepted. He was happy to get away from the cold and see some old friends: George Bruyn, Sigvald Refsum, MacDonald Critchley, Yves Agid.

Most of the first two days, Paul sat beside the pool and looked at his notes and tried to make some sense of his two months in Jerusalem. He still felt bitter. The entire inquest had been a sham and he had gone along with it. They would have outvoted him had he not gone along. He had had the right to submit a minority report. To what end? A tempest in a teapot. No one would have paid any attention. It was as rigged as the 1919 World Series had been. And, of course, the White Sox had lost again. Now he knew what Shoeless Joe Jackson must have felt like when the Series was over and the Sox had lost. Jackson had not been paid and he was out of baseball for life. Shoeless and luckless Joe Jackson. Amateurs had no chance in that league. Jackson had been a fish out of water. So had Paul. He couldn't compete with the Eleazar Danins of this world. He did have one advantage over Joe Jackson, though. Paul had been able to go back to his own life, to his lab, to his patients, to the students at Austin Flint Medical Center. Joe Jackson had had nothing else to go back to.

It had now been six months. In those months he had tried not to think about Eleazar Danin. At least he had helped Eleazar prevent the near-tragedy that Avram had provoked by pulling the plug on Rabbi Eckstein. And Eleazar had introduced him to Sarkis. Paul often thought of his Armenian friend and those fruitful hours they had spent together above the jewelry shop.

At times he did think about his experiences at Mai-

monides Hospital. When he did, he didn't think about
the staff or the select committee. Instead Paul thought
about the patients. Especially about Mrs. Yousuf. What
had happened to her? Had his trick really worked? Had
they been able to get all of the toxin out of her spinal
fluid and out of her nerves?

He also wondered about the other patients and the residents and the students. About Dalia. She had been so
good for Joshua. Had she ever written that paper? It was
unlikely. Most often he thought about Sarkis. How was
he? And about himself. He was no longer angry and no
longer depressed, but he still didn't know when he would
be able to go back, if ever.

Paul spent those first two days in Puerto Rico reading,
remembering, thinking, and finally writing. He wrote
down the entire story of the Third Temple. He both posed
the questions and gave the possible answers. Then he
discussed each of them in order. It could have been an
act of God. Many people who had been there claimed
that this was the case, both Christians and Jews. He dis-
sected each alternative, giving the pros and the cons. He
gathered together every single piece of historical evidence that he could marshal, except for one. He just
couldn't bring himself to use that one. At first he convinced himself that this omission was because no editor
would accept an Armenian shorthand set of notes of an
archaic Arab document which was now lost but which
claimed to be a transcription of an earlier and also lost
set of fragments supposedly written in the year 411.

As he reached his conclusion, he began to understand
it all. It wasn't being done for any editor. It was what he
had to do. It was what was historically true for him. He
summed it all up in his conclusion:

> Undoubtedly, sometime during the second year
> of his reign, the Emperor Julian undertook to rebuild
> the Jewish Temple in Jerusalem. There is no doubt
> but that the construction was begun. There is equally
> no doubt that a sudden unexplained and dramatic act
> occurred which brought the project to a complete
> standstill. The death of Julian followed shortly there-
> after, and nothing more was ever done on the proj-
> ect. Different observers and different historians have

all made disparate claims as to what actually transpired. These vary from divine intervention to frank arson. Each of these is tainted by the inherent prejudices of the respective authorities.

An objective investigation of the evidence leaves little if any room for doubt as to what actually took place late that spring in Aelia Capitolina.

On May 20, 363, Petra, the capital city of the Nabateans, was shattered by a major earthquake during the early hours of the night. The city was so severely devastated that it quickly became a ghost town. Entire cliffs were shifted. Whole sections of the town were crushed into rubble. The city itself became no more than a mass of debris. A visit to the site, which lies some one hundred and twenty miles south of Jerusalem, across the river, in present-day Jordan, will afford even the untrained observer an unrivaled example of the destructive power of an earthquake, frozen in time.

At exactly the same hour, on exactly the same date, in the city then called Aelia Capitolina, the same earthquake, traveling along the northward extension of the Rift Valley, buckled the foundations of the Temple Mount, leaving not one stone of the newly built foundation of the Temple standing upon another. As so often happens, but miraculously did not occur at Petra, the smaller quake was followed by a great fire on the Temple Mount, which some observers misinterpreted as the primary event.

A close inspection of the site shows ample evidence that fire was not the initial problem. In the same way, there is no convincing proof of arson and no verifiable support for the claim that a miracle took place in Jerusalem, any more than a simultaneous one occurred in the city of Petra.

That done, Paul studied the program of the meeting. His paper was scheduled for the last day, in the second of two sessions entitled "The Bible and Medicine." The first he had already missed, skipping papers on Biblical leprosy, on plague in the Bible, on the nature of Goliath's head injury, on aphasia in the Bible. Aphasia. By Dalia Avni. She had done it. She was here.

He had to see her, to thank her for her kindness to Joshua.

He found her by the pool, sunning in a bikini. How could he have been unsure if it were a man or a woman playing catch with Joshua that first time? She looked very beautiful to him. Was it just that she represented most of what had been pleasant during those two months? She was happy to see him. She had hoped he would come to hear her paper. He apologized. Would she read it to him over dinner? Yes, she would.

Over the last three days of the meeting, he learned many things from Dalia.

Mrs. Yousuf had recovered and was in perfect health. Her husband had died in an attempt to infiltrate an Israeli position.

Mrs. Yousuf had not been the only person to develop Guillain-Barré syndrome from the poison. Several other people at her village came down with it. No one was sure how many. They had treated three more at Maimonides. Supposedly a couple more had become weak but had been too afraid to go to Israel. There were rumors that one of them, an old man, had died. A team of army doctors had been sent to the village to study the problem, but their report was still considered a military secret.

Ari Mashir, the Arab girl with Sydenham's chorea, was in perfect health and off her medication.

No one had seen Mrs. Fahoum since she left the hospital. She was probably doing as well as one could as a Palestinian refugee in Lebanon.

Dalia also told him about the staff. Only two important things had happened. Rivkah Geller had gotten married in December to a thirty-one-year-old resident after a six-week romance. Some people were scandalized by the age difference. Dalia wasn't. She had done some work with Professor Geller as a student and thought she was a remarkable woman, and was happy for her. Paul agreed on both counts.

The other news was about Romain Bernhard. He had retired. Paul was astonished. Bernhard had killed Zalman Cohen, he'd tried to kill Rivkah Geller, and then he'd tried to destroy the Dome of the Rock. Who knew what would have happened if he hadn't been stopped?

And his punishment for that was an early retirement. That was all. Why?

Paul knew why.

To avoid publicity.

To avoid all public exposure of what had been planned. Any hint of the plot would have been a disaster. Israel didn't need that.

Tisha B'Av seemed an age ago.

"Punish them, O Lord, according to the evil they have done."

After dinner, Dalia and Paul walked along the beach arm in arm and watched the waves roll in.

"I always wanted to take Joshua to the beach at Ashkelon so he could go swimming among the Roman ruins," she said. "But I never got the chance."

"He would have liked that."

"How is he?"

"He's doing fine, and so is Carolyn."

And, he realized, so was he.

All the way home on the plane, Paul studied what he had written. He knew it was the correct truth, the one truth that was worthwhile for him to believe. Sarkis had been right. The six-month wait had given him the right perspective. As soon as he got home, he would type it up and send a copy to Sarkis. Sarkis would agree. Paul was sure of that.

He sat in his office typing the manuscript from his longhand notes. The FM was playing. After six days without classical music, almost anything was welcome. It was a morning of film scores by classical composers, beginning with Copeland's *Red Pony Suite*, the score to the movie based on the Steinbeck novella, and followed by Walton's score for *Henry V*, the 1945 movie directed by Laurence Olivier.

Olivier's *Henry V*. That had been Paul's very first Shakespeare. What magic! When the camera moved from the closed-in stylized stage of the Globe Theater to the fields of Agincourt, he had felt as if he were there in the middle of the din and clamor of the battle. He had loved it.

Was that how Bernhard had fallen under the spell of

Shakespeare? With Berlioz it had been *Romeo and Juliet*. Which play had turned Bernhard on? Probably *The Merchant of Venice*. Bernhard, like Shylock, believed in revenge.

Paul's secretary brought in the day's mail after having carefully sorted out the circulars, bills, insurance forms, and occasional checks.

There were three letters from Israel. The first was from Hassan Rashem, postmarked from Abu Gosh. Paul quickly opened it, not surprised at his own excitement. Hassan repeated most of what Paul had already learned from Dalia. It was the last paragraph that meant the most to Paul:

> Dr. Richardson, I never got a chance to personally thank you for everything. The time you were with us was very meaningful to me personally and professionally. I would like to do a fellowship with you but first I am going to do some volunteer service for two years. I will serve on the border with Lebanon. I think I can help us all up there. May God be with you. Yuri and Dalia are both fine and send their regards.

The second letter was from Eleazar. Paul was not as anxious to read this one. Just as curious, but not as excited.

Father Dimitrios was back in Cyprus seeking revenge on the Turks there.

The Israeli government had been unwilling to create an international furor and instead had just quietly arranged to have Father Dimitrios transferred. He had been a terrorist in priest's clothing, but Israel could do nothing. Any other country would have tried him and shot him. But Israel couldn't. She would have been accused of being anti-Christian. Paul understood. Such understanding did not preclude either anger or frustration.

Father Dimitrios was no better than Professor Bernhard. Worse perhaps. And he did not even have to retire. Two embittered men acting out of revenge.

Was it always revenge?

Paul shifted through his desk drawer.

He still had a copy of all eight warnings.

BewAre tHe nInTh of AV

JerIchO

a plaGUe oN BoTh youR hOuseS

noW Fair hippOLYTa oUr
nupTial hoUr Draws apaCe

NOW IS ThE WINter Of oUr DisCOntenT
maDe GlORioUs sUmmEr by this
SUn of yORK

aLas PoOr YoricK I kNEW
hIm hoRatIo a FeLlOw of inFinite jESt

but sOFt what light thrU
YoNDEr windOw breaks
It is tHE East anD jUliEt
is the SuN

the kiNGs a bEggar
nOW thE PLaY is DONE

He was sure he had figured it out. He found his copy
of *The Merchant of Venice* and copied out the four lines
that were the answer. Then he very carefully went through
the eight warnings. Each time he got to a capital letter
he underlined the corresponding letter in the four lines
he had just written down.

It took him only ten minutes.

He was right. All the letters had lines under them.

If you prick us do we not bleed,
If you tickle us do we not laugh,
If you poison us do we not die.
And if you wrong us shall we not revenge . . .

It had been *The Merchant of Venice* that had turned
Bernhard on. And the character of Shylock. And the need
for revenge.

There were three letters left over.

A J.

An R.

A B.

JRB.

No, not JRB. But RJB.

Romain J. Bernhard.

He could picture him with his white shirt and tie. The direct descendant of Charcot. From Charcot to Babinski to Vincent to Bernhard. Bernhard was also the descendant of other things, of the Dreyfus case, of the Holocaust, and of a need for revenge that he could no longer suppress.

Revenge.

Triggered by a pulled plug.

But it had not been pulled by an Arab.

The last letter was from Vartan Boyajian. His father had died on December 21. Paul would never see Sarkis again. Sarkis had known that.

Paul had not even had a chance to send Sarkis a copy of his paper on the Third Temple.

He fingered the gold-encased Armenian coin he wore around his neck.

"My father spoke of you often, friend Paul. My family joins me in sending you our warm regards. We all hope to see you again in Jerusalem."

In Jerusalem.

When he had come home, he was sure he never wanted to go back to Jerusalem. That had been six months ago.

That was impossible.

He now knew that he would go there again.

He would not forget Jerusalem.

He would return.

It was noon. The news had replaced music on WFMT. The lead story was again Israel. The select committee had issued its report. It was not the whitewash the world had expected. The committee named names. It had placed responsibility. The major culprit was Defense Minister Ariel Sharon. He had made decisions on his own. It was his decision not to step in and stop the killing and not to keep Begin informed. Sharon had to go.

Democracy worked.

No whitewash this time. Some things had changed. Much of the world praised Israel.

Not the PLO, of course.

Arafat called for a war-crimes trial.
Paul knew they would go back next year.
Next year in Jerusalem.

■   ■   ■

JERUSALEM, MARCH 19, 1983. Forty-three Jewish right-wing political activists were arrested today by members of the Jerusalem security forces, supported by units of the Israel Defense Force. The Israelis were seized as they attempted to storm the Temple Mount through a little-known underground passageway. A spokesman for the group said that they had merely been planning to demonstrate the historical right of Jews to control the site of the Temple. The group was said to include members of a variety of extremist groups, including the Jewish Defense League, founded by American-born Rabbi Meir Kahane. Others had been among the protesters arrested at Yamit. A government spokesman said that such threats to Muslim religious sites would not be tolerated and that the forty-three would be tried, although the exact charges on which they would be tried were not known. Demonstrations were expected in both Jewish and Muslim parts of Israel, as well as the occupied territories.

This story appeared on a middle page of the New York *Times* and was not picked up by any other major paper in the United States. Even the overseas edition of the Jerusalem *Post* ignored it. As a result, the one American who would have really understood it never even read it.

One year later, Rabbi Meir Kahane was elected to the Keneset, Israel's parliament.

About the Author

Harold L. Klawans, M.D., is a senior attending physician and professor of Neurology and Pharmacology at Rush Medical College in Chicago. He holds the distinction of being the only American editor of the *Handbook of Clinical Neurology*, a seventy-volume neurology encyclopedia. Dr. Klawans is the author of over 325 scientific articles and an author/editor of more than 40 scientific books. His previous book, *Toscanini's Fumble*, a collection of essays, was widely praised. His novels *Sins of Commission* and *Informed Consent*, also featuring Dr. Paul Richardson, are available in Signet editions.

2501